Best wishes,
Sam Bledsoe

THE LAST SENOOBIANS
LIFE AND DEATH IN SECTOR 3309

Sam Bledsoe

SECTOR 3309 BOOKS
Lenoir City, Tennessee

Cover illustration by Ken Clayton
kwclaytongraphics@earthlink.net

Sector 3309 Books
782 Meadow Walk Lane
Lenoir City, TN 37772

Visit our web site: www.sector3309.com

Printed in the United States of America

First United States Paperback Printing: July 2012

To my lovely wife Charlene who has been with
me every step of the way on this long journey

Were it not folly, spider-like to spin
The thread of present Life away to win—
What? For ourselves, who know not if we shall
Breathe out the very breath we now breathe in!

The Rubaiyat of Omar Khayyam

A SACRED PLACE

O' Senoobis, majestic and divine,
Adored prodigy of ancient Karmut,
Proud mother of life itself,
You were the jewel of the Galaxy,
Precious and exotic beyond words.
Even now we embrace you in our dreams
And honor you in our eulogies.

We drank the clear waters of Deksabo.
We walked the beach at Manjikor.
With the cold surf against our feet
And the warmth of Karmut on our faces,
You made us fully alive.

At the top of a desert butte,
We sat beneath a gnarled anisee—
Like us, tenacious and defiant,
Clinging to the red stony tower
That presided over a mystical land.

We heard the whisperings of the wind
And waited there in silence
Until the Universe answered us,
Making us fully aware,
So we might know our destiny:
Senoobis, you will be reborn
While we wander homeless
Among the stars.

—Pansyn Vaberis

PLANETS WITH INTELLIGENT LIFE
IN SECTOR 3309

	Senoobis	Karyntis (Earth)	Nanzema	Peyr (Oblivium)	Krees
Star System	Karmut	Sarmadah (Our Sun)	Jestura	Gafor	Gafor
Diameter (miles)	7,600	7,926	8,891	8,206	5,153
Length of Year (days)	383	365.25	340	441	549
Moons (largest to smallest)	Portinyhe Pesh	Moon	Sart	Krophis Blo Nahgoon	Hys Thak Salopus Orz Ningeet
Distance to Earth (light years)	35	N/A	7	13	13
Population (millions)	630	6,500	452	2,100	.72*
Dominant Race(s)	Senoobian	Human	Shun Bretin	Peyrian	Ovlodian
Major Language(s)	Kuterin Pensoot	English Spanish	Vaboor Kuterin	Muthasi	Nejou

*The Ovlodian race on Krees was almost exterminated by the Peyrians. Out of 23,000,000 Ovlodians, fewer than 720,000 survived.

STARSHIPS IN SECTOR 3309

Starship	From	Mission To	Outcome
BALSERIOS crew: 21	Senoobis	Parkopia	fate unknown
SHANANIK crew: 20	Senoobis	Parkopia	fate unknown
SYZILIAN crew: 27	Senoobis	Karyntis	destroyed
VOLARION crew & staff: 65	Senoobis	Karyntis	destroyed by Pajputog
LANGORION * crew: 27	Senoobis	Nanzema	Mission Completed
MANKURIUN * crew: 28	Nanzema	Karyntis	returned to Nanzema
PAJPUTOG crew: unknown	Peyr	Attack Volarion	returned to Peyr
UPAKSANOCHIN crew: unknown	Peyr	Karyntis	destroyed by Mankuriun
GRUNASHAR crew: unknown	Peyr	Jupiter	unknown

* The *Mankuriun* was an upgrade of the *Langorion*.

See Appendix A for a guide on how to pronounce Senoobian names.

CONTENTS

PART 1: <u>LIFE ON KARYNTIS</u>

1	End of the *Syzilian*	1
2	Home Again!	9
3	The Montecarlos	23
4	The Franciscos	33
5	The Debate	38
6	Contact	47
7	The *Mankuriun*	52
8	The Perseids	73
9	The Nazca Lines	80
10	The Senoobians	86
11	Luke and Sonny	99
12	Senoobis	114

PART 2: <u>THE COLONY PROJECT</u>

13	Approaching Doom	123
14	The Colony Project	127
15	Report from Karyntis	137
16	Starships	142
17	The End of Senoobis	148
18	Lord Athrumos	160

PART 3: <u>DEATH ON KARYNTIS</u>

19	Karyntis At Last	175
20	Deathly Ill	187
21	Alberto Calderon	192
22	The Bretin	200
23	The Revenge of Calderon	206
24	The *Upaksanochin*	219
25	The Death of Bayn Kener	238
26	Return to Nanzema	252
27	Hayman-Angler	260
28	The Peyrians	287
29	Apanoo Vahleet	302
30	Detza Keeska	313

App. A	Pronunciation Guide	322
App. B	A Glimpse of Kuterin	323

PROLOGUE

Our solar system is just one among billions of star systems swirling within the Milky Way Galaxy that is itself only one of countless galaxies sprinkled throughout a vast, ever-expanding universe. That we inhabit such an incredibly tiny part of an infinite universe does not diminish the wonder of humankind, however, for each of us is unique, as are those distant stars that set the heavens aglow and kindle our imaginations.

The same chemical elements—the stuff of life—found here on Earth exist throughout the Universe, forged in those countless starry furnaces. The conditions that favor the existence of life, on the other hand, are exceedingly rare. Nonetheless, considering the vast number of star systems that exist just within our galaxy, it would be unrealistic to believe our star system claims the only planet with conditions that favored the evolution of intelligent life.

Indeed, it was within a star system much like ours and only a few light years away that a race of intelligent beings evolved thousands of years ago on a planet not very different from Earth. They were neither sinister nor angelic; they did not look very different from us nor did they possess extraordinary powers. In many ways, they were unremarkable; their problems were the same as those that have bedeviled every civilization throughout the centuries here on Earth.

No race will survive unless it has the wisdom to foresee the catastrophes that threaten it and the will to prevent them. If it does not adapt, it will perish as have many civilizations before it. Consider how many empires in the course of human history have risen to preeminence and then faded into obscurity, gods and all: Sumer, Babylon, Persia, Egypt, Greece, Carthage, Rome, China and Ottoman, to name a few. Are we foolish enough to believe that we are more perennial than all of these?

Humankind faces grave crises of its own making; after only 6,000 years of civilization, its very survival is in jeopardy. It is mismanaging and depleting the planet's finite resources as the global population continues its relentless growth. Human economies rely on sustained growth that strains the ability of our planet to support us. Our collective psyche manifests itself in short-term thinking, greed, competition and excessive consumption. And the threat of self-destruction from a nuclear war with an ensuing nuclear winter still hangs over us. With great hubris, humankind has ignored these looming crises and failed to address the manifold social problems that fuel them.

Our galactic neighbor, on the other hand, bore no responsibility for the catastrophe that threatened it with extinction. It crafted a unified government that solved the grave social problems that had plagued it for centuries and it learned to manage its planetary resources wisely. Its citizenry set self-interest aside in favor of the common good; instead of growth and excess, its economies were based on moderation and stability. Its societies planned for the long-term and thrived by promoting cooperation, diversity and respect for life.

The dinosaurs that dominated the Earth for millions of years were wiped out by a giant 7.5-mile-wide asteroid that struck the Earth 65 million years ago off the coast of Mexico. It was a similar catastrophe that forced our galactic neighbor to seek refuge on some other hospitable planet. It was the search for such a planet that brought it to Earth.

PART 1

LIFE ON KARYNTIS

1

END OF THE SYZILIAN

The three of them were the only survivors—the rest of the crew of the starship *Syzilian* was long dead, all 24 of them. Even those three were barely alive, clinging to life by the thinnest thread inside the starship's hyper-sleep modules. No one else had ever been in hyper-sleep for so long. Century after century they slept, cold and unaware, as the *Syzilian* continued her relentless race around Karyntis, locked in a slow downward spiral. Within their bodies, the virus that had pursued them to the edge of death also slumbered.

At her speed of 18,000 mph, the *Syzilian* made a complete circuit around Karyntis in 12 hours. In the beginning, her orbit was 340 miles above the surface; the air was so thin at that altitude that the drag it exerted on the ship's hull was imperceptible. The ship might have continued in this manner, frozen in time for millennia, except for one fact: with every revolution, that imperceptible drag slowed the ship by the most trifling amount and made her altitude fall by the slightest degree. But the effect was cumulative—the more she fell, the greater the drag; the greater the drag, the more she fell. There was no one able to start her engines and nudge her safely back into a higher orbit.

Since the *Syzilian* was not intended for atmospheric flight, it was not designed for aerodynamic efficiency. When the ship had descended to 45,000 feet, it crossed a critical threshold; heat sensors in the ship's hull began to register rising temperatures that would have been noted by those on watch if they were alive.

At 25,000 feet, the forward part of her hull began to glow a dull red that gradually turned into a bright red, triggering the long-silent alarms that were there to alert the crew in the event of danger. In the hyper-sleep modules behind the bridge, the automated wakeup process that would open the canopies and restore their occupants to full life began.

As soon as the piercing sounds of the emergency alarm began, three of the hyper-sleep modules came to life, lights on the master control panel began to blink and the canopies slid open, releasing their occupants to breathe on their own.

Groggy and aching in every muscle, Darz Tureesh was the first to react. The screeching of the alarms jarred his mind from its deep slumber and his eyes blinked open, recoiling at the sharp brightness flooding over him. The green pynambic liquid that supported his body and sustained his life had drained away. The mask that supplied the trickle of oxygen to his lungs had released and now he struggled to breathe on his own. His body seemed heavy as lead and, except for two fingers on his right hand, it would not respond.

He was the Operations Officer on the proud ship, a typical Senoobian, tall with a slightly elongated head that sported a thick bushy mane that tumbled down the back of his neck past his shoulders. He had a finely-shaped and sloping nose, pointed ears and large green eyes with narrow catlike pupils. He had a clef chin and normally was considered handsome but now he was gaunt and deathly pale.

Something was terribly wrong, but his thoughts were disconnected and he couldn't sort out what it was. The canopy of his module gaped wide open and he looked straight up as he tried to comprehend his situation.

He willed himself to think and grudgingly, over a period of several days, he began to remember their harrowing escape into the modules. He strained to lift his body enough to see if his shipmates were stirring within their own modules, but he could only raise his head painfully and ever so slightly. He tried to call to the others, but only a weak rasping sound escaped his throat as the sounds of the ship's alarms grew steadily louder and more urgent. He thought of his shipmates and became afraid. *Were they alive?* He thought about Jeliko. *Was she alive?* He rolled himself clumsily over the lip of his module and tumbled onto the deck with a painful thud. In a panic he crawled to her hyper-sleep module and lifted himself up to look inside, fearful of what he might see.

2

Jeliko Hanahban was the Communications Officer who used their radios to monitor various frequencies on their long journey to Karyntis. She possessed the same physical attributes as her crewmates but her hair was a little longer and thicker.

Darz looked down at her, worried; she neither breathed nor moved. The pynambic liquid was gone and her mask dangled from the canopy of the module. It was not pleasant to wake from hyper-sleep and it usually took a while. He took her hand and squeezed it gently, mesmerized by her pale, almost naked beauty. It was as if he were seeing her for the first time.

Suddenly her eyes blinked open, startling him, but they were too sensitive to make him out in the bright light. Her head ached terribly and her body felt as stiff and unresponsive as a wooden beam. She lay there, gasping, trying to awaken the long dormant synapses in her brain that would make her muscles move again. At last her eyes began to focus without stinging, allowing her to recognize the concerned face peering down at her. It was Darz! She smiled slightly, reassured.

Bayn Kener was the Executive Officer of the beleaguered ship. He was the oldest of the three and over the years he had become a father figure to the other two. It was another day before he awakened to extreme nausea and pain. He tried to move his head, but couldn't, and slipped back into a deep sleep. When he awoke, he lay there as a prisoner in his own body, still unable to move but beginning to grasp the gravity of their situation. When he was able to prop himself up so he could look around, he was horrified to see the skeletal remains of two of the crew on the deck near the modules. He realized then that all of the crew were dead except for the three who, like him, had retreated into the hyper-sleep modules.

With that realization, feelings of panic and loss overcame him, followed by a feeling of helplessness and then despair. The crew was more than his family; they and the ship were his whole life. He pulled himself up into a sitting position in a determined effort to find the others. Close by, Jeliko peered back at him with a thin smile and waved weakly. To his relief, Darz was sitting near her, obviously disoriented.

As Bayn lifted himself stiffly and painfully from the hyper-sleep module, he could barely keep his balance. The *Syzilian* was shaking violently as her metal hull groaned and twisted under the intense stresses she endured like a great beast tormented by fire. Darz crawled to him and together they rose, lurching back and forth while struggling to keep their balance. Hoping to gain control of the ship, they stumbled toward the control panel on the bridge. To their horror the altimeter indicated an altitude of only 19,000 feet, dropping fast. The ship's speed had slowed to 2,300 mph.

He felt the stifling heat pressing down upon him and wiped the sweat from his eyes. Glancing out the viewing port, he saw the hull glowing a fiery red. In desperation, he made his way to the pilot's module and tried to engage the engines, but the only response was from several warning lights that flashed stubbornly on and off.

As soon as he scanned the instrument panel, he knew it: the ship was doomed. "We've got to evacuate the ship NOW!" he yelled to Darz as they staggered back to find Jeliko still slumped against her module. He grabbed her by the shoulders and shook her frantically to bring her to her senses. "The cargo bay! We've got to get to a lander! It's our only hope."

"Amantis!" Darz yelled, motioning them toward the sleep module their shipmate occupied.

Jeliko nodded her understanding as she pushed unsteadily ahead of Bayn and Darz toward Amantis' module. When she reached it, she fell back in shocked disbelief. Amantis was dead! Only his bones remained.

The three of them slid down to the floor in utter despair at the death of their comrade. *There was no one more capable or loyal than Amantis Brazynis.*

Bayn glanced up at the date digitally displayed on the control panel and sat there stunned. Darz's eyes followed his. They couldn't believe what they saw—they had been in the modules for 720 years! They sat there for a few moments, confused and unable to move.

Bayn turned to them, his eyes wide with panic, "Come on. Come on. We've got to go now!" He looked around, trying to think clearly. "Wait! The disk library! We can't leave that!" he shouted.

Jeliko nodded, "Yes, you're right. I'll get it." Making her way to the data compartment that was near the bridge, she pulled the two levers that released the dull metal case that held the disk library. She

4

had forgotten how heavy it was and she swore as she struggled to free it.

Darz rushed over to help her and together they pulled it free. Then the three of them made their way down the long passageway, pushing the metal case toward the cargo bay that held the ship's two landers. To their relief, one of them was fully fueled. They closed the inside doors to the bay, heaved the disk library into the lander and Jeliko and Bayn jumped aboard.

The ship had begun to shake more violently. While Jeliko settled into the pilot's seat and quickly started the disengage sequence, Bayn secured the library against a bulkhead.

Damn it! Where was Darz? She looked out of the lander to see him desperately searching the cargo bay for anything that might be useful. "Darz, come on," she screamed, motioning frantically for him to board the lander.

There was a chest with a few tools, two DK-1 Krayzur handguns and some maps of the area stowed nearby. Darz gathered them up, threw them into the lander and leaped on board, sliding the door shut. He slipped into the seat next to Bayn and locked his own harness.

Jeliko was also moving quickly. As soon as Darz was aboard, she pressurized the cabin and completed the preflight checks. She started the procedures to open the bay doors to the outside and move the lander to the launch ramp. As the lander crawled toward the launch pad, she held her breath, expecting power to the launch pad to fail at any minute and the ship to blow apart; once the ship's hydrogen tanks overheated, the resulting explosion would be horrific.

When the lander reached the launch portal, they braced themselves. The engines balked at the first try but finally started with their familiar high-pitched whine. Jeliko pushed the throttle to maximum thrust and released the restraints. With a loud blast the lander shot out into space clear of the ship. After the initial turbulence, she extended the wings, raised the nose slightly for maximum lift and gained control.

As she did so, she looked anxiously back at Bayn and Darz. "Are you two okay?"

Bayn grumbled, "I'll live."

Darz answered, "I think so but that was a hell of a jolt! How about you?"

"I'm okay. Just a little shook up," she smiled weakly. "I don't know where we are, but we'd better decide fast where we're going and what to do."

She looked up to see the *Syzilian* streaking onward three or four miles ahead of them. *The Syz isn't looking good*, she thought. *She's going to blow any minute and we'd better put some distance between us fast.* The front third of the *Syzilian* was glowing bright red and there was a long trail of smoke streaming out behind her.

Jeliko glanced at Darz anxiously, "Let's divert to 25°/15° and try to figure out where we are. We'd better conserve every drop of fuel we can so I'm going to glide mode." She banked the lander sharply to the right.

Darz nodded, "Understood." He remembered the digital display of the date. "Bayn, is it possible we've been asleep for 720 years?"

Bayn was confused. "That can't be right! No one has ever been in hyper-sleep for more than 60 years. If it is true, no wonder my brains feel scrambled!"

They continued on for a few minutes in silence, puzzled, trying to make sense of their situation but still not thinking clearly. As Darz went over what had happened in his mind, it dawned on him: in his sickness and under the pressure of rushing to set the controls, he had failed to enter a specific duration, putting them all into a permanent hyper-sleep. By default, the ship's computers would awaken them only in the event of some emergency!

It was a design flaw in the units, he reasoned. *The controls should have required the operator to enter a duration.* He turned to the master control panel. *Units one through four were activated . . .*

His heart sank—*Amantis was in five!* In his haste, he had activated number four, not realizing that Amantis had thrown himself into number five. He felt sick to his stomach: he had let his comrade down, given him a death sentence. *I'm responsible for the death of Amantis— and how many more of my shipmates—as well as the destruction of the ship. I've failed them all miserably.* He was overcome with shame.

At that moment, Jeliko began a descending turn and within a few minutes they were only 13,000 feet above the surface. Racing on ahead of them in the early dawn and leaving a long trail of smoke behind her, the *Syzilian* suddenly exploded with a blinding flash into a great fireball, sending out streamers of fiery debris in all directions. They were struck by a shock wave of such force that it would have crushed them had they been closer. All three of them were knocked unconscious as their lander was slammed away from the ship as if by some giant unseen fist. When they regained consciousness several moments later, the great ship that had been their home for so long was gone. They watched the dark billowing cloud of smoke in disbelief.

After Jeliko had regained control of the lander, there below them in the heavily forested area, they could see the flattened trees pointing outward in a vast radial pattern. Trees nearest the center of the blast lay blackened and smoldering while those farther out were burning fiercely.

They and their lander were all that remained of the Karyntis Mission. They continued on for several minutes, overwhelmed at their loss and unable to speak. Finally, Darz picked up the map and said to Jeliko, "I think we should go back to our base site although I have no idea what we'll find there. Maybe there will be something salvageable, but I doubt it—not after more than 700 years. At least we know that area better than any other and that may be an advantage since we're going to be starting from scratch. If anyone has a better idea, let me hear it."

Bayn said, "Makes sense to me."

After a moment's thought, Jeliko responded, "Okay, here we go. Darz, see if you can figure out where we are and give me a heading."

He glanced at the instrument panel. A few minutes later he had their location. "Heading southeast at 800 mph, we should reach our old base in fifteen hours."

Stiff and aching, Bayn released his safety harness and stood up to stretch and look out of the canopy. He looked and felt like someone with a brutal hangover. "Ahggghooou!" he exclaimed. "Every time I go into a damn sleep module, it almost kills me. I hate the contraptions. I feel like I've been chopped into a million pieces and glued back together with the pieces all scrambled."

Jeliko couldn't help but grin. "Yeah, I feel like I've been chewed up and spit out too." She motioned toward Darz, feigning disgust. "It's a miracle we're alive. Our buddy here put us into a level 12 three-hour takedown. But I'm not going to complain too much because we're still alive thanks to those damn contraptions."

Before long they had passed over a wide stretch of ocean lying South of the area where Asia and North America almost touch at the Bering Strait. They followed the coastline southward, slowly descending, and before long they could make out small towns along the coast. When they had first arrived on Karyntis, they had observed not a single settlement within the northern continent. Now there were plenty of them.

After awhile there appeared below them on the coast the wreckage of a fairly large city; many of its buildings lay in rubble. *Was it recovering from a war or some major natural catastrophe?* They sped onward, not sure what to make of it. Years later, they learned that it was the city of San Francisco rebuilding after the great earthquake of 1906.

2

HOME AGAIN!

They were exhausted from their ordeal so Jeliko put the lander on auto pilot. It was some time before they drifted off into a fitful sleep. When they awoke several hours later, they were famished. There were some e-rations on board and, after they had eaten a little, they felt better. Before long they reached the coast that was only a few miles from the place where they had kept a small base for several years. As they descended, the familiar designs etched into the surface of the broad Nazca plain spread out before them, welcoming them home. It was a rough landing in a tight area. As soon as they were on the ground, they tumbled from the lander and fell to their knees, barely able to move but glad to be alive.

So, in the spring of 1908, they returned to the place where their ordeal had begun more than 700 years earlier. That area was now the Ica Province in the Southern part of Peru near a small, dusty town called Nazca. Neither the country nor the town had existed when they first arrived on the planet they called Karyntis. It was the place closest to being a home to them but it was far different now.

The plain was near the hills and woods they had come to know when their crewmates were alive. They looked around, half expecting the Nezeke, who had treated them as gods, to rush out and greet them but no one came. During the nine years they had spent in the area, they had enjoyed such a strong friendship with the members of the tribe that without them the place seemed deserted. They missed their old friends and wondered what had become of them. *Had they been wiped out by the virus that killed our crew? Or had the Hofut slaughtered them?*

Darz turned to Bayn and Jeliko with a mischievous grin, "Do you remember that time we coaxed Chief Kanzakek and one of his elders into our lander and flew them up to the *Syz*. It was a bad idea. The poor fellows were terrified and disoriented the whole time. When we got them onto the bridge and they looked down at the planet far below, they were dumbfounded, unable to grasp what they were seeing. To them the world was flat. And they couldn't understand why we didn't plummet to the ground."

Bayn chuckled. "I know, I was on the bridge that day and I tried to explain about our starship, the Earth's orbit and so on in simple terms but their language was far too crude to make any sense of it all. When they were safely back on the ground, they ran to their village like excited children trying, but unable, to describe to the others what they had experienced. I'm sure it was the origin of some fantastic myth."

The three Senoobians had a good laugh at the thought of two members of a primitive tribe thrust two thousand years into the future and totally overwhelmed by what they saw. Recalling the incident was a welcome diversion, but the gravity of their predicament quickly settled over them again.

Their situation was desperate: they were weak and exhausted and had to live out of their lander. On board there were only a few tools, some e-rations, a personnel transporter and a storage bin holding 110 pounds of gold that had been transported back to the *Syzilian*. Besides that, they had only the clothes they wore; they had no money to buy anything. After three days their e-rations ran out so they foraged for food and hunted small game without much success.

They were slowly starving so Bayn volunteered to go in search of food. He left in the morning and walked unsteadily, since he had not regained his full strength, for a long time until he came across a small house. This would be his first encounter with a human since their return to the surface, so he didn't know what the occupant who came to the door would look like or what he would do. *Would these humans treat them with the same compassion that they had treated the Nezeke so long ago?* After catching his breath, he dragged himself to the door and knocked on it until a roughly dressed human opened it.

Regarding him suspiciously, the man demanded gruffly in Spanish "Who are you? What do you want?"

This human looked no better than the primitive Nezeke but through the open door the aroma of cooking food made Bayn's empty stomach growl. He tried to communicate through gestures that he and his companions were starving and needed help but the human only glared at him with contempt and impatiently waved him away.

Feeling humiliated and discouraged, Bayn moved on. The second home he found was larger and better built but that human also treated him with scorn and shut the door in his face. *In 700 years, humans had changed little*. He began to feel bitter because of their predicament.

Farther on, beside a small stream, he sat down to rest, glad that Darz and Jeliko couldn't see him then—the Executive Officer of the starship *Syzilian* reduced to begging! He felt ashamed but he couldn't give up. If the next encounter didn't work out, he would have to take drastic measures—but what? He couldn't bring himself to steal food.

The third home he approached was a modest adobe structure owned by an aged farmer who lived alone and saw few visitors in that sparsely populated area. Bayn steeled himself for another rebuff. To his surprise, Javier Arenas cheerfully motioned him inside. Soon Bayn was trudging back to the lander, no longer hungry and with enough food to last them for a few more days. It was simple fare but they were grateful for it and they began to regain their strength.

Over the next few months, Arenas was their only friend in the new world. He continued to give them food as their health improved and, before long, they were able to repay his kindness by helping him repair his well. He taught them how to farm, their first words of Spanish and human social ways. When he died the following year, they missed him terribly but by then they were fluent in Spanish.

They desperately needed a permanent place to live so they sought out their old base camp in an overgrown and isolated area several miles from Nazca. The site afforded privacy and joined a wide and flat field that served as a good air strip for their lander. They made their home there by building onto what was left of the small metal structure that had been the heart of their base camp 720 years ago. They christened their new home Naksoris, after the village where Jeliko had lived as a child on Senoobis. Over the next few years, they improved and expanded that modest structure until it was comfortable and secure.

Their first years on Earth were difficult and survival in their new home was a daily challenge. They cut off the hair that grew down their necks and wore hats to cover up their pointed ears so they wouldn't stand out so much. The area was sparsely populated by humans but those they did encounter mostly ignored them or treated them with contempt because they were different. That frustrated them and made them bitter. The only thing that kept them from hating the whole human race was remembering the kindness of Javier Arenas.

After the death of Arenas, they felt even more hemmed in by the contentious humanity around them. After all, there were only the three of them, and they were forced to live among humans who were sometimes offensive and difficult to understand.

The place they called home was 30 miles of rough roads north of Nazca near the small village of Palpa, just off the stretch of road that would become part of the Pan-American Highway many years later. When they did venture out, it was usually in the late evening or early morning hours. Since they were taller than the Spanish-speaking Peruvians and clearly didn't fit in, most of the locals gave them a wide berth.

Occasionally they would run into a few toughs, however, who had been drinking and were behaving in a rowdy and provocative way. Sometimes the gang would insult and harass them until they snapped. Then they would abruptly stop in their tracks and the one of them who was the most angry would gesture toward the bullies and calmly enquire of the other two, "May I . . ."

The other two would politely reply, "Please do!" and the fight would begin. The three of them were highly skilled in martial arts so it wasn't unusual for Darz to take on four or five troublemakers by himself while Bayn and Jeliko stood by to ensure that no guns were drawn. Darz was quick and strong. In no time at all the troublemakers, who had expected an easy fight, would find themselves on the ground, beaten into submission and begging for mercy. Bayn and Jeliko were just as tough and eventually the word got around that it was best not to cross *the three odd ones* and the confrontations stopped.

For a long time, the three of them were distraught but Darz, who was more depressed than the other two, came to feel angry all the time. He still blamed himself for Amantis' death and the loss of the *Syzilian*. Finally Bayn pulled him aside. "Darz, we've had some tough breaks, but you know we've got to buck up and put the past behind us if we're going to survive here."

Darz looked at him with downcast eyes. "Yes, I know," he said, "but I still feel guilty about the mistake I made when we climbed into the sleep modules. If only I had programmed them properly, the *Syz* wouldn't have been destroyed and Amantis would still be alive. It's my fault that we're in this dreadful situation. I'm ashamed that I failed you and Jeliko."

Jeliko was comforting. "Look, you can't blame yourself. All four of us were ill. We were delirious. Our vision was blurred. It's unlikely that Bayn or I would have been able to get it right either. Forget it. It's not your fault. Besides we all need to focus on surviving here." She pulled him to her and hugged him tightly.

Then Bayn put his arm around Darz's shoulders, "Look, it was a bad break but we all did the best we could under the circumstances. You can't blame yourself. Get over it!"

In truth all three of them were mourning the loss of everything that defined who they were and gave them purpose. While they struggled to adapt to their new world, they were also dealing with emotional issues that made them despondent. They felt like helpless spectators with little control over their lives and, instead of a future, a dead end. What was the point of their existence? They felt marginalized and insecure and that made them bitter and cynical.

There were other things that worried them. They were concerned that the virus that had almost killed them had also revived and regained its virulent form. For several months, it was a ritual each morning to check their bodies as soon as they awoke for any symptoms that might be attributed to the virus. Eventually they regained their strength, concluding that the virus had either been killed or weakened, allowing their bodies to develop an immunity to it.

They continued to mourn the loss of the *Syzilian* and they wondered about the fate of their sister ship, the *Langorion*. *Had it reached Nanzema or had it also been destroyed by some Peyrian patrol? Or had it crashed on some inhospitable planet?*

They recalled the threat made to the CO of the *Volarion* by Lord Athrumos that the Peyrians would return to Earth and claim it for their own. *Had the Peyrians in fact returned to Earth while they were in the sleep modules? Was there a flourishing colony of Peyrians nearby? If not, would they come soon or had something happened to prevent their return?*

If the Peyrians did come, they could no doubt evade them indefinitely but to what good? It seemed the only thing left for them was to eke out a meager existence on Karyntis and then to die, accomplishing nothing.

There was a lot to learn about their new home. On Senoobis everyone spoke the universal language Kuterin and at least one of the three secondary language groups—Syptikaht, Dukasee, or Pensoot. Now that they were on Earth, they realized they would need to speak both Spanish and English to understand the world around them. Arenas had taught them some basic Spanish and they used it more and more. They studied old English newspapers and magazines from Lima and sometimes from Miami whenever they could get their hands on them. They jerry-rigged the radio from their lander and listened to both Spanish and English radio broadcasts. By 1930, they were fluent in both languages.

Not long after they had mastered English, they learned that Karyntis was called *Earth* by its human inhabitants. *Earth!* All three of them agreed it was an ugly guttural sound. It was hard to give up Karyntis, the name they had used for so long and one that was more pleasant to their ears. Even worse, abandoning that name was surrendering a small piece of their identity as well as their history.

The Senoobians had a hard time getting used to the human numbers system. Since theirs was a base-12 system, it took them a while to get into the habit of using the human decimal system for everything that had to be counted, measured or valued.

Adjusting to human food that was spicier than what they were used to was also hard for them. The three-meal regimen that is the human custom never appealed to them so they continued having only two meals a day. They felt self-conscious going out in public to eat so they mostly kept to themselves until they got to know Carlos Navarro and a few others at *La Taberna*, a local tavern. "I'm sure they thought we were fugitives of some kind at first," Jeliko joked.

Getting money to buy supplies and parts was an urgent problem. They soon realized, however, that gold was as valuable to humans as it was to them and that they could exchange it for the local currency. To their good fortune, they had 110 pounds of it on their lander, and there was a lot more to be found in Peru.

When the Spanish arrived in 1532, they were astonished to find that, even with primitive tools, the Inca Indians had amassed one of the greatest treasures of gold ever known. When the Inca king Atahuallpa was taken prisoner by the Spanish, as a ransom, he offered to fill a 22'x18' room with gold as high as he could reach. The Spanish gladly accepted his offer but killed him anyway.

The Senoobian race had a long history of mining on Senoobis; they were skilled at extracting and refining gold. The survey team from the *Syzilian* had found two rich veins of it, and before long they had set up a small but successful mining operation.

The three Senoobians found that some of the equipment left in one of the mines when they had fallen ill on the *Syzilian* so long ago was still serviceable. With it working, they managed to bring out modest amounts of the precious metal from the two small mines that had been worked by their shipmates before the virus struck. They found a banker in Nazca who paid no attention to how they looked and was glad to buy their gold. In 1969, they bought a used Ford pickup that made their explorations easier and safer, but they still had to be cautious because there was always the threat of being robbed.

The days on Earth were shorter than on Senoobis and perhaps that was why time seemed to pass more quickly for them here. One day they looked at their calendar and realized to their dismay that they had been on Earth for almost 50 years and that they had aged a great deal.

From their backwater vantage point in Peru, they could sense the pace of change was accelerating for humans. Because of the wide diversity and mobility of its ethnic groups, life on Earth was far more complex and bewildering than what they had known on Senoobis. There were cities sprouting up everywhere and the whole planet was becoming more *connected*. That didn't mean it was less dangerous, only that it was being profoundly transformed.

It was several years before they were able to overcome their depression but, as they became reconciled to their new lives, it gradually lifted. Sometimes when they needed a break from work, they would drive down to the ocean to relax and enjoy the view. Losing themselves in the rhythm of the waves, they would contemplate their own humble existence and the nature of the universe as well. They wondered how many distant civilizations like theirs had flourished and then faded into oblivion without leaving a trace. It was hard to accept that they were most likely the last of the Senoobian race, also poised on the brink of extinction.

One day when they were strolling along the beach, on one of their frequent visits to the ocean, Jeliko said, "I've been thinking about our situation. We were once proud and respected officers of the starship *Syzilian*. Now look at us. We look like vagrants! This isn't the way we should be."

At first Bayn and Darz were befuddled and looked at each other, as if to say, "What's gotten into her?"

Darz said, "Jeliko, I agree with you but we're not dashing young officers. We're older now. Consider our years on Senoobis, our years on Earth and all the time we spent in the damn hyper-sleep units. Who knows for sure how old we are?"

Bayn nodded at him. "Yes, you're right but she has a point. We can do better than this. We ought to do something meaningful with our lives. We've lived on two different worlds. I'll bet only a handful of beings in the whole galaxy can say that!"

From then on, they tried to put aside their anger and self-pity and worked hard to learn the ways of humans so that they might fit in and avoid confrontations. Bayn in particular became interested in the history of their region. "If you're going to understand a race, you have to know its history," he would remind them.

More than 950 years earlier, the survival of the Senoobian race had hung on the success of three starships that carried birthing units with embryos. The *Syzilian* and the *Volarion* were dispatched to found a colony on Karyntis where it was hoped the Senoobian race might eventually flourish again. The *Syzilian* had a small unit with embryos to birth twelve infants *in vitro*; the *Volarion*'s birthing unit carried 60 embryos. Sadly, with the loss of both ships, the embryos on both starships perished along with both crews—except for Bayn, Darz and Jeliko. The third ship, the *Langorion*, was dispatched to Nanzema but its fate was unknown.

These grievous losses were the death knell for their race—without children, there would be no future. Such terrible losses haunted the three of them and left them distraught on a personal level because they would never know the joys of having children.

In the spring of 1962, however, Bayn had an epiphany. While Darz and he were taking a few ounces of gold to their buyer in Nazca, they noticed a family with two children. The family was obviously poor, but the parents and their children chattered and laughed, seeming genuinely happy.

That evening after sharing their afternoon meal, all three of them sat down outside their home as the sun began to set. Noticing that Bayn seemed distracted, as if he were troubled by some problem, Darz said to him, "You haven't had much to say today. Is something bothering you?"

Bayn sighed heavily. "It's just that I've been thinking about our situation again," he said.

His two comrades gave each other an ominous look and rolled their eyes.

"We were sent here to found a colony but we failed at that." He paused, looking at each of them solemnly before continuing. "But I have an idea." He hesitated, as if he were unsure how to proceed. "Look, the odds are we're the only surviving members of our race. Once we die, our race is extinct."

"Really!" grumbled Darz, irritated at being reminded of their predicament.

Bayn assumed an avuncular tone. "Look, we need to have children," he declared. "Think what it would mean to have a child or two around! All we need is a healthy male and female and, well, here you are. It may be too late now but I think you two should take each other as mates and give it a try. Why not?"

Neither Darz nor Jeliko wanted to be the first to respond to such a proposition so they looked at each other nervously with blank expressions. Having children was a subject they had always avoided and, even though they were in their later years, parental feelings they had never before acknowledged were awakened, recalling the sense of purpose they had lost when the *Syzilian* was destroyed.

Bayn fixed his gaze on Jeliko. "Every member of our crew, including ourselves, longed to have children. And everyone left behind on Senoobis wanted to have children. We all desperately wanted families and children but were denied them by the destruction of Senoobis, the *Volarion*, and the *Syzilian*."

Jeliko responded with raised eyebrows. "Excuse me, but I'm getting a little muddled here. What exactly are you getting at?"

"I know that you and Darz have always had special feelings for each other. I'm just saying that maybe you two have more of a chance to have children than you realize."

Darz looked at Jeliko nervously. "Yes, you're right, of course. I've always loved Jeliko but we've never considered mating."

"And I've always loved Darz," she managed, glancing sheepishly at him. "Look, I admit that in a way I think of us as mates or," she paused as if to choose her words carefully, "maybe it's more like brother-sister feelings but, as for children, I wouldn't know where to begin. We have no birthing equipment and, even if we did, given my age and 720 years in a sleep module, whatever eggs I might have are probably no longer fertile."

"I'm sure you could say the same about my sperm," Darz stammered uncomfortably.

"Besides that, we don't have a DNA scanner or any of the other equipment we would need!" Jeliko declared brusquely.

"Wait! I didn't mean *in vitro*," Bayn interrupted. "I know it's a long shot but I was thinking of the old way, *natural birth*."

Jeliko's mouth dropped open. "You mean *sexual*! Are you mad? Not one Senoobian female had a natural birth in the 500 years before the launch of the Karyntis Mission. It's a painful and risky business."

Bayn looked at both of them apologetically. "I know and that's what has been bothering me. Look, I'm no longer your superior officer and it was presumptuous of me to bring up such a sensitive subject. It would be your prerogative alone to act on it. It's a shame we weren't emotionally able to act on this 50 years ago. We—I mean *you*—should at least try to have a child before it is too late for sure. It's time you thought about yourselves on a personal level. Even if you can't have children, why not be a real family."

Jeliko and Darz looked at each other shyly. Darz blushed. They both felt self-conscious, even a little embarrassed. They had never dared to think of each other in a *sexual* way but now they were forced to acknowledge feelings that, although long suppressed, now allowed them to see each other in that way. Bayn continued. "It would be a great risk to you, Jeliko, and by the *Mark of Dolahktus*[1] I would rather

---

[1] *Dolahktus* was a mythological figure who placed an occultic mark above the doors of those he resented to put a curse upon them. His name was often invoked when nothing seemed to go right.

die myself than lose you in natural childbirth. Of course, Darz and I would be there to assist you."

Jeliko was not reassured. She scowled at Darz. "Don't you think you and I should discuss this?"

Darz nodded, "Yes, of course," but his voice was unsteady.

Gathering steam, she turned to Bayn, "Look here. This sounds wonderful but, never mind my age, do we really want to have a child and then leave it here to fend for itself after we're dead? Wouldn't it be selfish on our part to have a child then?" She paused to let the impact of the question sink in.

Darz said, "Bayn, she has a point. Even if we were able to have a child, she couldn't have a mate when she growns up. Humans aren't an option."

Bayn said, "You're right but we don't know how much longer we'll live and I believe it would be worthwhile to have a child who can know what it's like to live as a Senoobian. Besides the pleasure it would give us, we have to pass on the disks to someone who can look after them."

Darz was skeptical. "Well, maybe so, but sometimes I think we should just destroy them so they don't fall into the wrong human hands. What good will they be after we're dead?"

Bayn was not dissuaded in the least. "I believe the disks may be valuable to some race in the future. Besides, I'd like to know that what happened to Senoobis and us won't be forgotten. And by the way, the files in the disk library on fertility, natural conception and natural birthing—you should review them before you two decide what to do."

Darz and Jeliko finally agreed to become mates and *give it a try*. In 1965, after a long and difficult labor when Jeliko almost died, a baby girl they named *Amara* was born. "By the *Mark of Dolahktus*," Jeliko declared when the painful delivery was over, "No wonder our females gave up natural birth!"

Bayn proudly assumed the role of uncle and the three Senoobians became among the most protective parents on the planet. Mara had sparkling green eyes and thick bushy black hair. Her nose was narrow and pointed like Jeliko's and she could wiggle her ears; her features were those of a pixie. She was mischievous, a little imp, but her smile was adorable and even the humans who saw her were captivated by her adolescent beauty.

She quickly learned to talk and by the age of 10 there was no end to her questions. Her curiosity was boundless so, using the disks, she learned mathematics, astronomy, physics and the history of Senoobis. She was so full of energy that she mastered the grace and agility of the Proxima—the communal dance forms that were at the same time physical, artistic and social expressions—and the martial arts. She took it all to heart and mastered it all.

She came to love hats and always wore one. By the time she was 15, she made them herself. But the hats she dreamed up were bizarre— they first surprised and then amused not only her parents but any hapless human she met. She grew to be tall and wiry like Darz.

At last the three Senoobians experienced the joys and frustrations of parenting. Amara was headstrong, always a challenge and sometimes a mystery to parents who had no experience with children. She often made them laugh. Sometimes she made them swear. They were often stumped about what to do with her but no matter what she did, they adored her. It was the happiest time of their lives.

By the 1970's, their two small mines had played out and they were forced to get out and prospect around the countryside. Their explorations were sometimes the source of strange experiences. One day, for example, they had been prospecting for gold around the *Poroma* riverbed near *Chauchilla*, some 18 miles south of Nazca. It was said that in the time of the Incas, the river had run yellow with gold dust. They found no gold but the area was historically rich in a macabre way.

The riverbanks had obviously supported a sizable population for the area was a vast cemetery. There were thousands of graves, most of which had been desecrated by *huaqueros*, or grave robbers, who left the skulls and other bones scattered about, exposed to the elements. The surreal landscape they saw all around them was gruesome evidence of a depraved and vile disregard for the dead. There was an air of violation and decay about the place that left them feeling sickened. What kind of person could commit such heinous crimes?

It seemed that wherever one went in Peru there were the remains of ancient civilizations that offered glimpses into the clouded past of the local peoples. Near the small village of *Trancas*, they found the ruins of a small ceremonial temple, called the *Huaca del Loro* by the locals, and they stopped there for a few minutes to rest against a stone wall that offered some relief from the blistering sun. The air was still and there were no animals or birds to be seen or heard.

As Bayn squatted down and leaned back against the wall to study the ruins around them, an uneasy feeling settled over him. *Who had built the small temple and what had happened here?* he wondered. He could almost sense the rituals that had gone on there hundreds of years ago and he began to feel like they were intruding. There was no sign of any living thing, but the hair on his neck and arms began to stiffen.

Jeliko sat up, bothered by a feeling she couldn't put her finger on. "We should go," she said. "I don't feel comfortable. Something bad happened here. I can feel it."

Darz was agitated as well. "I don't like this place," he said. His skin was beginning to crawl.

Jeliko's eyes grew wide and her voice became hoarse. "Human sacrifice," she declared solemnly.

"What?" Bayn said, his mouth agape.

"That's what happened here," she repeated firmly. "Human sacrifice!"

"How do you know that?" Darz asked nervously.

"I can feel it. Almost hear the horror in their voices. We shouldn't be here," Jeliko replied.

Suddenly there was an unnatural stirring in the air that seemed to gather around them. Without uttering another word, the three of them leapt to their feet as one, slung on their backpacks and set off down the path that had brought them there. They moved warily, not daring to break the silence, expecting some sinister apparition to confront them at any moment.

They continued their brisk pace until they heard the sounds of birds again. Kener put up his hand motioning for them to stop and they took off their backpacks and sat down to rest, relieved to be away from the ruins.

"What was that all about?" Darz asked, mopping the sweat from his brow. "I felt like we were being stalked by some invisible menace."

"I have no idea," Bayn frowned. "Whatever it was, it was close. But I was in a panic. I never experienced anything like that on

21

Senoobis. Perhaps we encountered some hostile psychic vortex manifested by some terrible evil that occurred there. Maybe it was human sacrifice; there was the stench of death about the place."

"Is such a thing possible?" Darz stammered.

"It must be," Bayn replied.

"Well, I've never felt anything like that before and I will never go back there," Jeliko said.

3

THE MONTECARLOS

In 1975, there were three humans who made a favorable impression on the Senoobians. Bayn and Darz first met the Montecarlos, whose modest adobe home was only a few miles from their own, one afternoon as they walked along the narrow road, tired and dusty, after their old gray pickup had broken down. Jeliko had stayed behind at Naksoris that day, as she often did, using the disk library to tutor Amara.

Alejandro and Ana María Montecarlo were sitting on their porch as their small son played nearby when they noticed Bayn and Darz passing by. Alejandro called to them, inviting them over to share their shade and a cool drink. The humans regarded the two Senoobians curiously but, before long, they were chatting with them like old friends.

Alejandro was from Ica, a kind and gentle young man who loved children and taught school. He was not ambitious; he wanted only a simple life, a happy family and a small plot of land. If he were not a teacher, he would no doubt have been a farmer. He enjoyed raising corn, potatoes and cassavas in the small garden behind his house, and was proud of his three alpacas.

He had a broad smile and a generous nature. The Senoobians needed a ride home for tools and then back to their truck. When he heard that their truck had broken down, he offered them a ride. They looked at each other, uncertain about whether or not to accept his offer. Alejandro was persuasive though, so they grudgingly gave in.

The Senoobians observed María closely, fascinated by her appearance. She was a small woman with smooth black hair and friendly eyes, plainly dressed but gracious in her demeanor. Although they had observed human females with considerable curiosity before, they had never talked to one at any length. María was different from the others and they felt a strong connection to her and liked her immediately.

As they chatted, the Montecarlo's son, who was two years younger than Amara, sidled up behind Darz and curiously touched the bushy hair that looked so different from his own." Darz flicked away the imagined insect in his hair. The little boy jumped back warily, giggling mischievously. Darz turned and playfully grabbed at the youngster.

Darz was surprised: the boy's intense brown eyes revealed a maturity and intelligence beyond his years. He thought to himself *I'm dirty and look strange. I probably sound gruff to him. Yet he's not afraid of me.* He smiled and spoke to the boy in Spanish. "What is your name, young man?"

The little boy hesitated for a moment and then replied in a steady voice "My name is Marco Montecarlo, Señor Darz." Then he pulled himself up straight and announced, as if he were privy to Darz's thoughts, "I am not afraid of you."

Darz was taken aback by the child's reply as the others looked on in amusement. For the first time, he was touched by the innocence and charm that could be found in humans and strong paternal emotions he had felt for the first time at Amara's birth returned. He bent down to look Marco in the eye, shook his hand and replied, "I am pleased to meet you too, *Señor Montecarlo*. And I am not afraid of you." Darz patted him on the head gently and tried to stifle a laugh.

Marco relaxed. "Good!" he proclaimed. "You can be my friend."

After Alejandro had given them a ride, the Senoobians repaired their truck and were soon back home. That neighborly meeting improved their view of humans and a strong friendship between them and the Montecarlos, but especially between Darz and the little boy, flourished. They visited the Montecarlos often from then on.

It was not long, however, before tragedy struck. A few months after they had first met the Montecarlos, the Senoobians were returning home early one evening from their new mine. As they approached the Montecarlo home, they could hear gunfire and the sound of cars racing toward them on the narrow road. Startled but curious to see what was happening, they pulled their truck off the road into the scraggly stand of trees near the Montecarlo home. They scrambled out of their truck just as two cars roared up the road, one swerving frantically to escape the barrage of gunfire that was directed at it, the other in pursuit.

A tire blew out and the car in front swerved sharply, hit a large rock and briefly became airborne. It landed on the driver's side and skidded to a stop near the old kiawe tree in front of the Montecarlo's house. Two men hastily pulled themselves from the wreck and ran toward the house, all the while firing back at the black sedan that slid sideways and came to an abrupt stop in a cloud of dust not far behind them. One of the men was either wounded or had been injured in the wreck; he was limping and unable to keep up with his partner.

Three rough-looking men leaped from the sedan and returned fire, using the overturned vehicle for cover. Several of their shots struck the man who had fallen behind before he could reach the porch. He yelled, twisted around to confront his attackers and fell toward them, instantly dead.

The man who was now dead had somewhat shielded his partner who reached the front door of the house, slamming into it with all his weight. The door flew open and he fell inside, tumbling to the floor, as the Montecarlo family looked on in shock.

Like a dropped cat, the man on the floor sprang to his feet. He found himself confronting a dumbfounded man, a terrified woman and a small boy. "Sorry to barge in uninvited," he growled in Spanish, "but they want to kill me. Can you imagine that!"

Alejandro planted himself in front of his wife and son protectively.

The man stood for a moment looking at Alejandro and then his face broke into a cruel smile, "Aren't you going to invite me to dinner, *estúpido*?"

The man was slightly taller than Alejandro and stocky. His voice was gruff and menacing. He wore a rumpled white suit and a soiled blue tie. His black hair was disheveled; his white fedora lay squashed on the floor. He was dark-skinned and his nose had been broken. His arrogant manner implied that he would just as soon shoot you as not.

He moved about methodically, sizing up the situation, with a frown on his face. His rumpled white fedora was in one hand, his pistol in the other. Instead of being afraid, he seemed annoyed that anyone would inconvenience him by shooting at him, as if that sort of thing happened everyday.

"Who are you? What do you want?" stammered Alejandro.

The man ignored him and calmly turned toward the window to see three men approaching the house with guns drawn. He broke out the window and fired through it, killing one of them.

A stream of profanities and threats from the men outside were followed by several shots. "Come out now, Alberto, or we'll burn down the house around you," one of them taunted.

The Montecarlos huddled together against the wall, more terrified than ever. Then it came to him. "You're Alberto Calderon, *el narco*!" Alejandro blurted out.

The man smiled, as if flattered. "Yes, yes, but I don't have time for introductions." He peered out the window and a sadistic look came over him. He motioned Alejandro over to him. "Look, here's what we're going to do . . ."

The man outside shouted again, "Damn you, Calderon, I'm running out of patience. Come out now with your hands up so we can talk."

Calderon turned to Alejandro, "Humberto thinks I'm stupid. He only knows how to talk with bullets. I'm going to tell him I'm coming out with my hands up. Then I'll open the door and you will walk out with your hands up. Don't say a word or I'll shoot you."

"No, no. He'll shoot me. You said so," Alejandro stammered in a panic.

"Shhhsh, *amigo*. I was just joking. Humberto out there wants to take me alive. It's getting dark and he's never met me so if you don't open your mouth, he'll think you're me. He'll take you to his boss who will see that you're not me and let you go when you explain to him how I fooled Humberto and threatened to shoot your wife. Then he'll shoot that incompetent jackass himself."

"No, *Señor* Calderon, please. He'll kill me. I know it. What will my wife and son do?"

Calderon looked at him coldly. "If you don't go out there with your hands up and your mouth shut, I'll shoot you right now."

The three Senoobians approached the house cautiously from the side, as the gunfight continued. "What should we do?" Jeliko whispered?

Bayn hesitated, unsure what to do. "Well, we did swear not to get involved in the affairs of the humans, no matter what? It can only cause us trouble. But . . ."

"Yes, we did agree on that," Darz blurted out, "And that would usually be the wisest course of action but . . ."

Jeliko interrupted, "Oh, to hell with that! We can't stand here and do nothing while they're murdered before our eyes. Besides, what about Marco?"

That was the last straw for Darz. "Yes, to hell with that!"

Alejandro glanced at his wife and son huddled together against the wall. "All right. I'll go. Just don't hurt them."

Calderon cautiously moved to the side of the door, nudged it open and yelled, "All right, Humberto, you win. I'm coming out with my hands up."

Alejandro stood up stiffly and approached the open door as Calderon shoved the fedora on his head. Looking at his family one last time, he turned and walked outside, his hands in the air.

A storm of bullets met him at the edge of the porch and he fell to the ground, dead.

There was only stunned silence and then the wails of a woman and child who had lost a husband and father to the heartless act of a psychopath.

The two men outside, looking around cautiously with guns ready, approached the body. "Damn you, Calderon," one of them yelled.

Calderon leaped through the doorway and shot them both.

María pushed through the door past Calderon and rushed to her husband's body, hysterical. "You monster!" she screamed.

With a smirk Calderon turned to María. "You're coming with me," he snapped, "So shut up. The brat can stay here." He reached down and pulled her up on her feet just as Marco charged into him, his small fists pounding at the cruel colossus towering over him.

Calderon backhanded the boy, sending him sprawling off the porch. María turned on Calderon, her arms flailing wildly, clawing his face and beating his chest, only making him furious. He slapped her hard, knocking her back down and then, standing over her, grabbed her hair and pulled her up again.

The Senoobians stopped in their tracks, unable to believe their eyes. "He's going to kill her!" Bayn hissed. He turned to his comrades, frantic to save her. "Come on!" He motioned to Darz and Jeliko. Darz circled around so he could distract Calderon as he approached. Bayn and Jeliko split up and moved in from different directions behind him.

Calderon drew his pistol and shot María. Then he looked up to see Darz rushing toward him, just as Bayn hit him with a crushing blow on the back of the neck. He crumpled to the ground, unconscious.

In a panic Jeliko reached the woman and slid down beside her. María gripped her hand and fixed her eyes on Jeliko's. "Please, take care of him," she pleaded. Her eyes closed and she was still.

Darz ran to Marco, sweeping him up into his arms. Bayn ran to Alejandro but there was nothing he could do.

Jeliko stood up slowly. "I will," she swore under her breath.

Marco pulled away from Darz and ran to his mother's body as big tears streamed down his face. As Jeliko looked down at him, the thought of an innocent and helpless child suffering such a terrible loss broke her heart; she made up her mind to protect him, no matter what. She put on a smile and hugged him tightly. "Marco, don't worry. I promise we won't let anyone hurt you."

Jeliko walked over to Calderon and picked up his pistol. She pointed it at him and pulled back on the trigger . . ."

"Jeliko, no! We'll leave him for the police," Bayn insisted. "It's not our business."

She dropped the pistol, slumped down and began to cry. Marco was watching her. She pulled him to her and hugged him. "It is our business."

Bayn and Darz tied up the unconscious Calderon and then called the police in Nazca.

Sergeant Luis Arturo answered the phone on the first ring.

"Six people have been killed at the Alejandro Montecarlo home on Solitaria Carretera Tres," Bayn rattled off. "Do you know the place?"

"Yes, I know it," Arturo replied. "Who are you?"

"A neighbor. Please hurry. Drug dealers, I think. One of the killers is alive. The Montecarlos are dead."

"Don't leave. I'll be there in 30 minutes."

Sergeant Arturo was feeling overwhelmed as he ran to his truck. *Holy Mary! Six murders and I'm the only one on duty.* He tried to call his boss but there was no answer. *With his mistress, no doubt.* He recalled the Montecarlos and his heart sank. *Good people.*

Being questioned by the police was risky for the Senoobians so Bayn took Jeliko by the arm and pulled her away. "We'd better go," he said.

Jeliko planted her feet and turned to face him. "What about Marco?"

"We'll have to leave him here until the police arrive," Bayn said.

"Leave him alone with Calderon unconscious and his parents dead!" Jeliko snapped. "I won't do it."

"Well, we can't take him with us. What would we do with him?"

"We can raise him," she blurted out.

"Raise him! Are you crazy! We can't raise a human child," Darz snorted. "He might murder us in our sleep!"

Jeliko glared at him, disgusted. "I can't believe you said that."

Darz turned red. "I'm sorry. I didn't mean it," he muttered, ashamed.

Bayn realized she was serious and her mind was made up. "Jeliko, uhh, I don't think that's a good idea," he tried half-heartedly.

"She's right," Darz said to Bayn. "We can't leave him."

When Arturo arrived and saw the carnage before him, he almost threw up. The Senoobians introduced themselves and told him what they had witnessed. Alberto Calderon had a long history of crime and violence in the Nazca area; Arturo recognized him at once.

"You'll need to appear in court," Arturo told them.

"We can't," Bayn replied. "We're not from around here, and we don't want to call attention to ourselves or make enemies."

"Well, the case against Calderon will be more difficult without your presence and, just by being here, you and I have already made enemies. From what I know about Calderon, if you testify against him, you will be taking a considerable risk."

Jeliko stepped forward, holding Marco's hand. "Okay, give us some time and we'll think about it. What we're most concerned about right now, however, is what we're going to do with *him*. Both of his parents are dead. As far as I know, the only living relative he has around here is his grandmother and she's very old."

"Umm, too bad. By the way, where are you folks from?"

"A place you've never heard of—we'll tell you about it some day when we're not so rushed,"

Arturo said, "Fine. Look, I've got a mess here to clean up. If you'll take care of the boy for a few days, I'll ask around about a permanent home for him. Then I'll stop by your place and we'll figure out what to do with him. A shame about the Montecarlos. Thanks."

"Glad to help, Sergeant," Bayn said.

Jeliko added. "You should call before you drop by. We're out a lot."

The Senoobians didn't have to testify against Calderon. Before Arturo could get back to them, the murderer had escaped from jail and disappeared. Thankfully, Calderon never found out who had knocked him unconscious.

No one else would take Marco in, so the Senoobians agreed to raise him. Although they had no idea what they were getting into, they became his family.

It was rumored that Sergeant Arturo was the only honest member of the local police force. The Senoobians came to know him well and, eventually, he gained their trust. It was the beginning of a strong friendship.

It took Marco a long time to recover from the trauma he had experienced at the death of his parents. He was insecure and the nightmares went on for years. It wasn't easy for him to adjust to his new life with the Senoobians or for them to understand a human child. Nonetheless, over the next few months, he grew to accept them as his own parents, and they took him as their own flesh and blood so much so that no one could have persuaded them to give him up.

For his part, Marco became so close to the Senoobians that he was blind to the physical and cultural differences between human and alien, seemingly unaware that he was not like them. In fact he came to feel closer to the Senoobians than to any of the other humans around him.

To their surprise, Amara was delighted to have a little *brother*. The first time Marco met her, he was quite taken by the elfish girl in her fancy round red hat and he pestered her with a storm of questions. To her amusement, he developed a crush on her and followed her wherever she went. He called her *Pokzahta*, which is Kuterin for *firefly*, because her eyes seemed to sparkle like fireflies at dusk. At first he was a pest, but eventually she took him under her wing and the two became inseparable, like a younger brother and older sister. There were no other playmates for either of them so, throughout their teen years, they spent a lot of time together, playing, fighting and exploring around their home, competitive but fiercely protective of each other.

The Senoobians taught Marco several skills that helped him become a smart and clever young man. He surprised them by quickly mastering their language. He and Amara spent hours chattering away in Kuterin, and Darz bantered back and forth with them, testing and teasing them. By the time he was 10, he could carry on a basic conversation in Kuterin. At 12, he was fluent in it and had mastered their numbers system. Bayn even taught him to fly the lander.

Amara taught him to play Zanoba®, the ancient strategy board game used by her ancestors to develop thinking skills. Unlike any human game, it was challenging and addictive. Marco and she were fiercely competitive and she was very good at it, but before long it was hard for her to beat him.

She also taught him to perform the basic *Proxima*, a communal dance that was a popular social outlet on Senoobis. Marco watched Amara and her parents perform it and, with their help, mastered several forms. It helped him develop his strength, stamina and coordination. Because of the attention and the training he received from them, he grew to be smart, confident and tough. They gave him plenty of encouragement and he thrived.

His desire to avenge his parent's murder coalesced into a dominant part of his maturing psyche; he and Amara often fantasized about taking revenge on Calderon. He was determined to never again be vulnerable and helpless the way he was when his parents were murdered.

The three older Senoobians practiced the martial arts and Marco begged them to teach him. They became his mentors and they helped him develop a style that would make him tough and fearless. He had a stubborn and competitive nature that drove him to practice relentlessly so he could excel at it. With his growing skill at martial arts came the strength and confidence to become independent and subject to no one.

Just as importantly, he refused to be outdone by Amara so he secretly vowed to become as good as she was. Almost every day, he practiced, coached first by her and then by Darz and Jeliko. He and

Amara grew closer but fiercely competitive as they continued to spar, each one determined to outdo the other, until they could win against Darz and Jeliko. He learned everything he could from them, becoming strong and fast, advancing, like Amara, through the four levels of skill. Not one of the four Senoobians went easy on him, nor did he want them to.

First Amara had to fight *Uncle* Bayn to qualify for the fourth level, referred to as the ᎣᏂᎢᎪᏍ (*Soojahn*). The next year, Marco was ready to fight him. The three old Senoobians were serious about their martial arts and Bayn gave him no quarter, making him earn every point; after the match, he too became a proud fourth level Soojahn.

Sometimes when Amara and Marco ventured out to explore the countryside, they would be pestered by some of the local human males who were often cocky and unruley. When the two of them had had enough, they would let loose a flurry of powerful kicks and devastating jabs to beat the troublemakers into submission in short order. Eventually it came to be a game to see which one of them could inflict the most damage on the troublemakers.

The Senoobians found the responsibilities of looking after two clever and headstrong children more challenging than they had expected. Since parenting made them more wary of the crude and sometimes menacing human culture that swirled around them, for the most part, they kept to themselves. They did connect with a few other humans, such as the Franciscos, who helped them see the good as well as the mean and parochial in humanity. As the years passed, their understanding of human nature became better informed and more nuanced, enabling them to avoid compromising situations.

By the time Amara and Marco were grown, most humans around Nazca paid scant attention to their Senoobian neighbors and that was the way they liked it.

4

THE FRANCISCOS

In 1979, the Senoobians met two other Peruvians who had a profoundly positive effect on them. The way they met is an example of how bad beginnings can sometimes lead to happy endings.

The human population was still sparse there so they didn't have many dealings with humans, except for the street urchins who were always into some mischief. Sometimes when they went into Nazca for supplies, the gangs of children that played in the streets would spot them and gather around, shouting cruel names.

Late one afternoon on such a trip, the perennial gang of young toughs that routinely pestered adults was playing in the street. That day they were more unruly than usual and as the tired Senoobians loaded their supplies, the ragtag group gathered around and began taunting them. This time their disrespect was particularly offensive and annoying. Some of them called the Senoobians names and even threw stones at them.

The Senoobians tried to ignore them but soon their insolence was more than Bayn could bear. He winked at Jeliko and Darz and began to put on an act that they understood they were to mimic. The three of them shuffled along, seemingly intimidated, until one of the older boys, a bully and the instigator, came too close. Suddenly Bayn sprang to life and pounced on him, seizing him firmly by the collar and yanking him off his feet before he could get away. As Bayn lifted him up to look him straight in the eye with his fiercest expression, the young tough yelled and kicked defiantly with all his might but he couldn't escape Bayn's grip.

As Bayn opened his mouth to chastise him in a stern voice, the young hoodlum spit in Bayn's face, just as a small man in a black cleric's robe appeared from the church behind them. He tugged at

Bayn's free arm and motioned them toward the church. "Don't be too hard on them, Señors," he said in a solicitous voice. "I will handle this."

Father Antonio Francisco had heard the commotion and, looking out the window in his office, saw the rowdy gang accosting them. Bayn loosened his grip and lowered the boy to the ground. The young troublemaker immediately pulled free and retreated a safe distance where he picked up stones and began throwing them at Bayn while spouting obscenities.

The priest called out to the young ruffian in a stern voice, "Ramon, why do you act that way? Show some respect!"

Ramon Maldonado was still cocky and pretended not to hear the priest. As if to say, "I'm not afraid of you," he slowly strutted over to rejoin his gang as he flashed hateful glances at Bayn.

The priest said, "Please excuse me for a minute." Then he approached the group and chastised the ruffians, sending them scurrying away.

Turning to the Senoobians, the priest said, "My name is Father Antonio Francisco; my friends call me 'Father Tony'. Please forgive the rudeness of the children, my friends," he said softly, "They mean no harm." He had thinning gray hair and a sparkle in his eyes.

Taken aback by his unexpected kindness, they relaxed and introduced themselves.

He said he had heard about them and that he was glad to finally meet them. Then with a kindly smile, he said, "Won't you rest for awhile and allow me to offer you a drink?" He was a kind and gentle man who seemed genuinely interested in them; he treated them with respect and gave them his full attention. They warmed to him immediately.

They sat down in Father Tony's small office. He called out through the door, "Phillipe, will you bring some wine for our guests?"

A pleasant young man with dark hair appeared and set some glasses and a bottle of wine before them. He was perhaps 5'10" and had fine features, a rather handsome young man. Father Tony introduced him with obvious pride as his son and Phillipe spoke to them with a charm and grace beyond his years—he was only 27—and seemed genuinely glad to meet them. For the first time they didn't feel different.

"Where are you gentlemen from?" Father Tony asked.

All three of them looked at each other, unsure how to answer. Finally Bayn said in Spanish, "Father, we live near Palpa but we are from a place far away. How we came to be here is a long story. Someday when you're not too busy, we'll be glad to share it with you."

He said that he was interested to hear their story when they were ready to tell him. It was the beginning of a strong friendship.

Eventually they did get around to telling both him and Phillipe how they came to be there and the two priests promised to keep their story to themselves. Father Tony said he was used to keeping secrets. They were honest men and the Senoobians grew to trust them completely. When they had questions about the human way of thinking or why humans behaved a certain way, they came to Father Tony or Phillipe.

On Senoobis religion had not been practiced for several hundred years, so the Senoobians had no concept of it. Bayn in particular became interested in the human practice of religion and, thanks to Father Tony and Phillipe, began to understand it. He studied everything he could find about the major human religions—Judaism, Christianity, Islam and Buddhism—and he peppered Father Tony and Phillipe with questions whenever he saw them.

He usually prefaced his questions with something like "Father, something's been bothering me. I wonder if you could help me out?" Bayn suspected that Father Tony and Phillipe came to dread hearing those words but they never seemed to mind. They were always patient and even claimed to enjoy their discussions.

Bayn recalled the first question he asked Father Tony. He had studied the New Testament and a few other texts in an attempt to understand Christianity. Then he took up the Old Testament, trying to better understand Judaism and how it gave rise to Christianity. He was aghast at how petulant and even blood-thirsty the Old Testament Jewish God seemed to be. *Why was it*, he wondered, *that the Christian God of the New Testament had become so much more peaceful than he was in the Old Testament? After all, he was the same god!*

Bayn was sitting in his office and said to him, "Father, I have a question." The priest seemed pleased at his interest.

Bayn said, "Father, the Bible says God is the same forever, but the God of the Old Testament is stern and fierce while, in the New Testament, he seems more benign. It is the same god, right?"

"After a moment, a serious look came over his face and Father Tony said, *My son, that is a very good question. Indeed it is too big a question for a simple man like me. I can only say that it must have been God's plan. I think God knew that He had to appear to humans in a form they could relate to and understand. I suspect that, since humans were primitive in those times, He had to be a more authoritarian figure. But I am only speculating. I live by my faith in things that I don't understand. We cannot possibly comprehend the mind of God.*"

That sort of conversation occurred on many occasions, sometimes with Father Tony, sometimes with Phillipe as well. The Senoobians always appreciated the two men's honesty when they didn't know how to answer a questions and their patience with the Senoobian's curiosity about human nature. Most of the time their conversations were helpful but other times they were left with more questions than answers. The one thing never questioned, however, was their kindness and goodwill. Their lives were based on a simple, unquestioning faith that some might have called blind or naïve.

One spring morning, they came to realize just how remarkable Phillipe was. Jeliko and Bayn had come to visit and, finding Father Tony indisposed with some minor illness, they chatted with Phillipe for a while. They were pleased to have a chance to get to know Phillipe better and they told him how much they appreciated him and how much they admired his father.

"Well, you're very kind," Phillipe said. "I love my father. He is a good man—probably the kindest man I have ever known. You know he saved my life. I lost both of my parents by the time I was 14 and I was forced to live on the street, literally starving. He took me in and treated me as his own son."

When they asked him about his work, he looked subdued and seemed disheartened. They knew that he was unusually sensitive for a human so they were not too surprised when he confessed that he was feeling discouraged. He confided that he was troubled about the leadership of their diocese.

Bishop Hervias had visited them the day before, but his concern was more for increasing tithes than ministering to his parishioners. There was an addition to be built, so he had urged Father Tony to ignore the poor and pursue the more affluent citizens of Nazca for their diocese. Phillipe had insisted: "What about our poor? Should we not minister to them first since they need us more?"

"The poor you will always have with you but you will not always have me. Matthew 26:11. We must serve the greater good," Bishop Hervias had insisted.

". . . in as much as ye have done it unto one of the least of these my brethren, ye have done it unto me. Matthew 25:40," Phillipe had retorted, disgusted.

They talked for a long time and grew to appreciate the young man's friendship even more. Compared to them in age, Phillipe was a child but he trusted the Senoobians without question. He assured them that, even if they were from some strange and distant world, it was of no more consequence than being from another country. That was one of the reasons they liked him: he seemed to understand their situation and didn't treat them as outcasts even though they didn't believe as he did.

5

THE DEBATE

After dinner one autumn day in 1982, Bayn said to Darz and Jeliko, "I've been thinking. Do you recall that message from the Peyrian lord that the *Volarion* forwarded to us?"

Darz nodded, "Yes, of course."

"He claimed the Peyrians had been to Earth more than a thousand years ago. Since he expected to capture or destroy the *Volarion*, there was no reason to lie about it."

Jeliko said, "Yes, I agree but what's your point?"

Bayn continued, "Do you remember, a couple of years ago, I found some old records giving the history of this region. There was one record in particular that was interesting. It was by Juan de Betanzos, a sixteenth-century Spanish writer who recorded some of the legends of the indigenous Indians in a book called *Suma y Narracion de los Incas.*"

"In it he describes the legend of a tall, thin, bearded and light-skinned man named Veracocha who wore a white robe, visited this area and taught the Indians many useful skills. His name meant *foam of the sea* and the Indians believed he was powerful, able to work miracles. There is a similar individual, although called by different names, who is mentioned in the myths of several other South American cultures."

"In fact the descriptions used for other deities who roamed South America and Mexico—gods such as *Quetzalcoatl* who was the primary deity of the Aztecs—are similar enough that they may be referring to the same individual. Aztec legends refer to a long struggle after which the evil god Tezcatlipoca defeated Quetzalcoatl and drove him out of Mexico. Tezcatlipoca required human sacrifice whereas Quetzalcoatl advocated peace and the sanctity of human life. The legends say that Quetzalcoatl, like Veracocha, sailed off in the direction from which he came after promising to return."

Darz stroked his chin, "Hmmm. Very interesting."

Bayn continued, "Now think about this. You know I've been studying various old religious texts, trying to understand the religious aspects of human culture. In the Old Testament, there is a book by Ezekiel, one of the prophets of the Jewish god. In the first chapter, Ezekiel describes a visitation by some sort of beings in a flying machine that is totally out of place for such a primitive time. It's a bizarre passage in which Ezekiel's god orders him to deliver various threats of punishment to the Jews. Ezekiel's god was angry because the Jews hadn't been paying enough attention to him or behaving the way he had commanded."

Darz said, "That's all very interesting but what are you saying?"

"Just that I can't help but wonder why this god in his awesome flying machine didn't just go to the people themselves and show off his power if he wanted to get their attention. Why send an illiterate prophet to harangue the people?"

Darz mused, "That's a good question. Maybe he was trying to establish a moral code so humans could become more civilized. If he wasn't going to be around very long, he would need someone to guide the people in his absence."

Bayn said, "And here's something else: this god is violent. He exhorts the Jews to go out and slay other peoples and take over their lands. He requires sacrifices, but as time went by he insisted on animal sacrifice rather than human sacrifice. Could there be a connection between the gods of Mexico and South America and the Jewish god?"

Jeliko shrugged her shoulders. "Who knows?"

Bayn continued, "Listen to this: there's another interesting passage in Genesis, the first book of the Jewish Old Testament, about giants. It says . . . *the sons of God saw that the daughters of men were beautiful, and they married any of them they chose . . . There were giants in the earth in those days . . .* Then their G od became angry with the humans and decided to destroy them all in a great flood."

"Now we have the Nazca Lines that must have been intended as a way of communicating with beings who could fly, since the designs can't be seen from the ground. The chronology is uncertain, but we're probably referring to a period in time a thousand years ago. There were no human civilizations capable of flight then."

Amara said, "So the Earth could have been visited by beings from another star system who contacted early human cultures and possibly inspired their early religious belief systems. But we know of only one advanced extraterrestrial race out there so . . ."

Darz exclaimed, "Yes, remember how the Nezeke treated us—like gods! Maybe they thought we were the Peyrians!"

Bayn said, "Exactly. What if Quetzalcoatl and Tezcatlipoca were actually Peyrians who had a falling out over how to deal with the primitive humans? And what if they've been planning to return ever since? The question is why haven't they returned before now? They were advanced then, so you would think they would be far more advanced by now."

Jeliko suggested, "Maybe they suffered some major cataclysm like we did. Or maybe they had a major intraspecies war and bombed themselves back to the Stone Age, or some pathogen wiped them out!"

"Well, there certainly are more questions than answers," Darz mused, "but there does seem to be some strong circumstantial evidence that the Peyrians have been here before and are coming back."

One dreary winter evening in 1983, there was an incident that revived their hopes that those on the *Langorion* might have survived. Jeliko was fiddling with the radio that she had removed from the lander years earlier. It was a good radio with a scanner but not very powerful. The Senoobians rarely flew the lander, so it had occurred to her that she could transfer the radio to their home and use it as a diversion. It was a habit she had picked up as a way to dabble in the field she had come to love as a young cadet at the academy in Senoobia. She found comfort in scanning the different frequencies and listening for communications from near space.

Why she sometimes tuned the radio to the handful of obscure VHF channels, she couldn't say. It was no doubt a matter of habit from monitoring the same frequencies for communications on the *Syzilian* for so long. Perhaps it was her only way of connecting with an almost forgotten life, so different from the isolated one she now lived. Nevertheless, the tinge of nostalgia she felt when she turned the dials always faded into disappointment after she heard only static.

It was getting late and she had decided to turn off the radio and go to bed. She gave the micro-tuner one last twist and, as she did so, she heard a message! The signal was weak and garbled. *Was it Kuterin?* She held her breath, pricked up her ears, turned on the record function and listened. A few minutes later, it came again, a little stronger, but then it faded away, lost to static, leaving her frustrated. It was definitely a message but from whom? She manned the radio for months after that but heard nothing else.

Sometimes the older Senoobians were so frustrated in their dealings with humans that their grumbling spilled over into their conversations with Amara and Marco, making them uncomfortable. Their only recourse was to air their grievances with Father Tony or Phillipe who always listened patiently and somehow managed to make them feel better.

By the late 1980's, their melancholy had worsened; they were dealing with several issues that stoked their malaise. Amara and Marco were grown and the old Senoobians no longer felt needed. Besides, they were feeling their age: they had less stamina and energy but more aches and pains.

Obliged to keep a low profile and unable to engage in human affairs, they were confined to a narrow and mundane existence. In the evenings when it was quiet and they were alone, it became their habit to relive the past when they were young, dashing officers, fearless and undeterred in the service of Senoobis. In those days, everything they did was urgent and exciting; now nothing seemed to matter. Their only relief from boredom was to tell colorful stories and perform the Proxima.

Bayn especially seemed to lose his spirit. One day when he was feeling more despondent than usual, he described his feelings so sharply that Darz and Jeliko were stunned. "We began our lives with so much promise, called to do great things," he said glumly, "but nothing has come of it. Here we are—only shadows of our former selves. I would rather have died like Amantis!"

It hurt Darz and Jeliko to hear him talk like that. They tried hard to console him with little success, perhaps because they were dissatisfied with their own lives as well.

In the fall of 1989, the three older Senoobians had an epiphany. They were setting up a new stage and sound system so all five of them would have a better place to perform the Proxima and practice martial arts.

During a break, Jeliko tapped Bayn on the arm and motioned Darz over. "I've been thinking about your theory that the Earth was visited by the Peyrians a thousand years before we arrived—we haven't considered the humans?"

Bayn replied, "What do you mean?"

Jeliko continued, "Don't you think we should warn them?"

Darz frowned. "Hmm, maybe, but I don't see what good it would do. I don't believe they could defend themselves against the Peyrians—even if they were warned."

One of the Nazca merchants had tried to cheat him the day before and the annoying incident had left Darz in a foul mood. He responded dismissively, "I'm not sure they're worth saving. If the *Volarion* had reached the Earth and we had successfully founded a colony, it would probably have been only a matter of time before we had to defend ourselves against the humans. I don't think they would accept us, even if we didn't look that different from them. Let their gods save them."

Jeliko said, "Darz, don't forget, for most of our history we were the same way. It was only after the overriding desperation of the First Tribulation that we managed to overcome our bloody past and pull together—it was *work together or die*. That was the great defining event in the history of our race. Perhaps the humans haven't yet experienced their own defining event."

He shrugged, "Apparently not. I would have thought that two bloody World Wars would have been their defining events and inspired them to work together to solve their problems."

Bayn said, "Look what they're doing to this planet. On Senoobis, the population was capped at 630 million and half the planet was set aside and protected in its natural state. Earth, however, is becoming more overpopulated by the day. No doubt humans would long ago have exceeded the planet's capabilities if they hadn't killed off so many of themselves in their wars." He shook his head sadly.

Darz said, "They are an odious species! I have sometimes wondered if there is some flaw in their genetic makeup. Too many of them are unable to control their destructive urges. Not even the gods of their great religions have been able to tame their violent natures."

"The worst flaw in humans is their hubris," Bayn declared. "They generally consider anyone different from themselves to be inferior and unworthy of the respect they grant members of their own group or race. Look, the Peruvians dislike the Chileans, the Chinese resent the Japanese, the Muslims detest the Jews, the Greeks loathe the Turks and everyone hates the Americans. Their arrogance drives their behavior more than their commitment to their religious beliefs.

"No civilization will endure if large segments of its populations work at cross-purposes with each other. I'll give you an example: although the health risks and the economic costs their societies incur by using illicit drugs are well known, millions of humans persist in using them. Why should we put ourselves at risk to help such an irresponsible species?"

"But I'm a human, Father," Marco protested, crestfallen. "Do you think I'm like that?"

Jeliko gave Darz a dirty look. "Of course not," she replied in a motherly tone. "We didn't raise you like that. Besides, your father is talking about irresponsible humans. Most humans aren't like that. Look at Luis and Phillipe."

Darz calmed down. "I'm sorry, Marco. I got carried away with my frustrations. I know you're not that way."

Bayn said firmly, "No, you're not like that, Marco."

"But Father, Mother's right: there are some good humans," Amara said. "And I've heard you praise the impressive art, literature, and architecture, as well as the beautiful music, they've created."

"Yes, yes, I'll grant you all of that," Darz conceded, "but, there are 6.5 billion humans living on this planet today. How many of them do you really think give a damn about anything but where their next meal is coming from if they're poor or how to put even more money into their own pockets if they're rich."

Amara said, "Father, I believe we should help the humans. Besides Marco, I know a few humans that I'm rather fond of. You said it yourself: the Peyrians destroyed the *Volarion* and, by doing that, murdered the few survivors of our species. They're our enemy—not the humans who have allowed us to live here on their planet unmolested for the most part. It's not their fault we were marooned here."

Jeliko said, "Amara's right. I wouldn't want anything to happen to Father Tony, Phillipe or Luis. And there was Arenas? Remember how kindly he treated us when we were desperate? Who's to say how many other humans there are like them, probably millions who shouldn't be harmed. Let's help them."

Darz said, "Not so fast. I don't think most humans will like the fact that other intelligent life forms exist in the universe. Out in the open, we might become so sensationalized and controversial that nothing would come of our efforts except a lot of trouble and risk to ourselves."

Bayn said, "I'm worried about that too, Darz. If we empower them with our technology, will we be creating problems for humans and putting ourselves, especially Amara and Marco, at more risk?"

Jeliko said, "Maybe we will be. But there's nothing we can do about our situation, so maybe we can do them a good turn. Darz, what about it?"

Darz looked contrite. "All right. Our children and our human friends are all that matter now. We can't ignore the possibility that the Peyrians will return. Maybe we should help defeat them any way we can."

Bayn said, "We have the technology; the humans have the resources to use it. If they will listen to us, then perhaps we should share our technology with them. If they're not smart enough to heed our warning, then at least we tried."

Darz responded, "Good point. If we're going to do anything though, we'll have to go through the Americans or the Russians since they are the strongest militarily and have the most experience in near space. If the Americans and Russians can cooperate, they might be able to defeat the Peyrians if they bring only one or two starships."

Jeliko remarked, "We will have to convince some influential government official that we're credible—prove to them we're who we say we are without compromising ourselves. I think we need a proxy—someone to represent us, with enough credibility to convince the leaders of the humans. I have no idea how we might find such a person without compromising our safety though."

Bayn thought about it. "A proxy? Someone we can trust to speak on our behalf without putting us at risk. Hmmm."

The Senoobians found themselves at a dead end and, before long, they had forgotten all about their debate.

During those years, Amara and Marco were struggling with their own issues. Amara had become a mature female who hungered to have a mate and children. That could never happen as long as she was stuck on Earth—there was no one suitable as a mate—so she grew increasingly frustrated and rebellious.

Marco was faced with a similar situation. He was a human who had grown up as a Senoobian. He spoke Kuterin; he had Senoobian values. He was not really comfortable around humans. The desire to have a mate and a family was strong in him as well, but what was he to do? Human females didn't appeal to him.

The reality was that, like their parents, they found themselves suspended in a kind of limbo, unable to find meaning or purpose in their lives. As young adults, their shared frustrations brought them closer together and made them more dependent on each other. Sometimes they would go for long walks in the evening, pouring out their anguished feelings to each other.

One day they went to the ocean near San Juan for a break from the gray days that were hanging over Naksoris. After a long walk and a spirited run on the deserted beach, they were ready for a swim. Laughing mischievously, they shed their outer clothes and slipped into the cool waters, almost naked. They swam until they were exhausted. Breathing hard, muscles aching, they dragged themselves from the water and collapsed on the soft sand, their thin underwear clinging to their bodies.

Amara lay back and closed her eyes, enjoying the warmth of the sun on her skin.

Marco propped himself up on one elbow, pleased to see her as he never had before; for the first time, he realized how beautiful she was. He blushed; feelings he had never before allowed were aroused.

When she opened her eyes, he was staring at her, fascinated, a guilty look on his face. She was amused; then she was pleased: he found her attractive. She didn't turn away; instead, she studied him unashamed, seeing him in a different way as well. He was handsome, his body pleasingly masculine. She scooped up a handful of sand and threw it at him.

He retaliated by pivoting above her and pinning her arms. They wrestled on the sand, fighting hard, with Amara giggling as she struggled to free herself. He held her tight, trying to hold her arms. As if on cue, they stopped, relaxed, eyes fixed on each other, mouths close, breathing hard, tempting each other.

Marco fell back onto the sand with a sigh, letting her go. "Amara, we're trapped. What are we going to do?"

They lay on their sides, facing each other.

She gently stretched out her hand, running her fingers through his hair and over his face, her eyes moist. "I don't know, but I'm afraid." She had never admitted a fear of anything before.

Marco furrowed his brow, puzzled. "Of what?"

"Our parents won't live much longer—what will happen to us after they're gone?"

His strong arms pulled her to him protectively.

6

CONTACT

It was not until late one evening, in early July of 1998, that the Senoobians received a second intelligible message. The three older ones were relaxing while Marco and Amara played the strategy game Zanoba©. Years earlier, they had all given up hope of receiving another message and no longer paid attention to their small radio.

Left on, however, it faithfully continued its digital vigil year after year, scanning the narrow frequency band that had delivered the first perplexing transmission fifteen years earlier. That night when it beeped the alert that it was receiving a transmission, Jeliko jumped, dropping her book. She raced to the radio, turned up the volume and hit the record button.

Calling Tyguta. This is Prolifigus. Urgent! Structural damage. Brosoros G213C. Can you help? Lepgeesh meertah. End.

Was it possible! Her hand shook as she picked up the microphone. "*Prolifigus! Prolifigus!*" she shouted, "Yes, we hear you!" Her voice trailed off into a whisper. *What am I doing? It can't be the Langorion. Ahgzahtu! What's going on?*

"Bayn, come here. Darz, get the Code Book. Hurry!" she yelled.

Bayn came running in. "What's going on?"

"Listen to this." She replayed the message.

Darz rushed in with the small booklet. She played the message again.

Bayn and Darz looked at each other, dumbfounded.

"After 800 years, can it really be the *Langorion!*" Jeliko exclaimed.

"It would seem so. I don't see how the codes could have been compromised. Let's have a look at the code book," Bayn said.

Darz stroked his chin. "Suppose the *Langorion* was not destroyed—only damaged, with her communications disabled. Suppose she managed to reach some planet or moon where some of the crew survived. What if the crew eventually repaired their ship and made it to Karyntis, looking for the *Syz*?"

Bayn was thumbing through the code book. "Highly improbable after more than 800 years, I would say."

"I agree but how else can you explain such a message?" Darz mused.

"I don't know but, odds are, it's from the *Langorion* or some force that has captured her. I expect we'll be able to tell when she replies," Bayn replied.

"But our signal is so weak, I'm afraid the *Langorion* hasn't received my reply," Jeliko said.

Amara came bounding down the stairs. "What's all the commotion?"

Marco stuck his head in from the kitchen. "What's happening?"

"Well, we've just received the most remarkable radio message! It's from *Prolifigus* to *Tyguta*."

"But I've never heard of *Prolifigus* or *Tyguta*," Amara said, puzzled.

Bayn chuckled. "You wouldn't have because they don't exist—it's a code! A way of contacting another ship without giving away your identity or location to someone listening in."

"Someone like the Peyrians," Darz said.

Jeliko explained, "*Prolifigus* is the code name for the *Langorion*. The code name for the *Syzilian*, for example, is *Nesfrezia*."

"I see," said Amara, "but who is this *Tyguta* that *Prolifigus* is calling?"

"An excellent question, my Dear. *Tyguta* is the code name for any Senoobian or Bretin ship receiving the message, a request for them to reply. And here's the other exciting part of the message—*Brosoros G213C*. That's the location code for Karyntis or Earth. They're approaching orbit!"

"The *Langorion* is coming here!" Amara exclaimed.

"Yes—if the message is authentic. The *Lepgeesh meertah* part means that they want us to authenticate our reply by including the correct key from our Code Book."

They continued to fret that *Prolifigus* might not be able to receive their weak transmissions. After thinking it over, they all agreed there was nothing they could do but keep calling *Prolifigus* and hope for a response. They took turns manning the radio and on the third day, Marco received the following message:

> Calling Tyguta. This is Prolifigus. Brosoros G209M. Ready for repairs. Parjat naktum. Lepgeesh karyat. End.

He grabbed the code book and yelled for Jeliko. "They've entered Earth orbit!" he shouted as Jeliko came running in. "They're requesting our global coordinates and authentication."

Together, Jeliko and Marco composed and transmitted the following message, giving the coordinates of their location on Earth:

> Calling Prolifigus. This is Nesfrekzia. We will assist. Naktum Vahsoog 3485 7201. Lepgeesh dyfak. End.

Profligus was close and coded messages flew back and forth using the prearranged codes to arrange a meeting. The Senoobians were jubilant but still mystified. *If this was in fact the Langorion, what was she doing here after 800 years?* In the back of their minds was the fear that the *Langorion* had somehow been captured by the Peyrians who had discovered their codes and set a trap for them.

On the third day a shuttle was dispatched to Naksoris. When it landed, Marco and the four Senoobians stood stiffly at attention, nervously and impatiently waiting to greet the three crewmembers who climbed out of it. The Senoobians were relieved—they were clearly Bretin.

The three Bretin seemed baffled at the appearance of the Senoobians. When the first one spoke in Kuterin, his enunciation seemed a little off. "I am First Lieutenant Ark Shurahp Navigation Officer on the N.S. *Mankuriun*." He gestured toward his two younger comrades, "This is Lieutenant Karseen Panzer, our pilot, and Ensign Nayta Agoyin, our Assistant Operations Officer."

They both stepped forward, smiling broadly. "We are honored to meet you," Panzer said. He was carrying a radio.

Shurahp continued, "If you don't mind my saying so, you're older than I expected."

Bayn tensed up. Something wasn't right. "If you don't mind my saying so, you're younger than I expected." He appeared to be only a few years older than Phillipe. "I'm Bayn Kener, former Executive Officer on the *Syzilian*. We were expecting the *Langorion*."

"Yes, well, the *Mankuriun* is an upgrade of the *Langorion*. We finished her rebuild 150 years ago."

Shurahp became suspicious. "I've read about Bayn Kener, the XO on the *Syzilian*, in our archives. That was 800 years ago! How can it be that you are alive after so long?"

"It's complicated, but, in a nutshell, while the *Syzilian* was in orbit around Karyntis, our whole crew was infected by a virus that we picked up on the surface. Except for the three of us, the whole crew died. We survived by getting into the sleep modules but we failed to enter a duration. After 720 years, the ship had fallen to such a low altitude that it overheated in the dense atmosphere. We were awakened by alarms and barely escaped in our lander before the ship exploded. We've managed to survive here for the last 90 years."

The three Bretin were aghast. Lt. Shurahp stared at him, "You're telling us that you've been alive for over 1,000 years, counting your years on Senoobis before the *Syzilian* launched!"

Bayn replied matter-of-factly, "Technically, that's correct but we were in the sleep modules on the *Syzilian* for about 870 of those years. By the way, this is Darz Tureesh, the former Operations Officer, and Jeliko Hanahban, the Communications Officer. We three are the only survivors of the *Syzilian*." Both nodded, feeling self-conscious.

Bayn waved Marco and Amara forward. "And this is Marco . . ."

Shurahp focused on Marco, noticing his eyes. "A human!"

Darz interjected, "Yes, a human—actually our adopted son *and* a master of Fourth Level Proxima."

"A human Fourth Level Master—Impossible!" Panzer exclaimed.

Marco blushed, "It's true—Fourth Level."

Darz cleared his throat. "And this is Amara Hanahban, mine and Jeliko's daughter, a Fifth Level Master. By a miracle she was born here on Karyntis *naturally* . . ."

"*Naturally!*" Lt. Shurahp exclaimed. Amara was wearing her brown, acorn-shaped hat and feeling a bit self-conscious. All three Bretin stared at her, fascinated, as if she were some sort of apparition.

"Yes, that's correct," Jeliko said, "And I don't recommend it."

"I'm sure it was difficult," Shurahp said sympathetically, at a loss for words.

After an awkward silence, Agoyin leaned toward him and whispered, "The invitation . . ."

Shurahp recovered, "Oh, yes. Well, this is all remarkable and we're eager to hear the details." He smiled broadly. "Our Commanding Officer, Captain Jandis Markovin, is anxious to meet you. He has asked me to invite you all aboard our ship."

Bayn said, "We're anxious to hear your story as well—and we are pleased to accept his invitation. We're ready to depart at your convenience."

Shurahp took the radio from Panzer. "Captain Markovin will be pleased. I'll radio him that you have accepted his invitation and that we will depart the surface in 30 minutes with all five of you."

"Excellent!" Bayn said.

While Shurahp was on the radio, briefing the Captain, Bayn said to Panzer, "So you used the *Langorion*'s codes."

"That's right. There was no *Mankuriun* when the codes were issued, so we continued to use the I.D. code for the *Langorion*."

"Well, that explains it," Jeliko said.

"You're from Nanzema then?" Bayn asked.

"Yes, sir, in the Jestura System. Obviously we have a lot to talk about."

7

THE MANKURIUN

At 1100, Marco and the four Senoobians boarded the shuttle for a visit to the *Mankuriun*. As the shuttle raced upward toward its rendezvous with the mother ship, they were unprepared for what they saw; the signs of a polluted and spoiled planet were everywhere they looked. The last time they had seen the Earth from such an altitude was when they escaped from the *Syzilian* almost a hundred years before. The planet looked far different now. Even in less-industrialized South America, the signs of a planet in distress were obvious; a huge section of the Amazon rain forest had disappeared!

With the clouds of Earth far below them, Amara and Marco crowded around a porthole, straining to make out the features of the Earth as it shrank below them.

The three older Senoobians, however, impatient for their first view of the *Mankuriun*, eagerly scanned the sky above them. They were curious to see how different she was from the *Syzilian* but they couldn't find her. Panzer was the pilot and Bayn, who was sitting behind him, leaned forward and tapped him on the shoulder. "Where is she?"

"We're almost there. You'll see her any minute now," Panzer replied.

Moments later the shimmering image of the starship appeared out of the nothingness of space, assuming the form of a dark behemoth looming over them. It was triangular-shaped, a little larger than the *Syzilian*, and obviously more advanced, a magnificent ship. As they slowed their approach toward the docking bay, its giant doors opened wide like a hungry mouth eager to swallow them whole.

Although the Captain had put the ship into stealth mode, he was still uneasy about the possibility of being detected by radar monitors on Earth or from outer space. What's more, there were hundreds of active, as well as defunct, satellites and thousands of stray parts and other debris in orbit around the planet, left over from countless missions, all posing a danger to the ship. A two-inch bolt whizzing around the earth at 15,000 mph—far faster than any earthly bullet—could easily puncture their ship's hull.

Panzer turned to Bayn, "If we weren't in stealth mode, we'd be sitting here exposed to everyone on Earth or in space."

A sitting duck! Bayn thought.

Panzer added, "It's quite effective unless you're within five or six miles of the ship.

On the observation deck of the *Mankuriun*'s landing bay, Captain Jandis Markovin, his aide Tavin Dolyvek, and Palander Stoveris, the Executive Officer, waited to greet their guests. They were eager to meet the only survivors from Senoobis—*they had actually lived on the mother planet 900 years ago! What stories they could tell.* Dolyvek was jubilant, "At last we'll find out what happened to the *Syzilian!*"

The Captain smiled, "Yes, at last the mystery will be solved. Palander tells me the Senoobians were in the sleep modules over 700 years!"

Stoveris nodded. "That's what they say."

Dolyvek said, "It's incredible. And we'll get a look at the human they're bringing with them. Imagine that: a human on board the *Mankuriun!*"

Dolyvek was nervous; they were going to meet time travelers from the distant past.

"I hear he doesn't look that different from us," the XO commented casually, "and that he's a master of the Proxima—Fourth Level."

"A human?" Dolyvek snorted. "Impossible!"

"Too bad you're not a master yourself, you'd be in better shape," the XO said without cracking a smile.

They watched as the shuttle arrived and the heavy doors to the docking bay slowly closed. When the shuttle was secured, air filled the bay again.

The three of them reached the shuttle just as its hatch opened and Shurahp appeared, followed by Marco and the four Senoobians.

Captain Markovin was not as tall as the old Senoobians, but he was younger and appeared to be in excellent shape. His dark hair was short but stiff and bushy, showing some gray. His manner was calm and unassuming, but he was keenly aware of everything around him. His friendliness and graciousness immediately put them at ease. It was obvious from the way he treated his crew, and in the way they responded to him, that they had the highest respect for him.

The Captain greeted them warmly and introduced his XO. Palander Stoveris was thinner and younger than the Captain, his hair was longer and his eyes were intense. He was also less garrulous than the Captain and seemed to scrutinize the Senoobians skeptically.

The *Mankuriun* was unlike anything Amara or Marco had ever seen before. Observing its inner layout and all of the activity around them, they were in awe of the ship and its crew. *How odd it seems here*, Amara thought; she was used to being surrounded by humans but now everyone around them was like her. There were several handsome young Bretin who caught her eye.

After the introductions and celebratory remarks, the Captain led them to his stateroom where they sat down with him and Stoveris to glasses of cold *chiska*. Captain Markovin was obviously pleased as he spoke to his guests, "I can't tell you how happy and relieved we are to have found you." He smiled broadly as he regarded his guests. "I hear that you three are survivors of the *Syzilian* and consequently of Senoobis."

Bayn nodded solemnly. "Yes, that's correct, Captain."

"He turned to Amara. "And you are the only Senoobian child born in the last thousand years by natural birth!"

She smiled, pleased at the attention. "Yes, Sir, as far as we know."

He regarded Jeliko and Darz with wonder. "What courage to attempt such a thing!"

Darz nodded proudly toward Jeliko, "It was brave on her part."

Jeliko said, "It was difficult and painful. I almost died; no wonder births on Senoobis were accomplished in vitro. And I was lucky—there was still a fertile egg or two in spite of my age. Darz managed to do his part and here she is. We had hoped to have another child, but it wasn't possible."

The Captain smiled first at her parents and then at Amara. "Well, I congratulate you all on such a splendid outcome."

He turned to Marco, smiling. "And you, Marco, a handsome young human raised by Senoobians! I know they're proud of you."

"Thank you, Captain. I am honored to be here," he replied in Kuterin.

"I must say, Marco, your Kuterin is excellent."

He became more serious: "My dear Amara and Marco, I beg your pardon. Your parents are special to us so Cdr. Stoveris and I are eager to ask them a lot of questions. I'm sure you've heard the stories of Senoobis and their exploits many times and may find our conversation boring. So it occurred to me that you might prefer a tour of our ship and a chance to meet some of our crew since you've never been on a starship before."

Amara's eyes lit up. "That's kind of you, Captain. Since this is all new to me, I would enjoy a tour."

"And so would I," Marco exclaimed.

The Captain turned to Stoveris. "In that case, Palander, perhaps Ensigns Dolyvek and Agoyin could be persuaded to escort them on a tour of the ship. I expect they might be delighted to do so."

Stoveris said, "Yes, Captain, I will be happy to arrange that."

He called Dolyvek on his communicator. "Tavin, find Nayta and report to the Captain's stateroom on the double. I have a job for you two."

Within minutes, the two young officers knocked on the Captain's stateroom door. Stoveris met them at the door and motioned Amara and Marco over. "Will you two please give Amara and Marco a tour of the ship, but have them back here by 1600 for dinner."

Amara and Marco heartily thanked the Captain and the four of them quickly excused themselves.

Captain Markovin turned back to his guests. "I couldn't help but notice that Marco has only five fingers on each hand?"

"That's right," Jeliko said. "Humans have four fingers and only one opposable thumb. The fact that they have ten digits is the reason they count by tens instead of twelves." She sighed, "It took us a long time to get used to their numbering system."

She wrinkled her nose, looking perplexed. "How odd, I haven't thought of Marco as human since he was a child."

Darz and Bayn nodded their agreement.

"So they count by tens! Interesting. I noticed his eyes too, round and dark brown. And his hair—I don't find it attractive. It's too flat.

Other than that he seems normal. Nevertheless, I'm quite impressed with both of them. I want to hear more about them, but first we want to hear about the *Syzilian*. For centuries, the fate of the ship and her crew has been a mystery. Please tell us what happened and how you came to be here, still alive after 800 years. How is it possible?"

Bayn related how the whole crew had become infected with the virus that killed everyone except for the three of them. He told about their desperate entry into the sleep modules and the mistake that led to the death of Amantis and eventually to the destruction of the ship. Jeliko told about their narrow escape from the *Syzilian* before it exploded and their return to the Nazca area where their base had been before.

The Captain said, "The *Langorion* received the same radio messages that the *Volarion* transmitted to the *Syzilian*, so the crew knew the *Volarion* had been destroyed. The *Langorion*'s orders were to operate under complete radio silence to avoid jeopardizing her mission so she never tried to contact the *Syzilian*. The *Langorion* never received a message from the *Syzilian*, so no one ever knew what happened to her."

Jeliko said, "And we've often wondered over the years what happened to you Bretin and the *Langorion*."

"Lt. Shurahp told us that the *Langorion* did reach Nanzema and successfully founded a colony," Darz added.

The Captain said, "Oh, yes, the crew was determined to succeed on Nanzema, no matter what. There was no other option—there wasn't enough fuel to divert to Karyntis. So our ancesters reached Nanzema and founded a settlement that would grow to 245,000 colonists over the next 200 years. They used the information contained within their disk library to jumpstart the colony and eventually to upgrade the *Langorion* into a more advanced starship, the *Mankuriun*.

"We Bretin were a gamble though. As you know, we're all the offspring of Jovan Bretin, the first genetically engineered Bretin. There were problems at first, but, over the next several generations, our scientists continued to improve our genome."

Stoveris added, "There were concerns that some unforeseen destructive trait might show up with tragic consequences for the colony. But that hasn't happened. It's been almost 800 years since the *Langorion* reached Nanzema and, as far as we can tell, we're pretty normal."

The Captain grinned at Stoveris, "Maybe we should let our guests be the judge of how normal we are."

Bayn laughed, "Well, you seem pretty normal to me."

Jeliko's thoughts drifted to the Bretin colony. "Captain, what's the population of your colony?"

"Just over three million," he said, "with about 75,000 square miles under our control."

"Any indigenous life forms of significance?" Bayn asked.

"Oh, yes. The dominant life form there is the *Shun*. They're brutish and warlike but intelligent, although not technologically advanced. They use large birdlike creatures called *Durahks* as beasts of burden and warfare. They're not happy that we've taken over a big piece of their planet. There has been increasing tension between us and them that may have escalated into a full-scale war by now."

"I'm sorry to hear that. Unfortunately the problems humans have here are mostly from each other."

"That's too bad. Of course, Nanzema is dangerous in other ways too. We lost almost half of our first generation of colonists. There are some nasty life forms there," the Captain said.

"There's the *yis*, for example: a large, harmless-looking plant that can snare a passing animal and hold it tightly until it digests the poor thing between giant leaves that secrete a powerful toxin. You'd better be quick with a machete if you come across one of those," the XO said. "We did manage to eradicate them around Pormidora though."

Darz said, "Hmmm, it sounds beastly. Speaking of life forms, any luck in getting some of our native species established?"

Stoveris seemed pleased. "Oh, yes, we were able to use the DNA masters we brought with us to create populations of several of our native species. On land, there are *penukri, geenahka, taygahpe,* and *chushevah*[2]; in the ocean, the *syrook* and *fanithus*[3] seem to be thriving."

Jeliko exclaimed, "You were able to save the *fanithus*! Bravo. Our DNA masters, as well as our embryos, were destroyed with the *Syz*." The *fanithus* was an intelligent aquatic mammal that Jeliko had played

---

[2] A large flightless bird, a bat-like mammal, a large butterfly-like insect and a bovine mammal

[3] A fish similar to a salmon and an intelligent porpoise-like acquatic animal capable of language

with and loved as a child. She had even learned to communicate with it on a basic level using squeals and whistles.

Stoveris replied, "It would have been a shame to lose a species so unique and intelligent."

"Yes, it would. What's the weather like there?" Bayn asked.

Stoveris said, "More tempestuous than on Karyntis, I believe, with occasional strong winds and violent thunderstorms. Nanzema is a little farther away from Jestura than Karyntis is from Sarmadah, so it's a bit cooler than here, but tolerable.

"At first our colonists struggled with the low oxygen level, only about 17 percent of the atmosphere. So, we've been working on a project to increase the planet's oxygen ratio and expect to have it up to 18.5 percent in a few more generations; we've genetically engineered three indigenous plants and two trees into photosynthetic powerhouses. They're efficient at releasing oxygen into the atmosphere, and we have several large established tracts of them."

"That's going well and, in another respect, we got lucky," the Captain said. "Our colony is called *Pormidora*. We chose its location because of several large geothermal vents there that we could tap into for much of the energy we needed. And for our water supply, there's a large lake—we call it Lake Kopadey—nearby."

"It sounds like an excellent location," Jeliko added.

Bayn abruptly changed the subject. "Captain, what about the Peyrians? Ever since we've been here, we've been expecting to look up and see a Peyrian starship. When Athrumos attacked the *Volarion*, he said they had been here before and they were going to come back. Frankly, we're surprised they haven't returned before now. Any thoughts about how to deal with that possibility?"

The Captain said matter-of-factly, "Maybe they've already returned—who knows? That's not something we can worry about now. We have too many other concerns, such as developing our energy resources, expanding our industrial base and strengthening our military. There's the likely war with the *Shun*. And we've started working on the next generation of starships to complement the *Mankuriun*. Since the Peyrians have advanced starships, we've got to be able to defend Pormidora. So we have a full plate; we won't be returning to Karyntis any time soon."

Jeliko thought for a moment. "Captain, is it possible that the peyrians have their own stealth technology and that they're around; we just can't detect them?"

"It's possible," he said, "but the Peyrians may be so arrogant they don't see the need for anything like that. It might not occur to them to develop that kind of technology."

He took a sip of *chiska*. "Our Space Agency sent the *Mankuriun* here to survey the planet; after what happened to Senoobis, we didn't want to face another catastrophe with no good options. Officially the case was closed but, off the record, the Agency still hoped to find the *Syzilian*."

Bayn was curious. "Captain, did your Space Agency ever consider establishing a colony here?"

"Yes, of course. There are advantages to having a colony here, but we don't have the resources to establish and support one now. Part of our mission was to survey this planet to determine its suitability for a future colony though.

"It's taken us 700 years of hard work to establish Pormidora, create an infrastructure, build our military, develop an educational system and build the Space Agency facilities to support the *Mankuriun*. That's why we haven't been here sooner.

"Imagine our shock when we arrived and discovered such a huge human population and that the planet's resources were being strained to the limit! Obviously humans don't bother to control their population; the planet's a disaster! I expect that, if we did have a colony here, we would soon be at war with them. It's obvious we can't coexist with them so I checked off that part of our mission.

"There was always the faint hope that we might find the *Syzilian* or at least learn what had happened to her. We hoped there might be a colony here somewhere or at least survivors, if the *Syzilian* was lost. The Agency knew that, with a war looming and our other problems, this would be our last chance for a mission to Karyntis in the foreseeable future."

Stoveris added, "This is an advanced model of the *Langorion*. Our communications technology is more advanced than before, so the Agency believed we might have a better chance of learning the fate of the *Syzilian* now. The *Langorion* would never have been able to pick up your lander's weak signals."

The Captain said, "We've been broadcasting our coded messages continuously on the old frequencies ever since our approach to Karyntis six months ago. We thought that, like the *Volarion*, the *Syzilian* might have been destroyed by a Peyrian warship. We had almost given up when, to our surprise, you responded to our message."

Bayn said, "We only have the radio from our lander; its range is limited. I thank *Inikeez* you didn't give up."

The Captain said, "So do I. There were several members on the Agency Board, however, who thought the mission was pointless after so long. Anyway, that's the main reason we've come here—to find you. And it's fortunate we've done so because our fuel reserves are becoming an issue. Besides, the humans are constantly shooting probes and satellites into space. If they somehow penetrate our stealth field and detect our presence, who knows what they might do?

"Our orders were also to learn if the Peyrians had established a base here since the Earth is only spittin' distance away from Peyr in cosmic terms.

"We've completed that part of our mission too. We've determined that the planet is unsuitable for a colony, learned what happened to the *Syzilian,* and found her only survivors. Although a Peyrian ship could appear at anytime, we haven't found any evidence of a Peyrian base. My only concern now is getting our ship home safely so we can assist in the war effort.

"I expect you're interested to see what life is like on Nanzema— quite different from here, I assure you."

The three of them answered in unison: "Yes, of course."

Stoveris said, "We have some video we can show you and perhaps you could share with us after dinner what it was like to live on Senoobis—we have our disks, of course, but even better to hear it first hand."

"A wonderful idea," the Captain said. "After all, it's quite an event to talk to the only three survivors of our mother planet. You're celebrities, you know—the last of the Senoobian race."

Bayn replied proudly, "It would be an honor."

Ensigns Dolyvek and Agoyin found themselves quite taken with Amara. They could feel the curious stares of other male crewmembers who seemed envious of them for being asked to show her around.

Marco sensed that most of the crew was curious about him as well. As they moved about the ship, most of the crew treated them with deference but not all of them. Some acted stiff and condescending toward them, and he detected a hint of resentment when they spoke.

Amara couldn't help but like Agoyin; he was more sociable and sensitive than she had expected for a Bretin. Their conversation gradually shifted from the ship and its crew to getting to know each other personally.

For the first time, Marco sensed a rival for her attentions and surprised himself by feeling jealous. Ensign Dolyvek was feeling a little jealous himself but he was no fool, and he grudgingly accepted the personal turn the relationship between Agoyin and Amara seemed to be taking. He winked at Marco as he tapped Amara on the shoulder. "Amara, I beg your pardon but I want to show Marco the Engine Room. Do you mind if I leave you with Ensign Agoyin to continue your tour?"

Amara smiled sweetly, "Not at all. Thank you, Tavin."

"You don't mind, do you, Nayta?"

Agoyin smiled broadly, "Of course not. We'll meet you at the Captain's stateroom at 1600."

When Amara and Agoyin reached the Bridge, they stood in front of the viewer and gazed down at the Earth quietly, each of them contemplating what lay ahead. Finally, Agoyin said, almost in a whisper, "Amara, it's not my place to tell you this but we will be leaving soon. Our Captain is going to invite you and the others to return with us. But Nanzema is nothing like Karyntis, so it's going to be a big adjustment for you if you go. I just want you to know that I'll help you. Your parents are old, Amara, but, if they come with us, I'll help them too."

It was the nicest thing anyone had said to her in a long time. He squeezed her hand and they both blushed."

In his stateroom the Captain assumed a sober tone. "These humans are a peculiar lot. What's it been like living among them?"

Bayn hesitated for a moment before answering as Jeliko and Darz looked at each other. "Well, I must say it's been a remarkable experience. Sometimes happy, other times tragic. In some ways the humans are like us, but in other ways they're quite different."

Turning to Jeliko and Darz, he smiled, "Would you agree?"

Darz said, "Sure, there are some humans that I respect, but too many of them think only of themselves, instead of what's best for the whole human race."

Jeliko nodded and Bayn continued, "I think the biggest differences between us are psychological; they don't seem to think the way we do; too many of them are irresponsible. And there are a few minor physiological differences, of course, such as their unattractive round ears and their unusual eyes."

After a while, Bayn said, "That reminds me of an issue we should discuss: should we warn the humans about the Peyrian threat, give them further assistance, or do nothing at all? What do you think?"

"Until we found you, these weren't options so I haven't thought about it," the Captain replied.

Jeliko said, "Before you arrived, we concluded that we should warn them. They've struggled mightily at enormous cost to rise to their present level of civilization. We're not concerned about saving the human species as it is now so much as saving it for what it can become. Only now have they evolved to where we were a thousand years ago."

Bayn said, "On Senoobis we had several visionary leaders step forward and lead us into the future, unlike the humans who seem to have had more tyrants than benefactors. If they can ever overcome their social problems and their destructive natures, they may yet become a great species. They are resourceful; perhaps if they get a helpful nudge, they will achieve their true potential."

"We've discussed this a lot," Darz said after a moment's thought. "The Peyrians are a brutal and powerful race, determined, I suspect, to conquer and enslave every intelligent life form they encounter. Given the resourcefulness of the humans, however, if they are forewarned, they may be able to defend themselves. Otherwise, they face almost certain annihilation."

The Captain said, "Well then, with regard to the humans, I defer to your superior knowledge. I don't know what else you could do, short of giving them information from our disks. And that makes me uneasy—I don't believe we should technologically assist a race that might become our enemies in the future."

Bayn replied, "I'm inclined to agree with you. Before you found us, we thought we were the only survivors from Senoobis. We considered contacting some human in one of their major governments, warning him about the Peyrians, and letting him follow up through the proper channels. What would be the harm? We were going to die off anyway. But now the situation is more complicated—we have to consider you Bretin."

Jeliko said, "And there's a downside for the humans as well: if we do share our technology with them, it might be misused and destabilize the balance of power on the planet."

The Captain said, "Well, I have more immediate concerns. Do what you think best; just keep us out of it. Who knows what the humans might do if they discovered we were in orbit around their planet? Except for your closest human friends, I would rather the humans not know we're here."

Bayn frowned. "I'm concerned about that too: there's no need to stir things up by mentioning you Bretin."

The Captain nodded. "Agreed." He seemed to relax. "We'll be leaving in a few days. You've been marooned here on Earth for almost a hundred years. How do you feel about leaving this planet?"

They were taken by surprise. "Captain, are you inviting us to return with you to Nanzema?" Bayn stammered.

Markovin smiled. "Yes, I am—BUT, with the limitations of our life support systems, we can only take three of you. Otherwise, it would be too risky for all of us."

Bayn said, "The chance to go to Nanzema is a dream come true!"

"Well, it occurred to me that some of you might want to return with us where you can live out the rest of your lives with your own kind. I can't say that you would be safer there since there may well be a war going on when we arrive."

They looked at each other, speechless but overjoyed. They hadn't considered the possibility of giving up Earth for Nanzema at all.

Jeliko beamed, "Can you imagine: we would surely be the only life forms in the whole galaxy to have lived on three different planets!"

The Captain smiled broadly. "Well, that's something to celebrate. Palander, a toast to our guests this evening!"

"Wait a minute," Jeliko exclaimed, "There are five of us! What about Marco and Amara?"

Bayn's face reddened. "*By Inikees.*" He slumped in his chair and rubbed his chin. "If anyone goes, it should be Amara and Marco."

The Captain was taken aback. "Take a human with us? Hmmm. I don't know about that. I'm afraid the physiological differences between him and us might make his use of the sleep modules problematic. What do you think, Palander?"

"Who knows how a human might fare on a starship? Even if he survived the trip, how would he manage on Nanzema? Can't say I recommend it."

"Captain, we raised Marco. We can't leave him behind," Darz protested, crestfallen.

The Captain screwed up his face in a frown. "Look: we can only take three of you. You'll have to decide among yourselves who goes but Marco can't be one of them."

Darz said, "Well, living among our own kind again would be a dream come true but . . ."

Bayn nodded. "Captain, we've all fantasized about living freely as Senoobians again. We should be with our own kind, but there are our human friends . . ."

Jeliko said, "We've got to think about Marco. He wasn't raised as a human—we can't leave him. I don't want to go if he can't go."

Bayn said, "Yes, there's Marco. And what about Detza Keeska? We've worked like dogs for several years to build a new home there."

Darz nodded, "Yes, we have. Besides all of that, at our age we will have to start over on a new world. I don't know if I . . ."

Their enthusiasm had clearly waned and the Captain was becoming irritated. He raised his hand, "All right, I know how hard your decision must be, and I will respect it, but you must be sure of it. Once we leave, there's no turning back. Let's talk about it at dinner. Perhaps you have more questions about what it's like on Nanzema and how you might fit in."

Bayn said, "Thank you, Captain. That would be helpful."

During dinner, the Senoobians described their youth on Senoobis before the launch of the *Syzilian*. Then Cdr. Stoveris and Lt. Shurahp discussed life on Nanzema and answered questions. After dinner, Ensigns Dolyvek and Agoyin escorted Marco and Amara to their parent's stateroom and then excused themselves.

Her parents were tired and confused; it had been a long day. "So, what do you think of the ship?" Darz asked.

"Impressive," she said, "but it was weird seeing all of those Bretin, I mean being where everyone looks like us."

Darz smiled, "I know. It feels weird to me too."

"I didn't like the way some of them looked at Marco and me though. Made me feel self-conscious."

Marco said, "Yeah, me too. Looking different from everyone else made me uncomfortable. Now I understand how you've all felt on Earth. As for the ship: yes, it's impressive."

"By the way," Bayn said to Marco and Amara, "The Captain has asked us not to mention the Bretin or this ship to anyone except for our closest friends. He's concerned that, if some "big shot" human learns they're here, there might be a confrontation that would compromise the ship and its mission."

They both agreed to honor the Captain's request.

Darz cleared his throat. "Now, we have a big decision to make: the ship is leaving in a few days and the Captain has offered to take three of us on the return to Nanzema. Unfortunately the ship's life support systems can sustain only three more . . ."

Marco and Amara looked at each other apprehensively.

Darz continued, "I must confess that at first, the three of us were thrilled at the chance to live with our own kind again. Then it dawned on us: we can't go and leave you two behind."

"We're too old; I don't believe we could survive the trip anyway," Bayn added. "Or all of the stress we would face trying to adapt to a new life on another world."

Darz nodded, "Let's face it: the three of us don't have much longer to live. Besides, Nanzema is far different from Earth. For example, its atmosphere has less oxygen than Earth's; an oxygen deficit would be hard on us."

Jeliko said, "It would be better for us to live out our remaining days on Earth. It's not a perfect place, but it's the only home we know now."

She took on a solemn look. "Marco, in your case, there's another issue. The Captain's not sure you could survive such a long trip in the sleep modules—most of the trip will be spent in them, you know. Your physiology may be incompatible with the way they work, making them unsafe for you. And you're different from the Bretin; he thinks the social and cultural adjustments facing you would be too much."

She turned to Amara and drew a deep breath. "The truth is, going to Nanzema only makes sense for you. If you remain here on Earth, without the three of us, you will be the only Senoobian, growing old alone, always at risk. You and Marco will always be close, but someday he will want his own family. Amara, you're the last of the Senoobian line. Our mission was to continue that line. Now, only you can do that."

Darz said, "She's right but it's your decision. We don't want to give you up, but this will be your only chance to live a full life."

Amara thought about it for a long time, her brow furrowed. "You have always told me that duty must come first. I know that. We have to honor the sacrifices made by our ancestors: I will go to Nanzema. I do want to have my own family someday and, if I can continue our line, all the better."

She thought about how hard it would be to leave her parents and Marco. She turned away, her eyes moist.

"What about me?" Marco asked, trying hard not to feel abandoned—or betrayed.

Amara swallowed hard, trying to find the right words, "Marco, Mother's right. Someday you'll meet a human female and want to have a family of your own too." As soon as the words were out, she regretted them.

He felt a knot in his stomach. *I don't want a human female!* he thought angrily. He had hardly spoken to one since he was a child. Thoughts of Amara leaving and the Senoobians dying left him feeling cast adrift. *His life was falling apart!* He had lost his human family and soon his Senoobian family would be gone as well.

They are old he admitted to himself, facing for the first time the reality that they wouldn't live forever. *What will I do?* he wondered as he tried to process the implications of losing all four of them. He could feel the old fears he had suffered into his mid-twenties of being left behind creeping back into his mind, sure to summon the old nightmares when he managed to sleep.

Already feeling empty inside, he studied her, memorizing every feature. "If going to Nanzema is a good idea for you, I'm all for it, even if I can't go with you. Sure, I'll miss you. I'd rather be there, fighting the Shun beside you, but I'll be fine," he said, forcing a smile. *Inside he wasn't so sure.*

"I'll miss you too," she whispered

Bayn cleared his throat. "It won't be easy for any of us to give her up, Marco, but it's the right thing to do. The Bretin are like us; she will be happy there."

Jeliko repeated, "The important thing is she can have a family and continue our lineage through the Bretin."

Darz said, "Marco, remember, you can have a human family and friends here."

He thought to himself, *I may have a human body, but I'm a Senoobian at heart—I don't want a human family. I want to be with Amara.*

The next evening, the XO took them to the Crew's Lounge where they sat down with him and the Captain. "So, who is going with us?" the XO asked.

Amara spoke up. "I am, Sir. I hope to have a family on Nanzema."

Darz said, "We three, on the other hand, don't think it makes sense for us to go—we're too old. There's not much we can contribute on Nanzema. Bayn doesn't believe he can survive the trip and Jeliko and I don't want to leave him behind. Nor do we want to give up Marco or the human friends we've known here for so long. We deeply appreciate the extraordinary efforts you and your crew have made to find us, in fact, we owe our lives to you, but—"

"So only Amara will be going?"

Bayn nodded. "That's right. The rest of us will remain here."

Stoveris said, "Then it's settled: our shuttle will return you to the surface tomorrow morning. We'll say our goodbyes to you then."

Jeliko glanced around her. "Where's Marco? Amara, have you seen him this evening?"

"No," she said, "but I'll go and look for him." The thought of leaving Marco behind was eating at her.

As he got up to leave, Darz hesitated. "By the way, Captain, how long will it take to reach Nanzema?"

He thought for a moment. "About 30 of your Earth years, most of it in the sleep modules."

Amara saw her father grimace at the thought of using the sleep modules again. She turned to Stoveris before she reached the door. "Sir, are the sleep modules as bad as my father says?"

"I don't like them myself," he said, "but don't worry. I believe you'll find ours better than those he had on the *Syzilian*. Besides, we sedate our crew before they enter them. You won't experience those dreadful claustrophobic and suffocating feelings as much."

Bayn said, "Well, I'm not keen on climbing into them either."

The Captain chuckled, "I agree, they're not for the faint of heart, but the technology is improved and they are more reliable."

"That's a relief," Amara said, as she excused herself. She disappeared, walking briskly down the passageway, anxious to find Marco. She was confused and knew he was too.

Bayn had an idea. "Have either of you been on the surface?"

"No, we haven't," Stoveris replied. "We've always believed our presence here was too critical for us to leave the ship. Why?"

"I was thinking that you might enjoy a brief tour of Naksoris. We would be pleased to show you around—with the proper security, of course. You might find it interesting to see what the surface is like, and it might be a good break before you leave."

The Captain shrugged. "I'm nervous about leaving the ship but I'll consider it. Our presence here is problematic with so much human surveillance. That's why I've always elected for the XO and me to remain on board, although I am curious about conditions on the surface."

Bayn said, "No doubt, this will be your last chance to experience the planet first hand. You could meet some of our human friends. They've respected our privacy for years and, unlike most humans, they're completely trustworthy."

He seemed to warm to the idea. "It would be interesting to meet them—and I could visit the ocean. That's what fascinates me about this planet: such vast oceans. There are no oceans like these on Nanzema. When I was a young adult on Nanzema, I loved to sail off the coast of Kopadey; there were such good winds." He sighed heavily, "but now, because of the Shun, it's too dangerous. We'll see. Leaving the ship seems risky but Palander and I will discuss it."

The Senoobians left the Captain and XO and trudged back to their compartments. Compared to Naksoris, their accommodations were cramped and spartan. The three old Senoobians were restless so they made their way to the bridge. Watching the Earth slip into darkness, they felt unsettled. They stood there for a long time, brooding about their situation.

Finally Bayn looked at his two comrades, heavy-hearted. "I hate to give up Amara; now I'm worried about Marco."

Jeliko and Darz nodded solemnly.

Bayn said, "There's nothing we can do to help her and all we can do for Marco is encourage him and give him advice if he asks for it."

Darz lowered his voice, "Quite right."

Jeliko said, "You know, I find our talented Bretin friends a little stuffy, not the spontaneous and emotional types we were at their age. Of course, it's not their fault; Senoobis was only a distant memory when they were born. I'll bet they've never experienced the joy of a well-executed Proxima or known the exhilaration of hang gliding over snow-capped peaks like those of Mount Dorvusha."

Jeliko replied, "I'm sure you're right but I can't blame them. They've lived their whole lives under siege. Yet I've never known any finer officers or crew than those on this ship. I would gladly place my life in their hands and I'm grateful they're here. Can you imagine the sacrifices they've made in trying to find us?"

Bayn frowned, "Maybe we're bothered by the fact that they succeeded in their mission while we failed in ours—maybe we're just feeling a little inadequate next to our *brothers*."

Bayn cleared his throat. "The Bretin have made such an extraordinary effort to find us that I felt guilty about declining their invitation. But now it's okay; we won't put the *Mankuriun* at risk or have to leave Marco behind. And Amara will have a bright future."

Darz said, "It's still going to be damn hard, giving her up."

Bayn nodded, "It is indeed."

The thought of never seeing her again was hard for them to bear. "I don't know how I can let her go," Jeliko said, "but, I have to admit, if I were in her shoes, I'd do the same thing."

Since the *Mankuriun* was securely in orbit around the Earth, no navigational duties were required; the navigation compartment was unmanned and dimly lit. After a methodical search, Amara found him there, alone, staring at the huge holographic display of Sector 3309 with all of its star systems. Earth in the Sarmadah System and Nanzema in the Jestura System were connected by a plot of the long voyage that would take the *Mankuriun* back to Nanzema. There was even a small grey icon, blinking where Senoobis had been.

She paused in the doorway, enveloped in the light from the corridor behind her, looking angelic and alluring, as her eyes adjusted to the darkness. "I've been from one end of this ship to the other looking for you. What are you doing in here?" she scolded.

"Just looking at the big picture," he grinned, gesturing toward the huge display. "Trying to sort through my feelings and, frankly, missing you already."

She slipped inside and closed the door, drawing near him, slowly, deliberately. "I've been worried about you," she whispered softly when they were close, face to face. Their eyes met—her green feline eyes eager, glowing in the dark.

"I had to find some place where I could think things through without being disturbed. This is the only place on the whole ship with any privacy."

"Really?" she purred, a sly smile on her face, the tip of her tongue wetting her lips.

He started to protest, but she placed an index finger firmly against his lips. He could taste the sweetness of her skin, feel her hot breath close to his mouth, his own breathing becoming more hurried. Some unknown force seemed to possess them, holding them transfixed, their feelings for each other transcendent, their emotions merging into a singularity of passion that neither could resist. He took her hands in his, pulling her to him; they kissed long and hard. Craving the smooth touch of her skin, he slipped one of his hands inside her shirt.

"Wait!" she commanded, her voice raspy. With her eyes still fixed on his, she pushed away from him and turned toward the door.

His heart sank.

But she stopped. To his relief, she looked back at him hungrily, as if making up her mind; then she turned quickly and locked the door behind her. Before he knew it, his arms were around her again, squeezing her tightly, kissing her deeply.

Stars exploded violently in his mind, leaving only his awareness of that moment unshattered. Breathing hard, he surrendered eagerly to her openness.

"What happened in there?" Marco stammered, as they left the navigation compartment, their bodies depleted, their legs wobbly.

"A *mishugah*," Amara managed, as they walked arm in arm.

"A what?"

"It's a Kuterin word; it means literally an opening or unveiling: seeing someone in a whole new way by discovering their hidden and private side and feeling an intensely personal bond with them."

"You mean *sexual*?"

She laughed. "That's only part of it. It's also a commitment to each other. Mother once told me that most people live a lifetime without ever having a mishugah. Uncle Bayn never had one. Mother and father had been together for most of their lives before they had their mishugah; she always said I was born because of *it*." She sighed, "I never dreamed I'd experience one."

"Well, I've never had such intense feelings," he said, "and I'll never again think of you in the same way."

She grinned weakly. "Nor will I, you."

A few steps farther along, he stopped and searched her eyes. "Amara, did we do something wrong back there?"

She spun around and took him by the shoulders. "Marco, look at me—I'm not your sister."

He relaxed and grinned. "You're certainly not. And I'm glad."

When they reached their compartments, the three Senoobians were still awake. They knew the decision they had just made would affect their lives in a dramatic way. "Ah, you found him," Jeliko exclaimed.

"Marco, where have you been?" Darz asked.

His face flushed. "In the navigation compartment, thinking things over. Amara found me there. I'm sorry—my feelings are a little jumbled right now," he said, his voice uneven.

For a moment there was an awkward silence. Eyeing her mother and father nervously, Amara paused and drew a deep breath: "Uhh, I don't know how to explain it, but something remarkable just happened to us."

Jeliko's ears perked up. "Oh, what was that?" she asked, puzzled. She looked at both of them more closely; there was a glow about them.

"We had a *mishugah*!" Amara blurted out.

"A *mishugah*? You and Marco!" Jeliko gasped.

They both nodded sheepishly.

"It was incredible!" Amara said.

Darz jumped up from his chair. "Is *that* possible?" he ventured.

"Darz, of course, it's possible. Marco was raised like us—he's more Senoobian than human—but I never expected *that*."

"How can she go to Nanzema then? It's not right to have a mishugah and be separated!" Bayn exclaimed.

Jeliko gave both of them a dirty look and turned to Amara. "Look, I want you both to be happy and it's your decision but, mishugah or not, duty has to come first . . ."

Amara threw up her hands and gritted her teeth. "Mother," she snapped, "I know what I have to do." She turned and rushed from the compartment so they wouldn't see her tear up.

Marco ran after her. When he caught up with her, he pulled her to him.

"Marco, I'm sorry. I don't know what to do," she sobbed.

"Nor do I. I can't bear to give you up," he said, "but our mother's right—you have to go."

8

THE PERSEIDS

August 12, 1998: At 12:30 a.m. Dr. Martin Winslow Connor, his wife Ellen, their daughter Karen and her friend Angela toasted each other with a round of sangria, settled into their folding chairs and took in the quiet beauty of the summer sky. So far, it had been a hectic year for the Connors and they had looked forward to finally relaxing and enjoying what had become a family tradition each August. They chatted about the events of the past week and their upcoming trip to Peru as a Yanni CD played soothingly on Martin's aging boom box. The lake before them was calm and the sky above them was clear, laying out before them a tapestry of bright summer stars.

For the past several years they had driven out to their favorite spot on Cherokee Lake, far from any distracting lights, and enjoyed the Perseid meteor showers. Some years they were spectacular; other years, if the sky was cloudy, there was nothing to see. Although the best hours to view the showers were between midnight and dawn, usually too late for the likes of Martin and Ellen, they still managed to turn the outing into a festive occasion.

After 21 years at Carson-Newman College in Jefferson City, Martin had retired at the end of the previous semester as head of the History Department. The school was a small Southern Baptist liberal arts college that had been founded in 1851 as the Mossy Creek Missionary Baptist Seminary. That unwieldy name was changed a few years later to Carson College, however, and eventually to Carson-Newman in 1888, through the happy union of the all-male Carson College and the all-female Newman College. The school became the heart and soul of Jefferson City, a small Southern town in the foothills of the Appalachians, 25 miles from Knoxville.

Besides history, Martin had been fascinated by astronomy ever since his teenage years. His interest had been inspired by reading Ray Bradbury's novels and Carl Sagan's 1980 book *Cosmos*. He was intrigued by such mysteries as how the Earth was formed, how the building blocks of life were forged in the stars and how life and consciousness evolved from that lifeless matter. He still recalled the majestic statement in *Cosmos* that stoked his yearning to discover the grand saga of human experience: *Human beings, born ultimately of the stars and now for a while inhabiting a world called Earth, have begun their long voyage home.*

Now he was retired; he had anticipated and planned for this time for several years. Sixty-five years old and still in good health—he never smoked—he felt good and looked fit for a man his age. He was tall and trim with a touch of gray in his thinning hair and in his dress favored a yellow bowtie and navy slacks. He was full of vigor and always gave the impression that he was in a hurry.

When Martin had proposed one last trip to Peru to his wife, she was neither surprised nor disappointed. She was well aware of his fascination with the histories of Central and South America; besides, she was itching for a get-away herself. It was the kind of thing she had come to expect from Martin—she had often accused him of being the most curious man alive, always eager to be off on some new quest.

Martin's wife of 36 years, Ellen was an RN at Jefferson County Memorial Hospital in Jefferson City. She was a perky brunette, trim and attractive, 61 years old but still full of energy. She was the practical one, a take-charge kind of woman who seemed to know what to do about everything. She and Martin complemented each other nicely. He was the dreamer, always in awe of the mysteries of the universe; she was the planner, brimming with common sense. For the past several days, she had been busy arranging the logistics of their three-week trip to Peru. In only two days, Martin, Karen and she would board a plane in Knoxville for their flight to Lima. Then they would rent a small car and drive south to Nazca.

Their daughter Karen taught history and was the Assistant Principal at Jefferson County High. Thanks to a difficult divorce two summers past, she was a single mom with a nine-year old daughter and a seven-year old son. She had taken a break from teaching to sort out her affairs, so when Martin and Ellen invited her to accompany them, she had readily agreed.

She hadn't taken a vacation in over four years, so she was ready for a long get-away. Since the children were older, Karen had decided to accept her neighbor's offer to take care of Sean and Lindie while she was away. The Andersons lived two houses down from Karen and their son was Sean's best friend.

"You're not going to leave me here while you two have all the fun!" she teased. "Besides, I want to get in a vacation before the millennium brings on the end of the world!"

Her mother laughed, "That's a good idea. You never know what might happen!"

Just then, Karen heard her friend giggle at some story her father was telling. Angela was also a teacher at the high school and her divorce had become final only a few weeks before Karen's. In trying to console each other, they had become close friends even though they didn't have much else in common.

Karen had an agile mind but Angela had agile feet. Karen regarded her friend with a touch of envy. Angela was no scholar but she could dance with the best of them; she probably knew 50 or 60 line dances, as well as the East Coast Swing. Her drop-dead gorgeous figure was the result of many nights spent dancing at Cotton Eyed Joe's in Knoxville.

Now as she sat there, feeling relaxed and listening to her father pontificate about this and that, Karen began to reminisce. Like her father, she was inquisitive from the day she could talk and she enjoyed asking questions to test him. Each year her questions became tougher.

Karen had learned all about the Perseids from her father. In fact, she probably knew more about astronomy than any one else in Jefferson County, except for her father. She had gradually come to enjoy their spirited conversations and speculations about historical and astronomical subjects almost as much as he did. She even caught herself becoming animated as he did when they talked about the wonders of the universe.

As Karen gazed up at the Southern part of the sky, lost in her thoughts, Angela yelled excitedly, "There's one!" as the first meteor of the evening suddenly appeared, gliding silently across the sky. Angela had never seen a meteor before so she leaned toward Karen, "Where do they come from?"

Karen took a deep breath before beginning her explanation, "Our solar system has two kinds of small objects: asteroids and comets.

Both can cause meteors but it's the comets that cause meteor showers."

Karen continued, "Both asteroids and comets consist of matter that was left over when our solar system was formed billions of years ago. Asteroids are usually found in an area between the orbits of Mars and Jupiter called the *asteroid belt* so they don't move around like comets. They're usually the size of pebbles like the one you just saw, but they can be hundreds of miles wide; Ceres, the largest known asteroid, is the size of Texas!"

Angela was amazed, "Wow! If the meteor I just saw were that bright but only the size of a pebble, I can't imagine how bright Ceres would be if it hit the atmosphere."

Karen laughed, "Me either."

Angela was intrigued. "Well, what about comets then?"

Karen continued, "Well, comets are sort of like big dirty snowballs, made up of frozen water, gases and solid matter mostly like dust or grains of sand. Most of their solid matter is in a core that's three or four miles wide."

"Comets travel in long flattened orbits that take them far outside our solar system. The closer they come to the sun, the bigger and brighter they become. The sun's heat boils off the frozen gases and water, releasing the solid matter and forming a long tail called a *coma* that streams out away from the comet for thousands of miles.

"When the Earth runs into these bits of matter left behind by a comet, they burn up in the atmosphere producing the bright streaks that we call meteors or *shooting stars*. We call them *meteor showers* because there are so many of them.

She paused a moment to give Angela a chance to process the information. "In the case of the Perseids, there's this comet called Swift-Tuttle—Swift and Tuttle were the guys who discovered it—that takes about 120 years to make a complete trip around the sun. Every year in mid-August, the Earth passes through some of the debris left behind from its previous orbits. The resulting meteors seem to come from the Perseus Constellation and that's why they're called *Perseids*. They aren't the only annual meteor showers but they're the most impressive of the ones we can see. On a good night at their peak, we've seen as many as 50 or 60 in an hour."

Angela was becoming more intrigued. "Do any of these meteors ever hit the ground?"

Karen replied, "Oh, sure, sometimes, if they're big enough, but most of them burn up in the Earth's atmosphere because they're no bigger than a speck of dust or a grain of sand. If they do reach the ground, they're called meteorites and they usually cause a loud explosion and leave a crater"

Angela felt a twinge of apprehension. "Has anyone ever been killed by a meteorite?

"I don't know," Karen replied.

Martin and Ellen were listening to their conversation and Karen glanced toward her father, inviting him to respond. Martin couldn't resist: "Well, as far as we know, no humans have been struck by a meteorite. But in 1911, there was a meteorite that exploded into about forty pieces before hitting the ground near Alexandria, Egypt. It was called the Nakhal Meteorite and it appears to have originated on Mars where it was blasted into space eons ago by the collision of another large body with the planet." His expression became downcast. "A farmer saw one of the fragments strike a dog and vaporize the poor animal." He paused for effect. "The dog's name was *Lucky*!"

Karen frowned at her father, "Daddddd! That's not funny."

Ellen was accusatory, "Martin, you made that up!"

Martin kept a straight face. "Honey, it's a true story." Then he laughed, "Of course, I can't swear to the dog's name."

Turning serious again, Karen said, "Dad, tell her about that crater we saw in Arizona."

Martin scratched his chin thoughtfully. "Oh, yes. Well, a few years back, we took a family trip out west and one of our stops was at the Barringer Meteor Crater near Flagstaff, Arizona. The crater is impressive, even after 49,000 years. It's about three quarters of a mile wide and over 500 feet deep. It was formed by the impact of a 150-foot wide meteor that hit the ground at a speed of roughly 45,000 mph. If a meteor only 150 feet wide made a crater that large, what do you think would happen if Ceres struck the Earth?"

Angela gasped, "We'd all be killed?"

Martin pointed into the air dramatically, "Yes! Without a doubt."

Ellen looked at her husband in mock horror, "Honey, should we be worried?"

Martin smiled at her, "No, the odds are pretty small that we'll be hit by one large enough to wipe us out. At least in the next few thousand years."

"Well, that's a relief!" Angela giggled as another meteor streaked across the sky.

Martin added, "More importantly for us, humans might not exist today if it weren't for the huge six mile wide asteroid that struck the earth 65 million years ago. That collision created a crater 3,000 feet deep near the coast of the Yucatan Peninsula about 120 miles west of Cancun. Its shock waves sent debris hurtling thousands of miles, eventually throwing the whole planet into a kind of nuclear winter that lasted more than a year. Astronomers believe that the massive impact of that asteroid killed off the dinosaurs, allowing small shrew-like mammals to evolve over millions of years into humans."

Martin looked up as another meteor streaked silently across the early morning sky and disappeared. "I've been fascinated by them ever since I was a kid. I remember a preacher at the little Baptist church I attended in Tazewell then. He said the *showers* were a sign from God that we had better be on our toes because He might destroy the Earth by fire at any time. Every time I see the Perseids, I get a twinge of anxiety that there may be a big asteroid out there ready to wipe us out like the dinosaurs. Kind of makes me feel like we're living on the *edge*."

By 3:30 a.m. they had seen enough of the Perseids to last them for another year and by 4:30 all of them were in bed sound asleep. It was almost eleven when a ringing phone rendered Martin fully awake. It was almost noon when Karen sat up in her bed, awakened by her two children. Ellen had been up since ten a.m., busily making preparations for their trip.

But Martin was in no hurry; all he had to do was finish packing and go to the bank for money and traveler's checks. He poured himself a glass of iced tea, threw open the screen door and shuffled outside to his favorite rocker where he could enjoy the fresh air and avoid the storm of activity taking place inside. He looked around the neighborhood and thought about how much he had enjoyed the years spent teaching history at Carson-Newman. During his tenure there, he and Ellen had traveled to Peru twice before to explore the rich history of that country. Now he was eager to return once more to explore the lines that have been a mystery since their discovery from an airplane in 1927. The Nazca Indians had never founded an empire on the scale of the Maya or the Incas but the mystery surrounding them was compelling: *what was the purpose of the huge ancient project that had created the Nazca Lines?*

9

THE NAZCA LINES

One morning Jeliko was scanning *La Voz de Ica*, the local newspaper. There was a short article about a retired American college professor who was coming to Nazca to study *the lines* and other local archeological sites. She read the article again and then yelled to Darz.

Two days later the Connors flew into Lima, arriving at Jorge Chávez International Airport in the evening. The outskirts of Lima around the airport were not impressive but the downtown area was a historic mecca bustling with activity. They spent the next day visiting the *Museo Nacional de Arqueología* in *Pueblo Libre* and strolling about the *Plaza San Martin*.

The next morning they rented a Toyota Corolla and began the easy five and a half hour drive along the Pan-American Highway to Nazca, the small dusty town of 100,000 that lies 150 miles south of Lima just off the coast. It was a cloudless day and a scenic drive. With a stop in Ica for a visit to a local *bodega* and lunch, it was early in the evening when they arrived in Nazca.

They checked into the *Hostal Sol de Nazca*, took a shower and then went to a local tavern to get something to eat and to savor a real Pisco Sour, Peru's national drink. The excitement of being back in Peru and his eagerness to see the lines made it hard to go to sleep and harder to wake up the next morning.

They arrived at the small airstrip five miles south of Nazca at 11:00 the next morning. It was a warm and pleasant day with just a hint of haze in the air. Their pilot was waiting for them by the aging Cessna.

Martin and Ellen climbed into the rear seat and Karen took the front seat for a better view.

Martin felt a strange sense of déjà vu. He and Ellen had been here seven or eight years ago and since then he had thought about this mysterious place and *the lines* hundreds of times—he had kept an aerial photo of the lines on the bulletin board in his office until he retired. Now he and Ellen would see them again and Karen would see them for the first time. He was curious as to what her reaction would be as they came into view on the plateau below.

The lines were a giant puzzle that had eluded solution by him and countless others. To those who grasped the mystery they posed, they were awe-inspiring. To others, however, who saw the lines as mere scrapings in the barren soil of the plateau, they were little more than primitive graffiti on a monumental scale and of passing interest.

As they waited while Roberto did the preflight checks, Martin couldn't help but recall the anticipation he had felt over the last few years of seeing the lines again. It felt good to be back in Peru, a country so rich in history.

The sputtering sound of the Cessna's engine starting up snapped him back to the present. Five minutes later they were racing down the runway and then they were airborne. The single-engine Cessna slowly climbed to about 1,600 feet and within 20 minutes they were able to catch the first glimpse of the objects of their journey.

The Cessna began a slow descent to about 900 feet and there before them on the Nazca plateau emerged a vast collection of designs etched in the pampa. Scattered apparently at random were well over a hundred designs, many in the shape of animals, easily recognizable as snakes, lizards, monkeys, spiders, several kinds of birds and even a whale. There were also numerous geometric designs such as rectangles, triangles, trapezoids, and spirals. But there was one design that didn't seem to belong. It was the odd figure of a man—*or an alien*—with large round eyes and wearing what appear to be boots and a space suit, his right arm raised as if in greeting.

Because of their great size, the designs only become apparent from a height of 400 feet or more. There are straight lines more than three miles long. There is a 165' long hummingbird, a 150' long spider, a 600' long lizard and a 400' long monkey. These easily recognizable designs were painstakingly made by scraping a continuous shallow furrow into the surface, even through rough terrain. Yet there are no hills or structures from which the designers could have overseen their work.

Most of the designs occupy a 200 square mile area defined by the *Rio Ingenio* to the north and the *Rio Nazca* to the south and bisected by the Pan-American Highway that cuts through the plateau.

The mystery of the origin of the lines has baffled scholars and visitors to the region for almost 100 years. Their age is uncertain at best, but based on studies of pottery fragments found in the lines and inconclusive radiocarbon dating of a few organic remains, the lines have been dated at between 1 and 500 A.D.

Just as no one knows their real age, no one knows their purpose. Numerous theories have been advanced since the lines first captured the attention of a few travelers in the 1930's when the first commercial air flights began between Lima and Arequipa. Since the lines can only be properly observed from the air, they have been described as landing strips for extra-terrestrials. They have also been described as terrestrial maps intended to represent the constellation of Orion and track the declinations of the three stars in Orion's Belt. Local legends say that they were created, not by men, but by the Viracochas, a race of demigods, who are said to have founded a great civilization in Peru thousands of years earlier.

The lines have survived the ravages of the centuries because the Nazca plateau is a barren and desolate area with little plant or animal life of any kind to disturb them. Besides that, the Nazca plateau has only about ½" of rainfall every two years. The area can be windy but the pebbles in the designs become heated by the sun and give off heat waves that deflect the wind.

Ellen found the lines curious as she had before but since there was no practical benefit in them, she soon lost interest. Karen, however, was visibly impressed. After an hour of viewing the designs and taking numerous pictures, they returned to the small airport. As they drove back to their hotel, there were no answers to the same questions that had baffled Martin since his first visit to Nazca. *Who had made the lines? How had they made them? Why had they made them? When had they made them?* There was only wild speculation.

Finally Karen looked at Martin with an air of resignation. "Okay, Dad, what do you think?"

Martin responded with a smile, "I'm not going to tell you what I think—not just yet! I want to know what you think first while we're on our excursion tomorrow. Then I'll tell you what I think."

The next morning they made the 30-minute drive along the Pan-American Highway to the plateau. When they had reached the first design that appeared to be a stork, Martin pulled out a map that he had created from several past aerial photographs.

Viewed at ground level, the lines themselves are hardly noticeable and appear as little more than grazes on the surface made by scraping away black volcanic pebbles to expose the desert's paler base of yellow sand and clay. None of the cleared areas were more than a few inches deep and the soil was soft. It was difficult to reconcile the impressive designs they had seen from the air with the unremarkable scrapings they found before them.

After studying the great spider design for some time, they decided to take a lunch break. As they sat down to a sandwich, all three of them were in a thoughtful mood. Martin looked at Karen, "Okay, what do you think? Any ideas?"

Karen thought a minute. "Well, there are no ruins anywhere on this plateau so it seems that no one ever lived here. Apparently they chose this place specifically to create these designs. But you can't even see them from the ground. I don't know."

Ellen noticed the curious expression on Martin's face. "What are you thinking, Dear?"

"Ellen, this is one of the driest places on Earth and it's probably been this way for thousands of years. It's a terrible place for hunting or farming so it has probably never been permanently inhabited. And yet somebody went to a lot of trouble to come here and create these designs over a long period of time. What would be the point of expending limited labor resources this way?"

Ellen thought about it. "This was obviously a pretty special place."

Karen asked, "But what was special about it?"

Martin replied, "Well, it's flat and open—no hills, mountains or forests. Nothing in the way of geological features to recommend it, so maybe it's special because something important happened here."

Karen interrupted, "But what in the world could have happened way out here? Why would anyone even come here?"

Martin laughed, "I wish I knew. But think about it. Where did the people who did this come from? We would naturally expect that they lived near a river or along the coast where there would have been fertile land and abundant fresh water with lots of things to eat—game and fish, maybe crops. The fact that we've seen designs representing a heron, a pelican and a whale seems to confirm this. But there is also the image of a monkey and an Amazonian spider so perhaps they lived in the jungle. Obviously whoever did this traveled around.

"When humans want to communicate with someone who doesn't speak the same language, they use pictographs or drawings that visually represent the ideas they want to communicate. I think that's what was going on here hundreds of years ago. But look: the people who did this were obviously trying to communicate with someone, real or imagined, who could fly back then. These designs weren't intended to be seen by anyone on Earth because no one then could have gotten high enough to notice them—there aren't any hills around here. So the mystery is who the heck were they trying to communicate with and what were they trying to say."

Karen frowned, "Dad, are you thinking *aliens*?"

Martin laughed again, "Well, there is one theory that the lines were created as a kind of landing area for alien travelers but that's too far-fetched, even for me."

"Well, what do you really think then," Ellen prodded.

Martin paused for a moment, "There is another theory. There were two cities that were important to the Nazca: Cahuachi and Ventilla. Built on the edge of the desert plateau, Cahuachi lies 45 miles inland from the coast and is bound by two lush valleys. Excavations have revealed a treasure trove of clues about the Nazca culture and have connected it with the construction of the lines. It appears to have been abandoned around 500 A.D. after a devastating flood and earthquake destroyed the city some time around 350 A.D. That's when the Nazca religion seemed to lose its hold over the people.

"It appears that the Nazca were governed by a powerful class of priests who controlled the precious water resources and thus the agricultural productivity of the area. The Nazca built an impressive irrigation system consisting of 80 miles of aqueducts, most of them underground, to control the distribution of water in the different valleys so that agriculture could flourish and support the growth of the civilization itself.

"Cahuachi appears to have been solely a religious and pilgrimage center for the Nazcas, probably a lot like Chichen Itza, the Mayan religious center. Apparently, its population was quite small except during major ceremonial events when the population swelled to several times its usual size.

"On the opposite side of the pampa from Cahuachi, archaeologists found the site of Ventilla—an ancient settlement that appears to have been a large urban center. One long pathway links the ruins of the two cities, apparently serving as a pilgrimage route between the two sites."

Ellen said, "Well, I don't doubt that the Nazca culture and religion were centered around water. If there was a severe drought, the people might die. Like the Maya, I'm sure they were encouraged by their priests to believe that some god controlled the rain or flow of water from the mountains."

Karen added, "Now that I've seen the lines up close, I can see that they're narrow and they don't seem to have been disturbed as they would have been if a lot of people had used them as paths. Surely they would have venerated two or three of the most reliable and closest water sources. Like the Maya, agricultural productivity was very low so I doubt if they had the time or manpower to go rambling about the pampa to draw water from distant springs; that's why they built aquaducts."

"I agree," Martin said. "In order to survive, primitive cultures like the Nazca were concerned mainly with water, food, shelter and fertility. Their food came from hunting and gathering, as well as from crude and limited agriculture and fishing. We don't know anything about their religious beliefs since they had no writing system as far as we know. But my guess is that they believed that their gods lived in the heavens and that they controlled the four necessities of life: food, water, shelter and fertility. Maybe by creating these huge designs that their gods could see from the sky, they hoped to encourage them to provide those resources."

Karen said, "I keep going back to the spaceman figure—I can't help but believe that it's the key to the puzzle but I don't know how."

All three of them were stumped by the sprawling mystery before them. They wandered about, pondering different explanations until their thirst and hunger put an end to their explorations.

10

THE SENOOBIANS

When they returned, hot and tired, to their hotel late that afternoon, there was a message waiting for Martin. It read: "I have some important information for you. Please meet me at 8:00 tomorrow evening at *La Taberna*. Ask the bartender for Bayn Kener."

How strange, Martin thought. He couldn't recall anyone he knew named Bayn. *Probably another academic in town who's heard that I'm studying the lines. Maybe he wants to discuss some new theory about them or some other archaeological site?*

After dinner, Ellen and Karen went back to their room to relax while Martin went to his meeting with the mysterious Mr. Kener. Arriving at *La Taberna*, it was 10 minutes 'til nine and the bar was dimly lit inside. Spotting the bartender, a small dark man with a heavy mustache, Martin approached him and asked in Spanish, "Can you tell me where I can find Señor Kener?"

The man glanced up at Martin and gestured toward a figure seated with two others at a corner table, "Over there—the one in the middle."

The three people in the corner were talking among themselves and paid no attention as Martin approached. The one in the middle appeared to be in his late 70's with a full head of graying hair; his face had a weathered but patrician look that reminded Martin of an older Peter O'Tool. All three were dressed in plain, well-worn shirts and trousers that Ellen would have pronounced *plain*. Their features were nothing like those of the locals. Their heads had an elongated shape with a slightly sloping nose that separated bright green eyes with slits for pupils. Their hair was coarse and followed their necks down below their shoulders in a sort of bushy mane. Out of the hair on the sides of their heads poked two pointed ears. And there were the prominent chins and lips that appeared slightly pursed as if to keep some secret from escaping.

"Señor Kener?" Martin asked, taken aback by their appearance.

All three of them stood up and the middle one offered his hand. His grip was firm and somehow different. "Yes, I'm Bayn Kener. Please call me Bayn. You are Professor Martin Connor."

"Yes, that's right," he stammered. His mind was reeling. What kind of people are these? He had met all kinds of people in his travels around the world but none that resembled these three."

He gestured toward the other two as they nodded. "This is Darz Tureesh."

"Pleased to meet you, Dr. Connor," Darz said with a self-assured smile as he looked Martin over and extended his hand.

A little younger than Bayn, perhaps in his early '70's, Martin guessed, Darz appeared wiry and athletic for his age with a firm grip that seemed to envelope Martin's hand. He looked different, even handsome in an exotic way. His eyes were bright green and intense.

"And this is Jeliko Hanahban."

Martin turned to Jeliko and shook her hand. "Pleased to meet you—Jeliko?"

She smiled broadly and replied. "Yes, Jeliko will suffice. Glad to meet you, Dr. Connor."

What odd names! he thought. *Not a normal name among them.*

He held his gaze a moment too long, fascinated and rendered speechless by her mature but eloquently feline appearance.

Noticing his stare, Jeliko looked back at him amused and questioning, as if to say, "Whaaat?"

Martin blushed. "Sorry, I didn't mean to stare but your appearance is rather striking, I mean distinctive but attractive."

There was indeed something intriguing about Jeliko whose mane was a rich bronze color, longer and fuller than Bayn's or Darz's. There was a silver pendant, hexagonal-shaped with the words, ⲭⲛⲁⲭⲑⲔⳑ OⲟⳘⳆⲉⳆⳑⲟ̄ in some unknown language etched on it, hanging from her neck. Martin sensed a toughness but at the same time femininity. Her soft facial features and small breasts reminded him of an aging tomboy. He guessed she was about his own age, perhaps in her sixties.

Bayn's voice was deep, his speech was precise, almost English-sounding, and his manner was gracious. "Please join us," he said, motioning toward the empty chair.

"Thank you," Martin replied.

As he sat down, his eyes were drawn to a polished blue stone, the size of a quarter that hung on a silver chain around Bayn's neck. It was in a silver hexagonal setting, forming an unusual amulet.

As Bayn seated himself again, Martin was startled to notice that he had six fingers, including two opposable thumbs, on each hand. Glancing quickly at the other two, he saw that they were the same!

Bayn cleared his throat, "Martin . . ."

"Uhhh, yes. You have some important information for me?"

Bayn replied, "Yes, I believe we have some information that may be important to you. We read the article about you and your interest in the Nazca Lines in the local paper. We hope you are someone who has an open mind and can be trusted . . ."

"And frankly we didn't know anyone else to call," Jeliko continued.

Martin became suspicious, "What do you have in mind?"

Bayn smiled. "Oh, don't worry. It's not illegal—strictly above board. But it may be critical to the future of humankind. We're going to tell you some things that you may find hard to believe but they're too important to be confused or misunderstood. If the information we give you gets into the wrong hands, it may be dismissed as preposterous and its benefit will be lost. Therefore I must ask that you keep what I tell you completely to yourself until you're ready to trust us and we can explain everything to you."

The phrase *critical to the future of mankind* stuck in his mind, filling him with uncertainty and apprehension. "Wait a minute, Bayn, I'm just a lowly history professor and retired at that. I'm not sure I'm the best person to handle matters extremely critical to the future of mankind. Who are you all anyway?" His voice was strained and his face was flushed.

Bayn lowered his voice, "Professor Connor, please relax. We want to help you and everyone else on this planet so don't make this any harder than it already is. Look, before we go any further, here's what I want you to do to establish our credibility. Every human being on this planet has the same number of chromosomes, 23 pairs, right?"

Martin nodded, "Of course."

Before he could protest, Bayn pulled out a medical syringe and a small vial and without flinching stabbed the needle into the largest vein in his arm, drawing a small amount of blood. Martin was aghast! "What the hell are you doing?" he half yelled in surprise.

Bayn methodically laid the needle aside, capped the vial and handed it to him. "Get this analyzed as soon as you can—you'll find my blood cells have 25 pairs of chromosomes. You'll also find that all the major constituents—red blood cells, white blood cells, platelets and plasma—are different from yours. I suggest you drive to Lima. Get back to us as soon as you can. Then we'll talk. Don't tell anyone where you got this sample." He nodded toward the bartender. "His name is Carlos. Let him know when you're back. He'll notify us and we'll meet you here again. Do I have your word that you'll keep our conversation to yourself until we can talk again?"

Martin was too overwhelmed to think clearly. He had a sinking feeling that he was into something way over his head but all he could manage was, "All right, you have my word."

"Good," Bayn said. "Nice meeting you. Don't worry; we only want to help. We'll talk again soon."

All three of them stood up to leave and shook his hand. Then they were gone. Martin sat there for a few minutes mystified, trying to make sense out of their meeting, relieved to be alone. These three were odd-looking characters. What were they trying to prove? That they weren't human? That was an unsettling thought. If they weren't human, what the hell were they? What had he gotten himself into?

From the bar Carlos regarded the man at the table with amusement, recalling the first time he had met the Senoobians. "A drink, Señor?" he called out.

But Martin didn't hear the offer. He rose slowly as in a trance and ambled out into the night air.

When he reached the hotel, Ellen and Karen were still awake. Ellen was reading the novel she had brought and Karen was writing a postcard to Sean and Lindie. As he entered the room, they looked up. "That was a short meet- . . . What's wrong?" Ellen asked when she saw the bewildered look on his face.

His voice was flat. "Uhh, nothing really. I just don't know what to make of the three individuals I just met. They were the strangest people I've ever seen. catlike green eyes and odd hair. Definitely not from around here. Oh, and, oddly enough, they all have six fingers on each hand. And one of them is a woman, rather tomboyish, but I would guess about our age."

Ellen seized him by the shoulders and shook him. "Martin, Martin, are you on drugs!"

It was as if the dam holding back his emotions suddenly burst and a torrent of words came rushing out. "They want me to drive to Lima and get a sample of their blood analyzed. The one named Bayn said that his blood isn't like ours, that it has 25 pairs of chromosomes instead of 23 pairs, and . . ."

Ellen raised her hand to ward off the barrage of words. "Stop!" Her expression became a scowl. Now he felt a little foolish mentioning the whole thing. "25 pairs of chromosomes!" she whooped. "That's impossible. Every human being on this planet has 23 pairs of chromosomes. The only way he could not have 23 pairs of chromosomes is if . . ."

The two women gasped, "He's not human!"

"Then what is he?" Karen asked, mostly to herself.

"I don't know. He didn't say and I was so dumbfounded I didn't think to ask," Martin said, a little embarrassed by his lack of information.

Ellen was becoming alarmed. "And the purpose of this trip to Lima would be . . ."

"Well, he wants to prove to me that I can believe what they tell me. And he wants me to have the proof I need to convince the appropriate authorities. He said he has some information that may be critical to the, uhh, future of humankind."

It was all too bizarre for her; she was becoming suspicious—and irritated. "Martin Winslow Connor, if this is a prank of yours, you've gone too far. Now what's going on?"

There were the operative words: *you've gone too far!* He had learned long ago when that phrase popped up, he'd better seek cover. "Honey, I swear to you, this is not a prank. I don't know what's going on. I know it's highly unusual . . ."

"This doesn't have anything to do with drugs, does it?" she interrupted. "The last thing we need is to get sucked into some drug smuggling operation."

"Honey, I don't think this has anything to do with drugs." He paused, feeling foolish. "Apparently it's about, uhhh, saving the human race."

Ellen stared at her husband in disbelief. "Saving it from what?"

"He didn't say exactly."

She scowled at him. "Well, unless he knows how to save us from ourselves, I don't want to hear it! Martin, for God's sake, why would they pick you? What's wrong with the CIA, the FBI, the Department of Defense? Or Interpol?" She was on a roll and she was getting madder by the minute. "Martin Winslow Conner, are you making this up? Does this have something to do with that theory of yours about aliens and the lines?"

"Whoa! Ellen, I'm not making this up. I don't know why they singled me out except they said they had read the article about me in *La Voz de Ica*."

She began to calm down and he began to feel more confident. "Anyway, I've got a gut feeling that I need to follow up on this. Why don't you and Karen come with me to Lima tomorrow? While we're waiting for the results, we can do some sightseeing and Karen can visit the University. Then we can see the blood results together. I can call Roberto at Universidad de Lima in the morning. Maybe he can get me into a lab there that can rush this through for us. We can be in Lima by early afternoon."

Then it occurred to him, "Better yet, why don't we spend a day at the Museo Rafael Larco Herrera. It's a prestigious archaeological museum with the largest private collection of pre-Columbian art in the world. It's in an old mansion built over a pre-Columbian pyramid and surrounded by lush gardens of bougainvillea. The museum houses a wide assortment of textiles, precious metals, jewelry and pottery."

He winked at her devilishly. "It's also renowned for its collection of ancient erotic pottery representing various sexual relationships. Maybe we could learn something. What do you think?"

Karen feigned disgust and went back to reading her novel.

"Hah! I should have known. If you learn any more about sex, you'll be dangerous."

"You mean, beyond the missionary position?"

"Yes, dear, you might hurt yourself!" she teased, finally calming down.

"So! I can afford to take risks; that's why I married a nurse," he shot back.

"Yes, that's why I'm trying to protect you from yourself. By the way, why is it called the missionary position?"

Martin replied with a smug grin, "Because missionaries in the last century taught that it was the only natural position—with the man on top! Anything else was unnatural and sinful!"

"I knew you'd have an answer for something like that."

Martin laughed. "My dear, you'd be amazed at how much useless trivia this magnificent brain holds!"

"Well, the museum does sound like a good idea. Besides making me curious, you've also made me paranoid; I think we'd better go with you. I don't think Karen and I should stay here by ourselves with some inhuman weirdoes on the loose. And I want to go to your next meeting with Mr. Kener and his friends as well."

"That's right, Dad, and I'm coming too," Karen chimed in.

The next morning Martin phoned Roberto and asked for his help in arranging a blood analysis. Roberto agreed to direct him to a clinic near the university where a lab technician he knew could expedite the analysis.

Four days later, Martin and Ellen had the results in hand. There were in fact 25 pairs of chromosomes and the white blood cells were definitely not human. As Roberto gave Martin the results, he asked, "Where did you get this sample? I can't match it with any animal I know. I've never seen anything like it!"

Martin could only mutter coyly, "Neither have I—it's a new species!"

On their way back into town, they stopped off at *La Taberna* to quench their thirst and to ask Carlos to notify Bayn that Martin had returned.

Later that evening Bayn telephoned Martin to set up a meeting the next afternoon at *La Taberna*. Martin agreed and then asked if he could bring his wife and daughter. Bayn readily agreed and then hung up. Martin turned to Karen. "It's all set. Are you sure you want to come along?"

"Why not?" Karen replied.

The next afternoon, the three of them arrived at *La Taberna* to find the three strangers seated together in the same place as before. Karen stared at them in spite of herself. Ellen was also startled at their unusual features, but she managed to smile without looking uncomfortable as Martin introduced her. She noticed the brilliant blue gem hanging around Bayn's neck. *"Buenas tardes*, this is my wife Ellen and my daughter Karen," Martin said, feeling a little tense.

Karen waved an anemic *hello* and Ellen said meekly, "Pleased to meet you."

Bayn smiled back at them and said, "Ellen, Karen, my name is Bayn Kener; this is Darz Tureesh and Jeliko Hanahban. We're glad you could join us."

Turning to Martin, he asked, "Did the blood test turn out as I said it would?"

Martin said, "Yes, it did, so we're ready to believe whatever you tell us. But who are you? And why are you here?"

Ellen finally summoned the courage to join the conversation, "And why did you choose Martin to contact?"

She had been looking them over, incredulous and unusually shy. On the drive over, she had felt nervous. *Were they really aliens?* she wondered. *If they were, what do you say to an alien the first time you meet him? How was the trip from Alpha Centauri?* Now she was feeling a little disappointed. These aliens weren't very exotic.

They looked different, definitely not quite human, but not that different. Mentally she took inventory: bright penetrating green eyes, long sloping nose, thin lips, pointed ears that slanted backwards and odd hands with SIX fingers! They were strange for sure but not scary strange. They seemed friendly enough and they spoke English and Spanish flawlessly. But their clothing was plain like that of the locals.

Jeliko regarded her solemnly. "Those are all important questions, but, Ellen, I think your question deserves to be answered first. Martin, your questions will be answered fully as we tell you our story.

"We believe that our message is of such importance that it should be delivered to someone in the American government who will know the best way to respond. After all, Americans seem to occupy a position of leadership in the world community, at least militarily, right now. We didn't know any Americans, however, so we put the whole issue aside."

He smiled at Martin. "Then one day we saw the article about your interview in the local paper *La Voz de Ica*. It occurred to us that you might be a good choice to act as our proxy by conveying our warning to the proper authorities. You were educated and we speculated that you might have the necessary connections."

Bayn said, "That's when we decided to contact you. We all agreed that, once we had revealed what we knew to you, we would have discharged our moral responsibility. From then on, it would be up to you humans to decide how to respond to the potential threat."

"But what *is* your message?" Martin asked impatiently.

The three Senoobians, slightly perplexed, looked at each other, not quite knowing where to begin. Bayn was the first to speak. "Please be patient. We have a lot to tell you, but I promise we'll answer all of your questions."

Jeliko began, "As you can tell from our appearance and from the blood test, we're not from Earth. We're from a planet that *was* 35 light years away. It was totally destroyed when our star system collided with a vast cloud of space debris that we believe was left over from an ancient nebula in our sector of the galaxy.

"Our astronomers searched for a planet we could colonize before the destruction of our own planet so that our species would not become extinct. They found Earth and we were part of a mission that was launched to found a colony here. The rest of our crew died and our ship was destroyed as the result of unfortunate events. As far as we know, we're the only surviving members of our species."

Ellen looked incredulously at Jeliko, "So, you really are extraterrestrials! Aliens! You don't look like aliens and you don't talk like aliens. Is this some kind of joke?"

Bayn looked directly at her and in a slightly condescending voice said, "Ellen, what did you expect, some kind of monsters? May I remind you that, to us, you're the aliens. It just so happens we're not so different from you humans. We chose to reveal our information to Martin because we believed he would have an open mind as a result of his familiarity with the different cultures he has studied. We also believed that, being educated, he might know how to best use the information we're going to share with you. I'm glad you're here, Ellen, because he will need your support if he decides to follow through on this."

She was not reassured.

Bayn turned to Jeliko and Darz and began speaking to them in an unfamiliar language: ᏜᎪᎯᏞ ᎬᏁᏜ ᒼᐧᎤ ᏦᏋ ᎢᏝᏇᏐᏜ ᏜᏏᏗ ᏭᏔᎢᒪ ᏟᎢᎢᒪ ᏜᏭ ᏜᏁᎬ 3Ᏼ ᏁᏜᎢᎬᏐᏪ ᏜᏞᏛᏘ ᏯᏛ0 ᏦᏗᏗ ᏰᏭ ᏯᏁᏫ ᏜᏭ ᏜᏧᏜᏔᒪᏜᏗ It sounded like *nahshee loon azu tho jahmin noo. Koga dayga no nool cho english neeku rus thoo. tay do doom no naybu pan.*" (I don't know if they believe us. The fact that we're speaking in English may be throwing them off. What do you think we should do?)

Darz replied: ᏅᎯᎤᏞ ᏏᏍᏇᎻᎻᏙᎯ ᏞᎬ ᏦᏅ ᎦᏞᎢ ᏅᏅᎠ ᎬᏞ ᎬᏝᎠᏅ ᏏᏅ ᏙᏅᏅᏅ ᏙᎯᏅᏅᏙ ᏅᎯᎠᎻᏪ It sounded like *nahshee peytinah eel tho veeg nosha zee labu yehksoray kahter nahmay.* (I'm not sure they're capable of understanding but maybe some explanation will help.)

Darz turned back to the three humans who were looking baffled at what they had just heard. "What language was that?" Karen asked.

Bayn replied, "It's Kuterin, our native language. We were just trying to decide how we might convince you that we're who we say we are."

Ellen was still suspicious. "Mr. Kener, that could be Sanskrit for all I know. Show me what your language looks like." She nudged her napkin toward him. "Here. Write something on this."

Bayn obligingly took it, pulled a pencil from his shirt pocket, thought a moment and began to write: ᏥᏅᎢᏅᏏᏅ ᏞᎤᎢᏠᎤᏞᏅ Ꮕ ᏙᏓᎤ ᎢᏅ ᏅᎠ ᏅᏣᏞᏅ ᏞᎤᏣᏃᏲᏞᏅ Ꮕ ᏙᏓᎤ ᏞᏘ First he translated: how many fingers do I have on my hands? I have six." Then he pronounced it slowly: *dogepu eejooseeo nah kays geh nye kotao eekopota nah kays eem.*"

The three humans leaned over, intrigued to see what he had written. "Hmmm, very interesting. I've never seen a language quite like that," Martin said.

"I expect not," Jeliko replied.

Ellen searched Jeliko's eyes for any sign of trickery. "How come you all speak English so well if you're from some other planet?"

Jeliko was amused at Ellen's feistiness. "Actually, we've been on your planet for almost a hundred years now and we learned to speak English and Spanish a long time ago. We've made it a point to learn about you humans and your planet; we read newspapers and watch T.V. just like you do."

"Think of us as inter-stellar immigrants," Darz chuckled.

Ellen was incredulous. "Wait! You've been here for almost a hundred years? How is that possible? You don't look that old—how old are you, by the way?"

Bayn looked at her, knowing his answer would be hard to swallow. He gestured toward Jeliko and Darz. "Well, Jeliko is 155 years old, am I right, Jeliko?"

Jeliko nodded, "Yes, that's right."

Bayn continued, gesturing toward Darz, "Darz here is 159; and I'm the oldest at 168—as best I can tell."

Ellen and Karen gasped.

Martin was puzzled, "What do you mean as best you can tell? You're not exactly sure how old you are?"

Jeliko said, "Well, it's a little confusing because, first of all, our years on Senoobis were 18 days longer than your Earthly years. And our days were almost two hours longer than your days. Besides that, on our way here we spent about 150 years in sleep modules—or extreme suspended animation—and another 720 years the same way before our ship was destroyed." He smiled slightly.

Ellen stared at all three of them as if they were insane.

They said no more, giving her time to process everything.

Martin searched Bayn's face for any sign that he was joking. But there was no hint of a smile. It was obvious that all three of them were dead serious. His skepticism turned to wonder? At that moment he heard Ellen saying to him, "Martin, Dear, it's time for us to go," as she gave him a short, swift kick under the table."

Martin yelped, "Ouch!" and startled everyone. Annoyed, he turned to Ellen, "Wait a minute, if they are from another planet, things would be totally different from the way they are on Earth. Remember the blood test. And their hands! I believe we should hear them out."

Karen spoke up, "Mom, I think they're telling the truth. Why would anyone go to all this trouble to convince *us*? I mean, what's the point?"

Darz looked at all three of them seriously. "Look, we know this is a lot to comprehend but Karen's right. We don't have anything to gain from going to all this trouble. We're the only survivors of our race and we have no future here. Nevertheless we believe humans are in grave danger. We decided we should try to warn you humans, even though we have suffered numerous indignities from your kind. It's the right thing to do."

Jeliko said, "Yes, all three of us were quite bitter from time to time because of what we have been through and because of the coarseness and cruelty we have found in some humans. We thought for a long time that it would be best to keep our silence and let you humans sort things out on your own. But, over the years, there have been a few humans who have treated us with kindness and we finally

96

concluded that we should speak up for their sake and for all the others like them."

Darz replied, "Yes, that's right. There are some intelligent and compassionate humans whose lives shouldn't be jeopardized. So we only want to help by warning the proper authorities of a serious threat but we're not in a position to do that ourselves."

"But why do you need me?" Martin asked. "Why can't you just contact someone in authority yourselves and deliver your warning?"

Darz responded, "Martin, we don't need you; you need us. We can very easily walk away and forget this whole situation. We have nothing to lose. And if you don't choose to take us seriously, that's what we'll do."

Bayn added, "We just want to get our information to someone who will know what to do with it. But to pass on this kind of information you have to know someone who will take you seriously. And that someone has to have credibility or they will be dismissed as a crackpot.

"Do you honestly think anyone in any government is going to take me seriously if I call and say I want to warn them about an impending invasion from an alien race? And when they ask who I am and I say, *My name is Bayn Kener. I'm from the planet Senoobis*, I expect they're going to hang up on me. Can you imagine their snide remarks as they slam the phone down: I'm sorry, sir, we only take alien invasion calls on Tuesdays. *Weirdo!*"

Ellen relaxed. "I see what you mean. Well, why don't you just walk into the CIA offices? It's easy to see that you're not human."

Bayn gave her a patronizing look. "Ellen, if we did prove we were members of an alien race by showing up in person, can you imagine the sensation it would create? Or the kind of treatment, even confinement, we would have to face, on display like freaks. I shudder to think what any government that got its hands on us might do to us. Besides all three of us are old—and cranky; we want to live out our last years in peace."

Jeliko joined in, "Exactly. We don't want the hassle we would have to deal with."

Darz nodded his agreement.

Bayn looked directly at Ellen and Martin. "I'm sure you have a lot of questions but, if you'll permit us to tell our story, I believe all of your questions will be answered in due course."

So that was it—a possible invasion from another alien race, Martin thought. The three humans sat back in their chairs, mulling over everything. They looked at each other, lost in thought and overwhelmed, not sure whether to take what they had heard seriously or not.

Bayn, growing impatient, said to Martin, "Look, I know all of this is hard to swallow. And I know most humans would dismiss us as freaks but we're just trying to help. Sometime in the near future, this planet may meet the meanest bastards in the galaxy and, if you humans don't get your act together, it may be *sayonara* for the human race!"

Ellen interjected, "Wait a minute. All of this is pretty scary. How sure are you that this invasion is going to happen?"

Bayn said, "We may be wrong about all of this but this alien race does exist, as surely as we exist. Maybe for some reason they won't return to Earth and for your sake I hope they don't. But if they do, it could be tragic for the human race. We believe that someone at the highest level should be aware of this and look into it. We aren't sure that you humans can manage a united front against a threat like this, but we believe you should at least be warned; then it will be your responsibility as to how you proceed."

Finally Martin said, "Okay, what do you want us to do?"

Bayn said, "Since you Americans have the most powerful military now, we thought you might contact someone in your government and get them down here. I think it would be best if we all sit down together and you and they hear our whole story. So if you will arrange for someone in authority to meet with us, we're prepared to tell you and your contact everything we know."

Jeliko added, "Call us when you're ready and we'll meet you here again. Here's our phone number." He handed Martin a piece of paper.

Martin glanced at it and then at Ellen. "Well, if the fate of the human race is at stake, I guess we'd better get crackin'."

He scratched his chin thoughtfully. "The only person who comes to mind is Floyd Cates in Spring City. Maybe he can tell me who to contact. I'll give him a call and see what he thinks."

Ellen's voice took on a sour note: "Floyd, your old fishing buddy? Of course—I knew he'd be good for something someday!"

Martin muttered to himself, "I think he will be in this case."

11

LUKE AND SONNY

That evening Martin emailed Floyd Cates who had retired in Spring City, Tennessee. His friend was helpful; two days later he had the name of a contact in the CIA:

> Email Luke Pearson and tell him I said to contact him. He's an analyst with the Directorate of Intelligence, one of the departments in the CIA. I was his section chief before I retired in '94. He's a young guy, pretty smart, but he's not far up the ladder. You won't be able to reach the Director of the CIA or anyone else with any seniority anyway. You'll have to start with someone like Luke and hope that he can carry the ball further up. The good news is that maybe he'll listen to you because he hasn't gotten jaded yet with all the crap that goes on there. The bad news is he won't have much clout and, even if you can convince him to take you seriously, his bosses may blow him off. You know some of these guys get lost in the bureaucracy and are just putting in their time until they retire. They can't see the big picture and don't want to be bothered. Here's his email address: lpearson1412@cia.gov. Good luck.

The next morning, Martin composed an email to Luke Pearson:

> Mr. Pearson, I'm contacting you at the suggestion of your former co-worker, Floyd Cates. I have some information that I believe will be of utmost importance to the CIA in the pursuit of its intelligence-gathering mission. I am a retired history professor from Carson-Newman College in East Tennessee. A few days ago while on a trip to Peru, I received some information that I believe deserves your urgent attention. If

you will email me your snail mail address, I will forward it to
you. I believe you will find it most interesting. Please let me
know as soon as you have received and reviewed it; I will be
glad to answer your questions then. I will be in Peru for three
more weeks. Dr. Martin W. Connor.

The next day, Martin received an email response from Luke:

Dr. Connor, I don't have a lot of time but if Floyd says I
should talk to you, I will. Here's my address . . .

That Tuesday evening Martin and Ellen met with the three
Senoobians again and put together a package of information to mail to
Luke Pearson. It included a short narrative that Martin had composed
with their help, a copy of Bayn's blood test, a photo of Martin and
Ellen with them and a videotape of the three with Bayn delivering a
short message in English.

To save time Martin and Ellen drove back to Lima the next day
and stood in line for almost an hour so they could ship the small
package to Luke by UPS Worldwide Express. As Martin paid the
$85.00 shipping charge, he turned to Ellen with a frown, "Ouch!
Dahling, this isn't what I had in mind for our vacation!"

As they left the UPS store, Ellen punched Martin in the ribs. "You
know, we must be whacko for doing this. I just hope your Mr. Pearson
doesn't think we're whacko."

It would take three days for the package to reach Luke in
Alexandria and probably another couple of days for him to digest the
contents and respond to Martin by email. Then it would take a couple
more days for Luke to make the arrangements for the trip to Nazca, if
he would come.

Martin and Ellen decided that, while they were waiting for his
response, it would be a good time to make a quick side trip to Cuzco,
only a two hour flight from Nazca. Whenever they were in Peru,
Martin and Ellen always managed a trip to Cuzco so they could stroll
about the city and enjoy its unique blending of Inca and Spanish
history.

A beautiful city of almost 300,000 and the second largest in Peru,
there is much to recommend Cuzco. But there were two aspects of the
city that Martin and Ellen disliked. Since the city is nestled high in the

Andes at an altitude of 11,000 feet, it takes a day or two to become acclimated to the higher altitude that causes weakness and nausea. The other aspect is the extreme poverty of the proud and friendly Peruvians living in hovels and wretched conditions around the city.

Cuzco was the capital of the Inca Empire until the Spanish conquest in 1532 when Francisco Pizarro and his men massacred thousands of Inca warriors. The craftsmanship of the Inca stonework, some of it still visible throughout the city, never failed to impress them. Unfortunately the Inca foundations of precisely cut stones were the only remains of far older Inca buildings and temples that the Spanish had destroyed. The more recent Spanish stonework used to erect buildings atop the Inca foundations was crude by comparison.

One site that Martin and Ellen always visited was the wall in the narrow alley of *Hathun Rumiyoq*, near the *Plaza de Armas*, that had a large boulder cut with no less than twelve angles in its jointing with the stones around it. How the Inca builders could achieve such precision without metal tools, they could not fathom.

On the crest of the hills overlooking Cuzco to the north was another mystery that had intrigued Martin from the first time he saw it. The ancient fortress of *Sacsayhuaman* was said to be shaped like the head of a puma, an animal sacred to the Incas. Not a lot was known about it; most historians attributed its construction to the Incas but others speculated that it predated them.

The most impressive feature of *Sacsayhuaman* is its great size. It is constructed of huge granite boulders ranging in height from twelve to 28 feet with some weighing well over 300 tons. The huge stones were somehow transported over rough terrain from quarries as far as 18 miles away and lifted into place one above the other by Indians who didn't have the wheel, horse, or ox. Nor did they have steel or iron tools with which to cut the stone. And yet the stones were cut with intricate angles that matched the adjoining stones perfectly.

As Martin thought about their trip to Cuzco, he realized it would give him a welcome break from the perplexing situation he found himself in with the Senoobians. It would be a pleasant distraction that would help him sort through feelings that ranged from disbelief one minute to apprehension the next.

Luke Pearson was not your typical Washington bureaucrat. After a stint in the Navy, he had settled in Charleston, South Carolina for a few years before moving on to D.C. to look for a job. Now he was 36 years old, fairly muscular and still in excellent shape, in spite of having held a desk job with the CIA for the past 8 years. He managed to stay physically fit by playing racketball twice a week and jogging on the weekends. And he still loved to water ski whenever he had the chance.

Luke had sandy hair and a broad smile. He was easy-going and loved to dance; it was his way of letting off steam from the mountains of paperwork he managed. His friends described him as the kind of guy who would give you the shirt off of his back. They also joked that he had a way with the ladies. Nonetheless, he had never married, even though he had been engaged a couple of times. In spite of having lots of lady friends, he couldn't seem to find the woman that made him want to settle down.

The following week when Luke received Martin's package, his first reaction was one of disbelief. *Who are these people and what do they want from me?* He sat back in his chair with a cup of coffee; the blood test results looked legitimate. Of course, the photos could be easily faked. And the tape could be faked as well but why would anyone go to so much trouble? He went back and forth: one minute ready to throw the whole package into the trash can and waste no more time on the kooks; the next minute, ready to take the information seriously. After all, was it really so farfetched that there might be highly intelligent life else where in the universe. He couldn't resist thinking with his dry sense of humor, *if they're so damn intelligent, why would they want to come here?"*

Finally he decided to take the tape to his friend at the National Security Agency in Ft. George Meade. Joe "Sonny" Campbell spoke five languages and was a linguistics hotshot at the NSA. His job was to look for patterns in the millions of communications from around the world every day. Luke thought to himself, *Sonny's a smart guy; I'll see what he thinks."*

Luke picked up the phone and called, "Sonny, I need to talk to you. Can you meet me at Potter's at 6:00?" Sonny agreed.

Sonny was slightly shorter than Luke and not as physically fit. They had met when they were stationed on a destroyer based in Charleston. Sonny was the Communications Officer and Luke, the

Weapons Officer. They were both single and from the South so they hit it off. Sonny, who was from Tuscaloosa, married a petite blond, a typical southern belle from Birmingham, soon after he got out of the Navy. Friends hinted it wasn't a good match; sure enough, they divorced after only three years. Luke and Sonny did stay in touch, however, and wound up working only a few miles from each other in the D.C. area.

Luke was already at Potter's, waiting on a bench outside, when Sonny arrived. As Sonny sat down beside him, there was a serious look on Luke's face that was out of character for his usually jovial friend. Luke got right to the point, "Sonny, will you do me a favor and give this a listen. I need you to tell me what language it is and if you can make any sense out of it."

Sonny smiled at Luke, "Nice to see you too." Not missing a chance to tease his friend, he rolled his eyes back in his head cynically and muttered, "Only calls when he wants a favor." Then he jabbed Luke in the stomach, "Okay, but it's going to cost you a couple of rounds."

Luke slid the tape into the player he had brought with him and they listened to it, sitting on the bench. After a few minutes, Sonny hit the stop button. "Okay, I'll bite. What is it? It's not Russian, not a Romance language, not German, not Mandarin, definitely not Hindi. It's not Farsi or Arabic. Not Greek or Hebrew. I've never heard anything like it. Where did you get this?"

"Sonny, you won't believe me when I tell you. Besides I've got some more info I want to run by you. Let's go in and get a table. We can talk about it while we eat."

Sonny's curiosity was aroused. "Sounds good to me."

Soon they had a table by a window, a margarita for Sonny and a long neck for Luke. Sonny was all smiles as he took the first sip, "Boy, do I need this. Perry's been bustin' my chops all day." Sonny's specialty was Farsi and the volume of communications his department monitored out of the Middle East was overwhelming.

"So, tell me, what is this weird language you've got? I thought I had heard almost everything but that's a new one. What's going on?"

Luke opened a large envelope and handed a photograph to Sonny. "Take a look at this. This is history professor Martin Connor and these are the three hombres who speak the language on the tape." It was a large photograph of Martin and the three Senoobians standing next to their shuttle. They were a full head taller than Martin.

"Well, they are three odd-looking fellows. Where are they from?"

Luke looked Sonny in the eye and in a matter-of-fact voice said, "This picture was taken in Peru, if we may believe Dr. Connor, and these three fellows are from a planet 35 light years away. They're aliens. At first I thought Connor was just another crackpot and I started to throw his package away but, before I did, I called Floyd Cates who referred Connor to me. Floyd is retired in a little town in East Tennessee and it seems he knows Connor quite well. He says Connor is no crackpot, just a typical small college professor and pretty conservative at that. He's pretty familiar with South America and has made several trips to the area to study the history and culture down there."

Sonny sat back in his chair. "What else you got?"

Luke continued as he handed Sonny a copy of the blood test, "Well, Connor wanted me to take him seriously so he had a blood test done on one of these "guys" at a clinic in Lima and here's a copy of the blood test. Basically it says that the blood sample is not human. It has 25 pairs of chromosomes and none of the other blood components match human blood. I can't imagine why anyone would go to the trouble to fake something like this."

"Very interesting. Okay, so what do these *aliens* want you to do?"

"I asked Connor the same thing. He says he has some important information for me. Wants me to come to Nazca to see these guys for myself—where the hell is Nazca?"

"It's a small town in southern Peru, near Cuzco."

Luke looked puzzled, "Where the hell is Cuzco?"

Sonny frowned at him. "My God, man, you don't get around much! It's the second largest city in Peru. It's in the South in the Andes Mountains about 14,000 feet up. It was the capital of the Inca Empire until the 1500's when the Spanish vanquished them. Ever heard of Machu Pichu?"

"Well, sorta'."

"It's the ruins of an abandoned Inca religious center high in the Andes Mountains, a three-hour train ride from Cuzco. It's one of the most beautiful and haunting tourist sites in all of South America. It wasn't discovered until 1911."

"Well, it sounds charming but what do you think? Should I go and check this out?"

Sonny didn't hesitate. "Uh, yes, you should and I'm going with you. Besides you'll want someone with you who speaks Spanish."

"Sonny, I'm sure Connor speaks Spanish—but I would feel better if there were two of us. Who knows what I might be getting into? Can you get off from work, this Friday and all next week?"

"Yeah, I think so. I'll let you know as soon as it's worked out."

"Great, I'll get Marlene to get us a couple of tickets."

The next morning Luke gingerly entered his harried section leader's office. "Lou, I need to take a few days off. Is it okay if I take off a week starting this Friday?"

Lou Broucelli was usually irritable. "Sure, why not?" he said with mock sarcasm from behind a desk piled high with reports. "There's nothing going on around here! Business or pleasure?"

"Well, business, I guess. I have something I need to follow up on."

"And that would be . . ."

"Uh, just a report of some aliens that may involve security issues."

"Damn it, Luke, this is not the immigration service. Can't you just say your grandmother died like everyone else? Go on! We'll try to limp along without you for a week."

"Thanks, Lou. I'll give you a full report when I get back."

"I can't wait," Broucelli mouthed to himself. As Luke reached the door, Broucelli yelled, "Hey! Don't be late on the MEDINT reports!"

At 2:30 that Friday afternoon at Dulles International, Sonny and Luke boarded Delta flight 1077 for Atlanta. From there they caught a connecting Delta flight that set down in Lima at 10:45 that evening. After sleeping in on Saturday morning, they had a leisurely breakfast, then packed and rented a Toyota Yaris for the five-hour drive to Nazca as Martin had suggested.

Martin, Ellen and Karen met them at the *Hostal Sol de Nazca* for dinner that evening. Luke and Sonny were pleasantly surprised to meet Karen and she was just as pleased to meet them. Karen was attractive: she had bright brown eyes and dark brown flowing hair, a cute smile and a turned up nose. Her figure was gorgeous and when she talked, her voice dripped with honey. Immediately the trip became more interesting for all three of them. For the next few minutes, the two young men forgot all about aliens.

"What kind of work do you do?" Karen asked Sonny.

Infatuated with her, Sonny made a clumsy attempt to be funny. "I could tell you but then I'd have to kill you,"

Luke choked and Karen gasped. Luke thought to himself: *the man's brilliant but he's a bumbling idiot around a good-looking woman!*

Finally Luke managed to salvage his friend's faux pas by quickly changing the subject and putting Karen at ease again. They all decided to get down to business. Luke began, "Martin, what the hell is this all about? Are these aliens for real?"

Martin smiled, "Luke, I'm still not sure what to believe myself anymore. When I'm with them, I'm totally convinced they're who they say they are but, when they're not around, I start wondering if this is all my imagination. It all seems too bizarre. But don't worry; I'm going to let you guys decide for yourselves. They should be here . . .," he looked at his watch, "any minute now!"

Luke looked at Sonny, not knowing what to expect, "Ohhhhh-kay. I can't wait." He was feeling a little apprehensive. Just the word *alien* conjured up images of mysterious and formidable creatures from strange worlds. He recalled some of the science fiction movies he had seen such as *Alien, Star Trek* and *Star Wars*. At the same time his mind was reeling. If these guys are real, this is a big deal. A historic event!

Luke had to ask, "Martin, how long have these aliens been on the Earth and how did you find them?"

Martin replied matter-of-factly, "Well, according to them, they've been here about 90 years—their starship was destroyed in a huge explosion over in 1908."

Ellen added, "And, Martin didn't find them. They found him."

Sonny looked at Martin, "Okay, let me get this straight. These guys are from some distant planet that was wiped out when it collided with a monster cloud of space garbage left over from some . . . nebula? Anyway, when their astronomers realized what was going to happen, they started looking for a planet they could colonize before their own planet was destroyed and they became extinct. They found the Earth and these three were part of the crew that was sent here to found a colony. Their ship was destroyed in some kind of accident and the rest of the crew was killed. And they're the only surviving members of their race. Am I right?"

Martin nodded at him, "That's about it."

They all looked up as the door opened and the four Senoobians came in. As they reached the table, Luke remembered the photo he had received from Martin: *Except for the eyes, they're not that different.*

Darz immediately saw the five humans and pointed them out to Jeliko and Bayn. Upon reaching the table, they greeted Ellen, Martin and Karen and then introduced themselves to Luke and Sonny. Then, Darz said proudly, "And this is our daughter, Amara." He smiled and gestured at her hat. "We call her the *hat maker.*"

The conversation stopped as all five humans focused their attention on the remarkable young female who stood before them. Amara did indeed wear an unusual hat; it was the size of a basketball, shaped like a Hershey's kiss, and made from six alternating sections of silvery fabric that came together at the top. There was a narrow flange of another textured fabric around the sides and in the back. Her thick black hair was short on the sides but long in the back where it flowed down past her shoulders. The tips of her ears peeped out just below the flange. She wore a thin jacket made from the same fabric as the flange of her hat, giving her the look of a gypsy.

Her costume and her exotic features were mysterious and alluring. Luke and Sonny couldn't take their eyes off of her. *If only they were Senoobians,* she sighed to herself.

She stood straight, projecting an air of confidence and clearly alert to everything around her. She was tall and lean with thick black hair, long eyelashes and bright green eyes that bored through them.

Karen was fascinated by her.

Ellen was taken aback. She turned to Jeliko, "You didn't tell us you had a daughter! She's lovely."

Then turning to Amara, she said, "We're pleased to meet you, Amara, and that is a remarkable hat! I like it." She laughed, "Of course, I'm too old to wear anything like that."

Amara smiled and bowed slightly. "It's my pleasure to meet you too."

Five humans and four aliens! It was a meeting none of the humans there would ever forget. After all, the Senoobians were the strangest beings they had ever seen—not *strange* in a scary way. Maybe *unusual* would be a better word. The humans studied the aliens cautiously, incredulously. Sonny marveled at their flawless English. Luke couldn't help staring at their facial features and Karen was speechless.

After the formalities, Darz turned to Luke and Sonny. "I know we look a little different from what you're used to. I hope that doesn't make you uncomfortable."

Luke said, "No, not at all. It's just that you're not quite what I had expected. Martin sent us a picture, but it's not the same as seeing you in the flesh. Actually, I expected you to look a lot different from us but you're not that different, really."

Bayn smiled, "We'll take that as a compliment."

"I hope you're not disappointed," Darz added curtly.

Luke stammered, "No, no. It's just that I've never seen a real live alien, I mean, someone actually from another planet, that is, another solar system. As humans, we've speculated for centuries as to whether or not we were the only intelligent life in the Universe. It's just hard for me to believe that you're really from another planet. Meeting someone like you is a very big deal—a historical first. Please don't take offense."

"None taken," Darz added drily.

As the older Senoobians and humans began to talk more freely, Amara and Karen moved off to the side and struck up a conversation. "Actually, I was born here on Earth, Amara confided, so I don't think of myself as alien." She chuckled, "Actually we think of you humans as the aliens."

Karen was amused. "Well, I can see why you would. Actually you really don't look that different and your English is better than mine. Are you married?"

Amara sighed, "I would like to be but it's not possible. After our planet was destroyed, my parents and Bayn were stranded here on Earth. I was the only Senoobian baby born after our planet was destroyed. In fact, not a single child was born in the 60 years before then. There are only the four of us so there's no one to be my mate. There's no one my age to talk to or do things with except for Marco."

"Bayn is your uncle?" Karen asked.

"No, not really. I refer to him as my *uncle* because in a way he's part of our family. My parents wouldn't have had me if it weren't for his encouragement. Actually he was the Executive Officer on the ship that brought us here."

"What about Marco? He's your brother?"

"Uhhh, no, not really but I think of him as my *brother* because, well, he's part of our family too. Actually he's a human my parents adopted but I don't think of him as human; we're very close."

"I'd like to meet him. How come he didn't come with you?"

"He's helping one of our human friends, Luis Arturo, with one of his cases. He's a policeman in Nazca."

"You sure have an interesting family." She was looking at Amara's hat. "Say, that's an unusual hat. Where did you get it?"

Amara laughed. "I made it myself," she said. "As you can see, I like to be a different, you know, to stir things up. I do like hats. I have 45 of them, one for whatever mood I'm in."

"Wow, what an exciting life you must have," Karen exclaimed.

"Uggh. It's boring! Don't get me wrong. I love my parents and Uncle Bayn. And I appreciate Marco, although he can be irritating. Actually, if it weren't for him, I'd go crazy. I mean he's the only one I know my age, but he's a male. It's depressing not knowing one female my own age to talk to or one male for a courting ritual."

She seemed to perk up. "How old are you, Karen?"

"Why, I'm 37," she grinned. "How about you?"

"I'm 33," she sighed, "but I feel older than that."

Amara was interested to learn that Karen had been married and had two children. She had a lot of questions, including "What's it like to be married? And what about children?" She knew Senoobians had no more than two children, unlike humans who often had several.

Just then Father Antonio Francisco and his adopted son Phillipe came in and, seeing the group in the corner, came over to say *hello*. Bayn introduced them to the five Americans. "We were just talking about the history of our people," Bayn said, "Won't you join us?"

Father Tony glanced at Phillipe who nodded his approval. "Yes, of course," he said, regarding the Americans warmly. "Please, my friends, call me Father Tony."

Phillipe replied in Spanish, "Please, call me Phillipe." He was a little thin for his 46 years, but he had a sturdy look about him and there was a calmness in his manner that he had acquired from years of working with Father Tony. His hair was black; his eyes were bright blue and there was a small scar near his throat. The humans liked him immediately.

While Phillipe appeared virile but genteel, Father Tony seemed fragile but resolute. He was 63 years old with graying hair—a small, gentle man with a warm smile and a friendly manner. He and Phillipe pulled up two chairs and ordered a glass of wine. Then Father Tony nodded at Bayn, "Please continue."

Martin and Ellen were a little surprised. The Senoobians seemed to know the priest well. "How long have you known each other?" Martin asked the priest.

"Oh, we've known these three for several years. They're close friends."

She gestured toward the Senoobians. "Do you really believe that they're from some distant alien world?"

Father Tony smiled at the three Senoobians with genuine affection. "Yes, of course. I believe they are truthful. I don't know where they're from but it doesn't matter. Who they are is more important than where they're from."

Jeliko winked at him, "Thank you, Father.

Once they were all comfortable, Bayn looked at Sonny and Luke solemnly. "We want to share some important information with you. Feel free to ask us anything you like. We only want to help. Why don't we have a drink and we'll tell you our story. Then it's up to you what to do about it."

Bayn beckoned Carlos over to take their orders. While they were waiting for their drinks, Luke noticed the dark blue stone that hung from a silver chain around Bayn's neck. It reflected the light in a hypnotic way. "That's a beautiful stone," he said. "What is it?"

"It's mirytakite, a rare stone on Senoobis, somewhat similar to your diamond except that it's blue. It's several centuries old, passed down to me by my father. It has always made me feel calm. Every family on Senoobis had some kind of amulet that they favored, somewhat like a coat of arms"

All of the humans agreed it was a beautiful stone.

Sonny turned to Jeliko, noticing the unusual silver pendant she wore. He was intrigued by the words engraved on it in some unknown language: ⅄Ω⊤ꓱKΛ·OΩΞⵏ€⊦⅃ᵹ "What does it mean?" he asked, pointing toward the engraving on the hexagonal-shaped pendant.

"Oh, the words mean *Starship Syzilian*. The hexagonal shape represents our planet Senoobis. I wore it on our ship as an officer and I haven't been able to give it up. I'm too sentimental, I guess."

Bayn paused, glancing proudly at Jeliko and Darz, and smiled. "Would you believe that these two, and even myself, were once considered the crème de la crème? We were all young then but these two especially were dashing in their red and gold uniforms. They performed their duties with distinction and I never worried when they were on duty. Of course, everyone aboard was dedicated and proud to serve on the *Syz*. After all, the survival of our race rested on the shoulders of everyone who was a part of the Colony Project."

Sonny was curious, "All of you must have been relieved and proud to have been chosen out of all those who applied for duty on the *Syzilian*—and to play an important role in helping your race survive. Preparing to sail off into the vast unknown of space—what an exciting but scary time that must have been!"

Bayn said, "Oh, yes, I was proud to be one of those chosen and it was an exciting time. But that was not my only reason, or even my greatest reason, for going. I would have gone on that ship some way, even if our race weren't facing extinction. You see, I watched the *Syz* being built. She was beautiful and alluring and seemed to come alive before my eyes; I fell in love with her. I wish you could have seen her. I became so obsessed with her that I never even considered the sacrifices she would require."

Visibly moved, Sonny turned to Jeliko, "What about you?"

Jeliko grinned, "Well, I'm not sure I'm normal either. I was always deeply curious, eager to discover something new. To explore some strange new world was always my dream. Like Bayn, I guess, the heavy costs of pursuing that dream never occurred to me. After all, a starship is no place to raise a family. Once you're on the way to some mysterious new world, there's no turning back. By the time you realize what you've given up to pursue your dream, it's too late."

"What did you do on the *Syzilian*?" Sonny asked.

Jeliko said, "I was the Communications Officer which suited me just fine; the *Syzilian* was exotic and seductive and she fulfilled my dream. On my first flight, I was awed by the countless stars shining brightly and clearly all around us, undistorted by the atmosphere of Senoobis. There were so many more than could be seen from the surface and they looked so brilliant! I knew then that I was where I should be. When I wasn't on duty, I spent hours peering out of the viewing port on the bridge, enchanted by the beauty of the starry beacons that surrounded us."

Luke lifted his glass in salute to her.

"What about you, Darz?"

Darz seemed a little uncomfortable. "Maybe we are misfits but we were treated like heroes and that was enough for me. I was the Assistant Navigator. Our world was doomed; someone had to go. All of my life I was the tough one, the one everyone else looked up to and depended on. But for once I just wanted to run away. The impending destruction of our world was something I couldn't deal with. I couldn't bear the thought of our whole civilization being snuffed out. For the first time in my life I felt helpless and afraid. The *Syz* seemed to offer the only way to redeem myself from such feelings."

Bayn smiled, "The truth is, each one of us would have found a way to be on that ship whether or not Senoobis was doomed. I think we were all driven by a sense of adventure. Darz loves being where the action is. Nothing fazes him and he responds to every crisis with a cool head."

Martin cleared his throat. "Let me get this straight. Even a starship as advanced and powerful as the *Syzilian* took many years to reach the nearest star systems? Surely the *Syzilian* could travel at warp speed or something—you know, the speed of light?"

Bayn was glad to move on to a happier subject. "You're referring to Captain Kirk and the starship *Enterprise*, aren't you? We've seen a few episodes of Star Trek and had some good laughs. I wish space travel were as easy as that show made it seem. In reality even a ship like the *Syz* had limits.

He paused, his voice betraying a hint of resignation, "We were never able to travel at anything approaching warp speed. The Laws of Physics dictate that the amount of energy required to approach the speed of light approaches infinity because the object's mass itself approaches infinity. Despite their best efforts, our engineers were never able to achieve sustained velocities of more than 22 percent of the speed of light. I expect it will take some radical new technology in the future to make that possible." He slumped back a little and his face took on a look of disappointment. But then it turned into a mischievous grin, "And, in case you're wondering, we can't beam people up! Sorry."

Jeliko chimed in, "No, we can't compete with the *Enterprise!*"
Everyone laughed.

Bayn continued. "Anyway, since it took light 35 years to get here from Senoobis, it took us five times as long, or 175 years, to actually travel the same distance."

Darz added, "That's why we only considered star systems within 48 light years of Senoobis. There wasn't enough time to travel any farther."

The Senoobians spoke with such candor and reason that they no longer seemed *alien* and the things they said didn't sound farfetched. They were transformed into common travelers with tales of some distant, exotic land and the enthralled humans were eager to hear more.

They began with a brief history of their race, and how it suffered through terrible times. Once they began, it was hard for them to stop. The more they talked, the more memories they dredged up; some of them had been buried since the loss of the *Syzilian* and were painful to recall.

12

SENOOBIS

Our home was on Senoobis, the second planet from the star Karmut in sector 3309, a small jagged arm of the Bortuks Galaxy, which you call the Milky Way. It was a medium sized planet with two moons: Pesh, the smaller and nearer of the two, and Portinyhe. Karmut was a bit smaller than your sun, and Senoobis was a bit smaller than your Earth. Senoobis was also a bit cooler since it was farther from its star and its year was a little longer—by 18 days to be exact. In cosmic terms, it was not far away at all from Earth."

"In the Forty-First Century, the path of our star system carried it into an area littered with vast clouds of gas and cosmic debris. Our astronomers named that area the *Orgrot*—a Kuterin word that means *destroyer*. Those clouds of cosmic clutter were probably the remains of some ancient nebula that had birthed distant star systems like our own millions of years ago.

"One day without warning, clouds of meteors began to rain down on the surface of Senoobis. Sometimes the skies would light up in a spectacular display as dust storms from outer space caught fire and mercifully burned up before reaching the ground. At other times, meteors the size of houses would streak through the sky and strike the surface so violently that the fiery explosions killed thousands.

"Many more died from the rush of the tidal waves that swept over the low-lying areas along the coasts. Others died a slow death from starvation as great clouds of dust swirling around the planet shut out Karmut's life-giving light and played havoc with its climate, destroying most of the plant and animal life.

"Our ancestors called that time of suffering the *Tribulation*. It was almost 100 years before our star system reached a less dense and destructive part of the Orgrot. But civilization on the planet had collapsed and our species tottered on the brink of extinction; the slate of life on Senoobis was almost wiped clean.

"Four out of five Senoobians perished during those hard years but Senoobians slowly clawed their way back from the great disaster. With a newfound unity and peace forged in their common effort to survive, our ancestors began to rebuild and within 150 years they had risen above their precarious condition and even surpassed their former greatness."

Jeliko picked up the story. "But the more the planet prospered, the more frequent and widespread war became. At last, a group of determined visionaries cried *enough* and vowed to end war on the whole planet forever. They decided that the best way to prevent war was through a strong central world government that could mediate disputes among member states instead of allowing intractable independent nations to start wars by encroaching on each other's sovereignty. Besides, dealing with the major problems endemic to a complex global population required a central government that could coordinate the efforts of member states and give equal representation to a diverse group of constituencies."

Martin interjected, "In other words, a central government of the planet with authority over global issues and member states with authority over national issues."

Jeliko nodded in agreement. "Yes, it's a simple concept but a difficult one to realize. Kurmythia was the superpower of its day, but it had suffered enough from war to realize that all of Senoobis would benefit if the planet were united under one government. So Kurmythia was the first nation to support the visionaries in pursuing world unity. After several years, Kurmythia and three smaller nations managed to form a confederacy and create a Supreme Council to govern it.

"The problem was how to convince the other 126 nations to give up some of their power and independence and join the new confederacy. There was a great deal of mistrust and fierce resistance to giving up any authority. Those who were in power in the independent nations refused to relinquish the powers that the new government would assume; they were more interested in preserving their own power than in pursuing any long-term vision of unity and world peace.

"But the Supreme Council eventually succeeded because its goal was not to secure power for itself but to be an effective government for all the peoples of Senoobis. Once it was victorious and on a solid footing, the Kurmythians and their allies, who had been the driving force toward a world government, did a remarkable thing: they voluntarily relinquished their dominance without prejudice, placing themselves on the same level as the conquered states, and subjecting themselves totally to the authority of the new central government.

"Sorting out the new world order so that it worked fairly and effectively to the benefit of everyone on the planet wasn't easy. Once the younger generation that had grown up with the new government began to fill positions of authority within it, however, the dust began to settle. The Council still struggled through 45 contentious years before it worked effectively enough to deliver the promised benefits of unification to all its member states."

"The Council reasoned that, besides having a common government, having a common language would make it easier to communicate more effectively and would promote a stronger sense of fraternity among all of the peoples of Senoobis. At that time, there was a confusing hodgepodge of languages—as there is here on Earth—so the Council ordered the creation of a new language to be adopted as the official language of the whole planet. It was called Kuterin, from *kuterah* that means *global*. After a generation had grown up using it, everyone on the planet could communicate effectively with everyone else."

Darz spread his arms as if delivering a benediction. "It worked! At last war was only an ugly memory—a shameful testimony to our former barbarity."

"With a common language and a strong central government that served them efficiently, all Senoobians became members of a worldwide group. That sense of global community connected our ancestors more strongly than all of the small groups within it, and reduced the opportunities for conflict. Without the terrible distraction and waste of constant war, the people prospered."

Martin was intrigued. "Your politicians must have been very effective; they must have taken a long-term view of things. The government must have been free of the partisan politics that hamper our human governments."

Jeliko replied, "It was an effective government, but it took time to create the culture of trust needed to make it work. From what I can tell, it was quite different from the democracies and dictatorships that are the most common forms of government here on Earth."

Sonny was curious. "What about political parties?"

Bayn laughed. "We didn't have any. Our ancestors never saw the need for them. In fact, from what we've seen of your human politics, political parties only encourage adversarial relationships, partisan choices, and corruption instead of cooperation. Our political process was not competitive and adversarial like yours. We identified the most promising candidates, elected them quickly and efficiently, minimized corruption, and avoided divisive posturing. Candidates didn't have to finance expensive advertising campaigns or spend long months campaigning; all candidates were given the same amount of state-sponsored publicity. Politicians were able to give their full attention to the job for which they were elected and were able to make objective and sound decisions for the benefit of all the people because they weren't beholden to any group or individual."

Darz scoffed, "But our culture wasn't materialistic like your human cultures. Individuals were admired for their contributions to society, not for their material wealth. Serving in public office didn't make you wealthy, but it could bring you great honor and the gratitude of your people. In fact, it was the law that government officials could earn no more in office than they had earned in their previous employment."

Martin exclaimed, "In other words, since the candidates didn't have to organize and finance expensive and prolonged campaigns, there was no need for campaign contributions, lobbyists, special interest groups or *pork*! And without the distraction of trying to get re-elected so they could hold on to all their power and *perks*, it was easier to vote their conscience. Right?"

Bayn said, "I'm not sure what you mean by *pork* and *perks* but otherwise you're correct. The government financed the whole electoral process for all candidates; the process was straightforward, and inexpensive. It was neither contentious nor obtrusive. The point was to elect officials who could spend all of their time doing their jobs, instead of wasting their time in office trying to get re-elected, and to have candidates with the experience, vision and leadership qualities that the government needed."

Jeliko continued, "Anyway, a few hundred years after recovery from the Tribulation, the Supreme Council was working smoothly; its organizational and jurisdictional issues were settled and an effective political system was in place to bring qualified candidates to public office. With the whole planet at peace, it had the resources to confront the perennial social problems that were consuming fully 40 percent of its resources."

Sonny was curious. "What kind of problems are you talking about?"

"Oh, our social problems were pretty much the same as yours here on Earth: crime, drugs, birth defects and emotional disorders, the infirmities of old age, natural disasters, domestic violence, etc. By then, the population was growing so fast that the ecological systems of the planet were beginning to fail."

Jeliko smiled, "The Council knew that the government couldn't last unless it resolved its other problems. It named a commission of the most brilliant social scientists of that time to develop programs that would finally solve its growing social problems."

Bayn said, "Some jokingly referred to it as the *Utopia Commission*."

Darz chimed in, "But the Commission was up to the challenge."

"So the first mandate given to it was to double the longevity of our citizens, which at that time was about 105 years."

Sonny was stunned. "That's more than 200 years! Surely that's impossible."

Bayn replied, "I realize that does sound unlikely since human longevity seems to have reached a limit of about 80 years in your advanced nations and far fewer years in your poorer nations. But we did it."

He gestured toward Jeliko and Darz. "We weren't kidding when we told you that Jeliko is 155 years old; Darz is 159; and I'm 168, not counting the time we spent in sleep modules."

Luke gasped and Sonny's jaw dropped.

Ellen exclaimed to Jeliko, "I know what you said but it's still hard to believe. I would have guessed all three of you to be in your '70's!"

Jeliko said, "That's kind of you, Ellen, but it's true. I'm 155 years old. There were several factors that increased our longevity as a race. There was a global program that prohibited all addictive substances, promoted a healthy diet, encouraged an active lifestyle and provided equal health care to everyone. And the people engaged in lifelong activities such as the Proxima that kept them healthy."

Bayn said, "Besides all that, our culture was not competitive like yours. Our world was at peace and in many ways our lives were simpler than yours so there was less stress."

Darz added, "While a healthy lifestyle was being embraced by the people, our geneticists worked hard to discover other ways to dramatically extend life spans. They discovered that the main physiological cause of aging was the shortening of the ends of the chromosomes, or telomeres, that contain redundant DNA. They discovered a way to restore the telomeres and our longevity soared."

"There are several benefits from living longer but at least one downside. There is a natural tendency for any species to multiply until it has reached the limit that its habitat, in our case the whole planet, can support. If our race was going to live twice as long, that would increase the population if reproductive rates continued at the same level.

"Our scientists determined that the optimum population for our planet was 630 million, a level that ensured its ecological stability. Senoobis had ample pure water, clean air and agricultural resources to support that population indefinitely, so the Council gave the Commission its second mandate: to limit the population to 630 million."

Martin was dumbfounded. "You capped the total population of the planet at only 630 million!"

Bayn winked at Martin, "Yes, it seems like a paltry number compared with your six billion humans, doesn't it?"

Martin nodded, amazed.

Jeliko continued, "To maintain the population at or below that number, the Council first limited the number of children families could have to two. There was a census every twelve years and then the birth rate was adjusted as needed.

"Crime was a particularly pervasive problem that imposed a staggering economic burden on our race and inflicted great suffering on its individual victims. It undermined the collective psyche by inciting fear and distrust among our people, demoralizing them and making them cynical. And the economic costs of crime in terms of unrealized potential, lost productivity and the costs of security systems, law enforcement, judicial and prison systems was staggering. Oddly enough, the more we prospered, the more widespread crime became."

Darz said, "No one knew why there was so much crime or how to stop it so the Supreme Council's third mandate to the Commission was to reduce crime to no more than 5% of its level for the benchmark year."

Father Tony said, "Well, in our case, the answer is in the Bible: there is an evil one called Satan who is at war with God and seeks to corrupt all of humankind. He leads the whole world astray by appealing to the sinful nature of humans."

Jeliko smiled. "Our ancestors never knew such an entity. Maybe he's at work on this planet but he didn't bother us on Senoobis."

Bayn laughed, "Maybe our ancestors were so terrible, he never felt the need to go there."

"Maybe so," Jeliko said, chuckling. "Anyway, the Commission did an exhaustive study that enabled our social scientists to understand the causes of crime—at least on our planet—and to create a program that would eliminate virtually all of it. I won't bore you with the details of their study; I'll just tell you that the program they created worked."

They were all intrigued and Father Tony was thinking—*Things must have been different on Senoobis. The Devil must have been too busy with his struggle on Earth to bother with Senoobis.*

Jeliko paused for a moment to collect her thoughts and said, "I believe we need a break and another round."

The Senoobians had intended to give only a passing summary of how they came to be in their present condition and how they discovered the threat to humans and themselves. To their surprise, in sharing their story, they found a cathartic release of the repressed memories that had festered within them since the loss of the *Volarion*. For the first time they felt liberated from their past.

After refreshing their drinks and briefly stretching their legs, the humans heard about the massive do-or-die Colony Project that occupied the Senoobian race for three centuries.

PART 2

THE COLONY PROJECT

13

APPROACHING DOOM

By the Forty-Sixth Century, the social programs created by the Bashydun Commission were a success; there was a unified government for the whole planet, crime was almost non-existent, war was a thing of the past, and the planet's ecology was in balance. There had never before been such a happy time to be alive—Senoobians were prosperous, peaceful and secure. But such a glorious time would not last.

If it is to become great, every race must have either a challenge or a dream to inspire it. For the Senoobians, it was the challenge of surviving the passage of their star system through another part of the Orgrot that would ravage their planet again as it had in the Forty-First Century. This time the planet faced frightening meteor strikes that continued off and on for 72 years. Beleaguered Senoobians called it the *Second Tribulation.*

During that time, the Supreme Council questioned whether the Second Tribulation was a fluke or a forewarning of worse destruction to come. Their technologies were quite advanced by then so the Council directed their astronomers to begin the intensive research that would allow them to better understand the cosmos in general and the nature of the Orgrot in particular.

The astronomers knew that their universe was vast on an unimaginable scale and surprisingly dynamic. They learned that within their galaxy—humans call it the Milky Way—Karmut was two-thirds of the distance from the center to the edge of its flat spiral shape. Years earlier, the astronomers had mapped out their galaxy into sectors. Senoobis and Karyntis were only 35 light years apart, occupying the same sector, designated 3309.

They learned that their galaxy was roughly 100,000 light years in diameter and that it contained some 300 billion star systems, many with planets. They also discovered how *cluttered* some areas in their galaxy were. The Orgrot was one of those areas, several light years across. If their star system were not destroyed during the journey, it would take more than 450 years to travel through it. Besides its clouds of cosmic gas, dust and debris, there were also asteroids, some as much as 20 miles in diameter.

Imagine their alarm when the astronomers discovered that their star system was approaching yet another dense part of the Orgrot that would batter their planet again. They warned that in 300 years the planet would suffer the first major impacts of the *Third Tribulation.*

As Karmut reached deeper into the Orgrot, Senoobis would encounter larger meteors and the impacts would become more frequent and devastating; thousands of Senoobians would be killed.

Polimydis, the Minister of Astronomy, made a full report to the Supreme Council:

Mr. President and honorable ministers, as you know, in the Forty-First Century we entered the outer fringes of the Orgrot and suffered the First Tribulation. In the Forty-Sixth Century, we reached another dangerous area within the Orgrot and suffered the Second Tribulation. In about 300 years, we will reach a third region that is heavily populated with matter that is coalescing through the forces of gravity into denser matter that will eventually form new stars and planets. It is all part of an ongoing cosmic process that extends over billions of years.

As we pass through this dense part of the Orgrot, our whole star system will be battered again in varying degrees. The result will be the Third Tribulation, the worst of all. I regret to report that our data indicates that our whole star system, including Senoobis, most likely will be destroyed and all life on our planet will perish.

I believe that passing through a less dangerous part of the Orgrot is unlikely but, at this time, I cannot speak with any certainty about our fate . . . so I can only recommend that we prepare for the worst and hope for the best. In another hundred years, our fate will be more clear but we must act now.

My friends, Senoobis simply has the misfortune of occupying one of the more active and densely populated regions in our galaxy. If our worst fears are realized and our planet is subjected to multiple collisions with large masses, I don't believe anything can be done to save the inhabitants of this planet.

Now, as to what we may do. I don't yet have any good answers. I believe that the best we can hope for is to avoid the extinction of our species. I recommend that a commission be appointed to begin studying our options as soon as possible. I now open the floor to questions.

Considering the terror that their ancestors had endured from the Orgrot in the two previous tribulations, the report caused great distress. The Council appointed a commission of top astronomers and scientists to present to it the best option for surviving the disaster. Eventually, after studying the few options they could identify, they decided that their only hope was to locate in a nearby star system another planet capable of supporting life and to colonize it. Thus, if the expected cataclysm did destroy all life on Senoobis, at least their species might survive, even though it would be on another world.

Months later after thorough study, Polimydis, as head of the new commission, made the following report to the Council:

Our Commission has determined that colonization is our only viable option. We recommend conducting a search to find within 48 light years another star system with a planet that can support life as we know it. There must be a stable surface and an atmosphere with sufficient oxygen. There must be abundant water. There must be adequate natural resources for food. And the planet must be located at the proper distance from its star to assure a viable range of temperatures. If there are indigenous advanced life forms, well, we'll have to deal with them when we get there. We will, of course, need to carry defensive weapons in the event of hostile actions by those life forms.

The best we can hope for is to discover a hospitable planet in time to send a contingency of Senoobians to colonize it. Anyone who does not leave Senoobis as a colonist will probably not survive but there is nothing we can do about that. There are no other options. If the colony doesn't survive on the new planet, our species will become extinct.

If the Council accepts our proposal, we must begin planning for such a mission immediately by appointing the most qualified individual we have to head that project. Once we have located such a planet, we will need to colonize it with the bravest and best of our species. We will need to build the next generation of starships, large enough to carry our colonists safely with the resources they will need to found the colony.

One of the council members raised his hand. "Polimydis, what are the odds of our finding such a planet within 48 light years?"

Polimydis didn't hesitate in answering; this was no time to shrink from stark reality. "In the time we have to carry out such a search, I estimate no more than five to ten percent," he replied gravely.

The council member was shocked. "No more than that!"

"No more than that," Polimydis repeated firmly.

After a strained silence and no further questions, the Chairman of the Council said, "Polimydis, on behalf of all our people, I thank you for the valuable service you and your staff have rendered. We will consider your recommendation."

At the next meeting, the Council accepted the recommendation of colonization as their only option. The Chairman's instructions to the council were brief:

"At our next meeting, please bring a nomination for Director of the Colony Project and be prepared to draft the articles that will establish the framework for the project. This meeting is adjourned."

14

THE COLONY PROJECT

At the next meeting of the Supreme Council, after several hours of discussion, the decision was made to offer the Project Director position to Armahs Judasis. After all, the Council wanted the most qualified individual and Judasis had proven himself time and again as he wisely guided his ministry in its long-term projects.

Judasis was tall and lean with prominent features. He had a long friendly face, bright grey-green eyes, a jutting chin and high cheekbones. There was a kind but patrician look about him. He sported the same kind of beard that all the other top officials wore but his beard and his hair were turning gray and fatigue was etched into his face. After all, he was 135 years old and he hadn't slept well for several years.

His position as Minister of Strategic Planning was demanding and stressful. It required someone who could grasp the broad sweep of events and look into the future. It also required the ability to consider unorthodox perspectives and to develop new approaches to long-term problems. But now, considering the urgency and enormity of the challenge they faced, most of his former projects simply weren't needed anymore. After all, if your house is on fire, what you're having for dinner is hardly relevant.

Judasis was conflicted about assuming the new position because he felt that someone younger might be more capable and, besides that, he was thinking about retiring. The new position was of enormous consequence though and he believed it was his duty to accept if the Council asked. It was not customary to decline an offer by the Council so he graciously, although reluctantly, accepted the position and immediately resigned his position as Minister of Strategic Planning.

Since the Colony Project was so complex and risky, Judasis was determined that everything possible would be done to ensure the success of the colony. There were four stages of the project: (1) find at least one suitable planet, (2) design and construct starships that would assure the survival of the colonists during their long voyage, (3) select the best colonist candidates, train, and equip them, and (4) successfully establish the colony after their arrival on the new planet.

As the first stage of the project, Judasis instructed his astronomers to survey all of the star systems in Sector 3309, and identify any planets that might be suitable for habitation. There was simply not enough time to consider missions to more distant parts of the galaxy. Out of the 31 star systems they surveyed, the astronomers found only six with planets worthy of further investigation. Considering their Space Agency's limited capabilities for extended space travel, however, it was a stretch to reach even those six planets.

The astronomers couldn't glean enough information from their telescopes so Judasis directed his engineers to design and build long-distance unmanned probes. These would be dispatched to the six planet candidates to gather first-hand information and transmit it back to them for further analysis.

The probes would be able to reach a sustained speed of no more than 22 percent of the speed of light, meaning it would take five times as long for the probe to reach the star system as it would for light or radio signals. Radio transmissions from the probe, however, would return to Senoobis at the speed of light. The Sarmadah probe, for example, traveling at 1/5 the speed of light, would require 175 years to reach that star system and another 35 years for its data to reach Senoobis—210 years in all.

When Judasis presented his plan to the Supreme Council, he showed them a table that listed the six star systems and their planets.

The "Time to Reach" column gave the number of years it would take the probe to reach the planet, traveling at 1/5 the speed of light. The "Time to Receive Rpt. from Probe" column gave the total number of years required to receive the probe's report. That total included the number of years from the previous column and the time required for the radio report from the probe to return to Senoobis at the speed of light.

PLANET CANDIDATES IN SECTOR 3309

Star System/Planet	Distance from Senoobis	Time to Reach	Time to Receive Rpt. from Probe
Darisoti A&B[1]/Parkopia	7 L.Y.[2]	35 S.Y.[2]	42 S.Y.[2]
Gafor/Oblivium	13	65	78
Kabriolis/Moksena	22	110	132
Parfis/Paksadorus	27	135	162
Sarmadah/Karyntis	35	175	210
Jestura/Nanzema	41	205	246

[1] Darisoti is a binary star.

[2] L.Y. = light years, S.Y. = Senoobian years

The success of the program depended on finding the best planet candidates, so Judasis relentlessly pressed his design and construction engineers until the probes were ready. Ten years after the beginning of the project, probes were launched to each of the six planets to gather critical information about them and transmit it back to Senoobis.

Karmut was expected to enter the dense part of the Orgrot in 300 years, but it would be 246 years before they even received a report from the *Nanzema* probe. By then, the Colony Project would have to be ready to launch.

Inconclusive results were received from the probe sent to Parkopia, the nearest planet, but data seemed to indicate that the planet couldn't sustain life as they knew it.

A few years later, Judasis dispatched the intrepid old *Balserios* to Parkopia to see if the planet had any redeeming attributes that the probe could not pick up, such as geothermal vents or thorithium deposits that might render it habitable. The CO's orders were to collect data on the planet's *vitals* for sixty days and then, barring any game-changing revelations, to head for home. The *Balserios* reached the planet but then disappeared; there was no clue as to what had happened to her. Her only report described a young planet with a harsh climate—a rather unpleasant and barren place, too cold.

But something strange was going on there. Darisoti was a binary star system so it tended to be a little screwy anyway. There were some wildly fluctuating gravitational forces, mostly Fervakin Aberrations, but the CO didn't know what to make of them. The Agency suspected that those unusual phenomena might have caused the *Balserios'* instruments to fail, sending her spinning out of control.

Further research indicated that Fervakin Aberrations were symptomatic of a wormhole. Yet no one was sure that wormholes even existed since no one had ever encountered one. There was a research project on wormholes once, but it was shelved when the Orgrot mess panicked everyone. The astronomers detected an anomaly near the edge of sector 3309 that emitted unusual radiation and acted like a wormhole but nothing came of it.

A couple of hundred years later, the *Shananik*, another aging freighter, was dispatched to Parkopia. Her mission was to discover what had happened to the *Balserios* and to collect more complete data on the nature of the planet. Of course, Senoobis was destroyed before the *Shananik* reached the planet so no one survived on Senoobis to learn the fate of either of them.

For the second stage of the project, Judasis directed the engineers to begin design work for a new generation of starships. There would be three of them. All three would have to be fully operational before data was received from the probe sent to Nanzema, the most distant of the six planets.

The first one would be an improved version of the aging starships that had been in service for many years within the confines of their own star system. It would be named *Syzilian* in honor of Mandolus Syzilias, the astronomer who had discovered the Orgrot. The engineers were given 85 years in which to design and build her. Her mission was to reach the chosen planet first, explore it to confirm its suitability for the colony and prepare for the arrival of the second ship.

That ship would be the *Volarion*—the actual colony ship, the heart of the Colony Project. It would be more advanced than the *Syzilian*, having benefited from improvements developed and tested on the *Syzilian*. It would carry the most assets and offer the best hope for success.

The Colony Project would span 200 years and was so daunting in its complexity and size that it required the restructuring and mobilization of the entire Senoobian workforce. During the first few years, Judasis was overwhelmed, uncertain that the successful completion of the project was even possible.

After he had finished the design specifications for the *Volarion*, an incident occurred, however, that restored his faith in the leadership of the Supreme Council and his ability to see the project through.

When the ships were ready, one of the difficult jobs in the project would be deciding who would go. The population of Senoobis was 630 million but the future of the race would fall on the shoulders of the 119 crew members manning the three starships. Judasis called on Yonder Kosunatis who was still President of the Supreme Council.

After they had discussed the progress that had been made on the starships, Judasis informed him, "The design of the *Volarion* is complete. We have included accommodations for the twelve members of the Council; I expect those who are in office when the *Volarion* launches will want to accompany the colonists to the new world."

Kosunatis looked at Judasis in surprise, scratched his chin in thought and emphatically shook his head NO. "Do you imply that the Council is privileged, that we should be treated as more important than the average citizen of Senoobis? I assure you that we do not deserve special treatment. Every person who serves on those starships must be qualified to be there; we are not. It is our duty and our honor to serve our people and our place is here with them. Thank you for your consideration, but those accommodations must go to those who will serve the colony with more useful skills than we on the council possess."

Judasis smiled graciously, "I will honor your wishes." He was heartened; Kosunatis had responded as he had hoped. In truth, Judasis had not allowed for such accomodations.

The third starship, the *Langorion*, was to be experimental, nothing like the other two. It would be only slightly larger than the *Syzilian* but faster and more powerful. The *Langorion* was their contingency plan; it would carry the *Bretin,* the most controversial phase of the program, and serve as backup for the other two starships.

Judasis had charged the most unorthodox and brilliant engineer he could find with heading up the task force that would design the *Langorion*. That part of the program would be headed by Tarsun Masoolin who had recruited a couple of young geniuses to help with the engineering of the *Langorion*. While tried and proven technologies would be used for the *Syzilian*, whatever cutting edge technologies they could muster would be used on the *Langorion*.

Judasis had justified his choice of Masoolin to the Council by saying, "I know he's a maverick and, yes, he's difficult to work with, but he's brilliant; he sees problems in different ways. I don't want the *Langorion* to be anything like the *Syzilian* or the *Volarion*. I want a radical new design. I want to throw out everything we know about starship design and come up with a fresh approach." The Council was a bit uneasy about Masoolin, but it finally acquiesced; Judasis got Masoolin who relished the challenge and went right to work.

Most Senoobians were only dimly aware of the *Langorion* project since it was considered less important than the *Syzilian* or the *Volarion* and received far less attention. After all, they were the future of the Senoobian race—not the long shot *Langorion* that was radical in every way.

One of the most challenging aspects of prolonged space travel was hyper-sleep. Rovay Pikolis, an expert in physiology, was put in charge of improving the design of the hyper-sleep modules.

One day Judasis called Pikolis to his office. "I was just thinking about our sleep modules. Our best planetary candidate may turn out to be one of the two farthest away—Karyntis or Nanzema. If it is one of them, Senoobis will be only a dim memory by the time our colonists get there. On a trip lasting 200 years, I'm worried about whether or not our colonists will be able to survive the long hyper-sleeps required."

Pikolis replied solemnly, "Yes, I've been concerned about that myself."

Judasis stroked his beard in thought. "Rovay, I want you to push hard to improve our hyper-sleep technology even though there's not much hope of a breakthrough there. The way our sleep modules are now, I wouldn't want to crawl into one of them myself."

Pikolis smiled, "Nor would I but it beats the alternative."

Judasis replied, "Yes, quite right, but they're far too risky. Reliable hyper-sleep is critical to the success of this whole project. We've got to do better. I'm counting on you to find the breakthrough we need." Pikolis went to work with a vengence.

The third stage included selecting and training the best crews to man their starships, selecting the best candidates for colonists and preparing them to survive on a long voyage and then on a strange planet.

It also required compiling a complete record of the Senoobian civilization as a reference for future generations of colonists. After all, if they didn't have a complete record of their culture, how could they preserve their identity? The Minister of Information and Administration, Dr. Tanapis Jukasian, was charged with creating a complete but portable digitized library to be carried on each of the starships. It would contain roughly 300,000 one-terabyte data disks in holographic video, audio and text formats, a complete record of the Senoobian race.

It was a daunting project that would take 60 years to complete. It was called the Jukasian Archival System, or disk library, in honor of Dr. Jukasian. Four copies would be made: one for each of the starships and a fourth one that would remain in a time capsule on Senoobis.

The library contained its own access system with a panel that allowed the vast database to be searched and accessed quickly. There was a self-contained screen for viewing the videos or reading the text files and there was a high-fidelity sound system for the audio files. Yet it was only 24" wide, 60" long and 48" high. It was housed within a heavy, almost indestructible shiny metal shell with wheels that allowed it to be moved easily.

The third stage also included the Bretin. Judasis spent several months drafting the guidelines that would be used to develop the Bretin and their support systems. When he was finished, he called Lusyma Asigyus, who was the director of the Bretin Program, to his office. She was a leading authority on genetic engineering and had been instrumental in achieving several genetic breakthroughs. She was tireless and unflappable, infusing her research with integrity and vision.

Judasis was lost in thought when she appeared at his office exactly on time. She was tall and thin with prominent features and a generous smile that softened her intense nature. Judasis motioned her into his office and, after some small talk, they got down to business.

"I have the Bretin parameters for you: he handed her a thick folder. I know I'm asking the impossible, but we've got to have the Bretin ready to launch on the *Langorion* soon after the *Syzilian*. Who knows what they're going to find when they reach their destination? If something bad happens to the *Syzilian* or the *Volarion*, the Bretin are our last hope. I want you to spearhead the research for developing five generations of Bretin, each one smarter and tougher than the previous one. Pull Parabis into the project to help you with the genetics."

Lusyma grimaced slightly, "You know we're pushing our genetic capabilities to the limit and, if something goes wrong *out there*, nobody will be around to fix the problem."

"Yes, I know and I certainly don't want to put our Bretin at risk so I'm counting on you to get the genetics right."

"Thanks, Armahs, you really know how to apply the pressure."

He grinned. "That's my job, isn't it? I know what I'm asking you to do is nigh impossible, but we can't afford to put all of our colonial eggs in one basket. Don't forget I still want them to be 99.5% Senoobian—just smarter, faster and tougher. Parabis can help you with that. When this project is finished, I want our Bretin to be the toughest life form in the galaxy. Who knows what they may run into, so let's make sure they can survive anything."

She muttered drily as she turned to go. "Hmmm, impossible odds on the one hand and certain death on the other. No wonder I love this job."

Jukasis chuckled briefly as he stood up and wagged his finger at her, "Remember: all hush-hush, no publicity. The focus for the public should be on the *Syzilian* and the *Volarion*. No need to alarm our citizens—they have enough to worry about."

Asigyus' scientists built on advances that had been made in genetics by the Bashydun Commission to birth, over several generations, the Bretin, a group of 60—30 male and 30 female— genetically engineered, advanced individuals who would found their own colony.

Judasis considered the Bretin program so important that he and Asigyus handpicked each member of the small Bretin staff himself. The Bretin would be dispatched on the *Langorion* to the second best planetary candidate to found a Bretin colony. If the *Syzilian* or the

Volarion failed on the best planetary candidate, hopefully the Bretin would succeed on the second best. If they both failed or if there were no second best candidate, the *Langorion* would be dispatched to the best candidate. In the worst-case scenario, if none of the six planets turned out to be hospitable, the Bretin would have the best chance of surviving and continuing the Senoobian race, even though in a modified form.

Judasis had no idea how the Bretin Program would play out. It was the sociological and psychological aspects—not the genetic or physiological aspects—of the program that worried him; sociologically they were in uncharted territory. *By the time the fifth generation of Bretin had completed training and was ready to launch, how would they be perceived by most Senoobians?* he wondered. *What kind of social dynamics would emerge? Would the Bretin be resented for their unique status and enhanced abilities? Would they be considered abnormal, not really Senoobians? How would the Bretin come to feel about their mission to save the Senoobian race?* It was a huge gamble.

The program was controversial and there was considerable resistance to it at first, but Polimydis himself had told the Council that they must use the bravest and best of their race. So it was that after a long and robust debate, the council agreed that the Bretin would provide an important backup for the Colony Project and authorized that phase of the project.

Some considered the Bretin too different, not quite Senoobian, so there were questions: why bother with them when Senoobians could be sent just as well?

Truth be known, before long there was an undercurrent of resentment toward the small contingent of Bretin that bothered Judasis. The Bretin felt it too and sometimes there was a hint of tension in the air when the Bretin and Senoobians were together. But they were supposed to be different; that was the point—perhaps their differences, although considered minor by most, would allow them to survive where a Senoobian could not.

The fourth and final stage would be accomplished by actually reaching the target planet and founding a successful colony. The Disk Libraries would provide the knowledge and expertise that would make it possible to establish each of the three colonies much sooner.

Every Senoobian lived with the specter of extinction looming closer with each passing year, but many of them still hoped that somehow someone or something would save them. Although Judasis was resigned to their grim fate, sometimes even he gave in to despair and drank too much. Some people took up the old religions again. But there was simply no way to save the millions who would perish with the planet; he knew it as sure as night followed day and that reality gave him nightmares.

It was up to him to get the project off to a strong start. Although he would be dead long before Senoobis reached the point of destruction, he drove himself and his engineers relentlessly to create fail-proof systems that would ensure the survival of the colonists. With the long hours and pressures of his work, his health began to fail.

As their star system penetrated deeper into the deadly part of the Orgrot with each passing year, the meteoric assaults on the planet would increase in frequency and severity and the odds of annihilation would mount. As a result, Judasis and his wife Ansilea, like many other Senoobians, struggled with depression.

Sometimes they would awaken in a sweat from their nightmares and sit huddled together, staring out into the cool starry night, unable to go back to sleep. Ansilea knew Judasis was under enormous pressure so she tried to encourage and protect him. Sometimes when she held him close to her, both fear and anger welled up inside her and she couldn't let him go.

Judasis directed the Colony Project for 43 years and laid the foundation for its successful completion. He lived for 15 more years after retiring, just long enough to see the disappointing data from the first probe. "If only Parkopia could have been hospitable," he sighed.

After 220 years and several able managers, the gifted Mirdon Sadantis assumed responsibility for the project but time was running out.

15

REPORT FROM KARYNTIS

It was a historic day. As *Karmut* burned away the last of the lingering morning mists, Mirdon Sadantis felt relieved of a great burden as he enjoyed the view of the great Bay of Kurmythia from the balcony of his office in *Senoobia*, the planet's capital. Even before dawn, he had thrown open the tall windows of his office so he could breathe in the fresh air and admire the red brilliance of Karmut's ascent. It was the first day in many months that he had put aside his work to enjoy a few moments of reflection.

The decision to search for other worlds on which to live was at last vindicated. The message he had received a few hours earlier from the Astronomy geeks made his heart race with excitement as he absorbed every detail. At last, one of the six planets appeared to be enough like Senoobis that the chances were good that it would be hospitable.

There had been problems: the probe to Parkopia in the Darisoti system, the one closest to Senoobis, returned an incomplete report because of garbled data, but it hinted at a young planet only marginally capable of sustaining life. The starship *Balserios*, precursor to the *Syzilian*, was dispatched and the probe's report was confirmed: Parkopia was cold and its atmosphere thin. There were some simple plant forms but not so much as a lowly worm. Unfortunately, the *Balserios* suffered some unknown catastrophe and disappeared without a trace; its crew of 21 presumably perished.

The probe that was dispatched to Moksena in the Kabriolis system also returned unfavorable data. Its atmosphere was mostly methane and its surface appeared to be more liquid than solid so it was dropped from further consideration.

The probe that was sent to Oblivium in the Gafor System, 13 light years away, had transmitted signals confirming its approach to the planet but after that it was never heard from again. A second probe was launched but it was never heard from either. There was no other way to determine whether or not Oblivium was a potential candidate for a colony without sending a manned mission there, and they had neither the time nor a starship to do that, so they wrote off Oblivium.

The probe that was dispatched to Paksadorus returned only weak and unintelligible signals. There was a large area of intense radiation in the Parfis system that appeared to be the source of severe magnetic disturbances that interfered with its transmissions. Another probe was launched but it also failed.

There had not been enough time for the probe to Nanzema, the most distant planet, to return a report so that planet was still a mystery.

One problem they didn't have was getting volunteers to serve on the ships. In the past, only the most hardened Senoobians would consider going into space; it was a dreadful business. Even on short trips to planets within their own star system—extremely short compared with the long voyages the colonists would endure—some crewmembers had become claustrophobic and depressed. Others had simply gone mad.

But medications were created to deal with such problems. Besides, enduring the austere life of a crewman on a starship for several decades in order to live out the rest of one's life as a colonist on some new world was far more appealing than the grim alternative of perishing on Senoobis. Beyond that, being a colonist allowed one to serve the grand purpose of perpetuating their species. So there was a host of volunteers who were desperate to escape Senoobis, knowing that the planet was doomed and that everyone on it would die.

The 210th year since the launch of the Karyntis probe had come and gone with no report. It appeared that it had also failed; Sadantis and the Council were desperate. That is until, with great excitement, the astronomers received weak signals that faithfully delivered information about the mysterious new world before slowly degrading into unintelligible noise.

The distances between star systems are so vast that the odds of finding another planet capable of sustaining life within Sector 3309 were discouragingly small. Yet somehow they had done it. They had been lucky no doubt. But everyone on the Project had worked

138

relentlessly, generation after generation, driven out of desperation. The engineers and astronomers were heroes, all of them, so the Council commended them on their collective achievement.

When they had first discovered it, the astronomers named the star Sarmadah. Its alluring blue planet Karyntis was named after the deep blue Senoobian gemstone Karyntha. Sarmadah was the center of a system of six major planets, and somewhat larger than Karmut.

The Garzyee probe was not highly sophisticated; it was designed with simplicity to achieve reliability. Since it was a long distance probe, it was also small so its capabilities were limited—just the essential data. Its sensors had detected water, a temperature range of roughly -10° to 40° C, a gravitational field comparable to Senoobis, a stable surface and an atmosphere made up mostly of oxygen and nitrogen. There was no video and there was no information about the geography of the planet or indigenous life forms.

Sadantis was thankful that the probe had worked at all after its 175-year journey. It had transmitted its fading signals for only two hours and 15 minutes, but that was long enough to inspire renewed hope where there had been little before. There was always the possibility that unknown factors on Karyntis might render it inhospitable to their form of life.

Nonetheless, they were running out of time—in 80 years they would enter a denser part of the Orgrot where every planet in the Karmut System would begin to be battered into loose masses of rubble. Senoobis would lose its atmosphere and all life would perish. Eventually, after billions of years, that formless mass and other debris would coalesce into a denser mass that would eventually birth a new star system and the cycle would begin again. Perhaps in the far distant future another advanced civilization might arise from the grim remains of Senoobis.

The starship that would carry the colonists to their new home had been built and christened *Volarion*. The engineers, learning from the work done on the *Syzilian*, had applied every advance possible with as much simplicity as possible, knowing that simplicity and reliability go hand in hand. The *Volarion* would follow after the *Syzilian* was well on her way and the flight was going smoothly. If the *Syzilian* reached Karyntis and found the planet inhospitable for whatever reason, the *Volarion* would be diverted to Nanzema.

139

The entry chime to his office sounded and Munsos Gabriolis announced himself. "Mirdon, it's me. Permission to enter?"

"Come in, Mun. It's good to see you." He motioned to the most comfortable chair in his office, "Please . . ." Gabriolis was about the same age as Sadantis, who was 175 years old, but stockier with long grey hair. He had been disheartened for a long time but not now.

He landed in a comfortable chair. "Mirdon, the numbers look good, such as they are. And the Sarmadah System isn't anywhere near the Orgrot. Karyntis is definitely our best bet. I can have the *Syz* ready to launch in three years. What do you think?"

"Let's go for it! That will give the *Syzilian* a 15-year head start when the *Volarion* launches. Our plan is still risky but sound. If there's a major problem on Karyntis, the *Volarion* will have enough fuel to reach Nanzema.

"Yes, but we're down to the wire; the *Langorion* has got to launch when the *Syzilian* does so that both of them can skirt the edge of the Orgrot. With any luck, we'll have the report from Nanzema in another 24 years but by then both ships will be safely out of our star system. If the report's favorable, the *Langorion* can make for Nanzema; if it's not good, she can divert to Karyntis. But if both planets are a bust, all three ships will be out there with no place to go. That's when it really gets scary: the CO's will have to decide on the fly what to do."

Gabriolis frowned. "You're right. We won't be around to make the call."

Sadantis said, "Probably not." Their mood became subdued.

Finally Gabriolis said half-heartedly, "We'd better get busy; we're going to find ourselves in a meat grinder soon."

Sadantis stroked his chin. "I know. Well, it's time to bare down on the training for the crew and colonist designates. You've got three months."

Gabriolis nodded. "I know. We'll be ready."

That evening at his home in Residential Tower #4 off of Gengalus Square, Sadantis excitedly related the news to his wife Jiata as she busied herself in the dining center. She poured them a cold celebratory *chinchee* and began to sip hers slowly, hanging on his every word. This was truly a monumental occasion. Knowing that Karyntis appeared to be hospitable would raise the morale of every Senoobian."

"But we have to put this in its proper context," he reminded her. "There are lots of questions still to be answered. Is there intelligent life on Karyntis? Is there enough water? What will the weather be like? What dangers will our colonists face? What will the future be like for those who are born and die on Karyntis?"

That question bothered him. "They won't be Senoobians; they'll be Karyntians; they won't ever know what it's like to be a Senoobian," he said. "But it's our only hope. There's no other choice."

"His thoughts were interrupted by the happy voices of his son Jozee and his wife Ronasha as they entered the dining room. "Sorry to disturb you, father. Excuse us, mother," said Jozee. "We've only stopped by to chat for a few minutes. We hear that father is working too hard and not sleeping well."

Ronasha hugged her father-in-law. "Yes, we're concerned about you. Jiata tells me you've not been feeling well lately. Are there problems at work?"

Pleased to see the two of them, Sadantis became upbeat again and grinned mischievously. "Well, the usual things—you know, the end of the world and so forth, the kinds of things we old *noobs* dwell on—but I have some wonderful news! We've just received a transmission from the Karyntis probe—I was afraid it had failed—and thankfully it indicates that Karyntis is like Senoobis in some important ways. We don't know enough about it yet but the initial data are encouraging. It's still a long shot but I can't help getting my hopes up and it's certainly cause for celebration."

"Mirdon, that's wonderful!" Ronasha whooped excitedly.

"Why don't you join us for dinner?" Jiata pleaded.

"Of course," Jozee agreed after Ronasha nodded her okay.

As Sadantis watched his family at dinner, happy and hopeful, his love for them was overwhelming. He was proud that all of his hard work would help the Senoobian race survive. But there was deep pain too in knowing that his family would not. *If he could, should he bend the rules to save them?* he sometimes worried. The truth was that neither his son nor daughter-in-law would allow him to *arrange* a place for them on one of the starships and for that, he was grateful.

⅄ Λ Ⅹ Ⅹ ⁼ ⊥ ⚈ Ⅎ ℈ ⊥

16

STARSHIPS

The *Syzilian* had completed her shakedown flight and was ready to go. She had passed her trials with flying colors and her crew's performance was impressive. The orders placing Captain Rornan Mensykus in command and naming the ship's crew were received with both anticipation and trepidation; space travel is heroic and daunting but not the glamorous life one might expect.

The distances in space are so vast that missions to the nearest star systems can last 200 years or more. Duty on a starship requires the supreme sacrifice of foregoing every aspect of a normal existence. If sleep modules didn't allow hibernation for years at a time, it would be impossible for a ship's crew to endure such cramped quarters for so long, their existence limited to the confines of the ship, without going mad.

It was an ongoing joke that anyone who would apply for duty on a starship couldn't be *normal*. After all, why would anyone give up a normal life to spend most of his life cooped up on a starship?

The only way to overcome the mind-numbing isolation of long decades of space travel was for the crew to sleep through the greatest part of it. This was accomplished by using hyper-sleep modules, referred to simply as *sleep modules* by those who had never been in one and as *near-death torture* by those who had. The sleep modules reduced the demands on the life support systems so that, if the systems didn't fail, the crew had ample recycled food, water and oxygen for several hundred years.

While the *Syzilian*'s crew was in hyper-sleep for as long as 40 years, the ship would be on autopilot with only its scanners, sensors and computers fully functioning. Even its engines would be shut down as it glided silently and swiftly through space, dark and seemingly lifeless. Roughly every six months, deep within the core of the ship, its computers and navigation modules would communicate with each other, run systems checks, make any necessary adjustments to the ship's course and then shut down again while the crew remained in their deep sleep.

If the scanners detected a threat from space debris, such as a comet, or another starship, the crewmembers on call would be *awakened* by the ship's computers. *Waking up* was a process that normally took six months to recover to full functionality.

Crewmembers on call, however, were on a lower level hyper-sleep and one-month accelerated wakeups were possible, but they often suffered side effects such as muscle cramps and severe headaches for several weeks.

One extreme side effect, called *fractured consciousness*, was a month-long, skull-pounding hangover as the brain struggled to regain its synaptic integrity. It included nightmares, hallucinations and disorientation. Consequently whenever a crewmember was on call, the one thing he dreaded was an accelerated wakeup; it meant suffering through a painful wakeup because there was some urgent threat or problem to be handled.

Near the bridge in the hyper-sleep compartment, there were five sections of six modules—three of the modules were backups. Each gray metal module was cylinder-shaped with a clear canopy that covered the top one-third of the machine. At the front of the compartment, there was a large master console that controlled all 30 modules.

On one end of each module, there was a battery of large cables and tubes that serviced the module and gave it a sinister appearance. The inside of the modules were made of a rubbery material that conformed to the body of the occupant for maximum support. Without that support, the occupant's body would atrophy badly from remaining in the same position for years.

It was like crawling back into the womb. The ship itself was claustrophobic enough on a good day, but entering a sleep module could put almost anyone into a panic. The crewmember would completely disrobe except for his briefs, climb in, put on an oxygen mask, attach the monitors and close the canopy. The level one gradual shutdown, which normally took six months to complete, would begin with the introduction of a gaseous mixture through the facemask that began the process of slowing the body's metabolism almost to zero.

After the body's processes had slowed sufficiently, a cold green liquid would flood the module to lower the body's temperature even further and protect it during suspended animation. The sleep modules slowed the flow of life to a faint trickle—reducing the body's vital functions to $1/40^{th}$ of their normal level while maintaining the fragile line between life and death that preserved the body's tissues and slowed aging. If it weren't for hyper-sleep, the crew might arrive at their destination too old and infirm to perform their duties.

The hyper-sleep process itself was not physiologically difficult for Senoobians since they had evolved the ability to hibernate for several years. Three hundred thousand years ago, when the planet was cooler and more arid, their primitive ancestors were forced to survive by hibernating. Like a number of other species, they had evolved the ability to hibernate through long periods of harsh climactic conditions such as drought and famine. When a Senoobian fell terminally ill from a disease for which there was no cure, he would simply go into hibernation for a few years until a cure could be found. As the planet gradually heated up and became wetter over the last 100,000 years, Senoobians depended less on hibernation, although they were still capable of it.

Once a starship was free of the gravitational pull of the planet, the ship would gradually accelerate to 22 percent of the speed of light. Then the engines would shut off so that it could coast through space indefinitely. When the navigation system determined corrections were needed to the ship's course, small thruster rockets would fire for the brief periods required.

When it was time to begin the countdown to launch the *Syzilian*, families, friends and dignitaries gathered at the Launch Control Center on Pesh. As the crew filed through the center past those waiting to see them off, there was time for one last heartfelt embrace, one quick goodbye and one more handshake before the crew boarded the ship.

The crewmembers were handsome and dashing in their navy uniforms with red and gold trim. The music playing in the background was the *Seengher Symphony of the Stars*, always powerful and inspiring. It was the anthem for the whole planet, no doubt one of the most stirring compositions ever created. It gave chills to everyone who heard it playing over the PA system as the magnificent ship eased from her berth to begin the long journey to Karyntis.

In the meantime, the engineers who were responsible for the *Langorion* worked feverishly to prepare the ship for launch soon after the *Syzilian*. By the time she was ready to launch, a number of upgrades had been made to her.

The *Langorion* carried the same number of crewmembers and was the same size as the Syzilian but her engines were more powerful and her design was more advanced. On the other hand, her accommodations were more spartan than those on the *Syzilian* so she could carry more weaponry.

There would be little fanfare for the *Langorion*, however. She had been designed and built in the shadow of the other two ships and the public had almost forgotten about her. That was of no consequence to the Bretin, however; they were mavericks—proud and fiercely independent. The only Senoobians in the program were its director, the surly Kargin Kroovel, and several scientists. Out of the 60 Bretin, 27 were chosen to serve on the *Langorion*.

They were well on their way and Senoobis had already been destroyed when they received the long-awaited report from the Nanzema probe indicating favorable conditions.

The third starship to depart Senoobis was the *Volarion* that launched 15 years after the *Syzilian* and the *Langorion*. The engineers took the *Syzilian*'s design and modified it to fit her mission. The *Syzilian* was designed for research and exploration but the *Volarion* was essentially a cargo vessel.

The *Volarion* was considerably larger than the *Syzilian* since she had much more to carry. Her mission was to carry a contingent of colonists with everything they would need to establish a colony on the new world—communications, agricultural, textile, construction and medical assets—as well as six Hyperion missiles for defense. There was a birthing unit with 60 embryos that would become the first native generation of colonists. There was even a small genetics module that contained the DNA that would enable them to populate the planet with some of their most important Senoobian species such as the *penukri* and *taygahpe*.

One of the most important items on board the ship was the same Jukasian Disk Library that the *Syzilian* and *Langorion* carried. That information would be an invaluable resource for the colonists in perpetuating their species.

The Agency knew that Karyntis, as well as Nanzema, was a long shot but there were no other options. Even if the *Volarion* did reach Karyntis and conditions—water, oxygen, temperature, food, etc.—on the planet were favorable, some hostile, indigenous life form might pose a threat. And there was also the possibility that the colonists might be susceptible to some pathogen to which they had no immunity.

That's why the *Syzilian* was sent there first—to work out any such problems before the *Volarion* arrived. Since the *Syzilian* would reach Karyntis 15 years before the *Volarion*, she would explore the planet, choose the colony site and transmit periodic reports to the *Volarion* on the geography, climate, geology, indigenous life forms (including microbes), and energy resources of the planet. The *Volarion* would reach Karyntis thoroughly briefed and ready to establish the colony, thanks to the pathfinding of the *Syzilian*.

The *Volarion* carried a crew of 35, a Colonial Support Staff of 14, the elite 12-member Proturian security guard, and a research staff of 4 scientists—65 altogether. The Colonial Support Staff, or CSS, would be responsible for the care, safety, training and development of the 60 young colonists until they were all adults. In effect, the CSS would be the surrogate parents of the first generation of colonists.

After 245 years, the Karyntis Mission was ready. A magnificent ceremony took place in *Gengalas Square* in Senoobia, the capital and second most beautiful city on the planet, while joyous festivities played out across Senoobis in celebration of the completion of the their phase of the project.

The ship was fueled, the crew was trained, and all provisions were on board. Their star system had reached the outer limits of the Orgrot; it was time to launch; any delays would endanger the ship as it transited out of the star system into the space beyond Plimandia, the last large planet. Captain Gobetas took command of the ship and presented orders to the crew.

The *Syzilian* had begun her long voyage to Karyntis 15 years before. It was time for the *Volarion* to follow. Early in the morning, on the day of the launch, a crowd of family, friends and well-wishers gathered at the Transport Center to see the crew off. As the crew and support staff filed through the center to board the shuttles that would take them to Pesh, some cheered but many wept. Some focused on the festive part of the event as a celebration of the success of the Colony Project. Many felt only the sting of seeing loved ones for the last time and of facing the terrible reality that the end of Senoobis was near. For the last time, an orchestra played the stirring *Symphony of the Stars*.

The crew on the one hand and those remaining behind on the other, each weighed the challenges and perils that awaited them. From that day forward each would deal with his own struggles: those left on Senoobis, to face death; and those on the *Volarion*, to seek life by birthing a colony on a new world.

As soon as the *Volarion* had departed the Karmut Star System and was safely on its way to Karyntis, Sadantis retired. Narzis Angado served as Director of the Colony Project from then until the final days of the planet. He would not learn the fate of the three starships on which the success of the Colony Project depended.

17

THE END OF SENOOBIS

No matter how bad things became, Narzis Angado was always at his desk early in the morning. When the Chief Astronomer showed up at his open door and barged in without waiting for an invitation, Narzis feared the worst. Before Narzis could wave him in, Paleg Barzilay was in front of his desk, red-faced and wild-eyed. He was clearly upset.

Sixty years before, their astronomers had detected within the Orgrot a vast and dense cloud of solid and gaseous material that filled them with apprehension. Senoobis had passed into the Orgrot's outer fringes, bringing more frequent meteor collisions. As the planet approached the denser part of the cloud, it was encountering larger meteors and the impacts were devastating: more than 4,500 Senoobians had been killed in the last year. The government had been forced to use the last of its Hyperions to destroy the largest of the approaching masses.

As their astronomers monitored the advance of their star system into the swirling heart of the Orgrot, there was a growing fear in every Senoobian of what lay ahead. Over the last 90 years, the extent of the destruction had increased until it surpassed that which had occurred during the First Tribulation centuries before. Over the last five years, the astronomers had watched, fascinated and terror-stricken, through their telescopes as Plimandia, the planet nearest to Karmut, reached deeper into the Orgrot and was torn apart. It was a preview of what would happen to Senoobis. In fact, the *Volarion* had barely escaped the same fate as it traveled through the Karmut system.

During those five years the astronomers had also been tracking a loose group of five giant asteroids, collectively designated T-31 and nicknamed *the hammer*, as it sped toward a collision with Senoobis. The astronomers had described the masses as wreckage from a long-dead planet ground into dust and rubble by some ancient nebula millions of years ago. T-31 was a harbinger of death, coming closer by the day. It wouldn't destroy the planet, but it would likely end all higher forms of life.

Barzilay spoke in a voice that betrayed his anxiety, "Narzis, I have informed Markana, and she's convening a meeting of the Council tomorrow evening, but I wanted to tell you in person. Our projections are confirmed; we've run out of time. T-31 is going to impact us 45 days from today at 0925 in the morning in Bunjehy. It looks worse than I feared. The five masses are confirmed at three to 11 miles across—that's far larger than anything that's hit us so far. We're going to experience some major crust displacements and tidal waves far larger than anything we've ever seen before. I don't think we'll survive it."

Angado looked at him stoically. "We've known that day was coming for a long time, haven't we, my friend? And it had to happen on our watch! Sometimes I become depressed thinking that our children will be the last generation of Senoobians. I get angry thinking about how hard we *noobs* have worked to overcome our challenges and misfortunes and become a great civilization. And, damn it, we are a great civilization, Paleg. We've been responsible stewards of our planet. We've accomplished a lot—but for what? In a hundred years, we'll be no more than a fading memory, if any of our colonists survive to remember us at all."

He turned to the cabinet behind his desk, chose a bottle and filled two glasses. "I'd give anything to know how that story ends," he said as an aside. "Here, Paleg, we need a drink."

Barzilay took the bubbling green *chanchee* and settled down into his chair. "Yes, I feel the same way. Whether or not our brave colonists survive, Senoobis will be no more. They may flourish on Karyntis or Nanzema, but they will be transformed by their new world into a different species and Senoobis will be forgotten. No matter what, our race is doomed."

He stroked his chin and took a long drink before continuing. "Sometimes in my weaker moments, I mourn the tragic unfairness that we will pass away—into lifeless dust again—and everything we have achieved will be for nothing. I get angry, but eventually I remind myself that it doesn't matter. The Universe just keeps rolling along— creating, evolving, destroying—in a never-ending cycle, with or without us. How many civilizations in our galaxy alone have sprung up before ours and achieved greatness, only to be ground into dust again as we will be?"

Angado sighed and looked away, his eyes vacant. "Who knows? Nonetheless, when it's the demise of our own civilization we're discussing, I don't like it one bit."

The somber verse of Pansyn Vaberis, the old Kurmythian bard, came to him. He looked at the floor, unable to turn back the thought of his mortality, mouthing the words like a dirge:

Into the dark void cold death beckons us to grim repose
While in our hearts the mystery grows;
We pursue our fate without knowing why,
With barely a whimper as our goodbye.

He looked up at Barzilay. "Sorry. I do hate to go quietly. You know, when I was at the academy, I had a professor, I remember him like it was yesterday, who used to say, *Angado, the Universe is not sentient, it isn't aware of us and cannot care a tad about us. Therefore, you had better take care of yourself.* I didn't much like him then—he was too cynical I thought—but later on I realized that he was right. *Fairness* is just our fantasy that everything will somehow be set right in the end, proffered to ease the burden of our misfortunes. Beyond our contrived social context, there's no such thing."

Barzilay frowned. "Yes, quite right. That damned Orgrot! It's going to tear us to shreds and then in a few billion years another star will coalesce out of the mess to replace old Karmut and two or three new planets will form and there we go again. Maybe there'll even come to be new life on one of those planets and possibly a tiny bit of you and me will wind up in some of it."

His frown turned into a mischievous grin, "Come to think of it, Narzis, I suspect a bit of you would do well in a foul-smelling *groobut*. You wouldn't have to talk at all—you could just hop around, sticking your tongue out and croaking at whatever didn't please you. Now that's fairness for you!"

Angado feigned insult, "Hummph! Maybe so, my friend, but a mangy old *pisank* might suit you just as well. You know, scurrying around, poking its snout here and there and stirring up trouble. No, wait! A mud-wallowing, loud-grunting *hahksog* would fit your personality even better."

Now Barzilay pretended to take offense. "Well, there it is at last! I knew my social skills were unappreciated!"

They were on a roll. It was a ritual observed between the two old friends in times of stress, a testament to the strength of their friendship and a way of relieving the enormous pressure they felt. When they were angry or frustrated, a trivial comment from one might spark a contest to see who could outdo the other as a string of feigned insults and colorful invective flew between them. By venting their anger on each other, they managed to spare their subordinates and mates a great deal of abuse.

They both laughed and, as each lifted his glass in an unspoken toast to the other, Angado said with obvious affection for his old comrade, "Paleg, we've been a good team, haven't we? I've enjoyed our work together and your friendship. I could always count on you in a pinch."

Barzilay became more upbeat. "The same here. You've been a good boss and a close friend. We've worked hard, and I'm worn out."

They both lapsed into a sober mood again, their casual demeanor concealing the foreboding that was smoldering inside them. Finally, Angado said, "You know, I agree with you about that fairness business, and yet every so often something odd will happen and I get this uneasy feeling that maybe the Universe is sentient after all. Maybe we're just an insignificant cell in some vast cosmic organism that we can't begin to comprehend."

Barzilay replied, "Perhaps so. Sometimes I wonder if there has been any point to our existence at all. Senoobis has been our home for only a fleeting moment on the cosmic scale and what have we accomplished in that brief existence? Nothing of any lasting consequence that I can see!"

"Oh, well. No point in grumbling about our plight. Maybe just managing to stay alive is enough for now. Have you heard from Ranthus lately?

Barzilay brightened considerably. "Yes, a few days ago. Just before they went into the sleep modules. He wasn't looking forward to being cooped up on board for so long, and he can't wait to reach Karyntis so his unit can explore their new home. I've rested easier knowing they'll be there to protect our colonists."

"Yes, so have I. Nonetheless, I know it's been tough, giving up your only son.

Barzilay replied stoically, "No harder than what you face with your children, I'm sure. It was hard for a long time but Giloa and I finally resigned ourselves to it; knowing that he's doing something important for Senoobis has helped."

Angado lifted his glass to Barzilay again. "Yes, Paleg, and we've done our part—we've passed the baton on and now the future belongs to our colonists."

Barzilay stroked his chin for a minute. "Quite right. I believe we've given them everything they need to succeed but it's over for us. There's nothing more to do now but get some rest and wait for . . ."

Angado put up his hand to stop his comrade. "Paleg, there is one more thing we can do." He had a smug look on his face. "We don't have much time and we're not as young as we used to be but hear me out. Remember the *Balserios* that disappeared on the mission to Parkopia?"

"Of course," Barzilay said, puzzled.

"Well, before you die, wouldn't you like to know what happened to her?"

"Sure, who wouldn't?" Barzilay exclaimed. "So what?"

Paleg, what if we could go there and solve the mystery AND even start a new life there?"

"WE! Are you insane?" Barzilay exclaimed incredulously. "How would we even get there?"

"There's the *Shananik*. We could bring her out of mothballs, refit her and take her on a one-way trip to Parkopia with a Bretin crew. She's still a good ship: like you and me, old but reliable." He was getting wound up. "Paleg, why not do something bold instead of just waiting to die!"

"Narzis, *by Inikees*, she's a rust bucket—we'd never reach Parkopia!"

"Seven light years, Paleg. Only seven! We can make it."

"What about Vanjee and Giloa! Don't you think we should be with them when the world ends?"

"Of course. We'll take them with us!"

"Narzis, you're suffering from delusions of grandeur. You want to take Vanjee on a suicide mission! Besides, we couldn't get the ship ready in five days and what about finding a crew!"

"Paleg, I've already worked it all out. She can be ready in five days. Some engineers from Heshoti's group have been going over her for several months—a couple of them even want to go with us. And I know a few Bretin who are jumping at the chance to take the *Shananik* to Parkopia and find out what happened to their Bretin pals. I've talked with Argulis and he has no problem with some Bretin volunteers going. There are more Bretin than they can take on the *Langorion* so maybe some of those who will be left behind can survive on Parkopia *with us*—it's better than letting them die on Senoobis.

"No doubt about it, the chances are Parkopia is going to be a bust but, if something unforeseen ruins Karyntis and Nanzema doesn't pan out, Parkopia will be the only option. Besides, the *Shananik* is going to be destroyed anyway and, if we stay here, it's the end for us too. If we make it to Parkopia, at least we may have a fighting chance to survive."

"Narzis, be reasonable. Parkopia's cold, not enough oxygen—a terrible place! I'd rather be torn apart here in my home than die on some lonely chunk of ice!"

"Paleg, trust me. Bring Giloa. Meet Vanjee and me and our Bretin friends here at 1600. I've already talked to Markana. She has agreed to bring it before the Council."

The next evening an urgent meeting of the Supreme Council was convened, the latest of several meetings that had been called over the last few months to consider the worsening state of affairs. Over the last 90 years, Senoobis had come to be battered more frequently by the increasing density of cosmic matter strewn across its path as Karmut carried it deeper into the Orgrot.

The President rose to address the Council:

My colleagues, I now convene the 10th session of the Supreme Council in the year 4935 A.P. The primary business of this meeting will be to consider the actions we must take in regard to the impending collisions with the collection of celestial bodies designated *T-31*. Then you may bring before the Council any other matters you consider to be important. Let the Secretary record the names of those present.

Our situation is grim: we have 30 days to begin evacuations. The first asteroid is 6.5 miles across; it will enter

153

our atmosphere in 44 days at about 0925 in the morning, making a direct hit in the populated area of Bunjehy with devastating results.

Fifteen minutes later the second asteroid, three miles across, will impact in the ocean 250 miles from Herk, causing a catastrophic tidal wave. The third one, five miles across, will follow close behind, striking Potsuri in a sparsely populated area. The fourth one is the largest, eleven miles across. Unfortunately it is expected to strike 95 miles from Senoobia three hours after the third one. Its destructive effect will be unimaginable, obliterating our capital. The last one—nine miles across—will impact in Arkoli Province by the Thaxian coast.

I propose that orders to evacuate Bunjehy and Potsuri be communicated to the regional officials immediately. Since the level of particulate matter in the atmosphere is already dangerously high, and T-31 will make it worse, I also propose that respirators be provided to those near the impact area. Barring any major structural damage from a direct hit, our power grid will continue to supply power for communications and other vital functions.

Our food supplies are another matter. Since only 25 percent of our food resources are non-photosynthetic, we expect to experience serious shortages within three months. By blocking out the light from Karmut, the elevated particulate levels in the atmosphere have already reduced agricultural productivity by 20 percent.

Our medical supplies are adequate for a year. We've made all the preparations we can so, my friends, there's nothing else to do but wait and see what happens. Of course, we will continue progress reports to our starships as long as we can. Our global communications center will continue to be manned and will coordinate communications with any survivors here and with our starships. All citizens, except for essential emergency and power grid personnel, have been ordered to seek shelter. So, there it is. What say you?

The floor was open to anyone who wished to speak and those who did offered sound suggestions. At the end of the meeting, Narzis Angado rose to request permission from the Council for one more mission to Parkopia. Several members pronounced him *insane* but agreed to humor him. The President stood up. "If there is no further discussion, we will vote on the recommendations before us and the request by Narzis Angado."

The votes were unanimous in the affirmative. By noon on the second day after the meeting of the Council, all workplaces except for certain governmental agencies were shut down and everyone was at home with their families to make final preparations for the coming impacts.

The Ministry of Astronomy remained operational in order to monitor the progress of T-31. The ministry of Interior Security remained on duty to assess the damage resulting from the impacts.

Most everyone spent the remaining time in quiet reflection, bracing themselves for the destruction that would soon begin. Not all of them were ready to die, but they found some solace in their private expressions of hope for the safety of the crews of their starships, and in their confidence in the success of their missions. Thousands of personal messages were received and treasured by the members of the three crews.

A few days after the final meeting of the Council, the aging *Shananik* departed its orbit around Pesh and began its flight to Parkopia. It carried Angado, Barzilay, their wives, six younger Senoobians, ten Bretin and a generous stock of *chanchee*, the crew's favored drink. If they were lucky, they would reach the forbidding planet in 42 years.

A monthly status report from the Supreme Council had been transmitted to the startship crews to inform them of events on Senoobis. The day before the five Asteroids of T-31 were expected to strike the surface, a final message was transmitted to all three starships. Markana Ahkton, President of the Supreme Council, confirmed the prediction that 99% of the Senoobians on the planet would be killed by T-31. She thanked the starship crews for their service and wished them good luck.

At 0515 the next morning, four hours before the first asteroid was expected to strike the surface, she and her mate, Yun Neebor, stood on the balcony of their apartment in Residential Tower #4, and looked down at Senoobia after a sleepless night. They and everyone else had prepared for the coming of T-31 as best they could; now there was nothing to do but wait.

Their gaze lingered fondly over the wide expanse of Gengalus Square, heart of the capital, with its regal monuments and elegant fountains. Their eyes rested on the stately Council Hall at the West end of the square where they had spent so many eventful years. The capital was eerily silent; not a single person could be found in the square or a single transporter moving through the streets.

After three hundred years, the lives of every Senoobian had come down to this fateful day. It marked the end of everything they had labored for a millenium to build. The couple embraced and kissed warmly before pulling back to look lovingly at each other. They tried to ignore the bitter truth that they would likely never again see each other, their beloved city, or the dancing blue waters, brimming with life, in the bay that was to them paradise. But they could not.

At 0928, eastward beyond the horizon, they saw a bright flash of light as the first part of T-31 ripped through the atmosphere at blinding speed. It struck the surface in the Bunjehy Province with a violent explosion that staggered the planet. A huge billowing cloud of dust and debris reared up in the distance like a giant mushroom growing toward the sky. There was a distant boom and then a rumblingand quaking as the crust of the planet absorbed the enormous force of the impact.

As violent shockwaves spread out across the surface, the two of them clung to each other, helpless and vulnerable in their home. Taller structures swayed precariously and combustibles exploded into flames. They were knocked off their feet by the convulsions of the ground beneath their building. Huddled together on the floor, they were afraid of being crushed as their building collapsed around them.

At 0945, the second asteroid struck the ocean off the coast of Herk. A towering wall of water rose up from the ocean and raced toward the Bay of Kurmythia. They watched mesmerized as the mountainous tide slammed against their building, flooding the streets around them, and raced inland. Their building swayed but somehow remained upright. Then the tide reversed itself and rushed back to the sea, thick and dirty with awful debris. As they watched their gutted city emerge from the sea and heard the desperate cries of people drowning all around them, they covered their ears; it was too much to bear.

At 0954, before they could recover, the third asteroid struck Potsuri inland. Again the sky lit up in a frightening display as the ground heaved and the crust buckled in its convulsions. Any living thing within 50 miles of the impact was incinerated as hellish fires broke out, consuming anything combustible. Deep fissures opened in the surface, devouring roads, bridges, forests and buildings. Thousands were trapped or crushed under collapsing buildings.

The fourth asteroid was the largest, 22 miles across, a monster fireball, unimaginable in its destruction. At 1233, it struck less than a hundred miles from Senoobia and set off a chain of cataclysms that killed three-fourths of the population. Giant slabs of fractured crust were heaved skyward, only to slide back down, crushing buildings and leaving the capital in shambles.

Buried beneath the rubble lay the brilliant Markana Ahkton and her mate, the renowned composer Yun Neebor; no one would come to search for them; no one would call out their names; no one would deliver their eulogy. In an instant they would be swept away.

At 1340, the last asteroid razed Dargomeea, the beautiful resort city of a thousand faces, and delivered the final devastating blow.

In the year 4935 A.P., Senoobian civilization lay in ruins, its destruction complete. The billowing smoke and dust that filled the skies choked out the light from Karmut, causing most of the plant life to wither and die. In the months ahead those who survived the destruction from T-31 would starve by the millions. Those few who were able to carry on for a few more years, lived only to face a more terrible death as the ongoing cosmic barrage tore apart their beloved planet and its atmosphere bled away.

In the year 4954 A.P., the cosmic cycle was complete: after 5.2 billion years as a grand crucible of life, the battered planet returned to dust.

Drifting untethered through the dissipating remains of the doomed planet, a metal time capsule was the only evidence of the once proud civilization.

The handful of Senoobians and Bretin who managed to escape the Karmut Star System on the *Shananik* were well on their way to Parkopia. Whether or not they would reach the planet and manage to survive there depended on the resourcefulness and leadership of Narzis Angado.

On board the *Syzilian* Captain Mensykus sensed that things were going badly on Senoobis. The awful death his loved ones faced and his helplessness filled him first with rage and then despair. Instead of looking forward to the reports from Senoobis, he came to dread them. He knew that most of the crew felt the same way. It was not within the character of a Senoobian to entertain false hope. Nor was it the nature of their government to offer anything but a coldly realistic appraisal of the situation; the Council would not paint a hopeful picture where there was none to paint.

Knowing that he would never see Senoobis again had made it harder to leave than Mensykus had let on. The sadness that he had felt throughout their mission had gradually turned into depression, which had briefly yielded to the elation of finally reaching Karyntis. But his depression soon returned because the reports from Senoobis were more disheartening, serving only to remind him that he had seen Senoobis for the last time.

Mensykus was on the bridge, sitting heavily in the Captain's chair and brooding as usual, when a priority one message was received in communications. The fact that it was not due for another twelve days implied that it was the grim report they had been dreading. As soon as it was decrypted and printed out, Pandomis ran to the bridge to personally hand it to the Captain.

Seeing him approach with eyes downcast, Mensykus stood up with a heavy heart, took the message and scanned it quickly. Then he turned to Jeliko who was on watch and shook his head sadly. "It's over. Call everyone to a meeting at 1600 in the recreation compartment." Mensykus then slumped back into his chair and turned toward the viewer, unable to read the message again.

Most of the off-duty crew was relaxing in the recreation compartment when the announcement came over the P.A. system. At 1545 that afternoon, Jeliko reported, "Captain the crew is assembled." Not a sound came from the crew as Mensykus faced them and began to read in a deliberate and solemn voice.

CAT1 375802/FROM: MAhkton, Supreme Council TO Capt. RMensykus, Syzilian/LGobetas, Volarion: As President of the Supreme Council, it is my duty to report to you on the state of your homeland. This message will be brief and to the point. The first part of Asteroid Cluster T-31 will reach our atmosphere at 0928 tomorrow with the other parts close behind. Although the Council has ordered the evacuation of everyone within 1,000 miles of the impact area, the damage will be extensive and a large number will perish because they refuse to leave their homes. T-31 will be followed by a vast field of asteroids that will utterly destroy Senoobis within a few hellish years, leaving our planet too fragmented to hold on to its atmosphere.

This is the event that we have planned for and dreaded for 300 years. We are at a dead end and there is nothing more to do except to thank you for your brave and honorable service and to wish all of you success and prosperity in your new world. Be proud of what you have done because your courage and your sacrifices have sustained us in our darkest hours. By the time you receive this message, Senoobis will be only a memory to you but it will always be at the heart of who you are. You carry with you into the future the legacy of a proud and glorious race that, with your courage and spirit, will become even greater and prosper for millennia to come. Your Jukasian Disks will be your guide. This will be my last message to you. Whatever happens, you must prevail. MAhkton/Supreme Council.

Mensykus put down the message and looked up at his crew. They were all silent, mourning loved ones who had died 17 years before and their beloved mother planet that no longer existed. For the first time they felt alone and vulnerable in a vast and indifferent universe.

On board the *Volarion*, the message had been received with equal sadness three years earlier.

18

LORD ATHRUMOS

The *Volarion* was near the Gafor System when the alarm went off, filling the bridge with its shrill hreeuh-hreeuh-hreeuh sound. Things had gone smoothly since her launch 67 years earlier, but now the ship's radar detected something that required the attention of the crew on call.

Since the alarm was a category 1, indicating the most urgent response was required, the ship's computers had initiated accelerated bio-wakeup, a procedure no one cared to endure; it was exceedingly painful, disorienting and risky. An accelerated bio-wakeup was not possible from full hyper-sleep, so those on call were always at a higher readiness level than the rest of the crew and could return to full functionality within four weeks. Recovery from full hyper-sleep required six months but was not nearly as stressful on the body.

There were always five crewmembers on call, one of whom was either the Captain, the XO or the Operations Officer. Four weeks later, the five crewmembers were coming around. Pardan, the assistant navigator, was the first to regain full consciousness. His head throbbed unmercifully and every muscle in his body ached. He looked at the indicators, trying hard to focus, and saw that they had been in hyper-sleep for eleven years. He shut off the alarm and made his way gingerly to the navigation compartment. As he did so, he glanced over at Karomis, the Engineering Officer, and then at Larsyvus, the Assistant Communications Officer. Both of them were sitting up unsteadily, looking as if they had a hangover.

When he reached the large radar display, there near the top of the screen was an odd cloudy image that immediately caught his eye. The red brackets blinking around the contact designated BX1 flagged it as the cause of the alarms. It looked like a comet some 15 miles across with a long trail of gases behind it. It was streaking toward them at an oblique angle on a collision course. Factoring in both their speeds, the computer indicated that the mysterious object would reach them in only seven weeks—putting the ship at extreme risk.

Pardan was dumbfounded. "Where did you come from, you little son-of-a-bitch!" he muttered to himself. Then he yelled at the other two, "Come here. Look at this!" Karomis and Larsyvus stumbled over to him, still groggy but fully aware that something was wrong.

Karomis looked at the screen through dazed eyes. "What the hell is that?"

Larsyvus tried hard to focus. "Looks like a comet to me. Must have popped out of the Gafor System."

Pardan looked at Larsyvus, "I don't know where else it could have come from, but it's too damn close for comfort. We've got to take evasive action now. Look, I'll work out the course change, and you go and inform the Captain. Also, give Jander a call and see if he's coming around—we may need him. Karomis, check the stats on our visitor again."

Larsyvus frowned at Pardan. "If you don't mind, let's give the Captain a little more time. He's still groggy and cranky. I don't think any of us will want to be around him for awhile unless there's a damn good reason and I'm not sure this is a good enough reason."

Pardan managed a weak smile at Larsyvus, even though he felt nauseated and ached all over. Larsyvus was right, of course, but their mission was too critical to take any chances. Besides he wasn't sure how clearly he was thinking himself. As he sat down at the console to compute the course change, the icon representing Oblivium in the Gafor System caught his eye. "Karomis, we fired off two probes to Oblivium but, since we never received a single transmission from either probe, we wrote off Oblivium. After all, there was no time to send a manned mission there and Karyntis appeared to be promising anyway. Sure, there were still lots of questions about Karyntis but Oblivium remained a complete mystery."

Karomis scratched his chin. "Look, I think we're overreacting. Every star system has comets whizzing around it. They're not visible unless they're close enough to the star they're orbiting to be heated so that a tail of escaping gases and dust is boiled off and reflects the star's light. The stellar wind of the star pushes the tail away. We'll change our course, this unwelcome pest will whiz on by, and that will be the end of it."

Pardan thought a moment. "Yes, I'm sure you're right. I just don't want to take any chances."

A few minutes later, Pardan had the necessary course adjustments in hand. They would alter their course enough to miss the *comet* by 36,000 miles. He entered the changes into the navigation computer and immediately the ship began to move almost imperceptively but enough to carry it out of danger. The Captain was still unsteady and Pardan decided to wait until he had recovered enough to be briefed. There wasn't much to do except to wait for the minor course change to take effect and to verify that the near miss had been avoided. Karomis and Larsyvus decided on a few games of Purogus to clear their minds.

Two weeks later, when Pardan glanced at the large radar screen on the bridge, as he did every few hours when he was on watch, it hit him. Something was wrong; the angle between the *Volarion* and BX1 had not changed as it should have. They were still on a collision course! That could mean only one thing—the object had adjusted its course in response to their change. There was some intelligence driving it.

Pardan turned to the two crewmen, his heart pumping faster. "Larsyvus, get the Captain on the bridge. We've got a problem. That thing is still coming at us!"

Larsyvus looked up stunned. "What? That's impossible!"

Pardan yelled at him, "No, it's not. Get the Captain to the bridge. Karomis, look at this!"

Larsyvus jumped up and ran to the Captain's quarters near the bridge. Karomis rushed over to the screen. Pardan's mind was racing as he rechecked their course adjustment with his instruments. Had he made a mistake? He desperately hoped that Karomis would say to him, "Now look here, you've made a mistake. You see, the trinocular RBG sensors are not calibrated correctly. Everything's all right."

Karomis studied the screen and the computer's readout intently. Then he switched to the long-range scan. Finally, he turned to Pardan, his face ashen. "Uh, you're right, there's no mistake. And it's not a comet! Look. Its tail doesn't point away from Gafor the way a comet's would. Its tail points away from the direction of its flight, like the exhaust gases from a starship. I don't know what all of that garbage is around the core unless it's intended to throw us off by making us think it's a comet."

Captain Gobetas rushed onto the bridge with Larsyvus in tow. "BX1 has changed course. We're on a collision course again!" Pardan informed the Captain as he studied the screen intently for several minutes without uttering a word.

"Change course to avoid BX1, and notify me immediately if anything changes," he said to Pardan.

A week later, it was obvious BX1 was changing course to maintain the original bearings. That was enough. Pardan turned to the bridge intercom system and called Jander: "Weapons Officer to the bridge now!"

Jander responded immediately. "I'm on my way. What's wrong?"

Pardan filled him in as he made his way to the bridge and concluded his comments with "I believe it's hostile."

When he came onto the bridge, Jander regarded the screen intently. "If it is, we'll know soon enough. I'd better get to the weapons compartment and activate the Hyperions."

As Jander was leaving, Captain Gobetas came onto the bridge. "What the hell's going on?"

Pardan briefed the Captain thoroughly as he studied the screen for several minutes without uttering a word. Then, taking everyone around him by surprise, he exploded into action. "Pardan, I want everyone who's on-duty on the bridge at 1000. Have Larsyvus draft a Category 1 message to *Syz*, informing her that we suspect hostile action may be imminent. Also, have him start running scans of the radio frequency spectrum to see if he can find any frequencies our *visitor* may be using."

At 1000, all five of them were on the bridge. The Captain rechecked the large radar screen with a scowl and then looked from one to the other of them solemnly. "I believe we've encountered an advanced life form that we always expected to find one day but we have found it at the worst possible time. In the early stages of our project to find a planet to colonize, we launched a probe to Oblivium. We know it reached Oblivium but we never received any transmissions from it.

"We launched a second probe to Oblivium but never received transmissions from it either. Did both probes malfunction or crash into the planet? I don't think so. The probes were reliable. I believe they were intercepted and used to gain intelligence about Senoobis and our mission. It may be that they were reverse-engineered and converted into receivers for listening in on all of our communications. As a result we may have advanced life forms who know a lot about us while we know nothing about them. They may have known about our mission and decided to intercept us. I believe their intentions are hostile.

"We have essentially three options. First, we can try to outrun them but, of course, we have no idea what their capabilities are. Besides that, we're loaded down with cargo. Second, we can blast away and hope to stop them with our Hyperions. We have no idea what their weapons capabilities are. That's a huge gamble but I don't believe they know anything about our weapons capability either. Third, we can wait until they do something to reveal . . ."

At that moment, Larsyvus, who had been watching the screen, stopped him in mid-sentence, "Captain, there are three of them! It looks like they were in formation, sort of stacked one behind the other inside that cloud and now they're diverging!"

The Captain turned to his officers, "Well, there you are. The noose is tightening! Enough talk, gentlemen. Karomis, within the hour, have engineering ready to blast us out of here with everything we've got. Jander, get the Hyperions locked on those three ships. Pardan, prepare to resume our course to Karyntis. And all of you, look alive! Larsyvus, put the whole crew on bio-wakeup. This may get messy and everyone needs to be alert as soon as possible. Then draft another priority one to update the *Syz*. Quickly now!"

Two days later, the Captain and the officers on watch were gathered around the operations screen. The three contacts were only two weeks away and maintaining formation 300 miles apart. Suddenly, Larsyvus yelled at the Captain through the intercom, "Captain, we're receiving a message from them. I'm putting it through to you."

"Good, they can talk—but can we understand them? Pardan, put it on the speakers. Larsyvus, record it and tell me everything you can about it."

The speakers on the bridge came to life with a shrill whine that oscillated briefly before becoming clear. The voice was deep and raspy, but the message was articulated slowly so it was not difficult to understand:

ATTENTION VOLARION: I am Efydus Athrumos, First Lord of Peyr. We have come to welcome you. Please forgive our ruse but we did not want to alarm you. We have learned a lot about you since the first probe you sent to Peyr, our planet that you call Oblivium—a charming name. And then you were kind enough to give us another, improved version of the first. You are quite good at communications. You have kept a small staff of our linguists employed for many years interpreting your communications.

Perhaps your desperation has made you careless in your communications. We know about your unfortunate predicament and your plans to overcome it. Let me be clear. We will not allow you to succeed on the planet you call Karyntis. Why not? Because we were there to claim it with its untamed beasts and pitiful savages a thousand years ago. In the near future it will be an important part of our empire. As you have learned, our galaxy can be rather inhospitable so we prefer to diversify.

You may be curious as to our intentions. We want to inspect you and your ship before you become a small footnote in our glorious history—you probably have some curiosity about us as well. So, I invite you to change course toward Peyr, and we will provide an escort for you. If you decline our invitation, however, we will not hesitate to destroy you and the seed you carry with you. It is nothing personal, just the Universal Law of *Domination by the Superior*. I am not patient so you have one hour—not a minute more—to decide. EAthrumos/Pajputog.

The whole crew was stunned. Gobetas was livid. "That condescending son-of-a-bitch! I wonder how he would like a Hyperion up his ass!"

The Captain, flushed with anger, pulled the on-duty officers together on the spot. He looked at Pardan and then the others, "It seems we have been betrayed by our communications. Any grand ideas?" No one answered.

"Well, I'll be damned if we're going to windup stuffed and on display in a museum on Oblivium—or should I say Peyr? Larsyvus, send the following message:

To EAthrumos, First Lord of Peyr, since you outnumber us three to one, we accept your invitation. We are changing course. Captain LGobetas/Volarion.

He turned to Pardan. "Bring us about slowly to a course toward them. They will begin turning also. Jander, when we are within 1,000 miles of the nearest ship, on my command, launch a Hyperion at each ship, one right after the other. Ready the remaining three Hyperions in case one or more of the targets is not destroyed. Karomis, the instant the last Hyperion is away, get us out of here at flank speed on a course to Karyntis. Larsyvus, draft an update on our situation—include the message from Athrumos—and transmit it to *Syz*." He addressed them both, "Quickly now!"

Each officer rushed to his task and the *Volarion* began to change course.

Larsyvus called, "Captain, a short message from Athrumos."

The Captain put it on the speakers:

Captain Gobetas, you have chosen wisely. I look forward to meeting you on Peyr. EAthrumos/Pajputog.

And I look forward to seeing you as a cinder! thought Gobetas.

The Hyperions were armed, and the engines were made ready. It took the four ships two days to come about into the same formation. When the *Volarion*'s escorts had maneuvered into position, they were no more than 1,800 miles apart. Using a telescope on the bridge, Gobetas studied the three ships carefully as he thought to himself, "That's good, nice and close." They were not as large as the *Volarion* but they were obviously formidable ships.

Everything was in place. Gobetas turned to Pardan and, using Pardan's first name, said with a smile, "Barot, let's show our Lord that we don't appreciate his eavesdropping on us. Lock on targets BX1, BX2 and BX3. Launch Hyperions 1, 2 and 3 on my command."

He turned, pointing solemnly to Jander, "As ordered, now!"

Jander pressed the necessary buttons on his control panel and the doors to the launch tubes slid open quickly. The engines of the Hyperions ignited with a roar and in an instant they were gone, leaving the *Volarion* shrouded in quickly dissipating blue smoke. They would reach their targets in less than ten minutes, not enough time to get up to their full speed.

Gobetas pointed to Jander, "Now! Set course for Karyntis." The ship slowly began to turn.

He pointed to Karomis, "Flank speed! Everything you've got!" Karomis yelled to the engine room, "Flank speed!" The engines kicked in and the ship began to accelerate into a tight turn.

The officers on Lord Athrumos' flagship the *Pajputog* had been studying the *Volarion* just as intently and they detected the Hyperion's launch. *What a pity, we'll have to kill them*, thought Athrumos. His Commanding Officer turned to him, "Permission for evasive action, My Lord?"

"Granted," replied Athrumos.

"Targets acquired. Permission to fire, my Lord?" asked the CO.

"Yes, destroy them," growled Athrumos, becoming unnerved as the Hyperions blazed toward them faster than he had expected.

The *Pajputog*'s Weapons Officer entered the launch sequence, releasing three missiles, and the three ships began a twisting, evasive maneuver.

At that moment the first Hyperion struck the mysterious field of matter surrounding the three ships and exploded harmlessly although spectacularly. But in doing so, it cleared enough of a path for the second Hyperion to punch through and find its mark in one of the ships that was taking evasive action. The ship exploded violently and broke into two careening, gutted halves.

The third Hyperion followed the second one closely and could not avoid the expanding cloud of debris from the ship that was destroyed. It exploded prematurely but close enough to damage Lord Athrumos' ship and to destroy one of the three missiles. As he got back on his feet, he was furious. "Salvo 2. Fire!" he screamed.

The third Peyrian ship disengaged from the field of matter and, beginning pursuit of the *Volarion*, launched two missiles.

On board the *Volarion*, the Captain watched the intense flashes of light on the Peyrian ship that revealed the launch of the two missiles racing toward them. The *Volarion*'s speed was increasing but the missiles were gaining.

In the meantime, Larsyvus feverishly composed a brief update, encrypted it, and transmitted it to the *Syzilian*. Moments later a violent explosion rocked the ship; the large instrument panel on the bridge went dark, the engine room became an inferno, and the hull was breached. Damage Control was unable to contain the damage; the great ship rolled over and came apart, continuing on, perhaps forever, as a lifeless derelict.

Capt. Mensykus was on the bridge supervising maintenance on the ship's life support systems when Kastgar called from communications. His voice was frantic, "Captain, a Priority 1 message from the *Volarion*—She's under attack! I'm sending it up."

It took three years for messages to travel back and forth between the *Syzilian* and the *Volarion*. Whatever happened to the *Volarion*, it had occurred three years ago. Mensykus reached the printer just as it spit out the message. It read

CAT1 PRI1 4835-1211-1
FM Capt LGobetas/Volarion
TO Capt RMensykus/Syzilian
As we approached edge of Gafor System, detected unknown object that appeared to be large comet originating in Gafor System. Its trajectory placed it on a collision course with us and we changed course to avoid it but it also changed course and remained on near collision course. We changed course again with same result. I believe contact is hostile and that the two probes dispatched to Oblivium were recovered by unknown life form and used to intercept our comm. Have activated Hyperions. Will advise further. End.

Three hours later, Mensykus was still on the bridge. He was feeling totally frustrated that all he could do was wait for another message from the *Volarion*. He was exhausted and could feel the knots in his stomach tightening. Finally his communicator buzzed. It was Kastgar again, "Captain, another message from the *Volarion*! I'm sending it up."

Mensykus held his breath as he leaned over the printer to retrieve the message. It read:

CAT1 PRI1 4835-1211-2
FM Capt LGobetas/Volarion
TO Capt RMensykus/Syzilian

Unknown contact has separated into three objects that are still on course to intercept us. Have ordered battle stations and preparations for flank speed to evade. Hyperions are locked on targets. Have ordered wakeup for entire crew. Will advise further. End.

Two days later Kastgar buzzed the bridge again, anxious for Mensykus to see the latest category 1 message that he had decrypted. The Captain leaned anxiously forward to retrieve the message and began to read:

CAT1 PR1 4835-1211-3
FM Capt LGobetas/Volarion
TO Capt RMensykus/Syzilian
Received message in Kuterin from SOP Efydus Athrumos. 3 contacts determined to be warships from Peyr (Oblivium) in the Gafor System. Copy follows. Have responded that we will comply and change course. When we are close will launch 3 Hyperions and go to flank speed resuming course to Karyntis. I will advise you as soon as we have safely disengaged. If you do not receive a msg from me within 3 days, have most likely been destroyed. Has been an honor to serve with you. Whatever happens to us, you must prevail. End.

It was followed by a copy of the message from Athrumos. Mensykus read the message three times. They had made a tragic blunder in allowing their communications to be compromised. If the *Volarion* could not survive the attack upon it, the Karyntis Mission was doomed. The *Syzilian* did not have adequate resources to found the colony on Karyntis. Mensykus sank down into his chair, his mind reeling with the horror of the message. If he didn't receive a message from Gobetas within three days . . ., he couldn't bear the thought of it.

He agonized about his friend Gobetas and the terrible fix he and his ship were in. He thought about the mission and the great hope it had offered. Was it for nothing? He thought about the *Syzilian*'s situation. What would they do? It was difficult enough to survive in an alien world but, if they did manage to survive, at some point in the future, would they have to face a contingency from Peyr? As the hours passed with no message forthcoming, Mensykus and the whole crew became distraught. Four days after the last message, however, *Syzylian* began to receive a message. The Captain, full of hope, rushed to the communications center. It was not what he had expected. The message read:

> Captain Mensykus, I am Efydus Athrumos IV, First Lord of Peyr. This will be my only communication to you. I am sure you are anxious to learn the fate of your comrades. The Volarion is destroyed. Captain Gobetas and his crew are dead. Your mission is futile. We will soon return to the planet you call Karyntis to establish our own colony. We are clearly superior to you and you can expect no assistance from the primitive savages who inhabit that planet. Therefore, you would be wise to surrender upon our arrival. If you do not, you and your ship will be destroyed as was the Volarion. EAthrumos/Pajputog.

Mensykus was stunned. At first he felt emotionally numb, empty, unable to react; then he was overcome with sadness for the loss of the *Volarion*. He sat in his chair, watching his crew and mulling over the message, and wept.

He turned to Bayn who was standing nearby, struggling to contain his own emotions. "Bayn, inform the crew that I will address them in ten minutes."

The Captain's firm command snapped Bayn back to reality. Somehow he couldn't accept what had happened but he was relieved to have something to do.

Ten minutes later, the Captain began his address to the crew over the ship's PA system:

> This is your Captain speaking. You have all read the messages that we received from the Volarion and from the Peyrian ship. We've had a bad run of luck, some of it of our own doing. We've lost our homes, our loved ones, and our comrades. We don't know the status of the Bretin so it may be that, except for us, our race is extinct. Now we are facing a powerful and sinister race that intends to destroy us as well. I don't know how much time we have before we must face our new enemy. It doesn't matter. The arrogance of our enemy causes him to underestimate us. His threats will not intimidate us but only make us more determined to prevail. Let him come to Karyntis and he will be sorry he found the Syzilian! We welcome the chance to avenge the Volarion.

But we are the seed of Senoobis. First we must establish a colony. At 2000 there will be a farewell ceremony in Compartment four to honor the crew of the Volarion. That is all.

The crew returned to their duties, steeled against whatever the future might bring.

The three old Senoobians didn't know about, and couldn't bear to speculate about, the final days of those they had left behind on Senoobis. The only thing they knew for sure was that their home planet was gone and 630 million of their fellow citizens were dead. No one survived to describe the terrible events that marked the final days of Senoobis.

PART 3

DEATH ON KARYNTIS

19

KARYNTIS AT LAST

The Senoobians sat back in their chairs and relaxed without saying a word. They had finished their story. They were tired and emotionally drained, having talked far more than they had intended. They were curious about how the humans would react to what they had heard.

Finally Bayn said, "So now you see why we believe the Peyrians have visited this planet at least once before and that they may return at any time. What their intentions might be, we can't say. We can only urge you to consider this information in the context of our contact with them."

Jeliko said, "I was the Communications Officer on the *Syzilian* and I still remember the message from the Peyrian lord. He boasted that they had already been here and that they were going to return to the Earth and claim it for their own purposes at some time in the future. They clearly considered us as rivals and the Earth as their prize."

Darz added, "We can tell you how to identify the Gafor Star System that includes their planet Peyr. Beyond that, there's not much to tell."

The humans sat there fascinated, unsure what to make of the intriguing story they had just heard or what to do about it.

Finally Sonny spoke. "What happened to the *Syzilian* and its crew after the message from the Peyrian lord?"

Jeliko said, "Sixty-two years after receiving that final message, our crew had been out of hyper-sleep for several months so we were feeling pretty normal. The *Syzilian* was deep within your star system, approaching Mars, the small reddish planet we called Libdenyus. It was the next planet out from Earth—Karyntis to us then—and it followed Jupiter, the giant planet we called Kopurnitis. We quickly confirmed that Mars was a dead planet with only a hint of an atmosphere and a barren surface so we lost interest in it. As our view of Karyntis loomed larger, our anticipation of reaching it grew.

"Since we were reaching the end of the long voyage to our new home, we should have been jubilant, but the mood aboard the *Syzilian* was subdued. Our crew had spent most of the years since the loss of the *Volarion* in hyper-sleep with little time to mourn the loss of our comrades. The joyful reunion that we had anticipated when the *Volarion* reached Karyntis would never happen.

"When we were 36 million miles from Karyntis, the spectacular blueness of the planet was striking. During our approach over the months ahead, visual details of the planet began to take shape and its single moon, which we called Polyksia, grew larger. We saw that it was totally inhospitable, of course: there was no atmosphere and no water, although the surface appeared to be solid and stable.

"The *Syzilian* itself was not designed to operate in a dense atmosphere or to contend with the gravity of a planet like Karyntis. It would remain in orbit far above the planet's atmosphere while its two landers carried crewmembers and cargo to and from the surface. As we approached Karyntis, the Captain decided to enter an orbit about 420 miles above the surface in order to gain a discrete vantage point from which to survey the planet and to prepare our landing parties. At that time we had no idea whether or not there might be advanced and hostile species inhabiting the planet.

"There were more clouds and oceans than on Senoobis. We were astonished and relieved to discover that water covered three-fourths of the planet. An abundance of water was critical; it not only sustained life but was also the source of the hydrogen fuel we needed to power our ship and its two landers. Our hydraulic converters delivered the hydrogen through a controlled fusion process that mimicked, on a small scale, the process used in stars.

"In short order, we completed an analysis of the atmosphere: it was 21 percent oxygen, 78 percent nitrogen, and 1 percent argon with trace amounts of other gases such as carbon dioxide and methane. We spent several days studying the weather patterns and the geography of the planet. The results confirmed that the planet was similar to

Senoobis—the climate and the surface would be ideal for us! The crew's spirits quickly improved.

"We also studied the surface carefully to find any evidence of intelligent life and soon found it. First, we saw a few small cities. Then, we made a remarkable discovery on one of the large land masses: there was what appeared to be a road running for 5,500 miles. It was not until well into this century that we realized it was the Great Wall of China!"

Bayn continued, "On the two large continents that stretched from pole to pole and came to be the Americas, we saw no cities or any other evidence of advanced civilizations, except in what is now Mexico and Central America. It appeared that the whole of what is now South America was open to us.

"We also discovered several large pyramidal structures in the arid land on the Northern edge of the large continent that you call Africa, implying an advanced civilization; we only realized later in this century that they were the Pyramids of Egypt. It was soon obvious that all of Earth's human civilizations were primitive compared with ours. It was too good to be true. Our spirits soared!

"Captain Mensykus and our whole crew were growing impatient. After being confined on board the *Syzilian* for almost 200 years, we could hardly wait to set foot on the ground and explore our new home. After two weeks of orbiting Karyntis, our preparations were complete. We had fully surveyed and mapped a wide swath around the planet, deployed navigation and signal buoys and, after a great deal of deliberation, decided upon a place to establish a base. We seriously considered the Northern continent that appeared to be uninhabited. But we finally chose this site near the coast on the southern continent, between the Andes Mountains and the ocean, and accessible to a diverse range of geographies."

Darz continued, "Captain Mensykus believed there were numerous intelligent, but not advanced, civilizations on Karyntis but none on the continent that we intended to colonize. Finding such a fertile and hospitable land, empty of advanced civilizations that might pose a threat to us and ready to be claimed for our own occupation, was beyond our most optimistic expectations. We had been incredibly lucky."

Sonny was curious, "Darz, what year would that have been?"

Darz thought for a moment, "Let's see, according to your calendar, that would have been about the year 1188 A.D."

Luke was astonished, "That long ago—wow! Did you ever witness any of the wars or awful turmoil that was going on about that time?"

Darz said, "No, we didn't. From our vantage point it was hard to tell what was going on with humans then because they were very primitive. If our mission hadn't come to a bad end, we would have probably made formal contact with some of the nation states then. I suspect it would have been quite a shock for them but it might have given them pause from all of their wars."

Luke laughed, "You would have been like gods to them then. While you guys were asleep for the last 700 years, however, human civilization was making progress in catching up with you technologically—if not socially. At least we can talk intelligently with you now. There's no way humans would have been able to have an intelligent conversation with you in 1200 A.D.!"

Darz nodded, "Probably not. Anyway, when the long-awaited day that Captain Mensykus had designated for our landing arrived, everyone but the landing party crowded onto the bridge to watch.

"The lander could carry a crew of two, four passengers and enough cargo to set up a small base camp. Since this would be the first landing party to reach the surface, however, there would only be four on board—Jeliko, Tangen, Forstur and Pandomis—so the lander would have more room for cargo.

"At 0600, the crew received the launch directive. The flight bay doors opened slowly allowing the intense light of Sarmadah to flood the inside of the bay as the lander advanced toward the open doors. It had been a long time since they had flown the small craft and they were all slightly anxious about flying in the unfamiliar conditions of Karyntis. Lt. Forstur released the landing gear and they were catapulted safely away from the *Syzilian* with a jolt. It was a rush, like throwing yourself into the abyss and, having survived the experience, feeling invincible.

"As soon as they had fallen a few hundred feet, Forstur engaged the thrusters and they were snapped backward as they began a gradual descent that would last three hours and bring them to a spot on the mainland that seemed to be an ideal place to establish a base.

"As their altitude decreased and the atmosphere became more dense, they gradually slowed their descent to keep from overheating. It was a tense business at first but the two pilots quickly regained their former skill at flying the Lander and were able to concentrate on finding a suitable spot to land.

"Approaching the surface at an altitude of 12,000 feet, they began to see mysterious designs scattered about on the plateau a few miles farther inland, somehow etched into the surface. It was a collection of large line drawings representing a variety of animals and geometric designs. We didn't know what to make of them and we were too busy to give them much thought."

"The Nazca Lines!" Martin added, his curiosity growing.

Darz nodded, "Yes, that's right. Not far from the lines, in a shallow valley with a small river, they found a large flat meadow that offered a good place to land and they touched down there.

"Relieved to be safely on the surface, they sat back for a few minutes and studied the sparsely wooded area around them. It was a pleasant sunny day, brighter than what they were used to, since they had been on the ship for so long. The atmosphere was also a little richer in oxygen than on Senoobis and that made them feel slightly giddy.

"The landing party was to remain at their camp for a few days while they studied the area around them. Then the lander would return to the *Syzilian* for more equipment and supplies and a new landing party would take their place. They were first of all concerned about the resources available for food, water and shelter. They studied the plant life, looked for animal life—especially intelligent life—and checked the air and water for infectious microbes. They observed lots of birds and small animals but found no intelligent species. They were surprised that all of the flying animals they saw were feathered. On Senoobis almost all of its flying creatures were featherless, more like large bats than birds.

"They had settled into their camp and had expanded its perimeter sensors and become quite relaxed with their work. It was refreshing and exhilirating to roam about in relative safety and breathe fresh air but it was a curious new world."

"But what about the lines?" Martin insisted.

Darz replied, "Well, we were puzzled about the lines too. Several days after we had gotten our base camp set up and were acclimated to our new environment, we decided to go out and see the designs close up.

"As you know, the lines can only be seen from a considerable height. They are not impressive from the ground, but it was obvious that they were quite old even though they were undisturbed. In and around the shallow scrapings, we found a few shards of pottery with simple painted designs that gave us a glimpse into the culture that had created them. We immediately wondered why a primitive culture would expend so much effort over many years to create such works.

"Several years later we learned that the name of that primitive culture was the Nazca and that they had disappeared around 700 A.D., about 500 years before our arrival.

"As you know, there have been several theories about the origin of the lines. Some believe that they were religious in nature and that the Nazca were trying to gain the favorable attention of their gods. We suspect that they may have had contact with *gods* capable of flight—there was no one on Earth who was capable of flight then so it would have been some extraterrestrial race. Oddly enough, one of the designs seemed to represent someone wearing a suit like the ones we wore to protect ourselves in hostile environments. We suspect that there is a connection between local Viracocha myths and the comment by Athrumos."

Martin shifted in his chair and stroked his chin, wondering if the lines might indeed have an extraterrestrial connection. The more he thought about it, the more plausible it seemed; maybe the theory did make sense. He decided to investigate the Viracocha myths further.

Jeliko continued, "During twilight of the second day, we had our first encounter with the local inhabitants. Our landing party had come together to share the evening meal. Not being used to the amount of physical effort we had expended in our two days on Karyntis, we were all hungry and fatigued. Forstur was finishing a detailed report of the day's activities and the discoveries we had made for transmission to the *Syzilian*. Consequently, none of us saw the slight movement in the undergrowth around them.

"That is, until Tangen turned to Forstur to express his opinion that he expected we would soon find some form of intelligent, albeit primitive, life in the area because of the patterns of the lines we had seen. He suggested that Karyntis was quite old and might be teeming with intelligent life that would gradually reveal itself. He decided that we had settled in one of the quiet backwaters of the planet that offered a most suitable place to launch our colony. It was a place, he observed, free of any beastly inhabitants who might resent our *dropping in.*

"At that moment, in the corner of his eye, a slight movement and the sharp snap of a twig caught his attention. Tangen was not startled, however, since we had seen numerous small birds and even a few small furry creatures so he expected nothing more.

"Crouched down behind some undergrowth, the young Nezeke Indian named Menaksit was both startled and angry with himself because the sound he had clumsily made gave him away. He was so amazed by our appearance—we were impressive beings to him—that when Tangen turned to stare at him, he stood mesmerized, unable to move, only a few feet away. Tangen whispered to the other three of us and we turned to see Menaksit staring back at us from some bushes.

"Two days before, Menaksit and his tribe had seen our lander as a giant menacing bird circling over head, as if searching for a favorable place to nest. They had never seen anything like it and they were frightened at first, but their curiosity soon overcame their fear. They were superstitious and sometimes talked of unseen mythical gods who might protect them if appeased. They came to believe that the members of our landing party were the gods they had always imagined, able to fly and perform acts of magic.

"Finally, not knowing what else to do, he cautiously stepped out from the brush and slowly mouthed the only word that came to mind—his own name, *Menaksit.*

"All of us stared in disbelief. It was a being rather like ourselves except that it was almost naked. And it was trying to communicate with us. Tangen glanced at Forstur. It was obviously primitive—surely not the most advanced life form on the planet.

Jeliko said, "It reminded me of those historic simulations of our people 10,000 years ago at the Academy of Natural History."

"Forstur agreed, *Judging from the small cities we'd seen scattered about the planet, I don't believe this fellow is capable of building those kinds of structures, but let's see if we can communicate with him.*

"So he stood up and slowly extended his open hands toward Menaksit and gestured for him to come closer as he repeated *Menaksit* in a reassuring tone. Then he pointed to himself and slowly mouthed "F-o-r-s-t-u-r.

"Menaksit hesitated. It was clear that Forstur wanted him to come closer so Menaksit repeated Forstur's name and moved a little closer as he watched nervously for any hint of danger. All four of us were much taller than he and dressed in a smooth colorful material that probably amazed him. And around us were various kinds of objects he had never seen before. He didn't know what to make of us, but it was obvious we were powerful, and I'm sure he was afraid to offend us. So he moved closer still, cautiously, lowering his eyes and glancing from one to the other of us obsequiously.

"Our landing party didn't think we were going to learn much from him, but he appeared friendly so we reasoned why not offer him a seat and something to drink?

"Forstur sat down and the rest of us followed his lead as Tangen, in a slow, sweeping gesture, invited Menaksit to join us. We resumed our meal while offering him food that he at first declined by shaking his head, but eventually accepted as he gingerly eased down into one of our chairs that he no doubt found remarkably comfortable.

"A few days later, Menaksit appeared again. This time there were two shy young natives with him—they called themselves Nazeke. The next time he brought Kanzakek, the patriarch of their tribe, to see for himself the strangers who were so powerful.

"Eventually Menaksit led us to his village and, over the next few years, we came to know them well and visit them often. There were only 225 members in all. I asked Epsun to see if he could master their simple spoken language. He agreed and, along with several others, quickly mastered it. It was inadequate for expressing abstract ideas, however, and there was no system of writing.

"Our survey teams were always careful not to alarm the villagers who eventually realized they had nothing to fear and became friendly to us. We usually flew into their village using our yank-flier, a small personnel transporter that could carry two people several miles.

"Dr. Yornkin was responsible for all health issues relating to Karyntis. One of his tasks was to study indigenous pathogens that might pose a health risk to our crew. When I asked him if he would be willing to visit the natives and try to help them, he readily agreed. It became his custom to visit them perhaps once a month to give them any medical attention they might need and to teach them better dietary and sanitary practices.

"The Nezeke treated us like gods. After all, we could fly and we had all sorts of gadgets that intrigued them. I think they were most impressed by our communications gear. They never could comprehend how we could talk to someone who was far away; they thought the voices coming out of the small communicators we carried were some sort of magic.

"The Nezeke fed themselves by hunting small game, gathering nuts and berries, some fishing and a little agriculture. We gave them some tools and taught them how to improve their meager efforts at farming and how to construct sturdier shelters for themselves. Most of them used the fibers of local plants to weave simple clothing although some of them wore only animal skins. We even afforded them a certain level of security from the incursions of the Hofut, a hostile tribe that lived near them. That tribe of fierce and barbaric savages, who sometimes came in the early morning hours to raid the Nezeke village, was the one thing they feared.

"There were always ongoing discussions about how we should be spending our time. In fact, there were a few members of our crew who took exception to our spending any time at all trying to help the Nazeke. At one of our staff meetings, when I suggested that we check on them, Kastgar, who was our geologist, blew up.

"*It would be fine to help them,* he said, "*but we simply don't have the time or the resources. There is no Volarion. There are only 27 of us here and we're responsible for doing everything possible to establish a colony. That's our mission—to establish a colony so we can survive. We simply can't afford any distractions.*"

"*Besides that, look at them. They're savages! It would take us years to lift them out of their primitive state. We don't have the time to educate them or look after them. We have a whole planet to master. What's more, if we do manage to establish ourselves on this planet and the inhabitants advance with our help, mark my words, someday they'll pay us back by attacking us.*"

"I calmly reminded him that we all shared his concerns, but we shouldn't let ourselves become cynical. I agreed with him that our backs were against the wall, but I argued that we shouldn't abandon the principles that had been the bedrock of our civilization for 3,000 years—I reminded him of the First Rule: *Life is sacred; help whomever you can.*

"There was real anger in his voice. *How can I not be cynical,* he ranted, *considering what has happened to the Balserios, the Volarion and Senoobis? We've spent 300 hard years trying to see the Colony Project through with every day a struggle and little to show for it now. Yet you tell me we should worry about the Nezeke!*

"I assured him that we were doing the right thing. I reminded him that we were once in that pitiful condition ourselves. I insisted that we surely have some responsibility to help them improve their primitive existence. I urged him to consider that they were quite intelligent and deserved better than their meager existence." It was to no avail.

"He stomped off muttering to himself but eventually calmed down and later apologized.

"Besides being the Communications Officer, I was a biologist by training and I had always been fascinated by how life works. I had extensively studied the evolution of plant and animal life on Senoobis in all of its manifestations and now I was excited at the prospect of studying the various forms of life that had evolved on another planet.

"While Epsun and Kastgar surveyed, drew maps, took notes and looked for ore deposits, I wandered about collecting plant and animal specimens. Those ore deposits would be mined, processed into metals and used by the colony to construct various tools, utensils and housing. When they found a promising site that appeared to be rich in gold or other metals, they were elated as much as I was when I discovered some unusual new specimen.

"During our voyage to Karyntis, I had too much time, some would say, to think about what the new world might be like. I knew that life sometimes assumed bizarre forms in response to its environment. I didn't know what kind of climatic conditions we might find on Karyntis so I often speculated about the curious creatures and exotic plants we might find there. I was so anxious when we first landed on Karyntis that I had to force myself to leave the lander: I had halfway expected some ferocious predator to rush out and devour us. Consequently, when I found only small harmless animals crawling, running, flying and swimming, I was relieved.

"The local wildlife was important in the Nazeke culture, as it was in ours, and that common interest evolved into a strong connection between us. The Nazeke noticed that we were intrigued by the many forms of plant and animal life we found so they helped us to explore and learn about the region. The plateau was such an arid place that the varieties of vegetation and animal life there were quite different from those found farther afield in the wooded areas.

"They helped us collect and study a wide variety of wild life and sometimes they surprised us by bringing us some new indigenous creature. Some of those animals, such as the turtles, were unlike anything that existed on Senoobis. And in the ocean, there were great whales, porpoises and many kinds of fish that were also strange to us.

"One creature that I discovered after a few days of wandering about near our camp was like none I had ever seen before. It was a long thin harmless-looking creature with no limbs or any other visible means of mobility—it appeared to be no more than a head on a tail! I was amazed, however, to find it moving along rather well by wriggling its long body in a sinuous motion. When I bent down in front of it to have a closer look, to my surprise, it reared up aggressively, hissed at me viciously and tried to bite me with a deadly–looking set of fangs. When I later described it to Kanzakek, I learned that the natives called it a *sakobi* and that there were several kinds of them, including some that were poisonous. From that time on, I had a terrible fear of snakes.

"Another thing I didn't like about Earth was its bugs. There were hordes of them in incredible forms. I was amazed at how many different kinds of insects there were—spiders, wasps, bees, grasshoppers, ticks, centipedes, termites, ants, butterflies, roaches and on and on—as well as their vast numbers. I particularly detested the mosquitoes, the mites, the chiggers and the flies, all of which seemed to be drawn to me. From my first day on the surface, they made my life miserable.

"If I was outside and I stopped moving for a moment, the tiny predators descended upon me with a vengeance. And when I sweated, they were drawn to me in even greater numbers. I especially hated the tiny mosquitoes—although I couldn't feel them light on me, they made me itch unbearably. After weeks of constant irritation and spirited Senoobian swearing, however, I finally learned to wear light pants and shirts with long sleeves. I also prevailed upon Dr. Yornkin who soon came up with a concoction that repelled most of them, at last giving me some relief.

"Of course, my crewmates also suffered from the bites and stings of the tiny predators—we simply had not experienced that kind of creature in such large numbers on Senoobis. Many thousands of years ago, Senoobis had experienced a series of ice ages that killed off most of its insect-like creatures. Consequently, we never had to suffer vast swarms of insects like those that infest the Earth. Indeed, the insect-like creatures on Senoobis were much larger than they are here, but there weren't so many of them. That was most fortunate—can you imagine a housefly that weighed a quarter-pound or a mosquito with a three-foot wingspan? For some reason, thankfully, they avoided us, preferring instead other small creatures as their natural prey."

Luke said, "Whoa! Animal life on Senoobis and Earth was very different."

"Oh, yes," Bayn replied, "Just as humans and Senoobians are different. But ironically it was partly the compassion we felt for the Nezeke that led to destruction of the *Syzilian*. I'll tell you how it happened."

20

DEATHLY ILL

One summer morning our survey team stopped at the village that was in the same direction as the area they planned to explore. They were distressed at what they found: Chief Kanzakek and half of the village were seriously ill. The whole tribe was weak and demoralized.

"It was obvious that some sort of epidemic had broken out. Out of 225 members, fully a third of them were ill. They suffered from a high fever, nausea and headaches and several members of the village had already died. Dr. Yornkin was glad he had decided to accompany the team.

"Kastgar, the geologist, however, was impatient as usual to get on with their explorations and he complained to Amantis that they should be going.

"Amantis understood his frustration and tried to calm him down. *All right, if you're set on moving on, we'll go*, he said, *but I don't see any harm in leaving Dr. Yornkin here while we continue our work. Perhaps he can treat their illness and we can pick him up on the way back to our camp. Would that be all right with you, Dr. Yornkin?* he asked. He readily agreed and so did Kastgar.

"Observing the tribe in their pitiful condition, Dr. Yornkin determined to do whatever he could to help them. He instructed them to boil their water and cook their food thoroughly. He showed them how to make a simple soap that would improve their sanitary conditions. In the field, his medical equipment was limited but he examined several of them, took blood samples for analysis on the *Syzilian* and treated them with antibiotics. He had no idea whether or not the antibiotics he had given them would work, but he was confident that, in time, he could develop an effective vaccine.

"I'm sure he knew there was a chance that we Senoobians might also be susceptible to the pathogen that was making the Nazeke ill. And there was the possibility that he might not have an effective antibiotic. Nonetheless, his sense of compassion was so strong and his confidence in his own medical skills so great that he readily took that risk.

"The survey team returned late that afternoon to pick up Dr. Yornkin who promised to return to the village in a few days. The villagers were grateful for his help and those who were able came to see our team off.

"Within the hour, our team was back at its camp. The team secured the camp, gathered the newly acquired specimens, loaded them aboard the lander and lifted off for the *Syzilian*. Three hours later they were docked on board. The usual routine was to have dinner together in the early evening and to review the team's findings at the weekly meeting the following morning.

Bayn said, "Since I had been up late the night before, I decided to skip dinner and retire early. Darz and Jeliko, who had been on the previous watch, were still asleep when the survey team returned.

"After turning in their reports at the morning meeting, they were ready to relax in the afternoon, but Dr. Yornkin began to develop a high fever and the sweats. His body ached and he felt weak. The next survey team was unable to leave the ship as that experience was repeated with the rest of the crew over the next two days. Dr. Yornkin's condition worsened until he was delirious; less than 48 hours later he died. Before long, most of the crew was ill. Those who were able tried to care for the others but to no avail.

"In the recreation compartment, Jeliko and Darz were alarmed to find Lt. Maxsyn lying there, too sick to stand. He warned them that the whole crew was infected by some unknown pathogen and that we should not touch him.

"They ran to the bridge and found only Amantis Brazynis there feeling sick; the others were too ill to stand their watch. He told us that the other members of the survey team had fallen ill soon after arriving and that Dr. Yornkin was dead. The whole crew, except for the four of us—Amantis, Darz, Jeliko and me—had become extremely ill.

"I groaned in disbelief as the realization of what was happening sunk in. The survey team had picked up a lethal virus that had somehow gotten by Yornkin and infected the whole crew. Jeliko and

Darz were the last to be exposed to the infected survey team and the last to get sick because they were asleep when the team returned.

"Amantis had seen the crew get sick until they couldn't eat or care for themselves. The antibiotics they took didn't seem to have any effect; he found the other three members of the survey team dead in their bunks. He ran to the CO's stateroom to check on him; he was in bed, delirious with a high fever. *He's not going to make it,* Amantis thought, *and I don't know if I can manage much longer myself.*

"Darz was also getting sick.

"I turned to look at him and, although he was sweating profusely and losing strength himself, I gripped him by the arm to steady him.

"Jeliko was feeling unsteady on her feet and had to sit down. *Everyone I've checked on is down with this thing. We're the only ones still on our feet,* she said, *but I'm getting it too. I'm aching and sweating and starting to feel nauseous. It's some kind of virus. I'm afraid it's going to kill us all! If Yornkin hadn't gotten sick himself, he would probably have figured out a cure. I don't know what we'll do now.*

"I myself was feeling like I did when I recovered from hyper-sleep and was having trouble collecting my thoughts, but the thought of sleep brought a revelation. *Wait a minute,* I said. *The ship is on autopilot. Suppose we get into the sleep modules and time them out for 48 days with an accelerated draw down—our metabolisms will slow down drastically and so will the viruses'. The cryogenic gases will permeate every cell in our bodies and the virus as well. Maybe those gases will kill it before it can kill us. It's our only chance!*"

"Jeliko looked at me at first as if I were mad but, after a moment's thought, she said, *You may be right. I don't see that we have any other choice. It will give us a hell of a hangover but, if nothing else, it will buy us some time. It's worth a shot!*"

"Darz was willing to go along with anything that might make him feel better. He nodded his agreement, *Let's try it.*"

"Amantis said, *Okay, but we've got to do it now—come on!*" The four of us made our way as quickly as we could to the sleep modules. When we reached them, Darz's vision was becoming blurred. Sprawled on the deck near the modules were two crewmembers, one dead and one dying, who seemed to have had the same idea. The one who was still alive raised a hand toward us and moved his lips as if trying to speak but no sound came. It was Kastgar. He had recognized

Jeliko and for a moment there was a look of contempt in his eyes. Then he slumped back and was still. Darz bent over to help him up but realized it was too late. Motioning to the other three, he yelled, *Hurry! Get in. I'll set the master timer for 45 days and take us down to level twelve in one hour."*

"All three of us gasped! *Level 12 in one hour!* That was the most rapid takedown to the lowest level of sustainable metabolic activity. We would be barely alive. The shock from such a rapid drop in our metabolic rates could kill us. If the cryogenic gas didn't destroy the virus, it would kill us. Either way, we would never wake up but at least it would be a painless death.

"The first section had six modules in two rows of three: #1, in front of #2; #3, in front of #4; and #5, in front of #6. Jeliko, Amantis and I tumbled into a module and pulled the canopy down over us. I took module #1, leaving #2 for Darz. Jeliko took #3 but Amantis, in his feverish condition, took #5 which was at the front next to Jeliko's module.

"Darz steadied himself with one hand on the master control panel. His head was spinning, his free hand was shaking and his vision was blurred as he tried to make out the settings on the panel. He had to be sure he activated the correct modules, so he tried hard to focus as he entered the settings for the deepest sleep with a one-hour take down. Slipping into unconsciousness, he activated the first four modules.

"Staggering to module #2, Darz managed to roll his body clumsily over the flange into it. But in his haste, he failed to set the master timer. If no duration was selected, the module would not awaken its occupant until the emergency override was activated manually by a crewmember or automatically by the ship's sensors.

"The ship was in a stable orbit above the Earth but it began to lose altitude ever so slightly. After 700 years, it was only 19,000 feet above the surface. The friction from the thicker atmosphere at that altitude caused the hull to heat up so much that the emergency override was activated and the three of us were awakened. We barely managed to escape from the ship in one of its landers before it exploded. We lost everything except for some gear stored on the lander. We were in shock, of course, and didn't know what to do except return here to the site of our former base.

"But, after 700 years, the Earth had changed. We've managed to survive here since 1908, in spite of a soaring human population. Our future here is uncertain now so we're moving to a safer place. The information we've given you is our gift to the human race. I hope it will be useful to you."

At that point, Jeliko stood up to stretch. She said, "Now you know how we came to be here. What you do, if anything, with the information we've given you, is up to you."

Luke was curious. "Where are you going?" he asked.

Darz considered the question thoughtfully before answering. "Luke, I'm sorry but we can't tell you. Where we're going has to be kept a secret for now; too many humans of the wrong kind know where we live. We've spent the last few years building a new home, one that's safer where we can *disappear*."

Jeliko said, "After you pass on the information we've given you, I expect some humans, who may not have our best interests at heart, are going to come looking for us. It's best if you can honestly say you don't know where we are."

Martin, Ellen and Karen sat there for a long time, pondering everything they had heard. At last Martin stood up and said, "We will be leaving soon. I have a few days of research to do on the lines before we go so I can write a paper when we return to the States. Thank you for sharing your story with us. Whatever should be done now to alert humandkind to this threat is in the hands of these two young men. You've given us a new perspective on our small piece of the galaxy. I am grateful for that."

Bayn nodded. "You're welcome." He said, "I believe our information is in good hands. Now it's time to say *good night*." They shook hands and bade each other farewell.

After Karen said goodbye to Amara, she slipped aside to talk with Luke; she didn't want to lose touch with him. "I hope we can see each other again back in the States," she ventured.

"I was hoping the same thing," he said. "If you don't mind, I'd like to call you. Maybe you could come to Washington. I'd like to show you around the capital."

"I'd like that," she said. "Maybe you could come to Tennessee in the fall—we could go to an Eagles game." Their hug turned into a tentative kiss before they returned to the others.

21

ALBERTO CALDERON

Alberto Calderon and his gang of thugs were back in town. He checked into the *Hotel Cahuachi* wearing his customary white suit, white fedora and blue silk tie. In his hair there were hints of gray, and the lines etched in his face made him look older than his 54 years. At the hotel he drank a lot, smoked incessantly and often played cards until the early morning. He scowled when he spoke to the hotel staff but he gave lavish tips. When he fixed his dark brown eyes on those who displeased him, they were mesmerized as if by a cobra poised to strike.

It was his habit to return to Nazca at least once a year to check on the small operation he had there and to handle any problems that required his attention. It was the kind of homecoming that the good citizens of Nazca dreaded because there was always trouble. Besides that, there was a disturbing pattern of people disappearing when he was in town. Some of the old timers still recalled with distaste the young tough who had bragged that one day he would be rich and powerful no matter what it took. Calderon the young bully did grow up to be rich and powerful but also arrogant, cruel and corrupt.

His ambitions outgrew humble Nazca so he moved on in the early 80's to *Tarapoto* in the North of Peru, taking a couple of loyal thugs with him. The city was already well-known for its drug smuggling and violence and there, in that wild and lawless area near the Northern edge of the Amazon basin 210 miles northeast of Lima, he felt at home.

The *Huallaga Valley* around Tarapoto is dominated by coca barons who control the illegal coca-growing industry and make the valley one of the most dangerous areas in the world. The region remains beyond the reach of the government in Lima and more or less beyond law and order. Some locals have embraced the lawlessness as a way of life, even though drug money and automatic weapons have ruined many people's lives.

Vast tracts of rain forest in the region have been destroyed by increasing numbers of *colonos*, workers who clear the trees to grow huge quantities of the coca leaves that are their most lucrative cash crop. Calderon became involved in transporting illegal coca paste from Tarapoto to Columbia where it was processed into cocaine for the US market. Within a few years he was a major player in the Tarapoto drug smuggling trade.

But he still had roots in Nazca: there was some family, a couple of ex-girlfriends he had treated badly and some petty thugs who kept him informed about the goings-on.

The one person he always visited was his aged mother; he knew she worried about him and continually prayed for him. As a doting son, he worried about her and made sure she was well cared for. He didn't know why but the thought of her dying frightened him.

Calderon never knew the father who left his mother when he was a small child. And he never bothered to see his older sister Paulina, who feared him for his cruelty, or his young nephew.

In a shootout with the Vellejo cartel several years before, he had murdered Marco's parents, Ana María and Alejandro Montecarlo. He actually wound up in jail for a few days, charged with murder, but somehow he got off and made his way back to Tarapoto where he stayed until the trouble in Nazca blew over. He was busy running his rapidly expanding business in Tarapoto so he quickly forgot about the Montecarlos.

When he finally returned to Nazca, he bribed Pedro Gonzales, the police chief, so he no longer had to worry about being charged with the murders at the Montecarlo home. From then on, he returned with impunity twice a year, to check on his mother and oversee his business there.

It became his custom when he was in Nazca to hunt down anyone who had been a hindrance to his enterprises. If the word got out that he was coming to town, those who feared him would hide out until it was safe to return.

Before leaving Tarapoto, he made inquiries and, when he learned that Sargent Arturo was putting the pressure on his local minions, it was the last straw. He also learned that Arturo had been spending time with the three foreigners. When he was a boy himself, he had heard tales about them, how they had come from some unknown place many years before. He was not sure whether there were two or three of them but, as far as he knew, they had always lived near Nazca. He had never seen them himself, but he thought of them as monstrosities and wondered why Arturo consorted with such odd and insignificant people; he decided to kill them as well.

Sargent Luis Arturo was wiry, 45 years old and most of the local señoras thought him handsome. His black hair was short, he had a strong chin and he had a friendly smile for everyone he met. He was a deputy with the small Nazca police department when he investigated the murder of the Montecarlos 23 years before. It was he who had hauled Calderon off to jail only to have him escape. He was still determined to arrest Calderon again.

Most of the local police were intimidated by Calderon and afraid to interfere with his criminal activities. But Arturo took his job seriously and stood up to Calderon's organization. First Calderon sent threats to him. Then an exasperated Calderon ordered his lieutenants to arrange a meeting with Arturo to warn him that he could either back off or suffer a fatal *accident*. But Arturo had refused to be intimidated, and Calderon decided that on his next visit he would take care of Arturo himself.

Besides Arturo, there were two other men on Calderon's hit list. His informants had told his lieutenant, Rodolfo Flores, about the *gringos* who had come to town and were snooping around. Flores made a few calls to contacts in the States and eventually learned that the two men worked for the U.S. government. He told Calderon that he suspected they worked for the D.E.A. and that they had been seen at *La Taberna* with the strange ones. Flores was proud of his efficiency.

Calderon suspected that something was up. *Had Arturo talked to the authorities in Lima about his drug trafficking? Were the Peruvians cooperating with the Americans again? It didn't matter; he had his informants in Lima as well.* Tonight he intended to have a leisurely dinner while his minions rounded up his victims. He would take care of all of his *problems* at the same time and fly back to Tarapoto the next day.

Before this visit, Calderon planned to catch Arturo by surprise so he kept his trip to Nazca a carefully guarded secret. Usually when he came to town, he would relax and drink whisky for a day or two before getting down to business so those he was gunning for had time to get away. As soon as he arrived this time, however, he ordered his thugs to bring Arturo to him.

Later that evening as Calderon was having dinner with Pedro Gonzales, Flores approached his boss with the news. In hushed tones Flores informed him, "Arturo is at *La Taberna*."

Calderon nodded approvingly, "Good. Now what about the two *gringos*?"

"The boys will be pickin' them up any time now, boss."

Calderon was pleased and flashed a sinister smile at Gonzales. "Good. Bring all of them to me at midnight. This time I'm going to finish some old business. Everyone in this town will know better than to cross me."

Gonzales shifted uncomfortably in his chair at the implied threat; he considered Calderon a cocked pistol that could go off without warning. Flores nodded enthusiastically as he stood up to leave; he had things to do before the meeting at midnight.

Indeed, as Flores was leaving Calderon, on the other side of town one man knocked on the door of Sonny and Luke's hotel room while two others stood in the shadows with guns drawn.

Carlos Navarro was tending bar as usual at *La Taberna*. Luis Arturo and his younger brother Juan were there, relaxing. After the murders of Marco's parents, Luis and the Senoobians had become close friends and he was pleased that, under the parenting of the Senoobians, Marco had become a well-adjusted and competent young man.

At 8:00, Felipe, who was the assistant manager at the *Hotel Cahuachi*, came in. Carlos knew immediately by the expression on his face that something was wrong. Felipe had an anxious look about him as he leaned over the bar to tell Carlos in hushed tones, "Calderon is back in town."

Carlos didn't welcome the news that Calderon had returned. He gestured toward Luis, "You had better warn him."

Felipe nodded and then, getting Luis's attention, motioned him over.

As he reached the bar, Felipe took a deep breath. "Luis, Calderon's back in town, at the *Hotel Cahuachi*. He arrived earlier today with several of his thugs."

Luis grimaced.

"Luis, be careful. He's in a foul mood."

Arturo was both angry and worried as he returned to his table. He sat down quietly but Juan could tell by the downcast look on his face that there was trouble."

"Luis, what's wrong? It's Calderon, isn't it?" Juan asked, worried by his brother's somber look.

"Yes, I've got to arrest him," he said. Memories of Calderon's crimes and the death of the Montecarlos flooded back into his mind.

"Can't you get one of the others on the police force to help you?" Juan asked.

"No, Gonzales refuses to assign anyone else to help me."

There was no one else at the bar so Carlos and Felipe came over to join them.

They recalled all the crimes Nazca has suffered for so long at the hands of Alberto Calderon. "What do you think he's doing back in Nazca?" Carlos asked.

"I don't know but I'm sure he's up to no good. He knows I vowed to send him to jail. He's tried before and I expect he will try again to have me killed."

After another drink, Arturo got into his old pickup for the 30-minute drive to his home on the outskirts of Nazca. As he pulled away from *La Taberna*, a car parked in the alley suddenly turned on its lights, pulled out from the side of the building and came toward him. Alarmed by the suspicious appearance of the car, he made an abrupt turn at the next intersection and then a hard left at the next street. He was being followed; the car behind him also made both turns in an obvious effort to stay close to him. *Madre de Dios, what am I to do?* In a near panic, he thought *I can't lead them to my own home. They'll shoot me before I can get inside and lock the door!*

The faster he drove, the faster they pursued. He was terrified he would wreck and kill himself, but his instincts told him that, if he didn't escape his pursuer, he would be killed anyway. At the next intersection, the light turned red as he approached. He cursed the timing at first but then, seeing the stopped cars at the light, instinctively stomped on the accelerator and sped on through the light, barely avoiding a collision. The car behind him was forced to stop, but before he could make his getaway, its driver also slammed the accelerator to the floor and sped after him.

A few blocks later the chase was over. A car blocked the street and there were three men in front of it with guns drawn. Luis slammed on the brakes as he tried to find some other way out but there was none. In seconds the car that was following them skidded to a stop behind him and three more men with guns drawn leaped from the car. There was nowhere to go.

One of the three men from the car that had followed him, a burley man with a long thin scar down the right side of his face, opened Luis' door and angrily yelled at him to get out of the truck. As Luis stood up, the man cursed him and slammed his fist into Luis's jaw, knocking him to the ground. Then the man kicked him brutally in the side again and again before pulling him to his feet and dragging him away.

After binding Luis's wrists and roughly pushing him into the backseat, the burley man got into the driver's seat. Another man, smaller than the driver but more menacing, got into the seat beside him. Two other men got back into the car that had blocked the street. Then both of the cars backed up and started back the way they had come. Behind them the last of the thugs got into Luis' car and followed.

They had only gone a short distance when the man on the passenger side turned around while brandishing a pistol and snarled at Luis, "Good evening, my friend. My name is Juan Escobar. I'm warning you that I am not a patient man. Do you see this?" He waved a pistol in his face. "If you give me the least bit of trouble, I will be happy to kill you now. So don't try anything. Beeg mistake!"

Then, pointing to his accomplice, he said, "Actually my friend, the only reason I don't kill you now is that it would mess up his car. We're taking you to a place where it don't matter." And then he laughed sadistically.

The man who was driving glanced back at him. "He's a liar. He don't kill you right now because we have to deliver you in one piece so someone else can kill you."

Luis glanced at each of them, feeling powerless to do anything. He thought to himself, *what kind of men are these? They call you "friend" while they relish the thought of killing you!*

A few blocks later, the driver glanced at his watch and then at Manuel. "It's time."

Escobar turned around and pushed a cell phone at Luis. "Call your friends—the strange ones. Tell them to meet us at midnight or we'll kill you. Then give me the phone and I'll give them directions."

Luis could hardly think; his hands were shaking so badly he could hardly dial the number. Escobar turned on the dome light.

Bayn and Darz were tired, feeling more aches and pains than usual, although the hours they worked at their two small mines had grown shorter as they had gotten older. After a hot shower and a glass of Sangria, they were eager to forget the dust and grime of their work and rest their sore muscles.

Darz sat back in his chair and closed his eyes, trying to relax. Something didn't feel right. He felt restless and uneasy. He looked up at Bayn and Jeliko who also seemed unsettled and then at Amara who was sitting nearby reading.

As he tried to sort out his feelings, the phone rang, startling all three of them. Darz bolted upright and grabbed the phone. It was Luis.

"Two men have taken me as a hostage—they want you to meet them or they're going to kill me!"

Darz said, "Luis, is it Calderon?"

"Yes."

Escobar snatched the phone from Luis' hand. "That's right. We're going to kill him if you don't meet us at midnight."

Darz put his hand over the receiver and motioned to Bayn and Jeliko. "Calderon's got Luis!"

Darz spoke calmly into the phone, "All right, we'll meet you wherever you say. Just don't hurt him."

Escobar growled into the phone, "I thought you'd see it my way. Take Highway 26 East toward *Puquio* until you see the road to *Vilcanchos*. Turn left and go 15 miles until you see an entrance with rock walls on the right. Turn there and follow the dirt road for two miles until you see an old barn. Be there at midnight. Don't try anything or you'll never see him alive."

Darz yelled into the phone, "What do you want?" but he had already hung up.

He turned to Bayn and Jeliko, at a loss for words. He tried hard to collect his thoughts. "Calderon's men are threatening to kill him if we don't meet them at midnight at an old farm near *Vilcanchos*."

Bayn had an inspiration, "We have three hours to get there. If we use the lander, we can get there fast, scout out the area and come up with a plan. Darz, can you get it ready to go?"

Without thinking, Darz said "Sure!" Then he added under his breath, not quite sure that he could deliver on getting the lander airborne, "I'll see what I can do." He realized they hadn't flown the lander in several months. They hadn't been able to acquire the right kind of fuel; and the crude fuel they had managed to concoct was rough on the engines and caused it to sputter and jerk unreliably.

Bayn turned to Jeliko, Marco and Amara, "Stay here and secure the place. We'll get back as soon as we can." He grabbed the global positioning device they had gotten from the *Mankuriun* on the way out. "So you'll know where we are," he said. The G.P.D. would generate a signal that would make it easy to find them.

Jeliko nodded and begged them to be careful.

Ten minutes later, Bayn leapt into the lander as Darz started the preflight sequence. The two engines coughed and sputtered as the engines warmed and the lander rolled slowly toward the launch doors. Outside the hangar, they paused for a minute while Darz revved the engines. Then he pulled back on the yoke and they were airborne. The lander balked and sputtered for a moment and then, in a surge of power, rose quickly to level out at 500 feet as they began to follow the road toward the ocean. If Darz could keep the lander airborne, they would be there well before midnight, allowing them to gain the advantage of surprise.

22

THE BRETIN

When the car finally stopped outside the old barn, Arturo was dragged from it to face a man dressed in a white business suit. Enjoying the complete power he had over Arturo, Calderon eyed him coldly without a word.

The men threw Luis to the ground with his hands still bound behind him and a bloody cut over his right eye. His mind was racing as he tried to figure out some way to escape his captors while behind his back he struggled desperately to free his hands.

A few minutes later another car drove up; Sonny and Luke were pulled from it and marched inside. Luke had obviously been in a scuffle.

Calderon looked at his watch. It was almost 11:00, and everything was going as planned. Finally, as he proudly brandished a Walthen PPK pistol, Calderon addressed all of them. "You may be wondering why I brought you all here. We're waiting for a couple more and then we'll get down to business, so make yourselves comfortable." Around them stood two men with AK-47's and two others with pistols.

At 11:15, the Senoobians glided to a landing a mile from the barn and started off toward it at a trot. Twenty minutes later they could see the barn with five cars parked around it and light showing through the cracks between the boards in its walls. There was a board missing from one part of the wall and they approached it cautiously, hoping to see inside without giving themselves away. There against the far wall they could see Luis, Luke, and Sonny; all of them guarded by four men with guns. And there was Calderon talking to Flores.

Suddenly there was a rasping voice behind them. "Don't move!" They turned slowly to see a man with a gun pointed at them and another man coming up behind him out of the shadows.

The first man spoke in a sarcastic tone, "Well, what do you know? Here they are! Right on time."

"Let's go", he said, pointing to their left and prodding Darz with his pistol. "You don't want to keep the boss waiting."

As they came through the open door into the lighted area within the barn, the man with the gun yelled out to Calderon, "Look who we found hiding outside, boss!"

Calderon smiled at them with sadistic pleasure. "Ah, the *caballeros*!"

Calderon gloated, turning to Luis and making a fist, "At last I have you in the palm of my hand. You've avoided me for a long time and I don't like being avoided. Tonight you—", he gestured toward the others, "and they will all pay for your insolence."

Luis spoke up, his voice hard. "You are a bully, a drug trafficker and a murderer. God will punish you for what you've done."

Calderon only leered at him, "I don't think so, Stupido. I am not afraid, but you should be."

Darz knew they were all going to be killed unless they did something fast. He tried to control his growing rage so he could think clearly.

Bayn looked at Darz and then around him as his mind raced in search of some way to foil their captors.

Calderon continued his rant at Luis. "You meddling, insolent dog! I warned you to stay out of my business. You underestimated me. Now you'll die for it as I promised."

Luis spit at him. "You're not above the law, Calderon. You can kill me but I've turned over the evidence I have against you and your thugs to the Department of Justice in Lima. Your day is coming."

Calderon was livid and over Luis in an instant, seizing him by the throat. "Spit at me again and I'll shoot you right now. You're as stupid as you are reckless. Don't you know I can have your evidence *lost*. I have people in the Department who can fix anything for me."

Sonny yelled at Calderon, "Let him go!"

Finally, he let go of Luis's throat and turned to eye Luke and Sonny with contempt. "Ah, our *gringo* friends. Sent here to spy on us no doubt. Well, it makes my day when I can kill a *gringo* or two. On your feet!"

Calderon turned to the rest of his prisoners. "Get up! All of you," he snarled, "We're going for a little walk. This won't take long."

They stood up as the gunmen motioned them toward the door of the barn. Calderon moved through the door, smugly brandishing his pistol, and motioned for them to follow him toward an old pick up with a load of dirt, "This way, my friends," he said sadistically, "We have a job—" He paused in mid-sentence, looking around, startled.

There were several loud clanking sounds as metal canisters hit the floor and rolled into the middle of the barn. They exploded with a whoosh and a thick white cloud of gas filled the barn. *Nerve gas?* Bayn wondered dully.

Then came an iridescent blue light that seemed to settle over them. In the fog they were disoriented and couldn't see. The iridescent light faded into a dim glow and all of them crumpled to the ground, unconscious.

At first Bayn was having a dream: he seemed to be getting out of a hyper-sleep module. Several minutes later as he regained his sight and his balance, he looked up to see vague figures dressed in grey combat gear, looking down at him curiously. He recognized the Bretin from the *Mankuriun.*

Darz tried unsteadily to stand up but sat back down.

Agoyin appeared. "Sorry to have to use the canisters, Sir, but we had to knock everyone out so we could sort things out."

"Yes, well, that's quite all right," Darz said, still fuzzy headed, as he tried again to rise. "You saved our lives but how did you know we were in danger and where we were?" Darz asked, puzzled.

Agoyin was surprised. "Why, didn't you know? Jeliko radioed our ship and gave us your coordinates."

"Jeliko? Of course." He looked around, trying to grasp what had happened, and there to his surprise were Marco and Amara helping Bayn up. "What in the name of *Dolahktus* are you two doing here?" he scolded.

"We only wanted to help," Amara grinned innocently.

"Yes, we were worried about you and the others," Marco said, gesturing toward Bayn and their human friends."

"Well, call your mother and let her know we're okay," Darz snapped.

A few feet away Tavin Dolyvek was helping Luis to his feet. Two more Bretin were guarding Calderon and his henchmen who were sitting up slowly. Their guns lay in a heap against the wall.

Calderon, fully alert, pulled himself up straight and looked around, trying to make sense of the situation. "What do you think you're doing?" he growled at the nearest of the two Bretin as he tried to stand.

Dolyvek pointed at him sternly and motioned for him to stay down.

Calderon was furious. "You can't tell me what to do. Do you know who I am? I'll bury you here with all the others who have defied me!" Flores pulled himself up behind his boss. Realizing in the same instant that Dolyvek's weapon was in its holster, Calderon and Flores looked at each other and then lunged at him.

Dolyvek didn't flinch. As Calderon reached him from the front and Flores attacked him from the side, suddenly in an explosion of movement he leaped up and, whirling around, kicked Calderon in the stomach and followed that with a hard blow to Flores' jaw. Then like a giant coiled spring that had twisted as far as it could, he reversed the circular motion and in two sweeping kicks slammed them both again as they crumbled to the ground.

When Calderon came to his senses, seeing the Bretin preoccupied, he nudged Flores and growled in a whisper, "While they're having their little reunion, let's take them. Grab one of the guns." He nodded toward several guns that lay on the ground about ten feet away against the wall of the barn. Flores nodded.

Calderon sprang into action, rolling toward the guns and grabbing for a pistol, as did Flores. With pistols in hand, they twisted around, pointing at the Bretin, intending to shoot them before they realized what was happening. Before they could pull the trigger, however, Marco came flying through the air, knocking the gun from Calderon's hand and landing two hard blows to his head. He fell to the ground and stayed there.

Looking down at Calderon, Marco was overwhelmed by his emotions. This was the man who had murdered both his parents. This was the man he had hated and vowed to kill. He paused at first, unsure if he could do it. He remembered the desperate look on his mother's face as she tried to protect him. With a broad stance that would allow him to kick Calderon hard, he put all of his strength into it.

When Flores saw Calderon go down, he turned toward Marco, his pistol ready to fire, but Luis suddenly appeared and shot him.

Bayn motioned to Dolyvek, "Let's secure these murderers and then we can talk." Dolyvek nodded his agreement as Bayn walked over to Luis.

"Looks like you have a case for attempted murder and, I'm sorry to say it, but I believe you'll find some of Calderon's previous victims buried in that old well."

Luis nodded, "Yes, I'm afraid you're right about that. If your Bretin friends hadn't shown up when they did, we'd all be dead now at the hands of Señor Calderon. I'll take care of things from here."

Sonny and Luke conferred briefly; then Sonny spoke up, "Luis, we'll be glad to help you transport these guys to the jail."

Luis was relieved. "Thanks, I can use the help."

Dolyvek pulled Bayn aside and spoke to him at length in Kuterin. When he had finished, Bayn nodded and they walked over to Luke and Sonny.

"Now you've met some of the Bretin I was telling you about. This is Ensign Tavin Dolyvek. He and his comrades are from a Bretin starship orbiting the Earth. His CO is concerned that reports of their presence here might fall into the wrong hands and lead to panic and a dangerous confrontation. He does not want to meet with humans. Their ship is returning to their home planet in a few days. He requests that you keep their involvement in this incident to yourselves. Will you do that?"

Luke said, "Since they saved our lives, that seems like a reasonable request. What do you think, Sonny?"

"Yes, I'll agree to it," Sonny stammered. He had learned a little Kuterin from Bayn. Now he felt the urge to say *thank you* in Kuterin, but his mind was a complete blank.

Luis, Sonny and Luke with the help of the two Bretin and Marco stood Calderon and his gang together, bound their hands behind their backs and put them in the back seats of two of the cars. They placed Flores' body in the trunk of the car that Sonny drove. Luke drove the other car while Luis guarded Calderon and two of his henchmen who were bound in the back seat as they started for the Nazca jail.

As the two cars left the farm, the two Senoobians, Amara and Marco went aboard the Bretin shuttle and sat down to talk with the crew. Bayn related to the Bretin how they had happened to be there at the farm that night.

The lander and the shuttle were immediately flown back to the landing field at Naksoris. Since the Senoobian's lander needed service badly, the Bretin crew offered to spend the night there and help them work on it the next day.

Monday afternoon, they accepted an invitation from Captain Markovin to visit him aboard the *Mankuriun* again on Tuesday. He would dispatch their shuttle to pick the four of them up at 1500

When they arrived on the *Mankuriun*, the Captain was clearly relieved. "I understand you were almost murdered by a gang of humans!"

Bayn said, "Yes, your Bretin arrived just in time. They saved our lives and we thank you and them for their help. Of course, it was Jeliko who thought to radio for help. If she hadn't been able to reach you, Darz and I and four of our human friends would all be dead now."

"I'm pleased that we could help and that all ended well. Now, if I can just get our ship safely away before anything else bad happens, I'll be relieved."

He turned serious. "I'm beginning to believe this planet is bad luck. These humans seem to be a violent and corrupt species; too many terrible things happen here. There's a lot of crime and they seem to be irresponsible in managing their planet's resources. From our perspective, the ecology of the planet appears to be deteriorating."

Bayn replied sadly, "I would have to agree with you, although there are some reasonable humans. With regard to the planet, it does look spoiled now but if only you could have seen it when the *Syzilian* first arrived. It was beautiful! It's only in the last fifty years that it has taken such a dramatic turn for the worse."

23

THE REVENGE OF CALDERON

There was a whirlwind of activity playing out around Nazca. Luke and Sonny were leaving for Washington D.C. as soon as they had said goodbye to Marco and the Senoobians. Luke had worked on the report he was going to give Broucelli, limiting it to the Senoobians and omitting any reference to the Bretin or the *Mankuriun*. Luke and Sonny were careful not to mention them at all since the Bretin had saved their lives at the abandoned farm.

Luis was busy conferring with his boss as to the best way to bring Calderon to trial. Finally, he and Gonzales went to lunch, heatedly discussing the best way to proceed.

In his small cell, Alberto Calderon was also busy, planning both his escape and his revenge. He had recovered from the shock of what had happened at the barn and was intent on escaping. He was a street fighter who had learned there was usually some way, no matter who might get hurt, to deal with a problem. He also had an advantage, unknown to Arturo, which was the complicity of two members of the police department.

One of the jailors, Jorge Cabrera, had been his paid informant for years. If there were others around when Jorge brought food to Calderon, only a furtive glance acknowledging their connection would pass between them. If the other two guards were outside, Calderon would spout instructions to Jorge in quick hushed whispers.

Nor did Luis know that Pedro Gonzales was on Calderon's payroll as well.

Gonzales had told Calderon that the Senoobians would be leaving for good in a few days after saying goodbye to their friends. Calderon had replied that it was too bad they were leaving so soon because it didn't leave much time for him to get even with them. They had foiled his plans and they would pay for it with their lives. Calderon instructed Gonzales to summon Juan Escobar and two of his local henchmen as the agents of his revenge. He had employed them as assassins before; all three of them were excellent marksmen.

When the Senoobians returned to Naksoris, they were transformed; the three older Senoobians were dressed in informal but neat dark blue military fatigues. They seemed younger and their impeccable grooming gave them a distinguished look. Even Amara looked like a princess

As soon as the Senoobians had settled in for the day, they notified their small circle of friends that in three days Amara would be leaving Earth for good. They invited all of them to Naksoris to see her off.

Amara's emotions were in turmoil. She was excited about the adventure she faced, but the thought of leaving her Senoobian family and Marco behind was almost too painful to bear. *Could she even stand to be confined on a starship for so long?* she wondered.

She spent the next day packing and handling all of the details that had to be completed before she left. The next morning she couldn't find Marco so she took one last stroll around Naksoris by herself. It had been her home her entire life. Now, with boxes stacked here and there, it appeared dull and lifeless. There was a lonely and sullen feel about the place, as if it were peeved at being abandoned.

That afternoon, to their surprise, Bayn received a message from Commander Stoveris that the Captain had decided to accept their invitation for a short visit the day before their departure. Stoveris confided that the Captain had been against it at first but, in the end, his curiosity at visiting the surface and meeting some humans overcame his concerns. Commander Stoveris would remain on the ship to continue preparations for their departure the next day.

Amara spent most of her time visiting with Marco and reminiscing about their times together. Before she knew it, it was time to say goodbye. Before their human friends arrived at Naksoris to see her off, she put on a celebratory headdress that made her look like Cleopatra in spite of the air of sadness about the occasion.

As she opened the door to invite them in, a solemn Father Tony stepped forward and embraced her warmly. He was concerned that she was going to some distant, unknown world full of danger.

He recalled their walks and conversations over the years. Like her parents, he had been a teacher to her, but he had learned a lot from her as well. Thanks to the Senoobians, his concept of the Universe had expanded.

He spoke to her in a voice full of sadness. "My dear Amara, the day I never expected is here. I'm going to miss your friendship and our conversations. I have no idea where it is you're going but my prayers will go with you."

She said solemnly, "And I will miss you, Father. You've been a good friend and a great comfort to all of us." She thanked him profusely for his friendship and then hugged him warmly one last time.

She spent the next couple of hours reminiscing with Luis and Phillipe.

Sonny spoke to her in Kuterin, eager to show off. "Thank you for everything and good luck. I will never forget you. You are the most beautiful alien I know." In the last few days Bayn had spent several hours with him, teaching him their native language.

Amara laughed. "Not bad. Maybe I'll send you a radio message to let you know we've reached Nanzema safely. Let's see, it will take us 30 years to get there and another six years for my message to reach you here on Earth. Hah. You'll be an old man with a wife and lots of grandchildren by then."

When Darz walked up, Jeliko whispered in his ear: "36 years from now, I doubt they'll even remember we were here," she joked.

After chatting for a few more minutes, it was time to go. They all walked outside to the large field to meet the Bretin shuttle, carrying the CO for his brief visit to Naksoris. Then the shuttle would carry her to the *Mankuriun* for its departure.

Father Tony's thoughts went back to the first time he had seen the three Senoobians in the plaza near his church. He had thought them strange at first and was a little hesitant at approaching them, but he reminded himself that we are all God's children no matter how different we seem. At first he thought they were teasing him when they eventually confided in him that they were from a far away planet. When he got to know them better, however, they seemed no more different than travelers from Bolivia.

They had been eager to understand human ways and seemed particularly interested in religion because it was not practiced on their world. He smiled when he recalled some of the questions they had asked. They were tiresome at first, but he realized he had gained new insights by trying to explain confusing points of doctrine to them.

He had often wondered why their world had been destroyed. *Had his angry Christian God punished them for not believing in him? Surely that was not the case; obviously no one had introduced them to Christianity. He didn't know what to think. He did know that they were good—men? Should he even call them men? They really weren't men. They were from another world—but surely God ruled over their world as well. It was really pointless to wonder about such things. Only God could sort it all out. Nevertheless, whatever or wherever Amara was, he would miss her.*

It was just before 1600 when his thoughts were interrupted by the sound of the shuttle approaching from the west. Inside, the Bretin pilot brought the shuttle in slowly as the four Senoobians and the handful of humans surrounding them awaited the touch down.

Second Lt. Karseen Panzer was an excellent pilot. He had made several flights to Earth and he brought the ship down carefully near the group of people. There were nine people waiting to welcome the shuttle, and each one of them watched the ship intently. It settled gently onto the hard ground and, a few minutes later, the hatch opened.

From a brushy knoll 300 yards from the shuttle that sat in the grassy field adjoining Naksoris, three men watched as its hatch slid open. Without taking his eyes off the craft, Jorge Cabrera covered his mouth and muttered in a hushed voice to the other man who was only a few feet away, "Juan, what the hell kind of airplane is that!"

Juan Escobar was wondering the same thing. *Maybe it was some kind of new military craft.* He shrugged his shoulders *who knows?*

Diego León was crouched fifty or sixty feet away from them, partly hidden by a small stand of trees, as he nervously watched the odd craft.

The hatch was fully open, letting down a set of steps wide enough for two people to descend at the same time. They readied their rifles. Their instructions were to kill the Bretin crewmembers first so there would be no one to fly the shuttle. Then they could methodically kill the others who would be exposed in the open field.

As the small group led by Bayn approached the shuttle, Tavin Dolyvek, the copilot, opened the hatch and waved to those on the ground. A moment later, Karseen Panzer joined him at the opening and both moved aside to allow their passenger to descend first.

Bayn and Jeliko stood by patiently while Amara, standing safely a short distance away as the shuttle's engines shut down, hugged Marco tightly.

Captain Markovin stepped through the hatch into the sunlight and paused momentarily to adjust his eyes to the brightness and take in the scene around him. He watched with amusement as Darz pointed him out to the humans who waved excitedly to him.

At that instant, three gunshots rang out across the field, followed by a loud metallic ping as one bullet struck the shuttle and ricocheted harmlessly from its hull. A second bullet ripped through Bayn's left shoulder. Startled, Darz and Jeliko looked back to see him crumple to the ground, a wet red stain spreading down his left arm.

In the same instant Captain Markovin's head jerked backward as a third bullet struck him in the forehead, killing him instantly. Thinking he had stumbled, Karseen Panzer instinctively reached forward to steady his Captain as his body slumped down and an explosion of red enveloped his head. Realizing what had happened, in what seemed like a nightmare, he cradled the dead body of his beloved Captain against his chest.

Reacting quickly, he screamed to his copilot, "The Captain's dead. Lift off! Lift off! Now!" He dragged the Captain's body back into the shuttle as the hatch began to close and then, slumping against the bulkhead, still clutching his Captain's dead body, crushed with disbelief, he sobbed, "No, no, no!"

As the ship lifted off, three more shots were fired at the group of people who had rushed to the other side of the shuttle seeking cover and were now lying flat on the ground.

In the shuttle, Panzer's shock turned to rage. He carefully eased the Captain's body into a rack and scrambled into the cockpit. Dolyvek had already rotated the shuttle so that the white-hot exhaust from its engines would not incinerate those who were flattened on the ground. As the shuttle rose slowly, Panzer looked frantically for the source of the gunfire and when they had gained a little altitude, he saw it. "Over there", he yelled, pointing it out to Dolyvek.

The assassins on the ground, seeing that their bullets had no effect and that the shuttle was swinging around toward them, realized that the only thing left for them to do was to save themselves. They fired at it again as they turned to flee but to no avail. They raced toward the two cars they had left by the side of the road a few hundred feet away as it moved toward them, steadily gaining speed.

Panzer also saw the cars and, taking aim with the laser-guided cannon, fired at the first car that erupted in a brilliant explosion, knocking all three men to the ground and rendering Escobar unconscious. Seconds later, the second car exploded with a deafening blast.

Before the two men could get on their feet, the shuttle settled down near them. Its door dropped open and Panzer leaped from the ramp and, bellowing like a madman, rushed toward them as they fired at him while scattering in panic. Before Cabrera could get off a second shot, Panzer reached him and, in one quick blow, knocked the gun from his hand. Then whirling about, Panzer brought his fist down hard against his neck.

As Cabrera crumpled to the ground, Panzer continued on toward the second killer without slowing down. Overtaking him and spinning him around, Panzer's kick struck León in the stomach, doubling him over.

Looking around frantically, León saw a wooded area nearby, and broke free, running toward it. But Panzer, determined that the assassin would not escape, ran after him with such quick strides that he quickly overtook him. Once more, Panzer used a hard blow to the neck to knock him down.

But as Panzer stood over him, León jerked his pistol upward, firing point blank, hitting Panzer first in the side and then in the stomach. Panzer reacted so quickly that the sharp pain of the bullets ripping through his body only enraged him more. León fired again as Panzer slapped the gun from his hand. Three times Panzer hit him and then, with ebbing strength, slumped down beside him. León scrambled to his feet and resumed his frantic dash for the stand of trees.

Standing with binoculars on a small rise to the south of the field, Pedro Gonzales watched the unfolding events in disbelief; things had not gone as he had planned. The caballeros in the aircraft were more formidable than he had expected.

He quickly considered his options. He had released Calderon who was, no doubt, leisurely going about his affairs, confident that his plan was being carried out. The last thing he wanted to do was incur Calderon's wrath. He could lie to Calderon that they had killed the three Senoobians and that their bodies had been taken away in some unusual craft—to God knows where.

Not realizing that Gonzales was on Calderon's payroll, Arturo had told his boss everything he and Calderon needed to know to put their plan together: the Senoobians would get together with their human friends at their home one last time before they left the next day. It was too good an opportunity to pass up; everyone that Calderon wanted to take revenge on would be there and they would be sitting ducks. Then he could take care of Arturo at his leisure. What a pity Gonzales thought; the man was too trusting, too naïve.

Escobar appeared to be dead and León had escaped. Cabrera was the problem now; there was a good chance he would expose the relationship between Calderon and himself. It was clear what he had to do. He lifted the rifle to his shoulder, aimed carefully and fired. Still stunned, Cabrera was sitting on the ground, rubbing his neck when the bullet hit him in the chest, killing him instantly.

Seeing Panzer shot, Dolyvek set the shuttle on the ground, leaped from the cockpit and raced toward him, fearing the worst. As he ran by Cabrera, he was startled to see the man's body jerk backward from the impact of the gunshot and crumple to the ground. He looked around frantically, trying to determine the source of the shot from the sound and the direction of the bullet. Then he saw the small flash of sunlight reflected from the barrel of the gun that Gonzales had used.

Luis ran to Escobar as Darz and Marco reached Panzer at a run. They also heard the shot and, looking toward the sound, saw the flash of light. Since Bayn was in considerable pain and bleeding profusely, Jeliko and Father Tony had remained with him.

Dolyvek, upon seeing Darz and Marco reach Panzer, turned and sprinted back to the shuttle. Not knowing how badly Panzer was injured or even if he was alive, Dolyvek leaped aboard it and quickly maneuvered near Panzer so he could be evacuated to the *Mankuriun* for treatment by the ship's doctor. As they carried him aboard and laid him in the rack next to the one that held the Captain's body, however,

Panzer breathed his last. Dolyvek bent over him and closed his friend's eyes. They were like brothers. As Dolyvek turned to look at the others, he realized that Bayn had also been shot. He motioned for them to stand aside; as they lifted off, he could see the blue fiat speeding away from the rise where the killer had shot Cabrera.

Luis saw it too; the car belonged to his boss, Pedro Gonzales!

Dolyvek felt the rage rising within him. As he turned the shuttle and pulled back on the throttle, the lander surged forward toward the car. Flipping switches quickly and methodically, he activated the homing system for another of the lander's small missiles. The homing system quickly locked on the car and the missile launched. The car exploded in a shower of metal debris. Dolyvek turned the shuttle around and set it down near the spot where Bayn was lying with several others gathered around him.

As Luis reached the group, pushing a groggy Escobar in front of him, he pulled Jeliko and Darz aside. "It was my boss in the Fiat. I'm afraid Calderon is behind this." Darz clenched his fists, unable to speak.

Just then Dolyvek nudged Jeliko. "We'd better get him on board. He's lost a lot of blood." Amara followed teary-eyed as Darz and Marco carried Bayn on board the lander. When he was strapped into a cot, Darz and Marco leaped from the shuttle as the door closed.

Darz motioned to Marco, "Let's get the lander ready while Amara tells everyone goodbye."

She spoke to the small, unsettled group. "Don't worry, Bayn's tough. He's going to be okay. We're going to fly our lander to the *Mankuriun* so we can be with him. Father will bring him back as soon as he's been treated . . . ," she choked up, "but I won't be coming back."

When the lander was ready, Jeliko and Marco jumped aboard and Darz fired up the engines. Amara waved to her human friends, "I won't forget you. Good luck to all of you." With one lingering look and a broad salute to them all, she turned and disappeared inside. The lander's engines reached a fevered pitch and minutes later they were winging their way toward the *Mankuriun*.

As the lander disappeared from view, leaving the humans to deal with the shock of what had happened, they found themselves at a loss for words, saddened by Amara's departure and worried about Bayn's injury.

Sonny and Luke stood for a moment, unsure what to do next.

As Father Tony looked skyward, his eyes closed, his hands raised in solemn benediction, he silently prayed for their safety. Then he and Phillipe left for the church.

So much had happened in the last three days that Luis felt numb emotionally. The violence that had just occurred overwhelmed him at first, but it forced him to make a choice, causing him to dig in his heels and defiantly declare, "Enough! I will have no more of this." There were great challenges ahead, yet somehow he felt empowered.

Luke and Sonny were left standing there in the field alone at Naksoris. They looked around one last time before leaving for the airport in Lima. The next morning, they boarded the plane that would take them back to Washington.

As soon as the shuttle was on board the *Mankuriun*, Doctor Eyveer rushed Bayn to sick bay. He had lost a lot of blood and was unconscious, but two hours later, to their relief, he had survived the surgery, although his condition was still critical.

Darz, Jeliko, Amara and Marco arrived later in their lander and rushed to be with him. All they could do was wait for him to improve. Marco and Amara walked back and forth along the corridors, savoring their newfound intimacy, oblivious to the animosity of some of the crew.

A brooding Palander Stoveris sat in the XO's chair, staring down at the Earth. He couldn't believe their misfortune. His CO and one of his senior officers murdered! As soon as Bayn was well enough to return to the surface, they would be ready to begin their long voyage to Nanzema. His thoughts were muddled: *what would he say to his Captain's spouse? Or to Lt. Panzer's spouse? What action should he take in view of the Captain's death?* Over the last few hours, his shock at losing his captain had given way to denial, then to anger, and finally to a barely controllable rage. In fact, the whole crew was enraged. Some were pleading for retribution against the humans—any humans.

The *Mankuriun* transmitted status reports every twelve hours to Nanzema. The hardest thing he had ever done was to draft the report giving the details of the Captain's and Panzer's deaths. And there was Bayn; he was near death as well.

His thoughts turned to the criminals who had carried out the unprovoked attacks. Jeliko had informed him about the likelihood that the human named Calderon was behind the attacks. The attackers must be punished for such a heinous crime. On Nanzema the perpetrators of such violent acts would be dealt with quickly and harshly.

As the Earth moved deeper into night, yellow blotches and countless pin pricks of light appeared, sweeping across its surface. A huge patchwork of light grew brighter. He noticed a sprawling human city farther north. The anger continued to well up inside him. *What an odious species these humans are.* He hated them—all of them; he even resented Marco.

He glanced over at the weapons panel, focusing on the controls that would arm and launch their six Hyperion missiles. *Only one missile would be required to kill every person in the entire city.* His fingers moved smoothly over the master control on the small panel by his seat. He looked up at Nuferas, the Officer of the Deck, who was regarding him curiously. "Weapons Officer to the bridge! Get Darz and Marco up here too," he ordered.

Nuferas hesitated briefly, not sure what new crisis the XO confronted. He turned to the intercom and buzzed Doksolus, the Weapons Officer. "The XO wants you on the bridge."

Doksolus was alarmed. "What's going on?"

"I don't know. He was slumped in his chair with a blank look on his face; then he ordered me to call you and then Darz and Marco to the bridge. Sorry, I've got to go!"

The intercom buzzed, startling all three of them. It was the OOD calling. "Darz, the XO wants you and Marco on the bridge."

Darz said, "We're on our way. What does he want?"

The OOD replied, "Don't know but it's urgent."

When they reached the bridge, Doksolus and Dolyvek were there talking with the XO who was speaking loudly and angrily, gesturing wildly. When the XO saw them, he motioned them over to him. His tone was stern. "I've been mulling over what needs to be done about the deaths of our Captain and Lt. Panzer. What am I going to say to their spouses? When we return to Nanzema, I will have the unfortunate duty of offering my condolences to Ajuleta and Mirite for the deaths of their husbands. There will be no honor in any of this for me or this ship if I can't deliver their murderers to Nanzema to be punished."

Darz was confused. "What do you mean?"

Stoveris' face was flushed; Darz wondered if he might have a heart attack. "I mean that the murderers must be held accountable," he almost shouted. He strode over to the large viewing port on the bridge. In the distance, far below them to the North, a large city sprawled between the ocean and the Andes. I'm going to do one of two things: I will take the murderers into custody . . . ," He jabbed his finger forcefully toward a large map. "or I'll destroy that whole city."

Darz was aghast. It was Lima! "Sir, that's seven million humans—I don't think that's a good idea."

Stoveris was adamant. "At this point, I don't care what you think. I prefer not to take that course but, if we can't apprehend the murderers, I will destroy the city. If these human vermin choose to kill each other, so be it, but I will not allow them to murder my crew. I hold them all accountable!" He was ranting now: "I want both of you to return to the surface immediately. Dolyvek will be your pilot on one of the shuttles. I'll give you one day to find the murderers and bring them to me. I've postponed our departure until day after tomorrow at 1800; I suggest you leave immediately before he escapes. If you fail, I'll send a Hyperion into the heart of, uhhh, THAT human city."

Darz and Marco glanced at each other, stunned by the XO's orders. It was obvious there would be no further discussion. Darz snapped to attention, "As you command, Sir."

Doksolus stood stiffly at attention, looking uncomfortable, his eyes fixed straight ahead.

As they walked briskly from the bridge with Dolyvek, Marco gave Darz a questioning look, as if to say, "What do we do now?"

Darz's mind was racing. "We'd better call Luis. And Phillipe. We're going to need all the help we can get to find Calderon quickly."

Marco said, "I'll call Luis on his cell phone and ask him to contact Phillipe."

"Good idea. Maybe we can reach him while Dolyvek is doing the preflight. I'd better call Jeliko and let her know what's going on. She and Amara will need to be with Bayn when he wakes up."

After several minutes, Marco managed to reach Luis. "The XO's threatening to destroy Lima if we don't find Calderon and bring him to the ship. Darz and I will be landing at Naksoris in three hours. Can you or Father Tony locate Calderon and then tell us where to meet you?"

"He's threatening what?" Luis cried. His mind was still reeling from the shock of the day's events. In exchange for the chance to disappear, Escobar had told him everything. Their boss was on Calderon's payroll, and he and Calderon had used the information innocently provided by Luis to plan their attack. Now Luis felt guilty that he hadn't realized Escobar was corrupt.

He couldn't sort out his thoughts to think straight, but he heard himself saying dully, "Yes, of course, I'll see what I can do."

Luis had been trying to decide what to do himself. *What would he say in the report he would have to write? He had shot and killed Flores in self-defense at the farm. Cabrera had been shot and killed by his boss Gonzales, the police chief. Now Gonzales was dead. No one would believe that Gonzales had killed his own man or that aliens had killed him. How would he explain it all?*

Three hours later Darz, Marco and Dolyvek were landing in the wide field by Naksoris. Luis was waiting for them nervously by his old beat up Nissun pickup. He had learned from his inquiries that Calderon was at *El Huarango*, the finest restaurant in Nazca.

Marco said, "Father, you and Dolyvek stay here. Luis and I will handle this." He slid into the passenger side of Luis' pickup while Darz and Dolyvek remained with the shuttle. Luis warned Marco they would have to act quickly to capture Calderon before he left *El Huarango*, no doubt to spend the night with one of the fawning trollops he kept on call.

Calderon was ensconced on the rooftop patio with León, his new lieutenant and the only one of the assassins who had escaped the fiasco at Naksoris. After Flores' death at the farm, he had decided to place León in charge of overseeing his affairs in Nazca. He had hated to lose Flores who had always been loyal and reliable in carrying out his orders with unusual zeal. But León, who had worked closely with Flores, knew what he expected and had shown considerable promise. After the prerequisite bout of drinking, León would be properly installed as his surrogate and Calderon would leave for Tarapoto the next morning.

Marco waited with Luis in the shadows by Calderon's car behind the restaurant. As Calderon and León left the tavern and opened their car's doors, Luis stepped forward with his gun drawn, "Alberto Calderon, you're under arrest."

Calderon was drunk and unsteady. Looking up through glazed eyes and recognizing Luis, Calderon spat at him, "You again! So you're not dead! Well, I'll kill you myself, you meddlesome dog." He carried a Walther PPK in a shoulder holster as usual, but Luis reached him before he could draw it to fire and, in one smooth sweep, knocked it from his hand and gave him a sharp blow to the jaw. Calderon was stunned but strong; he straightened up and struggled violently but Luis had had enough. For once, he lost control and lashed out at Calderon, bringing his pistol butt down hard on Calderon's head, shoving him into the car as he slumped down unconscious.

As León pulled his pistol, Marco gripped his arm, causing his pistol to discharge into the air. After a brief struggle Marco subdued him and forced him into the back seat with Calderon. While Luis trained his pistol on the two dazed thugs, Marco called Darz on his communicator to let him know that they had arrested the two murderers and were on their way to the lander. Luis slammed the accelerator down and they sped off toward the shuttle almost 30 miles away.

24

THE UPAKSANOCHIN

On the *Mankuriun*, the crew was jubilant as preparations continued for their departure for Nanzema. They were fed up with Karyntis and anxious to leave it. On the other hand, they were pleased that the human murderer and his accomplice had been apprehended. Palander Stoveris had refused to leave his chair on the bridge for the past twelve hours; he had been unable to sleep after the Captain's murder and he was tired. He would be glad to leave this planet; after so many years of exemplary service, his Captain had been murdered—on his watch!

The XO's intercom flashed on; it was the ship's Operations Officer, obviously alarmed. "Sir, there's a large unidentified craft coming up fast from the Earth's dawn horizon. It's pinging all around us!"

The XO was instantly alert. "Do you think they've located us?" he yelled into the intercom.

"I don't think so. The pings seem to be in a random pattern. Recommend we go full passive."

"So directed," the XO replied tersely.

He switched over to Deratis, the Communications Officer. "Continue radio silence. Suspend all transmissions to the Council. Have you developed a radio signature that might give us a clue who our visitor is?"

"I'm running a scan now but nothing so far," Deratis replied.

The XO remembered the shuttle that would be returning soon. Damn! The *Mankuriun* was cloaked but not the shuttle and its radio transmissions might give it away.

He glanced over at the large Operations Display. The contact's speed was 1,800 mph; its range—2,900 miles.

"Well, let me know the minute you've got something. In the meantime, we'd better go to battle stations." He released the intercom button and turned to the OOD

"Sound general quarters. Any word from the shuttle yet?"

Nuferas turned to the alarm panel as he answered the XO "Sounding general quarters. Nothing from the shuttle yet, Sir."

The loud hair-raising *reeehro-reeehro* sound of general quarters erupted from the P.A. system catching the crew by surprise. The Ops Officer rushed onto the bridge. "It's not a human shuttle. It's too big to be anything but a starship," he announced.

The XO shot him a questioning glance. "Not a human satellite then?"

"No, definitely not. The contact's way too slow and it's not in orbit like a satellite."

The XO frowned. His voice was tense. "A Peyrian ship?"

"It could be the Peyrian ship we've been wondering about."

The XO nodded gravely. "Well, we can't do anything until the shuttle is on board."

On the surface, the two cars reached the waiting shuttle as Dolyvek lowered the ramp. The two prisoners were manhandled aboard in spite of Calderon's resistance and frequent outbursts. The two were securely strapped in and minutes later the shuttle was airborne again. Dolyvek radioed the *Mankuriun* to give a status report but there was no response. Ten minutes later, he tried again. No response. At first he was puzzled; then, alarmed.

Darz was sitting in the copilot's seat next to him. Something was wrong. He glanced at Dolyvek. "Do you have any idea why we wouldn't be getting a response?"

"I have no idea. I'll try again in a few minutes," Dolyvek replied.

On board the *Mankuriun*, the crew was on full alert, manning their battle stations. The ship was in cloaking mode, invisible.

The shuttle's radio frequency was patched into the bridge." When the message came over the speaker, everyone was relieved. "Shuttle two is airborne, returning to mother ship. E.T.A. 90 minutes."

Stoveris didn't want to risk revealing the ship's position by transmitting a radio signal so he ordered the ship's radio operator not to respond to the shuttle's messages. He sat deep in thought, considering their situation. They couldn't leave until the shuttle was safely on board. Another two hours. It would take that long for the shuttle to reach the *Mankuriun* and complete docking procedures.

The intercom next to the XO lit up and buzzed. It was Ops. "Sir, the contact has slowed to 1,200 mph. Range 1,100 miles. I think it's picked up the shuttle!"

"*Kruknogru!*" Stoveris exclaimed in exasperation. "She'll track the shuttle right to us." There had been a chance that the mystery ship might pass them at a distance and never realize they were there. But not now.

As the shuttle made its approach, Deratis called again. "Sir, she's changed course and is headed directly toward us."

"Damn bad timing for the shuttle!" Stoveris grumbled to the OOD

As they reached the *Mankuriun*, Dolyvek and Darz were puzzled to find that the approach lights were not on. The docking bay was ready for them, however.

Thirty minutes later they were on board. Stoveris was there to meet them. "We have a visitor. It may be a Peyrian ship. That's why we didn't answer your radio messages. But it seems they tracked your shuttle to us anyway."

Dolyvek was aghast. "I'm Sorry, Sir. I was so relieved to capture these two murderers that I didn't consider the need for radio silence."

"Nor, did I," he replied. At that moment, he saw Calderon and León being led away from the shuttle. The muscles in his jaws tightened and the anger in his eyes flashed a deadly warning. "So here are the murderers!"

Pointing to Calderon, Jeliko said, "Yes, Sir. That's the one responsible for the murders of the Captain and Lt. Panzer." Gesturing toward León, she continued, "And that is one of his accomplices."

Stoveris strode over to Calderon and stared him straight in the eye with obvious contempt. The temptation to strangle him slowly was hard to resist. He was inches from Calderon's face; his eyes burned with the warning *make one move and I will strangle you with my bare hands!* Finally he turned away in disgust, "Take this one to compartment D-15 and secure it. Take the other one to D-21. I'll deal with them later."

Calderon was afraid. His eyes darted around the small compartment, trying to make sense of what was happening. He had assumed at first that he was being flown to the United States for trial on drug smuggling charges. That didn't bother him too much. He had access to high-powered lawyers and he could bribe others in key positions. But something was wrong. There were no humans around him—only the weird ones speaking in their god-awful tongue. *Where was he and what the hell was going on?*

In his own compartment, León looked around him, feeling nauseated from the rough ascent in the shuttle. Claustrophobic and beginning to panic, he fell to his knees and prayed fervently for the first time in many years.

On his way back to the bridge, Stoveris' communicator buzzed: it was Deratis. "Sir, we're being hailed on the shuttle's radio frequency. It's Kuterin!"

"Kuterin! How can that be?"

Deratis said, "I don't know, Sir, but it doesn't sound quite right. It may be a Peyrian ship. They may think we're Senoobians. Maybe they have someone who speaks Kuterin like they did when they attacked the *Volarion*."

In Ops the officer on duty checked the display again. The contact's range was 700 miles. It had slowed to 575 mph. He called Stoveris to let him know.

Deratis broke in again, "Sir, their cloaking's good but we're getting a soft visual. It appears to be about a half mile wide, a flat round shape."

When Stoveris reached the bridge, Darz were already there by Jeliko.

Stoveris turned to the OOD "Replay the message, please."

The voice spoke in Kuterin; it was somewhat of a hissing monotone but the authority it expressed was clear:

Tyguta: This is the Starship Upaksanochin from the planet Peyr commanded by Captain Nezyrkipis Idannup. Please identify yourself. Do you require assistance?

"Peyrians!" A flood of emotions overcame him—apprehension, hatred, anger.

Stoveris said to Deratis, "He doesn't know who we are except that we're Senoobians . The less we tell him, the better. Send this message:

CAPT N Idannup: This is Commander Palander Stoveris, Commanding Officer of the Starship Tyguta. Assistance is not required. Please state your intentions?"

Stoveris looked at the Ops Display again. The contact's range was 210 miles. It had slowed to 175 mph. The tension on the bridge was palpable.

After several minutes, the reply came from the *Upaksanochin*:

CDR P Stoveris: Please state your home planet. We are here to investigate the attack on our colony. Do you have knowledge of that attack? CAPT N Idannup/PS Upaksanochin.

Stoveris struggled hard to comprehend the situation. His head was throbbing. *This was the race that had destroyed the Volarion.*

Finally he scribbled a message and gave it to Deratis. "Transmit this."

CAPT N Idannup: Our ancestors traveled on the starship Volarion from our planet Senoobis to establish a colony on this planet and save our race from extinction. Your ancestors revealed their hostile nature by using deception to destroy the Volarion in an unprovoked attack. We know nothing about your colony. Cdr P Stoveris/Tyguta.

Deratis transmitted it.

Jeliko thought to herself *Ouch! That's not very diplomatic.*

Stoveris glanced up at the Tactical Display on the bridge. The contact's range was 50 miles. It had slowed to 45 mph.

Stoveris switched on the intercom and called Doksolus, the Weapons Officer. "The Hyperions are armed?"

"Yes, Sir."

"And locked on target?"

"No, Sir."

Stoveris spoke sternly and decisively into the intercom, "Doksolus, arm Hyperions and acquire target."

After a brief wait, Doksolus reported, "Target acquired, Sir. Thirty-nine miles and closing slowly."

A half hour later, the reply came from the *Upaksanochin*:

CDR P Stoveris: I do not believe you speak the truth. The destruction of our colony was a senseless and reprehensible act. I have considered it in the context of the past contact between our races however and I understand that you might feel threatened. Although I consider such hostile action unjustified, we will take no action against you unless provoked. Let there be no hostilities between us. CAPT N Idannup/PS Upaksanochin.

Stoveris said to Jeliko, "Transmit this:

CAPT N Idannup: I speak the truth. Now I ask you: why did the Peyrians attack the Volarion and then threaten the Syzilian? Cdr P Stoveris/Tyguta.

After a while, the reply came from the *Upaksanochin*:

CDR P Stoveris: We bear no responsibility for the attack on the Volarion. At that time Peyr was controlled by the Frunjin, a ruthless faction that gained control of our government and pursued war with the goal of dominating our sector of the galaxy. Our people have a long history of contact with this planet—the one we call Chookuvot and you call Karyntis; when the Frunjin learned that your ancestors were also planning to colonize it, they ordered the attack on the Volarion.

There were many who opposed that hostile action. We had already suffered from a long and devastating war with another race on another planet when a rebellion broke out, triggered in part by the attack on the Volarion. It lasted for many years and almost destroyed our race before we were able to overthrow the Frunjin. It is only in the last 300 years that we have recovered from the wars that killed one-third of our people. Capt N Idannup/PS Upaksanochin.

Stoveris said to Jeliko, "Transmit this:

CAPT N Idannup: How did the Frunjin know that we planned to colonize Karyntis. Why did they not contact us about their colony? Cdr P Stoveris/Tyguta.

He studied the ship, only 30 miles away, through the televiewer on the bridge; the *Upaksanochin* reminded him of a dark dangerous predator, ready to spring.

A short time later the reply came:

CDR P Stoveris: Frunjin patrols intercepted both of the probes you launched to Peyr. Frunjin engineers converted them from transmitters to receivers. Their linguists were eventually able to master your language and learn about your mission from the messages they intercepted. They knew that if they attacked the Syzilian, the Volarion would escape, so they waited until the Volarion was near our star system.

We regret that hostile action was taken against the Volarion but it happened a long time ago. It would be to our mutual advantage to talk to each other in person so that we might avoid any future hostilities. May I suggest a meeting of envoys on the surface to disuss how we might repair our relations.

I am curious, CDR Stoveris: is your ship the successor of the Syzilian? CAPT N Idannup/PS Upaksanochin.

Stoveris angrily slumped back in his chair. "That's none of his business." He studied the faces of those gathered around him, stopping at Darz and Jeliko. "What do you think? Can we trust Idannup?"

They considered his question for a moment. Then Darz said, "There's no way to know. Nothing but gut-feeling to go on but Idannup seems to be straightforward. We ourselves have wondered why the Peyrians never showed up after their threat to the *Syzilian*. The story makes sense; after all, governments do change for better or worse—maybe their government did change for the better. After all, if they had their hands full with a rebellion at home, they might have suspended their missions to Earth."

"On the other hand," Jeliko said, "It could just as well be a deception. Since our misjudgment could be fatal, I recommend proceeding cautiously."

Stoveris glanced at the Tactical Ops Display again. The contact's range was 26 miles. It had slowed to 32 mph. He was feeling cornered. *The Upaksanochin was getting too close for comfort.*

Jeliko studied Stoveris as he and his officers heatedly debated the situation. She could imagine a similar debate going on between the CO and his staff on the *Upaksanochin*.

There was indeed a heated debate occurring on the *Upaksanochin*. The ship was on full alert and battle stations were manned. Idannup was pleased to have found the Senoobian starship but there were troubling questions. *How advanced was it? Were there others? What had happened to the Syzilian?* he wondered.

When his Communications Officer picked up radio signals in a part of the waveband unused by humans, Idannup was shocked. After analysis, the signals were determined to be Senoobian since the language was Kuterin. Their two linguists accessed their archives on the Kuterin language and studied it while the *Upaksanochin* searched for the Senoobian ship. Of all the 43 languages they had archived, it was the easiest to learn.

Now his patience was wearing thin. The dialog between the Senoobian CO and himself was not going well. Commander Stoveris was tight-lipped, not cooperative in the least.

He sat in the Captain's chair surrounded by several senior officers as they debated how to proceed. His greenish brow was furrowed and his yellow eyes intense as he considered his options. His orders were to investigate the loss of the colony that a previous Peyrian mission had founded several decades ago in an arid part of Chookuvot, the planet humans called Earth. The assumption was that humans had destroyed the colony in one of the frequent wars they waged. Now he suspected that it was Sennobians, not humans, who had destroyed their colony.

His orders included instructions that, if he should encounter another advanced race, although it was considered unlikely, he should avoid hostilities unless attacked. He should attempt to meet one of its leaders and suggest forming an alliance to their mutual benefit. He was to gather as much intelligence about them as possible.

Captain Idannup and his officers believed that a half-truth is always more useful than the whole truth. He was further instructed to reveal, as a matter of *urgency*, that there was a more powerful life form spreading throughout their part of the galaxy. The Peyrian High Command suggested that by misleading the other race about the threat, thus implying common ground, Captain Idannup might discover the extent of their capabilities and even influence them to lower their defenses. Now they were again dealing with Senoobians and the *Volarion* incident had come up. He decided to address the issue with half-truths and expressions of regret about the incident.

Idannup's XO said to him, "We're not going to get anything out of that son of a bitch. I recommend we attack the *Tyguta* now!"

Idannup said, "We must be ready to launch a surprise attack but we should proceed cautiously and learn what we can first. We don't yet know the extent of their weaponry, their home planet, or if there are other starships nearby. Let's continue our ruse and see what happens."

On the *Mankuriun* Commander Stoveris also reached a decision. He motioned to Deratis, "Send this message:"

CAPT N Idannup: Your explanation of the duplicitous conduct of your ancestors was informative but I do not trust you nor do I wish to meet with your envoys. Please withdraw immediately. Cdr P Stoveris/Tyguta.

Idannup's reply finally reached the *Mankuriun* an hour later:

CDR Stoveris: I understand your hesitation to trust us. My ancestors destroyed your ship; your predecessors destroyed our colony. Your race and mine have suffered enough. This must not go any further. The unfortunate event that framed the meeting of our races happened many centuries ago. We pursue only peace and our mutual security.

Besides, we face a threat to both our species. There is a yellow star that we call Afrundees 109 light years from Peyr. That star system is home to a kind of being who is nothing like us; we and the humans, and I expect you as well, are carbon-based life forms but they are not. They are dangerous and far more powerful than we are. The Imad, as we call them, have expanded throughout the adjoining sector and into this sector which contains both Peyr and Chookuvot. One of our ships found an obscure planet where the Imad had exterminated the local inhabitants except for a few who were allowed to survive on reservations.

Since our survival and yours is at risk, I had hoped to meet you so we could begin a dialog and eventually cooperate to our mutual benefit. I know now that is not possible. I believe you have been untruthful and that your predecessors destroyed our colony. We are departing this planet. Let there be no further hostilities between us. CAPT N Idannup/PS Upaksanochin.

Deratis came on the intercom, "Sir, the *Upaksanochin* is turning away."

As soon as Deratis rang off, Doksolus called the XO, "Shall I disarm the Hyperions, Sir?"

Stoveris didn't answer. It seemed that he had not heard. Instead, he clenched his teeth and scowled fiercely. "It won't end this way," he vowed under his breath.

"Sir, shall I disarm the Hyperions?"

Stoveris replied in a steady voice, "No! On my command, fire 1, 2 and 3."

Doksolus couldn't believe what he had heard. *Surely there was some mistake.* "Sir, I . . ."

Stoveris' voice, calm but insistent, came over the intercom to Doksolus, "Range, please."

"Range—18 miles, Sir. Speed—60 mph," Doksolus replied, feeling sick to his stomach.

His voice was firm. "Fire number 1!" Stoveris ordered.

"Sir, Are you . . ."

"Damn it! Doksolus, Fire #1, NOW!" he bellowed.

Doksolus was jolted into action. The order overcame his hesitation. He pulled the first release for Hyperion #1. He nodded to his assistant who pulled the confirming release. Immediately the *Mankuriun* shook slightly as the missile erupted from its launch tube in a puff of blue-gray smoke and raced toward the *Upaksanochin* only 18 miles away.

On the bridge no one uttered a word. Jeliko felt sick to her stomach—*We're taking revenge on those who weren't even alive when the Volarion was destroyed. How can we hold the Upaksanochin accountable for something that happened hundreds of years ago?*

Doksolus looked at the radar screen, still in shock, barely able to comprehend the visual display before him.

"Fire number 2," Stoveris ordered.

When that missile was safely away, he ordered, "Fire number 3."

On board the *Upaksanochin*, Idannup nodded his approval to his XO who turned to his Weapons Officer. "Ready all Lasers. When we are broadside to the *Tyguta*, on my command, activate Lasers. Target the bridge." The beams from the four powerful Arkonium Lasers would reach their target far faster than any missile could, quickly cut through the hull of the starship, breach the hull and kill the crew.

The Weapons Officer, replied, "On your command, Sir."

The status report Captain Idannup had composed minutes earlier was on its way to Peyr and to its sister starship, the *Grunashar*, at the speed of light. In less than an hour the report would reach the *Grunashar* as she explored Jupiter's moon Europa but it would take the starship itself three to five years to disengage and reach the Earth.

On the bridge of the *Upaksanochin*, just as he opened his mouth to order the lasers to be fired, Idannup was startled to see the flashes of light that signaled the launch of the *Mankuriun*'s missiles. *He had delayed too long!* He experienced a rush of anger and disbelief. *So it is another slugfest like the one under Lord Athrumos 700 years earlier*, he thought, regretting his misjudgment. "Fire all lasers!" he roared. "Flank speed! Launch V-3's."

Although they missed the bridge, the four laser beams struck the *Mankuriun* at four critical points and began to eat through the hull.

The metal began to soften from the intense heat and glow yellow; in 30 seconds the hull would be breached. Inside the ship, the sizzling sound was frightening.

But it was too late; seconds after the lasers fired and just as the engines engaged to thrust the *Upaksanochin* out of danger, the first Hyperion struck, rocking the ship in a violent explosion that tore apart the last third of its hull. Any crewmembers who were not killed instantly by the explosion were slammed violently against the decks and bulkheads.

Idannup's next thought was for the safety of his crew, but that concern was also too late.

The *Kornassin* sat on the flight deck of the *Upaksanochin* ahead of 14 other *Stokun V-3* gun ships, ready to launch. The *V-3* was dark gray with a flat saucer-shaped fuselage with rolled down wingtips and an odd-shaped air intake that gave it a sinister look. It was very maneuverable and heavily armed. Its crew had been ordered to stand by to lead the wave of *V-3*'s in case they were needed. There was a crew of three: Lt. Domaket Argrulee the Pilot; Lt. Apanoo Vahleet, the Navigator; and Lt. Epan Klyregit, the Weapons Officer. Argulee and Vahleet were two of the three crewmembers on board who had mastered Kuterin.

All three of them were intense and, arrogantly considering themselves superior to every other race, committed to dominating any race they encountered. When the *Upaksanochin* staggered under the first explosion with a wrenching sound, they reacted instantly.

"We're being attacked!" Vahleet yelled incredulously.

"Lift off! Lift off!" Argrulee shouted as he pushed the throttles to the max.

The *Kornassin* shot out of the flight bay as the second missile struck, ripping the stern of the *Upaksanochin* apart. None of the other gun ships were able to avoid being trapped and destroyed on the flight deck.

On the bridge, Captain Idannup struggled to his feet, dazed and bleeding from a concussion, as the ship descended into chaos. Moments later, the second Hyperion found its mark and then the third one. A raging inferno swept toward the bridge as he slipped into unconsciousness.

The ship erupted in a brilliant and horrific ball of fire; it was the end of the *Upaksanochin*. Below the explosion, wreckage from the ship rained down over the surface for miles around.

On the *Mankuriun*'s bridge, Stoveris digested the message from Idannup. *You may be an excellent liar, Captain Idannup* he thought *but we are not Senoobians—WE are Bretin.*

The crew on duty watched the display that showed the *Upaksanochin* torn apart by the three explosions. At first there was only a stunned silence but that quickly gave way to triumphant cheers and shouts of joy.

Stoveris sat in his chair with his eyes closed, relieved. His order had been impulsive and irrational. It occurred to him, *maybe there are destructive traits in our genetic makeup after all but I made the right decision.*

The OOD approached him cautiously, "Sir, are you all right?"

Stoveris looked up slowly and smiled slightly. "Yes, I'm fine. Thank you." His eyes were defiant. "I couldn't let them get away with destroying the *Volarion*. Couldn't trust them—Idannup was lying all along."

"That was a close call," the OOD ventured.

"Yes, it was," Stoveris nodded. "Get Damage Control to assess our damage from the lasers and report to me A.S.A.P."

He picked up the P. A. mike. "This is the XO speaking. Some measure of justice has been served for the loss of the *Volarion*. The *Upaksanochin* has been destroyed."

As Jeliko and Darz walked back to the compartment where Bayn was convalescing, the ship's doctor, Havat Eyveer, passed them in the concourse. Darz stopped to catch his attention. "Doctor Eyveer, may we speak with you for a moment?"

Eyveer paused, "Yes, of course."

Darz said, "Sir, the XO isn't acting rationally. He just ordered an unprovoked attack that destroyed the *Upaksanochin* as she was turning away. I'm not sure he knew what he was doing or that he is aware of the severe consequences such an action may have. Do you think he's suffered an emotional breakdown?"

Doctor Eyveer looked at them gravely. "I'm afraid it's the uridimace. When we Bretin are in a threatening situation, our hormone systems produce anprathumine which reacts with the uridimace to induce an aggressive fight response. The higher the stress, the greater the surge of anprathumine. The XO has been under a lot of stress with the death of our Captain and he's exhausted.

"I knew the Captain's death would trigger elevated levels of anprathumine in him—I understand he threatened to destroy a major human city. Thankfully, he reconsidered that order but when the Peyrians showed up, it was too much."

Jeliko said, "Couldn't you sedate him?"

Dr. Eyveer replied, "I could, if he would allow me to, but when a Bretin has experienced a jolt of anprathumine, it pushes him over the edge. You don't lightly stick needles in him. When the Bretin genome was being engineered, the goal was to enable a strong fight response for survival. The problem is that when an emotional fight reaction is triggered, it's difficult to make sound decisions. And the aggressive behavior that results is hard to control, especially as stressed as he is. There's not much that can be done about that, but there's also the risk of a heart attack, and I can do something about that. I'm on my way to the bridge to try to calm him down."

Darz said, "Thank you, Doctor. We won't detain you."

"The ship's blown up! It's gone! What do we do now?" Vahleet said, mostly to himself.

Klyregit frantically searched the skies around them in vain. "We're the only survivors," he exclaimed.

The *Kornassin* was streaking across the sky away from the flying debris. When they were safely clear, Klyregit began to replay what had happened. His anger welled up inside, choking him with hatred. "Wait! We've got to go back and make the bastards pay. That's what we're going to do! We'll kill all of them!"

"Yes, death to every one of them," Argrulee howled as he maneuvered the ship into a tight turn back toward the *Mankuriun*.

"Are you crazy? We can't take on a starship. They'll blow us out of the sky!" Vahleet yelled back.

"No they won't," Argrulee replied. "There's so much wreckage everywhere, their missiles won't be able to pick us up. Just keep us from getting blindsided by a big chunk of debris."

On the bridge of the *Mankuriun*, Deratis frantically waved the XO over, leaving his communicator on for Doksolus, the Weapons Officer, to hear. "Sir, a small craft escaped from the *Upaksanochin* and now it's turning toward us. I expect its intentions are to strafe or ram us in a suicide attack. We have two minutes to react. There's so much debris that our missile systems can't get a solid lock on it."

The XO grabbed the P.A. system mike. "All hands brace for impact! Damage control stand by!" he yelled. The alarm sounded *reeehro-reeehro*. "Flank speed. Hard to starboard!" he shouted at the OOD The ship started to turn but far too slowly to suit him. "Damn it, Nuferas! Come on. Bring her around!"

The *Kornassin* completed its turn and bore down on the *Mankuriun* only 15 miles away. "What are you doing?" Vahleet yelled.

"We're going to kill everyone of the bastards. I'm going to take us right into the bridge!"

"You idiot, you'll kill us too!" Vahleet yelled.

"Shut up, Vahleet. I don't care!" Argrulee growled.

"There'll be no one left to tell what happened to our ship! We don't need to die now!" Vahleet shot back.

The *Kornassin* was gaining speed. "Five miles to impact!" Vahleet gasped.

The *Mankuriun* was looming large in front of them.

Argulee swore like a madman. "I'll kill them all!"

"Three miles to impact!" Klyregit screamed. "Damn you, turn!"

They could make out the officers on the bridge. Vahleet braced himself."

On the *Mankuriun*, the XO and the officers on watch stared in disbelief as the fighter came at them fast, making straight for the bridge, like some giant avenging bird of prey. "All ahead flank. Hard to starboard. Come on, Nuferas, bring her around!" the XO implored. The thought spread through his brain like a nightmare in slow motion: *if it hits the bridge, we're all dead. We can survive anything but that— not a direct hit on the bridge!*

Doksolus had tried to get a fix on the *Kornassin* for their heat-seeking missiles, but the craft was streaking through a cloud of hot metal debris from the explosion. "No lock! No lock!" he yelled.

"Three miles to impact," Nuferas yelled. "Brace for impact! Brace for impact!" he roared into the P.A. mike. *Kruknogru! In ten seconds it will hit the bridge, killing everyone of us.*

The *Kornassin* sped like a bullet straight at the bridge, firing its four cannon but the *Mankuriun* was beginning to turn. Klyregit hit the buttons releasing two missiles.

With only seconds to react, Argrulee lost his nerve. *Damn it*, he swore to himself, slamming his fist into the armrest. He clenched his teeth, held his breath and swore mightily as he pulled the stick back with all his strength putting them into a 270° turn that would bring them behind and under the *Mankuriun*, plunging toward the Earth.

Pulling up at the last second, the gunship missed the bridge by only a few feet and skimmed over the hull of the *Mankuriun*, before rolling over and plummeting toward the Earth. Five G's . . . 10 G's . . . 15 G's! Time seemed to stop. Vahleet closed his eyes and braced himself to die. Klyregit put his head between his knees and blacked out.

On the *Mankuriun* the heavy splatter of cannon fire raked across the outside of the bridge pitting the viewing port but it held. The *Kornassin* was so close that the two bombs skidded across the viewing port like missiles and, with ear-shattering clangs, ricocheted high above the bridge before exploding, rocking the ship but doing little harm.

Vahleet slowly opened his eyes, shocked to find himself still alive. They were leaving the *Mankuriun* far above them. *Mother of Prasnogfa*, he thought, *now they'll destroy us with their missiles for sure!*

On the bridge of the *Mankuriun*, the officers and crew were still in shock, unable to move. Finally Deratis wiped the cold sweat from his brow. "*By Dolahktus*, how did they miss us? In all my life, I've never been so close to dying!"

The XO pulled himself together. "They didn't miss us," he muttered. "They decided they wanted to live."

He turned to Nuferas, "Damage assessment, quickly!"

Nuferas scanned the damage control status board.

Stoveris looked at the Ops Display. The target was descending toward the surface at breakneck speed.

Doksolus' voice came over the XO's intercom. "We've got a lock on it. Permission to launch a Hyperion?"

The XO paused and then said, "No. They've no place to go. We won't waste a Hyperion on them."

The crewmembers of the *Kornassin* expected to be blown out of the sky any minute but they reached the surface. When they were safely on the ground, they sat there with the canopy open and their heads back, unable to move for a long time, as the sun and a cool breeze brought them back to life. "Damn you, Argrulee, don't ever expect me to fly with you again," Klyregit groaned.

Vahleet relaxed. "Argrulee, I thought we were dead for sure. What changed your mind?"

"You did. Better to live and fight another day. We're worth more alive than dead. The information we have about the Senoobians may be useful. Besides, there's the *Grunashar*. With any luck, she'll find us. I was ready to sacrifice all three of us to destroy the *Tyguta* but why do that when we can live to enjoy our revenge?"

The three of them tumbled from the cockpit and collapsed, stretching out on the wings. "What do we do now?" Vahleet asked the others. They debated that question until they were tired of thinking about it. Suddenly an alarm in the cockpit went off. The ship's radar had picked up an unknown contact. Vahleet scrambled back into the cockpit. "It's the Senoobian lander leaving the *Tyguta*!"

They looked at each other as a twisted smile came over Vulujin's face. "That's what we need to do: we'll track them down and take our revenge on the lander." A few minutes later, they were airborne again.

At 1125 that morning, there were three brilliant flashes of light followed by a fiery cloud that appeared in the sky over the coast of Southern Peru. Long thin fingers of light gray smoke spiraled away in all directions and bits of burning metal and other debris rained down over a wide area. Many people on the surface saw the spectacular catastrophe and wondered what had happened. Small crowds were milling about on the streets of Nazca anxiously watching the smoldering conflagration dissipate in the skies above them.

In Houston, NASA had been tracking a contact that seemed to appear out of nowhere, then disappeared just as abruptly. The small blips made by the Hyperions, however, blinked on and off so quickly that they hardly registered. "What the hell was that?" one of the radar operators exclaimed. On their screens, no one noticed the small craft that sped away from the destroyed ship and then changed direction.

As Darz and Jeliko opened the door to Bayn's compartment, the ship was falling off to starboard. First there was the sizzling sting of powerful laser beams hitting the ship. Then there was the sound of bullets raking across the hull. Seconds later two explosions rocked the ship. "What's going on? Are we under attack?" Bayn asked, concerned.

"We destroyed a Peyrian ship," Jeliko said. "We didn't have to; she was turning away. Stoveris snapped; the stress of everything that has happened was too much for him. Now I'm afraid there will be war."

"War against whom?" Bayn asked.

"Against the humans, I suppose," Jeliko replied. "The *Mankuriun* is leaving but the Peyrians might use this incident as a pretext for attacking the humans. You know, the *if you don't hand the criminals over, we'll blow you to bits* kind of thinking."

"*By the Mark of Dolahktus!* What next?" Bayn groaned.

They sat quietly for several minutes, each wrapped in his own thoughts.

There was a knock on the door. When Jeliko answered, it was Agoyin. "The XO has asked me to advise you that we will depart this planet at 0600 in the morning. Your departure for the surface is scheduled for 1400. Please make sure that those who are returning to the surface are there 30 minutes early."

Darz thanked Agoyin and wished him well. "Come on," he said solemnly, "let's find the XO and say our goodbyes."

Darz and Jeliko hurried toward the bridge in long strides, while Bayn limped along behind them."

Near the bridge, an exhausted and conflicted Stoveris was shuffling toward his stateroom as the Senoobians approached him. Darz said, "Sir, excuse me. Permission to speak?"

"Yes, what is it?" he asked, irritated at being detained and continuing to move toward his stateroom near the bridge. Dr. Eyveer had given him a strong sedative. His speech was slightly slurred; the only thing he wanted was to get some sleep.

"We want to thank you for everything you've done for us and wish you a safe trip home. We are deeply distressed by the loss of Captain Markovin and Lt. Panzer." Darz said.

Bayn spoke up, "And good luck on the war with the Shun."

"Yes, yes, thank you. It's been an experience meeting you all. Good luck to you here."

Jeliko said, "Sir, if you don't mind, we'll fly ourselves to the surface in our lander."

"All right," he said, waving them away impatiently. "Be at your lander in one hour. I'll give the orders to the OOD to prepare for your departure. Of course, I'm disappointed that you won't be returning with us. But I'm pleased to have your daughter on the trip. We'll do our best to look after her."

He paused for a moment as if he had forgotten something, then abruptly disappeared into his stateroom, leaving the door ajar.

Before they knew it, he was back, pressing two DK-3 Krayzurs into their hands. "Just in case you need them—I understand your DK-1's are discharged. Forgive me if I don't see you off."

The three Senoobians thanked him profusely, shook his hand and wished him and his crew a safe return to Nanzema. Then they rushed back to their staterooms to gather their few belongings and say a final goodbye to Amara at their lander.

25

THE DEATH OF BAYN KENER

As soon as the three Senoobians landed, they rushed to put Bayn to bed at Naksoris and then called Luis to update him on what had happened.

Overjoyed at the chance to see them again, he arranged to meet them that evening at Naksoris. He had assumed that the *Mankuriun* had exploded and everyone on board had been killed. The last two days had been spent wondering what had happened and mourning the loss of his friends.

As soon as Darz and Jeliko met him at the door, he embraced them warmly. "I didn't think I would ever see you again!" he exclaimed.

"Nor did we," replied Jeliko.

"How's Bayn?" Luis asked Darz.

"He's coming along rather well for someone his age—he's pretty tough. Come and see for yourself," Jeliko said as she turned to lead him to Bayn's room.

Luis found Bayn lying propped up on his bed, his hair disheveled and his shoulder still dressed with wide bandages, but obviously glad to see him. "Well, you see we couldn't leave this troubled old planet after all!" he said weakly.

Luis said, "I thought you wanted to be with the Bretin."

"We did, until we thought it through. Then we had second thoughts. When it came down to it, we couldn't leave. We don't have that much longer to live and we realized that we probably wouldn't survive the trip anyway. Besides, we couldn't leave Marco behind."

Jeliko sighed, "Now Amara's on her way to Nanzema. We're heartbroken at losing her, of course, but it was her choice—I just hope it was the right choice."

Luis embraced Bayn gingerly, mindful of his injury. "Well, I'm pleased for her; I'm sure she'll be happy there."

Then he sat down on the foot of Bayn's bed and firmly squeezed his large foot. "I hope you're going to stay put for awhile. Now, what's the prognosis?"

"The doctor on the *Mankuriun* said I was lucky to be alive. An inch farther to the left and the bullet would have hit my heart and I would have died instantly. But, with the medicine I'm taking and plenty of rest, I should be good as new in a few weeks."

Luis could contain his curiosity no longer. "What happened up there? Was the *Mankuriun* destroyed and everyone killed?"

Darz took a deep breath. "That's what we wanted to tell you. While we were on the *Mankuriun*, something remarkable happened. We barely got Calderon and León settled down on board when a Peyrian ship appeared . . ."

"A Peyrian ship appeared!" Luis exclaimed.

Darz started again, "Yes, a Peyrian ship appeared and . . ."

"The Peyrians are here!"

Darz said, "They were: they had a colony here and their CO accused the XO of destroying it. Not knowing anything about the Bretin, he assumed they were Senoobians. The XO figured it best to let him think that.

"Anyway, the XO denied any attack on their colony. Instead of getting all upset and confrontational, Idannup said that things had gone too far and that we should all forget about the past and try to develop a peaceful relationship."

"Sounds fishy to me." Luis said.

"I know. He said the attack on the *Volarion* was carried out by the Frunjin, a ruthless group that controlled Peyr at the time, in spite of fierce opposition from a more peaceful group. A bloody civil war broke out after that and dragged on for many years before a more peaceful group came to power."

Luis said, "But the XO would have none of it, right?"

Darz said, "Nope, all of a sudden, things went to hell. Idannup broke off communications and the ship began to turn away."

Luis said, "That doesn't sound bad."

Darz said, "Except for one thing: as the *Upaksanochin* turned away, the XO ordered three Hyperion missiles fired at it. It was only 20 miles away. The ship was totally destroyed . . ."

Luis was aghast. "That's what I saw—the Peyrian ship blowing up! Why would he do such a thing?"

Bayn said, "Think about it. The XO has his Captain and First Lieutenant murdered. He's in shock, no doubt, and doesn't sleep for a couple of days. Suddenly his archnemesis shows up. He's angry and frustrated and now all of the hate and anger we survivors have felt toward the Peyrians becomes directed at the *Upaksanochin*. So he can't resist attacking it."

Luis said, "But that was a long time ago."

Jeliko said, "Maybe so, but consider the enormity of what they did: it was nothing short of genocide. And guess what: as the Peyrian ship was turning away, it attacked the *Mankuriun* with some sort of high energy lasers. If the XO hadn't launched the Hyperions when he did, the Mankuriun's hull would have been breached in seconds and we'd all be dead!"

Luis grunted in disgust, "So the Peyrian Lord's diplomacy was a sham?"

"Well, it was a bad turn of events, in any case," said Bayn. "I expect the *Upaksanochin* transmitted a report of their engagement with the *Mankuriun* to their superiors on Peyr. They're going to find out that the *Mankuriun* destroyed their starship. Peyr is 13 light years from Earth so in 13 years I expect they're going to be very upset."

Luis said, "But surely the Peyrians won't be upset with us humans. Won't they understand that we weren't responsible for the loss of their starship? Wouldn't they leave us alone if they knew it was the Bretin who destroyed their starship?"

Bayn said, "Maybe, but don't forget who we're dealing with. Here's a nice planet with lots of resources, populated with humans. What if they decide they want the planet badly enough to take on you humans? And if they do find out about the Bretin, won't that give them even more reason to take over the Earth and use it to keep the Bretin at bay or launch a war against them?"

The possibility of humans being drawn into a war between two advanced civilizations was unsettling. "But surely there's a chance our differences can be resolved in a peaceful way!" Luis said.

Bayn seemed to regain his strength, "There is that possibility, but you never know how these things will play out. Maybe the two parties will just go home and ignore the whole thing because they don't want to get into a disastrous and costly war. After all, they're a great distance from each other and supporting a starship is a major commitment. Can you imagine what it would take to wage a war between two different star systems?"

Marco said, "You know, humans have a saying that war ultimately comes down to *real estate*. I'll bet that principle applies on a galactic scale as well. The Peyrians might think *these humans are harmless; we've got our own problems. Let them keep their backward little planet to themselves?* On-the-other-hand, if they're sitting above the Earth in one of their starships, armed to the teeth, they might just as well decide they really would like to have our planet. There aren't that many inhabitable planets out there."

Bayn said, "That's why your government should be aware of the situation so it can develop a strategy for responding appropriately to whatever happens. If the Peyrians in fact have several starships and one or more of them are close by, they could show up at any time."

Darz said, "Quite right. If they have another starship in this solar system, they could be here in three or four years."

Jeliko looked at Luis solemnly. "Well, it's not our place to speculate about all this. We shared with Luke and Sonny what we know; it's up to them to handle it however they see fit."

Luis said, "Let's hope that they can get your information to the people who can best act on it."

Bayn nodded his approval, seeming to tire and grow drowsy. He slumped back against the pillows and closed his eyes.

"What will happen to Calderon and León?" Luis finally asked.

Darz replied, "I think the XO's intentions are to transport them to Nanzema and put them on trial for murder. I don't believe they will enjoy the trip. I have no idea what their punishment will be, but you can be assured that they will never trouble anyone here again."

Luis replied, "Whatever it is, it won't be severe enough for the likes of them."

The others nodded in agreement.

Luis asked, "What are you going to do now?"

Bayn replied, "We're going to leave as soon as I'm able to travel. We'll miss this place; it's been our home for a long time."

Darz said, "I know the Nazca police department is in turmoil and there's an investigation—hopefully, you can get through it okay. We will appreciate anything you can do to keep us out it. We'll be at great risk if we get dragged into it."

After talking for a couple of hours, Luis bid the three another emotional farewell.

The three Senoobians were still upset about the recent events and especially about giving up Amara; it was that very night that the dreams began. It had been a long time since Jeliko had been awakened from a dream. But that night was different; she had tossed and turned and sweated, even though it was not particularly warm. Suddenly she bolted upright in bed in a panic, instantly awake, with the dream still vivid in her mind.

There were the three of them, standing on the edge of a great rocky cliff, looking out over a vast restless ocean. But their faces were obscured and she couldn't make out which was which. Suddenly the earth gave way; one of them lost his balance and began to fall to a certain death. The other two reached out desperately to save their comrade but it was too late—they missed him by inches. It all happened in slow motion and their falling comrade slowly faded from view onto the rocks far below. She sat there for a long time, trying to convince herself it was only a dream.

Jeliko didn't take her dreams lightly. This was more than a dream; it was a nightmare and a premonition. She was from *Kundivar Province* on Senoobis where many, like her mother and her grandmother, were said to be clairvoyant. She had realized as a child that she had the gift of premonition through her dreams. Over the years she had learned to take them seriously; they often came true.

But she couldn't bring herself to mention it to Bayn or Darz. She didn't want to worry them needlessly and she hoped she would have no more.

A few nights later, she had a second dream. In this one there were only two of them and they were mourning the loss of their comrade. She awoke again in a cold sweat, feeling helpless and alone. The three of them had been together for so long and were so dependent upon each other that they functioned as disjointed extensions of the same body. The faces of the two remaining Senoobians were obscured but she never even considered whether or not she was the one who was lost. The only thing that mattered was that the two who were left would suffer the painful loss.

The third dream was more terrible than the others. It was a nightmare in which some sort of evil and menacing beast was prowling around in the darkness, seeking someone to devour. The other two rushed to warn their unsuspecting comrade about the murderous assault that the beast was ready to unleash. But they couldn't reach their friend before his death. Jeliko jerked awake, cold with fear.

Bayn and Darz, noticing that she seemed weary and depressed, were concerned. But she couldn't bear to tell them about her dreams. And she dreaded the revelation she knew was coming about which one of them would die.

In the fourth dream, the dreaded revelation came. The faces were more distinct and she saw to her horror that it was Bayn who would die. She and Darz reached out to him as he slowly faded away. A great bright light had been extinguished from their lives and she and Darz mourned terribly. She lay in bed a long time, distraught, unable to decide what to do.

Her only defense against such a tragedy was to try to convince herself that she was wrong. After all she had been wrong before. But she finally realized she had never experienced such a persistent premonition. She decided to reveal her dreams to Darz but not to Bayn. She knew that verbalizing her fear and sharing it with Darz would be a great relief. Perhaps together they could be vigilant and protective of Bayn so that nothing could happen to him.

That morning she arose early from her restless night, dressed and walked out to the meadow that was near their home. The first hints of dawn were bringing the field to life. There at the far end of it she could make out an alpaca, grazing peacefully. And nearby she saw a *Parihuana*, a native bird that was becoming extinct. The bird's plight reminded her of themselves—on the edge of extinction. *Was it a bad omen?* She knew what she had to do. She and Darz would resist the dreadful destiny she had glimpsed with so much will that it could not possibly happen. She felt defiant and determined, optimistic for the first time in days.

Darz and Jeliko spent the rest of the next day making Naksoris their temporary home. They had decided to remain there only until Bayn was strong enough to make the trip to Arizona. As they busied themselves in the arrangements for their move, however, they didn't realize that they were being watched. Ramon Maldonado and Raul Ramallo were thieves who had decided that Naksoris would be their next target.

Maldonado had grown up, tough and cold-blooded, on the streets of Nazca. When he was an adolescent, he refused to go to school; when he was a young man, he refused to work. Father Tony had tried to help him by finding small jobs he could do but usually he didn't show up. He became a *huaquero*, or grave robber, for a while, but found the field too crowded and the work too strenuous. By the time he was 18, stealing had become a way of life for him. Two years later, he committed his first murders. It was an old couple who confronted him while he was robbing their home. The fact that he was never caught and punished only confirmed him in his life of crime. And into that criminal craft he had mentored Ramallo.

Many things in life are a matter of timing and the events that unfolded at Naksoris were a sad example of bad timing. If the two thieves had cased Naksoris a day earlier, they would have found it empty and forlorn and would have no doubt passed it by in search of a more inviting place to rob. Unfortunately, the day they happened by, they noticed the three Senoobians going about, but they never saw Bayn who was still recuperating and bedfast.

As the two spied on the occupants from their hiding place in the heavy brush near the front of the house, it dawned on him. "I know those two," Maldonado muttered, mostly to himself when he saw Darz and Jeliko more closely. "*Los Condors*! They used to jump off the mountains around Cusco. They're friends of that stupid old priest, Father Francisco. I used to steal from him and make fun of him behind his back when we were kids. But these two—I remember them. They're the strange ones. There were three of them and once, when I was a teenager, our gang had a run in with one of them near the church. I've hated him ever since; I made up my mind that I'd kill him if I ever saw him again." His hand moved instinctively to the hunting knife that hung from his belt.

Ramallo said, "There's a younger man with them. What about the other old one?"

244

"I don't know. Maybe he died; I hope he has for his sake."

There were supplies they needed to buy and Bayn had assured them he would be fine until they returned from town. Actually the three of them had been hovering around him too much to suit him over the last few days; he was relishing the quiet time he would have to himself, time to reflect on their situation or read.

When Marco and the two Senoobians drove off toward town in their battered old pickup truck, Maldonado and Ramallo decided it was time to make their move. The windows on the side of the dwelling had been left open to admit whatever cooling breeze there might be. Without too much difficulty, they managed to climb up and slip through the window that was toward the back of the dwelling.

Bayn was dozing on his bed when he was startled by the noise; it was a suspicious sound. Someone was in the next room rummaging through their belongings! He raised himself up on his good elbow and listened—they were being robbed! The sense of an evil presence hung heavily in the air.

He had no way to defend himself—their weapons were still in the lander, as were most of their belongings. They had not bothered to move back into Naksoris since they only planned to be there two or three days. Should he yell at the intruder in hopes of frightening him away? Should he try to escape through the window or should he confront the thief? As he was debating what to do, a man appeared in the doorway. *There was more than one of them!*

Ramallo was not as experienced as his partner at this sort of thing. He saw the startled shape on the bed move and shouted a warning, "There's someone in here!"

Maldonado came running. Instead of unnerving him, being discovered always whetted his taste for danger and caused a surge of excitement that made him want to savage someone. He saw the figure on the bed and cautiously approached it with his knife drawn, ready, even eager, to attack.

Drawing close, he savored the look of surprise and fear he saw on the man's face. He saw the bandages and realized the man was not sick, but injured. As he looked triumphantly into the man's eyes, the man spoke and he recognized the eyes and the voice—it was the other old one, the one he hated. There was a dark blue stone on a silver chain around the man's neck, glittering seductively. He couldn't believe his good fortune: there wasn't much there to steal, but maybe God was giving him the chance to settle an old score.

Maldonado eased down onto the foot of the bed and relaxed as he studied the old man and savored the rush of power that washed over him. How delicious revenge was. *What a feeling of power swept over you when you could punish someone for past sins and watch them squirm.* "You don't remember me, do you? Oh, I'm sure I've changed a lot since you last saw me."

He leaned closer into the light. "Look at me; it's Ramon Maldonado. We met near Father Tony's church several years ago when I was still a kid. You tried to humiliate me in front of my gang."

Bayn remembered the incident. "I wasn't trying to humiliate you. You were the angry young man that I tried to teach some respect. It would have been much better for you if you had learned your lesson that day, but I see you are still angry and hateful, even as an adult," Bayn said. "What made you think that my friends and I deserved to be treated the way you were treating us? What did we do to you and your gang?"

"You looked strange and that was enough," Maldonado growled.

"Well, you and your gang behaved strangely toward us but we didn't throw stones at you or curse you for it."

Maldonado exploded. "Shut up! That's enough of your mouth! I swore I would make you pay for the way you treated me. I could slit your throat but that would be too quick. I want to watch you bleed to death slowly and feel the breath leaving your body."

Gripping the knife firmly in his right hand, Maldonado suddenly leaped upon Bayn, viciously stabbing the long, thin knife deep into his stomach in one quick motion. He fixed his eyes close on Bayn's and felt a rush of orgasmic pleasure at the pain and shock he saw in them. With his left hand blocking Bayn's good arm so he could not blunt the assault, Maldonado twisted the knife slowly and methodically for greatest effect. The warm wetness of the blood gushing out between them and the cold look of life draining from Bayn's eyes exhilarated him.

At last Bayn collapsed back onto the bed, the shock of his dying dissolving into a detached, unfeeling sensation. All awareness wafted into a remoteness that left him a stranger to himself. In seconds, all consciousness, like cool mists on a sunny morning, had dissipated into nothingness and he was gone.

Whether it was the awful finality of what he had done or the feeling of absolute power over his victim, Maldonado didn't know or care, but he felt intoxicated and keenly alive. He slowly pulled the knife from Bayn's body, wiped its blade lovingly upon the sheet and stood up, invincible and pleased with himself.

He walked to the bathroom and casually washed the blood from his hands. Then, returning to the bedroom, he unfastened the blue amulet from Bayn's neck and put it on himself. Turning to Ramallo, who had watched the murder with distaste, he said, "Let's get something to eat," and calmly strode toward the front door. Ramallo followed him outside but he had no appetite.

When Darz, Jeliko and Marco returned to Naksoris late that afternoon, they were tired and hungry. They had brought some food from the tavern so they could eat together. The house was unusually quiet as they entered, and there was no answer when they called to let Bayn know they had returned. Jeliko and Marco went into the kitchen to fix some drinks while Darz went to Bayn's room. There he saw their comrade, lying in a pool of blood, his face frozen in a gruesome mask of pain.

Darz stood there for what seemed like a long time, unable to speak, his mind transfixed, unable to process the horror that he saw. A scream welled up inside him until it came bursting out in a loud and long and desperate wail, "J-e-l-i-k-o-o-o." He fell forward onto the bed, hugging Bayn to him.

The mug she was holding fell to the floor and shattered; she and Marco were there in an instant. Entering the room, they both stopped short. Marco felt the wind knocked out of him by the gory scene, as if he had been slammed in the chest by some hard, unexpected blow.

It was obvious: they had been robbed and Bayn had been murdered. Their comrade, their soul mate, and their mentor lay in a pool of blood with vacant eyes that would never again sparkle with life. He was the father all of them had lost many years before. Even his amulet was gone.

Jeliko had never seen him cry but tears were streaming down Marco's face. "We can't lose him, Jeliko. We just can't," he wailed, refusing to believe that Bayn was gone.

Jeliko stood there: unable to think, unable to move, unable to feel anything but the grief that washed over her, leaving her so shaken and hurt that it felt like her insides were being ripped out. She too began to cry; the tears and the sobs came long and hard.

Perhaps it was the hot, wet sting of her tears that pulled her back from the surreal scene of death before her. The pain of her own loss gradually faded into compassion for Darz and Marco. Gently and insistently, she pulled them into a desperately needed embrace. They slid down to the floor and huddled together as Marco buried his head in her arms and held her tighter than he had ever held anyone before.

Darz, Jeliko and Marco were struggling with the loss of both Bayn and Amara. The funeral was two days later near the tiny town of San Juan, not far from Nazca, on a bluff overlooking the Pacific Ocean. Bayn loved the ocean and had expressed his wish to have his ashes scattered there. Only eight people attended the ceremony: Darz and Jeliko; Marco; Luis, his brother Juan; Carlos Navarro; Phillipe and Father Tony who officiated. It was a sunny and pleasant day, the kind Bayn would have enjoyed.

Father Tony didn't know how to hold a service for an alien non-believer, but he didn't have the heart to refuse the request of his friends. The loss of a friend who had become so dear had left him brokenhearted and confused. He began:

> My friends, we are gathered here today to mourn the loss of one who was dear to us. He never knew God but I believe that God knew him. Bayn Kener was a good person; his heart was full of love and compassion. To some of us, he was like a father; to some of us he was like a brother; to all of us, he was a loyal and trusted friend. He was a comfort and an inspiration for he suffered and overcame the misfortunes of life here on Earth with dignity. We all loved him as he loved us. We will miss him. We will never forget him . . .

He paused, unable to choke back his tears. They all came together in a circle and held hands. After a moment, he asked, "Is there anyone who would like to share an anecdote with us about Bayn?"

Everyone had a story. Darz told about his mistake with the sleep modules, ultimately causing the death of Amantis and the destruction of their ship. Bayn never berated him.

Luis told about the time he had been depressed, feeling like a failure. His job was going nowhere and he was lonely. Bayn listened to him and encouraged him.

Jeliko recalled the words from her dream, "A great bright light has been forever snuffed out."

Father Tony paused to dry his eyes. Bowing his head, he said, "let us pray."

Everyone there was distraught. They all stood silent for a moment and then turned toward each other, reflecting the pain in each other's eyes. Then, without speaking, they came together and embraced. After the brief ceremony, they remained a little longer, enjoying the view and each other's company as they reminisced about other incidents they had shared with Bayn.

Darz turned to Luis and pulled him aside. "We've surely had our problems of late, haven't we? How are you holding up, my friend?"

Luis said, "It's tough, Darz. That mess at Naksoris has become a huge headache. The investigation into the deaths of Gonzales and Cabrera by that unit from Lima has got me worried; it's obvious they don't think I'm giving them the whole story. And a forensic team has come to look into the remains in the well. There will be lots of questions, and I don't know if I can keep you guys out of it, but I'm trying."

Just then Jeliko came up and hugged him. "Luis, I know all of this has been hard on you. We're grateful for everything you've done."

"Thanks," he said. "I'm hoping I can explain it all away as the result of a turf war between two drug organizations. The big shots in Lima know there was bad blood between Calderon and some locals. He had his enemies. Now he and León have disappeared. What a coincidence! I've decided I'm going to turn in my resignation once this is over—I've had enough of the violence."

"I understand," she said "but what will you do?"

"I don't know. I just want to get away and start a new life."

Darz smiled at him, "We feel the same way: it's time for us to move on. We have too many bad memories of this place and there are the deaths of Calderon's cronies that will no doubt bring too much attention to us. The place we've been working on for several years is quite isolated, but it will be a good place to start over. After the investigation, why don't you visit us for a while?"

Jeliko nodded, "Yes, come and stay as long as you like. It would be a comfort to have you near."We'll fly down and pick you up when you're ready."

Marco joined them. "I'm going to miss you, Luis. Please come."

"Thanks," Luis said. "Let me think about it."

Father Tony and Phillipe walked up to them and Jeliko gestured toward Father Tony mischievously. "And we don't want to leave this stubborn old human either. It will be hard to give him up."

Darz smiled at Phillipe. "But, of course, he has you to look after him. We will miss both of you, my friends. May your God look favorably upon you and keep you safe. You have both shown us the good side of humankind and you have brought joy to our lives."

Phillipe hugged Darz and then Jeliko, unable to find the words he needed to say how much he would miss them.

Darz said to him, "Look, I know you have your work there at the church and you'll need to carry on for Father Tony, but, if you ever need us, you have our phone number."

"Thank you, Darz. I'll remember that."

The next morning, Darz, Jeliko and Marco busied themselves with collecting their belongings so they could leave Naksoris. Luis agreed to stop by and discuss the possibility of going with them to America.

When there was nothing left to do, they sat down with a drink to relax for a few minutes and reminisce about Bayn, Amara and Naksoris. Although Darz and Jeliko had been close ever since they had reported for duty on the *Syzilian*, it was only at Bayn's prodding that they had confessed their love for each other, and that love had given them Amara. Now Bayn's death had brought them even closer together.

They recalled with both joy and sadness everything that had happened to them since they had arrived on Earth. Now they were old, but their feelings for each other were as fresh and strong as they had ever been. The miracle was that they had conspired to spend their lives together without knowing it. Besides the few humans they had grown to love, they had only each other. Darz took her hand in his and they lingered there, basking in the warmth of Sarmadah.

26

RETURN TO NANZEMA

The *Mankuriun* was well beyond the moon's orbit and rapidly accelerating. Amara sat near the main viewing port as the Earth gradually receded into the distance. Every connection to the life she had known was through that small blue orb that would soon disappear. That thought made her sick to her stomach.

In spite of all the activity around her, she felt alone and useless. Her thoughts turned to Marco, as they often had the last few days, and how much she missed him. She recalled the *mishugah* they had experienced and how she had tingled all over. She thought of her parents and her few human friends. She would never see them or speak to them again; they might as well be dead. Never again would she breathe the air of Earth or frolic in the surf of the ocean that gave her such a sense of peace.

Desperate to choke back her growing panic at giving up everything she had known and cared for, she turned her attention to Agoyin who was busy on the bridge. She studied him intently, looking for some reassurance. *Had leaving Earth and giving up Marco been a mistake? She was duty bound to continue the Senoobian blood line— she owed it to her parents.*

The Captain and Nayta were the only two Bretin she had felt comfortable asking for help, but the Captain was dead, and she had known Nayta for only a few days. *Would there be differences between her and the Bretin that would create problems later on?*

Agoyin sensed her gaze and smiled as he waved at her. She smiled back, seemingly calm and assured while inside she felt weak and uncertain. She missed Marco so much that nothing else mattered.

The Bretin: of all the stories she had heard about Senoobis, she recalled the stories about the Bretin most vividly. They were stronger, faster and some said more disciplined than Senoobians. Supposedly they were also coldly unemotional. *Was Agoyin that way—coldly calculating and of no help in a crisis?* she wondered.

It was on the fifth day after their departure from Earth that Stoveris motioned Ponytis, the Officer of the Deck, over to him. At last Stoveris was rested, back to his normal self, and ready to consider the disposition of his two prisoners. He instructed Ponytis, "Keep our *guests* isolated from each other but tomorrow at 1500, bring León to me at the sleep modules. Have Amara meet us there to translate. After I have finished with him, bring Calderon to me."

Amara was lying on the bunk in her compartment trying to visualize what her new life would be like when she received the call from Ponytis. "The XO requests that you meet us at 1500 tomorrow in his stateroom to translate when we interrogate the two human criminals. The XO is going to hold a preliminary inquiry. You're the only one on board who is fluent in their language."

The thought of having to look at Calderon again, much less speak to him, disgusted her but she could not refuse. "Tell the XO that I am pleased to be of service."

The next day Ponytis and two security guards brought Calderon and León to Stoveris for interrogation. Calderon had overcome his fear and turned surly again. He glared at Amara with eyes hateful and threatening. "I'm going to enjoy killing you," he hissed with a crooked smile when he was near her.

Next he began ranting belligerently at Stoveris. Amara didn't bother to translate his words—his body language made his intentions clear. In a quick movement, he jerked free from his guards and started toward the XO with his fist clinched. Before Calderon could reach him, Amara parried his assault and slammed him into the bulkhead, following up with punishing blows to the face and stomach. Calderon went down with his nose bloodied and the wind knocked out of him.

As he eyed Calderon with cold contempt, Stoveris said to Ponytis and Amara, "Show him sleep module #23 in which he will spend most of his trip to Nanzema and explain his situation to him, Amara. Tell him if he makes another hostile move toward anyone on this ship or, if he does not cooperate fully, he will be ejected into space billions of miles from Earth and his body will explode from the lack of oxygen."

Stoveris knew that Calderon's body wouldn't really explode, but it was a threat that succinctly conveyed the horror of such a death—it was the lack of oxygen in the blood that would kill you in minutes. Left to die in the cold vastness of space, it would indeed be a horrible death. As Amara translated into Spanish, Calderon's eyes grew wide with fear.

When she turned to Stoveris and nodded that she was finished, Stoveris said, "Ask him if he fully understands the nature of his situation."

Amara did so and Calderon meekly nodded his understanding.

Stoveris said to Ponytis, "Now take him to the bridge and show him the speck that is his Earth. Then bring him to my stateroom." Ponytis motioned for Amara and the guard to follow him with their prisoner as the XO walked away.

On the bridge Ponytis nodded and the guard shoved Calderon toward one of the viewing ports. Pointing to the blue speck that was Earth, Amara said to Calderon, "There is your Earth. Look at it closely because this is the last time you will ever see it."

Before long, they were all seated in the XO's stateroom, as Stoveris conferred with Amara. After a few minutes, Ponytis rang a bell sharply three times, signaling that the tribunal would come to order. Amara stood and read in a solemn voice, "Alberto Calderon, you are accused of the murder of Captain Jandis Markovin, our Commanding Officer, and Second Lt. Karseen Panzer, the senior pilot of this ship, both of whom were killed in a cold-blooded and unprovoked attack."

She sat down as Stoveris stood. "As Commanding Officer of this vessel, I have convened this tribunal to judge the extent of your responsibility for this crime. You may be condemned to death. If so, when we reach Nanzema, you will face the wives of the two exceptional officers you murdered. The Criminal Division will then carry out your execution." He paused again while Amara translated.

Stoveris continued, "If you fail to cooperate fully during these proceedings, however, I will immediately conclude your trial and find you guilty of a level one felony. You will be ejected into space to die an agonizing death alone." He nodded for Amara to translate.

Then he continued, "Our Senoobian friends and your accomplice Diego León have already given me a full account of your role in this crime. I will now hear your testimony about your involvement in it. I require a complete and truthful account from you. If your story contradicts the information I have already received, I will find you guilty of a level one felony and you will be executed immediately by ejection from this ship. Do you understand?"

Amara translated and Calderon, realizing the futility of his situation and the prospect of a horrible death, meekly acknowledged his understanding. Then the interrogation began. With his attention secured by the precariousness of his situation, Calderon became fully cooperative. After two hours of questioning, Stoveris had heard enough; he was appalled at the sordid picture that emerged of Calderon the drug lord and the harm his drug trade had inflicted on humanity.

Ponytis rang the small bell again three times, signaling that the court would render its decision. The guard pulled Calderon to his feet. "Alberto Calderon, the court finds you guilty of *eksupathic* murder in the deaths of Captain Jandis Markovin, the Commanding Officer of this ship, and Second Lieutenant Karseen Panzer. Murder by ambush from a place of concealment without cause or provocation is the most cowardly and heinous form of murder and it requires the death penalty. You will be delivered to Nanzema where the Criminal Division will carry out your execution after you have faced the families of your victims. He turned to Ponytis and the other security guard. "Place him in sleep module #23."

As they led him to the module and Amara described in detail what would happen to him, he broke into a cold sweat. He was claustrophobic and, in his mind, the module was a high-tech casket, an instrument of death that would hold him lifeless, suspended in some god-awful liquid for 17 years. He was sure he would drown or that his heart would burst as the liquid filled the module and engulfed him. He cursed . . . he begged for an anesthetic . . . he prayed, to no avail.

Inside # 23, Calderon panicked as the cool green liquid filled the module. As the dark canopy snapped into place, it occurred to him that he wouldn't see his mother again and she would worry when he never came to see her; he was totally alone. For a moment he felt the terrible pain he had inflicted on so many others and regretted the evil he had done.

Amara was beginning to settle into her new accommodations. She was feeling less stress because Calderon and León were no longer a threat. They were securely confined in their sleep modules, slipping into lower levels of consciousness. Nor were there as many stares from the crew when she and Nayta were together.

A few days later, she was directed to report to Dr. Eyveer in sick bay for a physical and a review of any health issues that might be relevant on Nanzema. She and Nayta had just finished lunch when he said to her, "I have to meet with Nuferas for a couple of hours to update our maintenance logs in Ops. Why don't you go for a workout in the gym? Then you can see Dr. Eyveer for your physical. You won't be able to stay active here on the ship like you were on the surface. You'll need to follow a strenuous exercise routine to stay healthy when you're not in the modules."

"That's an excellent idea," she replied. She was feeling sluggish from her lack of exercise since she had come on board the *Mankuriun*."

At the gym, she changed into workout clothes and put her street clothes on a shelf in one of the lockers. After a vigorous workout, she showered and felt better. When she started to dress, however, she saw that her hat was missing! She was frantic. She had only brought her three favorite hats with her—she had left behind most of her belongings because of a lack of space—and now one of them was gone. When Nayta returned, she was standing in the middle of the gym looking befuddled.

"What's wrong?" Nayta asked.

"Someone took my hat from the locker. It's not here. I've looked everywhere."

"Amara, are you sure? Bretin don't *take* things. That's why we don't have locks."

"That may be, my dear Nayta, but my hat is gone. It didn't fly away by itself!"

Nayta looked around the locker room. "I know there's a reasonable explanation. Would you like me to help you look for it after your appointment with Dr. Eyveer?"

She was frustrated by losing her hat and found it difficult to concentrate during her appointment. Afterward, she and Nayta searched everywhere but it was not to be found. Nayta was baffled; it had simply disappeared without any explanation.

The next day she returned to the gym, wearing another hat. After her workout and shower, she went into one of the small stalls to change her clothes. Before she was dressed, two female crew members, chattering away, came in to work out. "Did you see that haughty Senoobian bitch this morning?" one of them scoffed. "She had on a hat that's even uglier than the one she wore yesterday!"

"Unbelievable," the other one laughed. "Who does she think she is?"

"I don't know but I'm not impressed. I can't imagine why Nayta hangs around with her."

It was Mahprah and Ekseez! Amara sat there offended, but too embarrassed to say anything.

"Me either," the first one replied. "The Captain thought they were hot stuff but look what it got him. The way I see it they blew their chances to make a go of their colony."

"Yeah, while we worked our asses off on Nanzema—Aybron says Karyntis is a cake walk compared with Nanzema—and then we have to save them from being murdered by humans. Pathetic! I don't know why we're taking her with us. She'll never survive in Pormidora!"

"I expect not. I bet the XO only brought her along to honor the commitment the Captain made to her parents."

Amara heard the locker doors slam shut and the two females going into the exercise area. The ship was becoming smaller, turning into a prison from which there was no escape. She took in a deep breath, put on her hat and walked out into the passage way, feeling self-conscious and vulnerable.

Amara began to spend more of her time alone in her compartment. A couple of days later, Agoyin found her there on the verge of tears. When she told him about the conversation she had overheard, he was aghast. "Nayta, I'm afraid I've made a bad mistake. The crew doesn't want me here," she sobbed.

He hugged her. "It's just that a few of the crew don't know what to make of you. But you'll win them over. Don't worry."

That night she couldn't sleep. *What have I gotten myself into* she asked herself. She lay there replaying what she had overheard in the gym. Then she got mad. *I'll go to the gym tomorrow and teach those two a lesson* she vowed.

That night Stoveris couldn't sleep. He felt sick; he had begun to feel weak and nauseous and, upon returning to his stateroom from the bridge, he decided to go to bed early. But he tossed and turned, troubled by odd dreams, until the sound of the intercom made him jerk upright in bed, soaked in sweat and aching all over. The OOD's voice was frantic, "Sir, Dr. Eyveer is dead!"

Confused and disoriented, Stoveris began, "Do you know what—" and then it hit him. He recalled what had happened to the *Syzilian* and that Eyveer had treated Bayn's wound.

Amara's sleep was fitful and wracked by nightmares. When the entry chime at her stateroom door sounded, she was too groggy to respond. Minutes later, she was startled by someone yelling her name and beating on the door. When she opened it, there was a panic-stricken Agoyin. He took her by the shoulders. "Amara, something is terribly wrong. The XO is dead. Dr. Eyveer is dead. Our crew is dying. Stay in your stateroom until I can figure out what to do."

She covered her mouth in shock. "Nayta, what are the symptoms?"

"Umm, a high fever, nausea, aching and delirium in most cases."

She remembered the stories she had heard from her parents and Bayn about the deaths of the crewmembers of the *Syzilian*. *The symptoms are the same*, she thought. *This happened after Eyveer treated Bayn. He could have been immune and carried it all of those years. If Eyveer or his orderly cleaned up after treating Bayn, they might have gotten infected by some of his blood.* The thought struck her like a bolt of lightning. *Ahgzahtu! Am I immune? Or am I a carrier too?*

"Nayta, this is what happened to the *Syzilian*. It's a human virus— a bad one! Our only hope is to get into the sleep modules with the fastest takedown."

"Are you sure?" Agoyin asked anxiously.

"Same situation. Same symptoms. Same result," Amara declared.

Agoyin's eyes met hers. "If you're sure, I'll put you in a mod," he replied "but I can't go myself until the ship is on autopilot. Hold on while I call the bridge."

The OOD answered. He sounded bad.

"Ponytis, is the ship on autopilot?" Agoyin yelled.

"Nayta? No. Tavin and I started the sequence, but we're both too sick to complete it. I've got to get to sick-bay."

"Ponytis, I'm on my way. I'll put the ship on autopilot. You and Tavin have to get in a mod now; sick-bay can't help you. Go!"

He turned back to Amara and grabbed her hand. "Come on," he shouted as he started off at a run for the sleep modules. When they reached them, he adjusted the settings and hurriedly explained how she would feel as she faded into a rapid hyper sleep. Then he gave her a sedative, kissed her, put a breathing mask on her, adjusted it, and nudged her into #21. He rattled off, "I'll be back in no time and settle into #19, beside you." He could feel the beginnings of a fever. The virus had launched its grim assault on his body and he was running out of time. He finished programming her unit and started off unsteadily for the bridge.

Outside the bridge he found Ponytis sprawled in the passageway, barely alive. On the bridge Tavin was slumped over the autopilot console, deathly ill. Feelings of nausea began to roll over him as he pushed Tavin aside and moved quickly to complete the procedure required to put the ship on autopilot. Sweat ran down his face and stung his eyes, making it hard to focus, so he had to restart the procedure twice. After the autopilot was engaged, he managed to transmit a brief message. *He had to get to Amara.* He staggered to his feet, swaying unsteadily, then stopped in his tracks and looked around, confused: *Where was he supposed to go?* He stood there, disoriented, unable to move and growing weaker. *If only he could sleep.* His vision became a blur; he slumped to the deck and slipped into unconsciousness.

Three days later, except for the faint hum of its electrical systems, the starship *Mankuriun* sped through space silently, mindlessly carrying its grim cargo to Nanzema. Within it there was neither sound nor movement. Only the bodies in modules 21, 23 and 25 were still alive.

27

HAYMAN-ANGLER

On Thursday morning, Luke called Lou Broucelli to let him know he was back and to schedule a meeting so he could brief his boss on his trip and turn in a formal report. As Luke walked into Broucelli's office, his boss scowled at him. "Okay, what's going on in Peru? You're three days late; this had better be good."

Luke winced. "Sorry, Lou. I had an experience there that was incredible; I had to see it through." He briefly related his contact with Martin through Floyd Cate's referral and his decision to go to Peru with his friend Sonny to meet Martin.

He described his meeting with the Senoobians, expecting Broucelli to throw up his hands any minute and say, *Hold on! Are you nuts? Do you expect me to believe that you went to Peru to meet some aliens from another planet. That's preposterous!* But he didn't.

Broucelli stood up and walked over to close the door to his office. "Go on," he said.

Relieved that Broucelli had not yet exploded in angry disbelief, he mentioned how he and Sonny would have been killed by the drug lord Calderon if Amara and Marco had not rescued them—he decided it was best to say nothing about the Bretin. Then he said, "Before I go any further, I want to show you something so you'll know I'm not imagining all of this."

He pulled out Bayn's blood test results and some photos from a file folder. "Take a look at this." Luke handled him the blood test results and the photographs. Broucelli studied them intently without comment.

Luke sat back and took a deep breath, unsure about how Broucelli was really reacting to everything Luke was telling him. "What do you think? You do believe me, don't you?" he finally ventured.

Broucelli slid open his desk drawer and Luke found himself looking down the barrel of a .45. "Oh, yeah, I believe you," he said matter-of-factly.

Luke was taken aback. "Lou, what the hell are you doing?"

Broucelli calmly cocked the .45. "Let's get one thing straight," he growled. "If you ever pull another stunt like that: running off without telling me when something like this is going on, I'll have you hunted down and killed! And don't ever bring in anyone from outside the agency without my permission. You got that?"

"Yes, sir," Luke stammered. He was terrified his boss would figure out that he wasn't getting the whole story and shoot him.

He thought to himself, *why did I have to promise Darz I wouldn't mention the Bretin? If Lou finds out about them, I'm history.*

"I'm sorry, Lou. It's just that it sounded like some crackpot story and I figured you would think I was an idiot for following up on it. But there was something about it that made me think I should check it out. For one thing, Connor, the guy who contacted me, is no nutcase."

Broucelli uncocked the .45 and laid it on the desk in front of him.

Luke took a deep breath and opened his mouth to continue, but, before he could say anything else, Broucelli stopped him by raising his hand. "Do you know anything about that big explosion that occurred two days ago over South America?"

Luke said, "An explosion! No, anyone killed?"

Broucelli related how a huge, high altitude explosion had been detected over the southern part of Peru. It was being investigated, but there was no explanation for what had happened.

It was almost two hours later before Luke finished describing his and Sonny's experiences with the three Senoobians. To his relief, instead of expressing disbelief and making him feel stupid, Broucelli actually listened with genuine interest.

Broucelli said, "So you're telling me that the Senoobian race was killed off except for the four Senoobians left on this planet and that another advanced race may be returning to Earth to take it over."

"That's what the Senoobians told us. The bad news is there are so many unanswered questions that we can only speculate about what might happen; the good news is that we've got a few years to figure out what to do."

"How much time do you think we have?" Broucelli asked.

"It's hard to say. According to the Senoobians, Peyr is 21 light years away—quite a distance—but who knows how long it will take the Peyrians to get here? If they are already operating within our Solar System, they could be here in four or five years. Bayn told us that Peyr is located in the constellation Libra; it's one of three planets that orbit the star that we call Gliese 581. Other than that, we know nothing about it.

"Well, it's obvious: we've got to find the Senoobians and get their disks!" exclaimed Broucelli.

He furrowed his brow and became silent. Then he swiveled in his chair and stared out the window, ignoring Luke. Finally, he stood up and paced around his office. "Luke, I don't want you talking to anyone else about what you've told me. I've got to sort through all of this before I pass it on to the higher ups. If the press got hold of this, I hate to think about the uproar."

He paused again as if he were trying to make up his mind. Then he lowered his voice. "I'm going to tell you something that must not be repeated outside this room. I have connections to the Hayman-Angler Corporation. It's a defense contractor, not a major player like Lockheed Martin or Ratheon but big enough and aggressive, way ahead of the curve. They mostly develop weapons systems and other advanced technologies. They're well-connected in Washington. There's one thing that sets them apart though; they take seriously the idea of *alien visitation*."

"You mean U.F.O.'s?"

"Yes. They accept the probability that Earth has been visited by other intelligent life whose intentions are unclear. Our government can't officially acknowledge that sometimes people witness things that we can't explain. Sure, 95% of what people see can be explained away as natural phenomena, the military conducting exercises, hoaxes and so forth but not everything.

"Just two and a half years ago—it was in March of '97, in Phoenix—hundreds of people, including Governor Symington himself, saw an enormous triangular-shaped craft cruise silently and slowly at a relatively low altitude over downtown Phoenix, Sky Harbor International Airport and several smaller towns. To this day, no one knows what it was."

"Anyway, a small group of astronomers—whose work just happens to be funded by Hayman-Angler—managed to arrange a meeting with the Vice President and a couple of other high level officials. The astronomers convinced them that there's something strange going on and that we should have some covert organization working on a strategy for dealing with the aliens they are sure we will eventually meet. What better organization than Hayman-Angler? I want to remind you: this is highly classified."

Luke had to ask, "Yes, of course, but what do you mean that you have connections?"

Broucelli frowned, "Think about it, Luke. Working for the CIA gives us access to information that could be valuable to a company like Hayman-Angler. Suppose the agency acquires information about some alien visitation. What's the harm in our passing it on to our contacts at Hayman-Angler. At this point, I can't say any more except that there are people a lot higher up than me connected to Hayman-Angler."

What's the harm! Luke thought. *Sounds like a conflict of interest to me and a dangerous one at that.* "Lou, I don't want to be involved in passing classified intelligence to unauthorized recipients."

Broucelli paused for a moment and appeared to be lost in thought. He drummed his forefinger on his desk and then moved in front of his computer and went on-line. A couple of minutes later, he had found the information he wanted and his face lit up.

"Luke, you said the Senoobians escaped from their ship just before it exploded in 1908. As a matter of fact, there was a huge airborne explosion over Tunguska in Siberia on the morning of June 30, 1908." He read from the site he was scanning:

A huge fireball streaked through the skies and disintegrated in a rapid series of deafening explosions at an altitude of eight km. No one knew what to make of it. The force of the blast felled trees in an outward radial pattern over a vast area and fires burned for weeks over a thousand square km area. One of the local nomads had 600 reindeer, his hunting dogs, and all of his furs incinerated. Whatever it was, if the thing had exploded over Europe instead of sparsely populated Siberia, at least a half million people would have been killed.

"There have been numerous theories over the years since then as to what exploded over Tunguska. We still can't say for certain what it was. The leading theory is that it was an asteroid but there's no crater or asteroid fragments. There have been other theories: that it was a comet, a black hole, anti-matter, or the nuclear power plant of an alien spacecraft. Maybe it *was* an exploding Senoobian starship."

They both sat there for a moment, considering the events that had occurred in Peru over the last two weeks. Finally Broucelli said, "Luke, this may be a defining moment in human history. Different civilizations have pushed up against one another time and again throughout history with dire consequences: the Macedonians and Persians, the Spanish and the Incas, the European immigrants and American Indians, for example. When that happens, winner takes all and the other fades into obscurity."

Luke said, "There's my favorite—the Punic Wars between Rome and Carthage, the super powers of their day, in the third century BC."

Broucelli nodded, "That's right. The clash of civilizations fighting to the death—now we may see it happen on an interplanetary scale and the question is what should we do."

Luke said, "Something big is going to happen when the Peyrians return. It's possible, things could get dicey."

"As I said, we may have only a few short years to develop a contingency plan for dealing with them. How can we ever reach a consensus as to the best way for all the developed nations to respond to something like this? It seems to me that the U.N. would be the natural forum, but it's hard to get agreement on anything there because every issue becomes so politicized. Maybe the Security Council with strong support from the U.S. could deal with it."

Broucelli said, "Don't be ridiculous. The best organization to handle this is hayman-Angler, and the smartest thing we can do is get our hands on those disks."

"Yes, they could be useful in a number of ways."

Broucelli nodded. "Tell me everything you know about them."

"Well, it's an indexed collection of 300,000 multi-media disks in a large metal case, the complete record of their civilization. Each disk is about the size of a silver dollar and each one holds a huge amount of information. The case contains the mechanism for accessing the disks by audio and holographic video as well as text . . ."

Broucelli interrupted, "If it is a complete record of the Senoobian civilization, including their technologies, as you say, can you imagine how valuable that could be to us? The Senoobians are obviously hundreds, or even thousands, of years more advanced than we are. Think how quickly we could progress if we had access to their technology—and weaponry. And to have the plans for a starship! Can you imagine? It boggles the mind. Besides all of that, we would be in a much stronger position if we had the benefit of all of that knowledge when dealing with the Peyrians."

Luke added excitedly, "Just as importantly, we could learn how they resolved their social problems, how they managed their planet's resources, how their government worked. What they've learned about the universe!"

Broucelli snorted. "Social problems! To hell with our social problems—we've got bigger fish to fry. If we had the kind of information I think they contain, the balance of power in the world would shift!" He thought a moment and then added, "Are you sure they still have them?"

Luke was appalled by his attitude. "As far as I know, they do. The disks are invaluable to them, of course; when their ship was about to be destroyed, the first thing they saved was the disks."

Broucelli was curious, "Did you actually see them?"

Luke said, "Yes, Sonny and I both watched a disk on their culture. They never volunteered, and we never asked, where they kept the case. I would guess that it's locked away in a secure place at Naksoris . . ."

Broucelli interjected. "Do you think they would share them with us? Maybe even loan them to us, I mean our government?"

Luke paused for a moment. "I don't know. If I had something that valuable, I don't think I would let it out of my sight. But I guess it never hurts to ask."

"Well, this is too important to wait; I'm going to talk to our Hayman-Angler people. I'll get back to you tomorrow."

As soon as Luke left his office, Broucelli made the call. Konrad "Ruger" Carlson was Broucelli's contact at Hayman-Angler, the go-to guy when a difficult mission required someone who could be counted on to get the job done, no matter what. Carlson was a man of few words, all business, always focused. He listened intently as Broucelli related his conversation with Luke. When Broucelli had finished, he asked a few brief questions and hung up.

Luke didn't have a phone number for the Senoobians, but he knew Father Tony would know how to reach them. When Father Tony finally answered, the first thing the old priest did was to tell him in

265

halting English about Bayn's death. When Luke understood the gist of how Bayn had been murdered, he was devastated. He gave the old priest a secure number and asked him to contact Darz and Jeliko. Father Tony promised to try to reach them and ask them to return Luke's call.

After Luke hung up, it occurred to him, "This probably isn't going to make Darz and Jeliko want to help us very much."

A few hours later, to his relief, he received a call from Darz: "Hello, Luke. How are you?"

"I'm fine, Darz. I'm awful sorry to hear about Bayn. He was an inspiration to all of us, and he will be sorely missed. Are you and Jeliko coping okay? And Marco?"

"Yeah, we're managing, but it's been rough. You knew him—he was unique in a lot of ways: a good Senoobian, our closest friend, our mentor. Yeah, we miss him, always will. He was a father-figure to all of us, you know; we'd been through a lot together."

"I can only imagine what you're going through." He could hear the fatigue in Darz's voice. *Probably hasn't been sleeping well.*

"Yeah, with Amara leaving, as I said, it's been rough."

What are you and Jeliko going to do now?"

"We're going to disappear—move away from Nazca to some place where we can live out our last years quietly. Marco is going with us, of course, and maybe Luis. The whole situation here is getting toxic for him as well. He's tried to keep a lid on it all, but there's only so much he can do.

"The Peruvian Police are investigating the deaths of Gonzales and Cabrera who were thought to be upright members of the police force. The situation is likely to blow up any day now and bring unwelcome scrutiny to us. People are going to start asking questions about us, and we could wind up being the scapegoats. Can you imagine the headlines: Local Police Killed by Aliens!

"Even though Calderon has *disappeared,* the only hope is to tie all of this to him, which is where it belongs."

"Darz, I'm sorry you and Jeliko have to go through all of that and give up your home."

"Well, Naksoris has some bad memories for us now, so it's just as well."

"Where will you go?" Luke asked.

"At this point I can't say, but we'll be in touch as soon as things calm down."

"Please do," Luke said. He paused. "Darz, not to change the subject, but I'm calling to ask for your help. I passed on the information you guys gave Sonny and me to my boss. He's trying to figure out what to do about it. He wants to meet you and Jeliko if you can possibly swing it, maybe some place away from Nazca where it's safe."

Luke took a deep breath. "Darz—"

"Yes?"

"I didn't mention the Bretin. My boss doesn't know anything about them or the *Mankuriun*."

"Luke, thanks for keeping them out of this, but I don't know what else we can do for you. You have the proof that we're for real. What good would it do for us to meet him?"

"Well, he's worried that there may be a war between humans and Peyrians. If they come back and try to set up a base here, our planet could become a battleground with millions of innocent people getting killed."

Darz was feeling his age; he was tired and his voice took on a sharp edge. "What's the big deal? You humans slaughter millions of each other every year in one way or the other. I'm sorry, but I'm a little put out with humans right now."

"Darz, I understand how you feel, but there are also a lot of good people on this planet."

He grunted and took a deep breath, his voice calmer. "All right, what does he want from us?"

"Well, he's hoping you might share some of the information from the Jukasian disks. Some of the technology they contain might put us on a more equal footing with the Peyrians.

"It might also be useful if some of us humans could speak Kuterin. Sonny knows the basics, thanks to you, but he can't carry on a serious conversation. We don't know anything about the Peyrian language but some of them may speak Kuterin. If we do have contact with them, being able to speak a common language might help."

Darz hesitated. "I wouldn't mind helping Sonny master Kuterin. The disks, however, are all we have left of Senoobis; we don't feel comfortable handing them over to anybody. I suspect that, if your government got its hands on them, we would never see them again.

We'll only give them to some organization we can trust. I'll talk it over with Jeliko anyway. Call me tomorrow around noon."

"Thanks, Darz. My best to Jeliko."

Luke called Broucelli to tell him about his conversation with Darz and that he wasn't optimistic about getting the disks. "He's hesitant to let the disks out of their sight, but he's going to talk it over with Jeliko and call me tomorrow to let me know their decision."

He told Broucelli about Bayn's murder and the bitterness that Darz felt. Besides, he continued, "The two of them are leaving Nazca. He did say he didn't have any problem with helping us learn Kuterin."

Senator Walter P. Gordon was at the White House talking to an aide about his upcoming trip to London when the call came from Montgomery Scott. Senator Gordon was Chairman of the Armed Services Committee and the major stockholder in Hayman-Angler.

"Monty" Scott, President of the Hayman-Angler Corporation, came from an old Virginia family that had been prominent in banking and politics for generations. His aristocratic upbringing was reflected in a genteel manner that, with his gray hair and prominent chin, gave him the kindly patriarchal look that disguised a hard and calculating nature.

Scott was upset. Broucelli had reported to Ruger Carlson who had reported to him that the Senoobians were reluctant to part with their disks. He briefed Gordon about Luke's call. "I want those goddamn disks," he growled. "We can't let something like this slip through our fingers! The Senoobians are leaving for God only knows where. We've got to move fast. If they won't give them to us, we'll have to take them by force. Walter, we may need some support on this. I'll be in touch."

That evening Darz briefed Jeliko on his conversation with Luke. It was clear that Luke was feeling pressure from his boss to acquire the disks. The more they talked about it, the more they realized how powerful the disks could be in the hands of one group or nation. They realized that if the United States, Russia or China possessed the technology recorded in the disks, they might dominate the planet. They were skeptical that any of those countries would share that information with the rest of the planet as Kurmythia had done centuries before.

At first they decided the only prudent course of action would be to share the information with the United Nations. After further thought, however, they realized that even the UN wouldn't be able to use the information to benefit all the nations of the world. They recalled the lack of progress humans seemed to be making in dealing with their major problems. Nuclear weapons technology from the former Soviet Union and from unstable nations such as Pakistan had fallen into the hands of terrorist groups and rogue states such as North Korea. They concluded that humans weren't ready to use such knowledge responsibly.

They next debated what to do with the disks to keep them secure until the time was right to share them with humankind. The safest course, they agreed, would be to leave the disks where they had been hidden for the last few years.

It had been Father Tony's idea. They had kept the disks in their lander for years, believing it was the safest place, but their lander was not easy to hide and times had changed. Now they realized that if some government or terrorist group learned about the disks, the lander might be compromised and the disks stolen. It would be safer if they were hidden where no one would find them.

They told Father Tony about the disk library and explained their dilemma to him. As they told him about its size and importance, he settled back in his chair, making a tent with his fingers. A moment later it came to him: "I have the perfect place in mind and I'm sure Father Navarro won't mind."

Father Luis Navarro had been the rector of the church some 60 years before Father Tony and there was a vault, intended for his remains, deep within the bowels of the church. Sadly Father Navarro never got to use his vault because he disappeared on one of his trips into the Amazon and his body was never found. The vault was eventually forgotten by everyone but Father Tony who discovered it by accident one day. When the Senoobians saw it, they readily agreed it would be the perfect place to keep the disks.

Darz phoned Luke to tell him they didn't think it wise to release the disks to any one government since the disks might disturb the balance of power in a world that was already unstable. Luke immediately phoned Broucelli.

The next day Ruger Carlson met with Scott to update him on the report he had just received from Broucelli. His boss was furious.

"What do you suggest?" Carlson asked.

Scott thought hard about everything Carlson had told him. "Ruger, I've got a plan. Broucelli told you that the Senoobians were close to a handful of humans in Peru, especially an old priest. Here's what I want you to do . . ."

Carlson called Broucelli back and explained the plan to him. "Take Pearson and Campbell—Gordon will clear his assignment with his boss at NSA—and two of my men with you and find our hard-headed aliens," he growled. "Offer them a million dollars or whatever it takes. If they won't sell, take them."

"What do you mean, *take them?*"

"Jesus, Lou! Do I have to spell out everything to you? That's what my men are for. Take the disks by force. Take the aliens to a safe house and make them talk. Take them to *Gitmo* if you have to. I don't give a shit! Just get the goddamn disks. You do understand, we want them alive, right?"

"Yes, of course. I'll get right on it," Broucelli stammered.

"Good. There's no time to waste. Get a chopper down there. Gordon will have our embassy contact the Peruvian government and tell them we're tailing some terrorists. If you have a problem, call me."

Carlson was a former Special Forces colonel; when the pressure was on, he could be mean-spirited. Just before hanging up, he said, "Lou . . ." His tone was ominous.

"What?"

"Get the damn disks—whatever it takes."

As Broucelli rushed back to his office to collect his thoughts, he groused to himself: *Jesus! What an asshole! The big corporations use their lobbyists to get whatever they want, and our congressmen are glad to oblige as long as the money keeps rolling in and they get reelected. It's a license to steal and the public is too dumb to know it.*

He sat at his desk, coolly trying to sort through everything in his mind. Then it occurred to him: *this is the opportunity of a lifetime! If I can manage to bring back two aliens and a cache of information that's probably worth billions, I'll be set for life—the fair-haired boy of the agency. Wait, if I can bring back the aliens AND the disks, it ought to be worth at least a couple of million to me. To hell with Carlson and Hayman-Angler!* His mind was racing at the possibilities.

The call Luke received from Broucelli was unsettling. There was a quasi-military operation in the works. He and Sonny and two Special Forces types were to form a small task force headed by Broucelli that was to leave for Peru early the next morning. "My head's on the block," Broucelli grunted. "We've got to get those disks, whatever it takes."

Even torture! Luke thought. *They came to us to help and this is what they get. Bullshit!* he muttered to himself angrily as he hung up.

Early that evening he finally decided what to do, even though he would be putting himself at risk. He had to go along with the operation to acquire the disks; there was no choice in that. But after his conversation with Broucelli, he was sickened by the thought of Darz or Jeliko being tortured if they wouldn't turn over the disks. He had to warn them but he didn't dare call them on either his office phone or his personal cell phone.

First he called Sonny and arranged for them to meet at Potter's in two hours. After checking to be sure he had his international phone card, he made his way to the small restaurant two blocks away from his apartment, seemingly for dinner. As soon as he had found a table and ordered a drink, he went toward the restroom as if to wash up but instead stopped at the payphone and dialed Darz's cell phone number. There was no answer so he left a brief message: "Darz, this is Luke. You're in danger. My boss is bringing Sonny and me there with a couple of toughs to get the disks from you. Don't call me. I'll call you again in a couple of hours."

After he had finished dinner, he tried the call again. There was no answer so he left another message: "Darz, we're leaving for Peru at 6:00 in the morning. If they can't buy the disks, they're going to take them from you by force. Make sure they don't find you!" As soon as he hung up, he rushed off to meet Sonny.

At Potter's he was relieved to find Sonny already there and motioning him over to his table. "Morris got a call from some big shot congressman. I hear we're going back to Peru with an escort— Broucelli and two security guys. What the hell is going on?" Sonny spit out before Luke could even sit down.

Luke explained everything. Then he suggested that they warn Father Tony. No doubt Broucelli will want to talk to him. They reached Father Tony and Sonny spoke to him in Spanish, explaining the urgency of their call and warning him that there would be men trying to find the Senoobians, men who might hurt him and Phillipe.

That night he couldn't sleep, worried by his failure to reach Darz and Jeliko: *Would they receive his message in time?*

By 14:00 the next afternoon they were in Lima and by 17:00 they were approaching Nazca in their small plane. The two security men sat behind Luke and Sonny. Hank Johnson was tough and wiry-looking with a short beard and big chew of tobacco. Mack Baker was a hulking man with huge arms and a sullen expression. Neither one was friendly or talked much.

After renting a car and a modest secluded house on the outskirts of Nazca, Broucelli asked Luke and Sonny to direct them to Naksoris first in case the aliens were still there. If not, they could look for clues as to where to find them. Luke and Sonny found it impossible to escape the scrutiny of Broucelli and the two security men who always seemed to be keeping a close eye on them.

When they arrived at Naksoris the next morning, the two toughs fanned out to search the area while Broucelli, Luke and Sonny approached the house. The door was not locked and they entered cautiously. There was a sad and empty feel to the place as they went from room to room, but it was obvious that it had been occupied recently. The toughs searched the hangar, which had held the lander, and the wooded area east of the house. There were no clues as to the whereabouts of the Senoobians.

That afternoon they stopped by the police station hoping to find Arturo but he hadn't been seen in three days. Next they stopped by the tavern where Carlos worked but he knew nothing about the whereabouts of the two Senoobians or Luis. Then they went to Father Tony's church. They found him in the small garden behind the church and he invited them in for something to drink. Broucelli questioned him thoroughly but he could tell them nothing about the Senoobians. As they left the church, it was obvious that Broucelli was getting frustrated.

Early that evening after dinner, they had a Cerveza and talked about their mission. Broucelli was adamant. Looking at the four of them, he declared, "Gentlemen, I've been in the bureau for 27 years and I have never once failed to complete my mission. And I'm going to complete this one, one way or the other. We're going to be here as long as it takes." He looked sternly at Luke. "You told me that Father Francisco is close to the Senoobians, and I'm sure he knows how to reach them. We're going to get the disks and we're going to take them and your two alien friends back to Washington. We can do it the easy way, or we can do it the hard way."

Neither Luke nor Sonny liked the sound of that. "What do you mean," Sonny asked cautiously.

"Well, you see Hank here; he's a talented guy. He knows how to make people talk. You enjoy making people talk, don't you, Hank?" The man was a brute and he nodded eagerly.

"Now here's what we're going to do: tomorrow, I'm going to kick back here with Luke and Mack and get over my jet lag."

He turned to Sonny. "You know your way around here and you speak Spanish. I want you and Hank to take the car and go see the Father. Tell him you need him to get a message to your Senoobian friends fast. The message is they had better bring the disks to us by 8:00 tomorrow evening or Father Tony's gonna get hurt."

Luke was incredulous. "Are you serious? Surely you're bluffing; you wouldn't hurt Father Tony! He's a priest for God's sake."

"I'm serious as a heart attack. We're going back with those disks or else."

Painful images of Father Tony being tortured flashed through his mind. "You don't mean water boarding!" He recalled the whole procedure with horror. The prisoner is bound to an inclined board with his head a little lower than his feet. Cellophane is wrapped over his face and water is poured over him causing him to gag and feel like he's drowning. Such panic sets in that the average prisoner is begging to confess anything within 15 seconds.

"Whatever. I wasn't thinking of water boarding but, now that you mention it, that's a good idea. There's plenty of running water here and, what the hell, it does get fast results."

Sonny exclaimed, "You're going to bring Father Tony here so you can torture him!"

"No, of course not—," Broucelli smirked, "You and Hank are gonna bring him here. I want him here by 6:30 tomorrow afternoon."

"What if he won't come," Luke exclaimed.

"Oh, he'll come because, if he doesn't, he *will* get hurt."

He winked at Johnson who nodded without a hint of a smile.

Luke stammered desperately, "But, Lou, we don't even know that they still have the disks."

Broucelli's voice had a sharp edge. "You sure as hell better hope they do."

After breakfast the next morning, Sonny drove off with Hank Johnson to find Father Tony. When they arrived at the church, he was in his study talking with great affection to a frail old grey-haired lady. When he saw them at the door, he motioned them in and introduced her with kindness and respect. She sensed that the two men were anxious to speak with Father Tony privately so she excused herself. Sonny finally persuaded Johnson to wait outside so he could talk to Father Tony in private.

As the old priest closed the door to his office, Sonny blurted out in Spanish, "Father Tony, you're in grave danger!" Then he explained the situation nervously as Father Tony listened calmly.

"It seems that we are all in grave danger," Father Tony continued in Spanish after a moment's thought. If I call Darz and Jeliko and they come in, who knows what will happen to them. If I don't reach them, I will be tortured and possibly killed by these men. I'm a frail old man; they could snap me like a twig. I could go into hiding but I'm a priest; I can't live that way. I could contact the local police but I doubt they could protect me. These men are obviously professionals. If I refuse to go with you, they will know you warned me and they might harm you."

Sonny said, "Father Tony, whatever else we do, I think we have to warn Darz and Jeliko. At the very least, they need to know that they are being hunted by these dangerous men."

Father Tony considered the situation briefly and placed the call. Darz answered and Father Tony quickly related everything that Sonny had told him. Then Sonny got on the phone. "Darz, I'm sorry. We had no idea things would turn out this way."

Darz said, "It's not your fault. I should have known this would happen. Hold on. Let me talk to Jeliko." The line went silent.

Finally he came back on the line. "We can't allow them to torture Father Tony. We'll come there with the disks."

Sonny gave him the address. "Be careful—these guys are serious. Luke and I will do whatever we can. There are three of them—Broucelli and two body guards. Darz—," he winced, not wanting to say it.

"What, there's more?"

"Yes, he intends to take you and Jeliko with the disks to Washington where they can interrogate you and have you interpret the disks. I shudder to think what they might do to you."

"Yeah, me too," Darz muttered. "We need to see Father Tony right after lunch so arrange with your security guy to pick up Father Tony at 5:00. Tell Broucelli we'll be there by 8:00 this evening with the disks. Let me speak with Father Tony again and then I'll go."

While Sonny paced back and forth nervously, Father Tony spoke to Darz and then hung up the phone. "It's in God's hands now."

Sonny said, "We're supposed to take you to meet Mr. Broucelli at 6:30. Can we pick you up at 5:30?"

Father Tony nodded and Sonny opened the door and spoke to Johnson, "We'll pick him up at 5:30. Let's get something to eat before we report to Broucelli." During lunch, Sonny's stomach was in knots as he tried to figure out what he could do to protect Father Tony and the two Senoobians from harm.

Father Tony went into the chapel where he sat quietly for a few minutes, deep in thought and then he prayed. At last he stood up and called for Phillipe who came and sat down beside him. After he had explained everything, he put his hands on the young man's shoulders and spoke with emotion, "My son, don't worry. If anything happens to me, I will go to a better place. I love you, my son, and I'm proud of you. If something happens to me, tend our flock and help our friends."

Phillipe didn't feel like helping their American friends, but he didn't know what else to do. The two men embraced as tears welled up in Phillipe's eyes. "Father, I beg you, let me go in your place."

"No, Phillipe. I'm an old man; I must go. You stay here."

When Sonny and the Johnson arrived at the safe house that afternoon with Father Tony, Sonny confirmed what Johnson had told him: the two Senoobians had agreed to be at Naksoris by 8:00 with the disks.

"Excellent," Broucelli exclaimed, licking his chops.

At 7:30 that evening, a black SUV sped up the narrow road to Naksoris and skidded to a stop at the porch. The two Senoobians got out and unloaded a large and heavy metallic case. They were angry that the humans had used Father Tony to get to them.

Broucelli gloated as they struggled to maneuver the disk library through the door. As Luke and Sonny rushed over to give them a hand, he studied them, surprised they were not the monstrosities he had imagined, in spite of the pictures Luke had showed him. "So you're the Senoobians I've heard so much about. I hear you're quite civilized; it was nice of you to come," he said sarcastically.

His demeanor changed: "Against the wall, now!" he ordered. "Baker, pad them down."

Baker pulled the Krayzur from Darz's side pocket, glanced at it contemptuously, and handed it to Broucelli. "That's it."

"Where's Father Tony?" Jeliko demanded.

Broucelli said, "He's fine. Bring him in, Hank." The man led Father Tony in.

Darz said, "Father Tony, are you all right?"

"I'm fine," he said. "Don't worry about me."

Darz turned back to Broucelli. "You have the disks, now let him go," Darz said.

"Not so fast," Broucelli said as he glared at Darz. He placed the weapon on the old table against the wall. "There are a couple of things I need you to do. You and Jeliko are going to go with us to Washington with your disks."

"What! Are you insane?" Darz demanded "Why?"

"We, I mean, our government, needs to debrief you. We don't have many authentic aliens drop by our planet, so it might be helpful if we could pick your brains for a few weeks. Besides we need you to be available while we review the disks in case we have questions."

Broucelli thought to himself, *you're too valuable to turn loose, pal. We won't let you go—ever.*

Darz was repulsed by Broucelli's arrogance. "It will take you years to go through the disks. There are 300,000 of them. If we show you how to access them, will you let us go?"

"No," said Broucelli "but I won't hurt you or Father Tony, if you do. How about a little demonstration?"

Reluctantly Darz stepped over to the metal case. He pressed a round recessed shape near one corner and a small control panel with a keypad and several buttons emerged from the top of the case. "This keypad is like the combination to a safe," Darz explained. "You get three tries and, if you enter the wrong sequence all three times, the case locks itself down. It's impossible to force it open and, if you try to, there's a mechanism that will instantly erase the contents of all the disks so the library will be worthless. The problem is I'm not sure I remember the combination."

"Don't hand me that crap," Broucelli threatened. "Open it up, now."

Sonny and Luke stood by the door, embarrassed at what was happening and frustrated by their helplessness.

Darz carefully punched in eight numbers. A slight clicking sound was heard and then one of the indicators on the panel slowly blinked five times. "That wasn't it," he said, looking exasperated.

"Don't jerk me around," Broucelli warned. "Hank, get the Father ready."

"Wait. Don't hurt him. I'm trying. The combination's been changed several times." He searched Jeliko's face, as if seeking her help and turned back to the case, his face a mask of concentration. He held his breath, closed his eyes for a moment and then carefully punched in eight more numbers. Once more the panel blinked five times. Darz straightened up, looking defeated.

"Damn it, Darz. Don't tell me you smart-assed aliens don't write down combinations. You'd better get it right this time or all three of you are going on the board."

He yelled at Hank who was in the kitchen with Father Tony strapping him to the bathroom door. "If it doesn't open this time, water board him!"

Father Tony was panicking. His heart was pounding faster; he tried to recite the Lord's Prayer.

Broucelli turned to Darz, "Then it will be her turn and then yours. It's a terrible way to die. You'll be begging to tell me everything."

Darz closed his eyes, his face betraying the tension he felt, and then his fingers moved to the keypad again. He hesitated momentarily and then entered the sequence, pausing only once to reconsider. Everyone in the room moved closer, feeling the tension and holding their breath. The indicator didn't blink. For a moment there was no response at all from the case except for a low humming sound that began deep inside it. The humans moved closer still, anxious to see the case open and disgorge its contents.

Suddenly there was a sharp bang, like the sound of a starter's pistol at a track meet, and a blinding flash as a small canister ejected from the top of the case and exploded, catching all of the humans by surprise.

At the sound of the explosion, Jeliko leaped toward the door that they had been careful not to close completely and reached the open air, still holding her breath. Darz lunged toward the table, snatched his Krayzur, and continued on through the open door, pushing it shut behind him. They landed on the ground outside gasping for breath. At first, there was loud coughing inside, but then it was quiet.

Fifteen minutes later, they eased open the door. All of them were semiconscious. Broucelli was lying on the floor near Baker. Luke and Sonny were slumped against the wall, unable to move. They stepped over Johnson, who was lying in the doorway to the kitchen, and rushed inside to assist Father Tony who was still lying tied to the door.

As soon as they saw him, they realized the worst. There was no movement, no sign of life at all. Darz checked his pulse; there was none. He was dead! Darz looked at Jeliko and said softly, "A heart attack—all of this was too much for him." *I could have saved* him somehow, Darz thought as a tide of guilt washed over him.

They looked at each other solemnly at a loss for words. Jeliko took Father Tony's hand in hers and sat down on the floor beside his body. "You shouldn't have died this way," she whispered as the tears began.

There was the sound of movement from the living room, and it sparked within Darz a rush of bitter anger. He stood up slowly and deliberately, shoved the intensity button on his Krayzur from *stun* to *kill*, and turned toward the door. Broucelli was there, still dazed, but lifting his pistol to fire at them. Darz was too quick; the sizzling blue bolt of energy from the Krayzur struck Broucelli, searing every neuron in his nervous system and emptying his mind of its memory. He slid back down to the floor, his eyes unseeing.

Baker lifted himself unsteadily from the floor, trying to grasp the situation. Darz fired again, point blank. The man's body convulsed for several seconds and then slumped forward.

He walked the few steps toward Johnson who fell back, desperately trying to escape his advance. Darz fired again.

Sonny and Luke watched the executions in shock. Darz's Krayzur fell to the floor with a heavy thud. Then he turned to them, his expression changing from anger to disgust. "We just can't stop the killing, can we?"

All four of them stood there in a surreal silence, staring at the floor. Finally Darz looked up at them. "We had better take Father Tony's body to the church and place it in Phillipe's care."

"Luke nodded, "Can we give you a hand?"

Darz said, "Thanks, no, we can manage. It's time for use to say goodbye to Nazca. Do whatever you need to do to clean up this mess; you'll have a lot of explaining to do about how your boss wound up dead in Peru."

Walking downcast back into the kitchen, Darz gently picked up the frail old man's body and carried it to their SUV. Then he and Jeliko picked up the disk library, loaded it into the SUV and drove off toward Nazca. They were anxious to return the disk library to the safety of the vault at the church.

Behind the wheel, Darz observed ruefully to Jeliko, "This is an ugly incident that brings shame to me as well as humans. It shows how depraved all of us can be. I'm no better than they are: they kill for greed; I kill for revenge." He was horrified at the thought of delivering Father Tony's body to Phillip. "I'm too ashamed to tell Phillipe what I've done."

When they arrived at the church, a distraught Phillipe was anxiously waiting for them outside the large wooden doors. "He died of a heart attack at the meeting—it was too much for him," Darz explained solemnly. Neither he nor Jeliko could bear to explain how his father had actually died. And Darz was too ashamed to admit that he had killed the three men who had tortured Father Tony. As soon as they had placed Father Tony's body in the small chapel, and secured the disk library in its vault, all three of them sat down for a minute as tears welled up in Phillipe's eyes.

He had been only a child, an orphan trying to survive on the streets, when Father Tony took him in, adopted him and raised him as his own son. It was a relationship that gave both of them a sense of family. He was a good man who deeply loved and respected his father. Now all three of them felt the terrible loss. Jeliko leaned over and placed her arms around him. "I'm sorry, Phillipe," she whispered. "We'll all miss him. You must carry on his work."

He looked up at her with sad wet eyes, wondering how he would manage without his father.

After Darz and Jeliko drove away, Luke and Sonny sat there for several minutes, still in shock at what had happened. Finally Sonny spoke, his voice shaky. "What do we do now? Our asses are in a sling for sure."

Luke thought for a minute. "Maybe our *friend* Calderon can help us out, in a manner of speaking, since the son-of-a-bitch tried to murder us all."

Sonny said, "In other words, blame the deaths of these three on drug traffickers? I'm not sure that would be smart. Besides I'm not sure we could pull it off. I think the best thing to do would be to tell it like it happened."

Luke said, "Maybe you're right. If we try to make something up, we'll just get caught. The truth is Broucelli tried to strong arm our Senoobian friends and he paid the price for it. Now they're going to disappear, so it doesn't matter how badly the corporation wants those disks, hopefully they won't be able to find them."

Sonny said, "Well, we'd sure as hell better tell somebody what's happened. Look, you call Broucelli's boss—Langford is it? Tell him everything. Then I'll call Morris. Let's give it to them straight."

Luke said, "Well, how do we explain the fact that . . ."

Just then the cell phone on Broucelli's belt rang. Startled, Sonny and Luke looked at each other as if to say, *what do we do now?* The phone rang three more times before Luke went over to Broucelli's body and gingerly removed it. "Hello, this is Luke Pearson."

The voice on the phone sounded surprised. "Pearson! What the hell are you doing on Broucelli's phone? Put him on."

"Who is this?"

"Ruger Carlson, Vice President of Operations with Hayman-Angler. Now put Broucelli on."

"He's dead."

"Dead! What the hell is going on down there?"

Luke told him what had happened.

Carlson was silent for a minute. "Where are the aliens now?"

"I don't know. They left in their lander with Father Antonio's body," Luke said.

Carlson hesitated. "All right. Sit tight. I'm coming down there myself. There's not that much air traffic in Southern Peru; if they're in the lander, we should be able to find them. Hang on to Broucelli's phone. I want you and Sonny to meet me at the Nazca airport tomorrow morning. I'll call you when we're a couple of hours out. If anything comes up, call me on this number. I'll bring a couple of guys to take care of the bodies." The line went dead.

Luke turned to Sonny. "It was Ruger Carlson; he's a big shot with Hayman-Angler! The fact that four men died here didn't seem to bother him too much. He said to stay put. He's going to fly down in the morning and wants us to meet him at the airport. And he's bringing somebody to take care of the bodies."

They looked at each other glumly, not happy about spending the night at Naksoris with three dead bodies lying about.

On the way back to Naksoris, Darz and Jeliko were silent, reliving everything that had just happened. Darz was distraught because he had killed Broucelli and his men. He glanced sideways at Jeliko, "Captain Markovin thought this planet was bad luck and I believe he was right. Too many bad things happen here."

As they entered Naksoris, Darz apologized to Luke and Sonny for losing control. Luke told them that he had truthfully reported to Carlson everything that had happened and that Carlson was coming to Peru to look for them. Darz and Jeliko agreed that he had done the right thing.

Luke said, "Look, we don't want to lose touch with you two, but don't tell us where you're going. I'll give you my sister's phone number in Tallahassee and you can leave me a message there. I'll give her a call every couple of weeks. I don't think it would be wise to contact me in Alexandria."

Darz and Jeliko nodded. Then Darz said to them, "We're going to leave the disks in a safe place. If humans ever become responsible enough to use the knowledge contained in them wisely, we'll turn them over to the appropriate organization. Until then, I believe they might do more harm than good. In the meantime, I expect that someday there is going to be another visit by a Peyrian starship. I think you should make the proper authorities aware of that. I doubt that they will be as cooperative as we've been.

"Darz looked solemnly at Sonny and Luke. Take care, my friends, we'll be in touch after things settle down." The four of them shook hands and wished each other good luck in dealing with the impending storm of trouble.

At 10:30 the next morning Luke and Sonny received a call from Carlson telling them he would be there in a couple of hours. They arrived just in time to see three helicopters landing near the small terminal. All three choppers and the crews were assigned to Hayman-Angler from DOD.

A Black Hawk UH-60 carried Ruger Carlson, his assistant, Clark Wentworth, and two burly security men with M-16's. The Black Hawk could carry the disk library, a couple of aliens and almost anything else that needed to be transported back to the states.

For more protection, there were two AH-64 Apache attack helicopters carrying a two-man crew and heavily armed with Hellfire missiles.

Puffing on a cigar, Carlson climbed out of the Black Hawk and strode over to Luke and Sonny, looking self-assured and in charge. He was trim with an athletic build and intense dark eyes, his slightly graying hair was in a crew cut. Behind him trailed Wentworth, and the two security men.

After the introductions, Luke and Sonny reviewed what had happened at safe house in more detail. Finally satisfied, Carlson said, "Okay, here's what we're going to do. I've gotten clearance to use DOD's recon satellite assets. The area within a 100-mile radius of Nazca is going to be scanned for unusual aircraft. They won't be far from their lander and we'll find it. While we're waiting to hear from our friends at DOD, let's scoot on over to Naksoris. I want to look around. While we're there," he gestured toward Wentworth, "Clark will take charge of the bodies. Make arrangements with your friend Arturo to help him *tidy things up*. Sonny, when DOD finds the lander, I want you to go with us to find the aliens and talk to them."

He waved them toward the Black Hawk and turned to Luke, "Okay, Sport, show us the way to Naksoris.

As they lifted off, Sonny turned to Carlson. "Sir, I don't know much about Hayman-Angler, except that it wants to acquire alien technology. Would you mind telling me a little more about the corporation?"

Carlson paused and chewed his cigar. "Okay, Broucelli's dead and I'm going to need your help even more now. He drew a deep breath. Hayman-Angler is a private company, a defense contractor, with some key personnel like myself who manage the government's secret program for investigating UFO's. It's founder and President, Montgomery Scott is the driving force behind the company—a real visionary in my opinion. Realizing the importance of having an ally in congress, he brought in an old buddy of his, Senator Walter Gordon.

"It was all Monty's idea. A few years ago he realized that there were too many events over the centuries that could only be explained as alien encounters. When you think about it, our own galaxy has billions of stars so the odds are that some of those stars have planets with conditions favorable for the development of intelligent life. Now, if some alien civilization is advanced enough to travel light years from its own star system to Earth, it must have some incredible technologies. If we could somehow track down our alien visitors and acquire their technology, wouldn't that be grand!"

Sonny thought to himself, *who needs millions of dollars for R&D if the technology is there for the taking!*

Carlson rambled on, "There have been clues from time to time down through the centuries, such as the Piri Reis Map which shows Antarctica as it would have looked about 6,000 years ago before it was covered in ice. The map was drawn from earlier unknown sources in 1513 by Piri Reis who was an admiral in the navy of the Ottoman Turks. There are other maps that imply aerial surveys thousands of years before humans could fly. And there have been unexplained events in this century, but he couldn't find anything concrete to follow up on until . . ." He paused, leaving them hanging.

"On March 13, 1997, early on a Sunday evening, a huge triangular craft with large lights on its underbelly was spotted near Henderson, Nevada, cruising silently in a southerly direction. By the time it reached Phoenix, it had been seen by hundreds of locals in small towns along the way. Later that evening it drifted across downtown Phoenix and the international airport and was seen by hundreds more people, including Governor Symington himself. You might guess it was some kind of experimental aircraft from Luke Air Force Base. Monty checked it out; it wasn't. From that point on he was a believer and that's when he recruited me."

The Mankuriun! Sonny thought to himself: *No point in bringing up the Mankuriun now.*

He changed the subject. He was curious to know how such a group had been received in Washington. "Does the President know you're on a mission to find aliens?" he asked.

"Hell no!" Carlson exclaimed. "It's a small group, strictly need to know and Top Secret. Except for Clark here, most of my department doesn't know what we're doing. As far as everyone knows, we're a typical DOD contractor. I've been sent down here to talk to the Peruvians about using some of our military assets to fight drug trafficking." He winked at Sonny: "We've had reports that some of the drug lords have gotten some high tech stuff, like stingers, RPG's, and C-4 plastic."

"There are several reasons for keeping this project under wraps. We're simply taking the information the government has accumulated and putting it to good use. We intend to be the first to acquire whatever alien technology may be available. Let me remind you that neither of you are to mention this to any one. I want to get control of this alien situation before word about it gets out and we have a media frenzy. I intend to get the disks and evaluate them for their military value. They could be priceless."

"But what about Broucelli and his men getting killed? Won't that raise questions?" Sonny asked.

Carlson feigned a look of disgust. "Drugs! It's a nasty business. Sometimes people get killed—that's why we have two Apaches with us. Don't worry. Clark here will handle the details when we get back."

Sonny thought to himself, *maybe Luke's idea wasn't so bad after all. But something doesn't add up.* "I don't get it. What's the real reason you want alien technology? Broucelli believed our government was incapable of dealing with the threat of a war between the Peyrians and humans."

Carlson smiled at Sonny in a condescending way. "Broucelli was an idiot! Think about it. I'm on the board of Hayman-Angler. Imagine what the company could do with some radical new technology—faster airplanes, more accurate missiles, new power systems. The technologies your Senoobian friends have could save us billions of dollars in R&D costs and put us years ahead of our competition. We could become the most powerful corporation in the world!"

"This isn't for the government then," Sonny ventured.

"Not directly, Sport. The information from the disks will be classified and controlled by Hayman-Angler. We will develop the technology and then, with Senator Gordon's connections, sell it to DOD on a no-bid contract and make a fortune. You've heard about those $500 hammers? Defense, Sport, that's where the money is! The government will pay any amount in the name of national defense— now there's a cash cow for you!"

Sonny was appalled as Carlson gathered steam.

"Look, if the Earth did become a battleground between two alien races, wouldn't humans be in a stronger position if they had the benefit of advanced alien technologies? Remember, we're not just making lots of money, we're building a stronger America by making new technologies available."

"Sounds to me like you're in the right place at the right time to make a *killing*," Sonny said as he thought to himself, *it's the greed of people like you that's killing thousands of innocent people.*"

"You can bet your sweet ass we are. Our government spends about $350 billion on contracts with 175,000 companies and about one-fourth of that total goes to only six companies, including Lockheed Martin, Boeing, Northrop Grumman, and General Dynamics. And here's the best part: less than 40% of the contracts that go to those companies are awarded in open competition. HAC isn't one of the top companies for government contracts now, but by God with the right technologies and Gordon's connections it will be."

Sonny was incredulous. "So the military-industrial complex is alive and well."

Carlson was almost preaching now, "That's right, Sport. And it's the military-industrial complex with the support of politicians like him that makes this country great; hell, that's why we're the only superpower in the world! We export more arms than anyone else; we supply almost half of the weapons sold to militaries in the developing world, three times what Russia, our nearest competitor sells . . ."

Sonny interrupted, "But, aren't we supplying arms to some of the most unstable regions in the world, to oppressive governments, to nations already involved in bloody conflicts, even genocide? And isn't it possible that those weapons could fall into the hands of terrorists and other enemies of the U.S., destabilizing friendly governments and putting our country at risk?"

Carlson regarded him as if he were naive. "Sonny, Sonny, they're going to buy their arms somewhere—don't you think it best that it be from us? Look at the beauty of it. Because we build good weapons, we can sell to both sides in those conflicts, like Pakistan and India, Israel and Egypt, Turkey and Greece. You boys have got to wake up to reality. We've got a huge opportunity here and, if you help me find these aliens and their disks, you'll be set for life."

Sonny was disgusted. He stared at Carlson in disbelief, feeling only contempt for the man who was lecturing him. *Another Merchant of death!* he thought. *Just like Alberto Calderon—he doesn't give a shit how many people die as long as he gets what he wants. That's how the system works and he knows how to work the system.*

28

THE PEYRIANS

The next morning Marco and the Senoobians waited to see their human friends one last time. They had invited Luis and Phillipe to stop by Naksoris for a final goodbye. Phillipe was the first to arrive; Darz asked him if he would look after the disks that were back in Father Navarro's vault until a safe place could be found for them at Detza Keeska. Then they would return to retrieve them.

They found him in a bad mood but he agreed. He had just had another run-in with Bishop Hervias over the use of the church's money. Besides, he felt lost without Father Tony and had become thoroughly disillusioned with the Church since Father Tony's death.

When Luis arrived, everyone came out to meet him. To their surprise, Luis looked tired and roughed up, as if he had been in a fight. His face had deep scratches, there were bruises on his neck and his hands were cut.

Phillipe, Marco and the two Senoobians looked him over, taken aback at his condition.

"I was in a scuffle last night but I'm okay," he explained.

"Luis, for God's sake, what happened?" Phillipe asked.

"Yesterday as I was leaving the *Pizzeri La Pua* on *Bolognesi Street*, a man brushed past me coming out of the restaurant. The pendant he was wearing around his neck caught my attention. Since I'd seen it so many times hanging from Bayn's neck, I recognized it immediately. I turned around and followed him. Late last night he left his apartment and I watched as he broke into a home on the edge of Nazca. I waited outside the window until he came out carrying a bag full of things he had stolen. As I stepped forward to confront him, he pulled a knife and attacked me.

"I found myself in a desperate fight for my life. He was vicious and strong. He tried to stab me repeatedly until at last I managed to get my pistol in position and shot him—twice. I'm sure he was the one who robbed you and murdered Bayn."

Phillipe and the two Senoobians were dumbfounded.

As they reached the front door, Luis stopped and turned to Jeliko. "By the way, Jeliko, I have something for you," he said with a grin.

"What is it?" she asked.

He carefully pulled an object from his pocket and held it out to show them.

Jeliko gasped. Darz was speechless. It was Bayn's dark blue amulet on a silver chain. Jeliko clasped it tightly in both hands, unable to believe her eyes.

Jeliko hugged Luis and then with tears in her eyes said, "Thank you, Luis. I was sure we would never see this again."

Everyone was silent, remembering Bayn. Then, with a sudden twinkle in her eyes, Jeliko turned toward Marco and beckoned him closer. "Marco, Bayn would have wanted you to have this." She held out the beautiful amulet to Marco whose face lit up.

"Thank you, Jeliko, I will always treasure it," he stammered, holding it up proudly.

Then they all sat down to talk about their plans for leaving Nazca. Darz said, "We've worked hard for a long time to build a new home far away from here because we knew that someday we would have to leave Nazca. It's ready and none too soon. Like every major decision in life though, there is both a good side and a sad side to it. Two days ago we almost left Earth to join our own kind on another planet, but, in the end, we couldn't do it."

"I'm glad you didn't go," Luis replied. The others nodded in agreement.

"Thanks, Luis. It's not easy to leave the only home we've known for more than 90 years but it's past time to go, to get away from here and start over. Too many people know about Naksoris. It's not safe there anymore," Darz replied.

"Can we tell them about it?" Marco asked.

"Yes, but they will have to keep it to themselves. It's in a wild unsettled valley on the Navajo Indian Reservation in the American state of Arizona—near a small town called Kayenta. The Navajos are the second largest tribe in America but there are only 240,000 of them occupying 27,000 square miles of reservation. There should be lots of privacy."

"And the landscape," exclaimed Jeliko. "It's austere; reminds me of Palophera on Senoobis where I grew up. I love the place! We've named it Detza Keeska—New Hope."

"So, that's where you all were when you disappeared for weeks at a time," Phillipe said.

"Yes, we've traveled there to work on the place for several years now. We first learned about the area when I was reading about American Indians. In the early '80's, we realized how crowded Earth was becoming so we flew there and looked around for a few days. We met several Navajo, including their chief, John Gray Wolf. He was a wise human who understood the predicament we were in. He eventually invited us to come and live on the reservation. It will be safer there."

Their conversation was interrupted by a faint rushing sound that came from the East. They looked anxiously in that direction as it grew louder and the wind swirled around them. Marco and Luis ran to the window. *An earthquake?* wondered Phillipe. There had been two mild ones in the Southern part of Peru in the last few years.

As quickly as it began, the rumbling stopped, followed by a loud hissing sound that fell in pitch and then faded away. "What a weird-looking aircraft!" Marco exclaimed.

Everyone else leaped to their feet and rushed to the window. It was a dark gray, flat saucer-shaped craft, unlike anything they had ever seen before. "What the hell is it?" Darz muttered. "Looks like a fighter!"

"Just our luck," Jeliko complained. "A state-of-the-art fighter and our obsolete lander!"

They all stared in fascination as a hatch in its side slid open and two figures emerged, looked cautiously around them, and then began to run toward their building. The two figures were dressed in green combat gear with gray helmets and the weapons they carried looked lethal.

"They aren't human and they aren't Bretin!" Jeliko announced.

"Who are they then?" Phillipe asked, obviously alarmed.

"Whoever they are, they're hostile and our Krayzurs are in the lander," Darz blurted out.

Luis pulled back his jacket. "I have my pistol," he said half-heartedly.

"Be careful," Jeliko implored.

The intruders reached their building and moments later the door flew off its hinges landing inside the room. Two figures with wiry bodies and greenish skin, stepped boldly through the doorway, confronting the small group inside and brandishing their weapons. At first, neither group moved, each regarding the other warily. The two intruders immediately focused on the Senoobians, the nearer one speaking to his comrade in some unknown language. It sounded like *pfyxinatu porgu axikjanbi*. He glanced toward his comrade who responded to him in the same kind of gibberish.

The first one began to speak haltingly in Kuterin. "At last, you are Senoobians, yes?"

Darz replied in surprise, "Yes, we're Senoobians. Who are you and what do you want?"

The second one appeared agitated and spoke in a stern tone to his comrade, "*zyklykal imuxtu!*"

Luis thought to himself *I don't like the sound of that.*"

The first one ignored his comrade, removed his helmet and spoke in Kuterin again. "We are from the *Upaksanochin*. I am Lt. Vahleet, the navigator of our craft." He nodded toward his companion. "This one is Argrulee, our pilot. Klyregit, our Weapons Officer, is in the craft out there. Both Klyregit and I speak your language."

He had long pointed ears that hung down from a crested head with no hair on it. His eyes were yellow and unusually large with a slanted shape above a long face with high cheekbones. His eyes appeared defiant and darted back and forth, taking in everything. His skin was green with a mottled pattern and there was a reptilian look about him.

"Peyrians!" Darz exclaimed. He was stunned; he had vaguely imagined some brutish, menacing creature. These two were menacing but not at all in the way he had imagined.

"Yes, Peyrians! You destroyed our starship and our colony. Now you will pay for that," Argrulee hissed.

"We didn't destroy your colony—we didn't even know about it," Jeliko retorted.

Argrulee sneered, "It had to be you Senoobians; humans couldn't have overcome our colonists."

Argrulee scowled at them. "You destroyed our ship and killed our crewmates. The *Mankuriun* is gone but we will kill you and every Senoobian we find." He advanced toward Darz with clenched fists until they stood eye to eye, the old Senoobian and the younger Peyrian.

Darz stood his ground. "I'm sorry to disappoint you," he said, smiling stiffly, "but we're the only Senoobians left on this planet."

Argrulee nodded malevolently toward Darz and pointed his side arm straight at Darz's head as if to shoot him. Suddenly he slammed it hard against the side of Darz's head, knocking him down. "You impudent fool!" he raged.

Luis slowly gripped the handle of his pistol, ready to use it if given a chance.

Darz sprawled on the floor, eyeing Argrulee with contempt and rubbing his jaw. "You're angry at us? Perhaps you have forgotten: when our colonists were traveling to Earth, wanting only to survive, they were deceived and their ship destroyed by your Lord Athrumos."

Vahleet said, "Yes, Lord Athrumos. A senior officer of the Frunjin who have ruled Peyr for centuries. Don't feel badly. Yours was not the first race the Frunjin defeated."

"You made war on the inhabitants of another planet!" Jeliko exclaimed.

"Yes. We overcame the Ovlodians in a glorious but costly war."

"*Ovlodians?*" Jeliko exclaimed.

"Yes, Ovlodians. They lived on Krees, the third planet in our star system," Vahleet said.

"Forget the Ovlodians and answer my questions," Argrulee growled. "What happened to your other ship—the *Syzilian*, wasn't it?"

Darz replied, "Yes, that's right."

Vahleet asked, "So, what happened to it?"

Jeliko determined not to mention the Bretin or Nanzema. "Almost 100 years ago, our crew became sick from a virus and all of them died except for us. The *Syzilian* was destroyed."

"So you are marooned on this planet as we are!" Argrulee exclaimed.

Darz replied, "Yes, we've been marooned here for almost a hundred years. I have no doubt that, like us, you too will die on this planet."

Argrulee said, "I think not. Our sister starship, the *Grunashar*, is near the largest planet in this star system and has received reports of the unfortunate engagement with the *Mankuriun*. I expect the *Grunashar* will be here in three or four years. All we have to do is survive until then."

"Surviving here won't be as easy as you think. You don't look at all like humans, so you won't be able to move around freely," Darz said, stalling for time.

"That does not concern us," Agrulee growled.

"If the *Syzilian* was destroyed, then what about the *Prolifigus*? And the *Nesfrezia*?" Vahleet said. "How many starships and how many colonies do you Senoobians have?"

"We don't know anything about those two ships. We've been marooned here for a long time and we've lost contact with our other starships except for the *Mankuriun*," Darz said. "Speaking of colonies, you've come here several times and still have no colony?"

"We started a colony on this planet three times but each one failed—destroyed by unknown forces," Vahleet said sourly. "When our ancestors learned that you Senoobians were going to colonize this planet, they couldn't allow it. That's why they had to stop the *Volarion*."

Jeliko turned to Vahleet, "We came here because we had to. Why did you come here?"

"We wanted an outpost to monitor this region of the galaxy and a refuge in case things go badly for us on Peyr. We had planned to populate this planet before it was overrun and spoiled by humans but a rebellion set us back hundreds of years. Now there are billions of humans ruining the planet. It doesn't matter; the next time we come, we will take it by force."

"What do you mean?" Darz asked, feeling sick to his stomach.

"The humans are vermin infesting this planet—one day we will exterminate them," Argrulee said coldly.

Jeliko said, "The humans may not be as easy to overcome as you think."

"I doubt that," Vahleet smirked.

Jeliko nodded toward the humans who stood aside listening to the exchange that only Marco could understand. "There are some good and intelligent humans here; you would do well to consider that."

Argrulee was growing impatient. "That does not concern us. If you want to live, answer my questions. Where is the *Mankuriun* going?"

"Then what are you going to do with us?" Jeliko demanded.

Vahleet smirked, "We're going to kill you, of course."

"What about them?" Darz asked, gesturing toward the four humans.

Argrulee glanced toward the humans with contempt. "Them? They must die too, now that they know about us."

"Why should we answer your questions if you're going to kill us then?" Darz said.

"Because we'll kill you all now, starting with the humans, if you don't cooperate."

"Well, at least answer our questions and then we'll answer yours," Jeliko said.

Vahleet glanced at Argrulee. "Why not, they'll soon be dead?"

"All right," Argrulee said. "Where is the *Mankuriun*'s base?"

Darz said, "If I were you, I wouldn't be so eager to find the *Mankuriun*."

"Is that so? I look forward to the day when the *Mankuriun* faces the *Grunashar*," Argrulee sneered. "Then we'll see . . ."

Argrulee's helmet communicator buzzed, alerting him to a call from Klyregitt. Vahleet glanced toward Argrulee and raised his hand, cutting him off in mid-sentence and urging quiet. Klyregit spit out the warning, "Three human military craft, inbound, less than three miles."

Argrulee quickly relayed the message to Vahleet who then translated into Kuterin for the Senoobians: "Three human aircraft approaching at low altitude less than three miles away." All of them turned toward the open doorway, straining to hear, as the rapid wump-wump-wump of helicopters approaching from the North grew louder.

Darz and Jeliko rushed to the window.

"What's going on?" Phillipe asked Darz.

"We have visitors. Looks like three helicopters!" he said.

From inside the cottage, all seven of the occupants watched as the choppers fanned out and approached them from different directions.

"Who are they?" Argrulee demanded of the Senoobians.

"Some humans that I don't trust," answered Darz. "All of us are in danger. We're going to have to defend ourselves."

Argrulee spoke rapidly into his communicator with Klyregit in the Peyrian fighter.

"The Humans will regret interfering with us," Argrulee swore.

In the cockpit of the *Kornassin*, Klyregit swore mightily. Because their ship was on the surface, their radar had not detected the low-flying craft until they were almost on top of him. He glanced at the blimps on his radar as he methodically activated his guns and missiles, locking them onto the three approaching targets.

Rugar Carlson sat anxiously behind the pilot's seat in the Black Hawk that led the two Apaches toward Naksoris with its sparse stand of trees. "Down there!" the copilot yelled as he pointed up ahead of them. In a large field just over a rise from the building were two unusual aircraft. He pointed toward the lethal-looking Peyrian craft, squatting like a giant predatory insect set to devour Naksoris. "I've never seen anything like them, especially that one."

Carlson's pulse raced with excitement. He had found the aliens and by damn they had two strange-looking craft. The one on the left appeared to be a cargo craft; the other had to be a fighter of some kind. The pilot turned toward Carlson, "What do you want me to do?"

"Let's come in from three directions. Put us down near the house and have the Apaches target the two aircraft. We can't let them get away. If they try to take off, shoot them down!"

The pilot grimaced apprehensively as he studied the Peyrian craft and muttered to himself. "Damn, let's hope they don't shoot back—especially that *junk yard dog* on the right."

The three choppers set down, their rotors still turning. Carlson climbed out with a bull horn in hand and directed it toward their building. "This is Ruger Carlson, representing the U.S. government. I want to talk to you. Come out peacefully and you will not be harmed. Come out now!"

The pilot said to him, "Sir, are you sure these guys speak English?"

"Oh, yes. They speak English."

In the Black Hawk, Sonny sat beside Wentworth, and tried to make sense of the scene before him. *The strange craft near the lander—where the hell did it come from? It was obviously heavily armed. Was it from the Mankuriun?* Then it dawned on him: *we're sitting here in Apaches training our weapons on an alien fighter. This may not be smart and I'm stuck in the middle of it.* He thought about bolting from the chopper. *Would Carlson's men shoot him?*

Inside the house, Darz turned to the humans and spoke to them in Spanish. "Look, Jeliko and I have to go out there but you don't. I don't think they know you're in here. Stay out of sight and as soon as the aircraft are gone, get away from here as fast as you can."

Then he turned to the two Peyrians who were in a heated three-way conversation and spoke to them in Kuterin. "They're looking for us; we have to go out there." He looked Argrulee straight in the eye. "We'll finish our business later."

Argrulee raised his weapon. "You're wrong about that, Senoobian, because I'm going to kill you now," he snarled.

Vahleet abruptly raised his hand, speaking in Kuterin, "Wait, let's make their deaths worthwhile. There's a lot we can learn from them." He gestured toward the choppers. "Let's take care of them; then we can handle this situation to our advantage."

Argrulee shook his fist angrily toward Darz. "All right. We'll deal with you later."

A moment later Darz and Jeliko stepped through the door opening into the morning light and walked calmly toward Carlson's chopper. The two security men jumped out of the Black Hawk, brandishing their M-16's, and joined Carlson. All three of them walked briskly toward the Senoobians. They stopped a few feet from each other.

"Darz Tureesh and Jeliko Hanahban. I must say, this is quite a reception, but you shouldn't have gone to so much trouble," Darz said calmly to the three men, "We can't stay."

"I've been anxious to meet you. My name is Ruger Carlson with Hayman-Angler, under contract to the U.S. Government. Is it true that you're from another planet in some distant star system?" Carlson studied the Senoobians intently, barely able to control his excitement at actually finding the elusive aliens.

Darz nodded, "Yes, that's right. What is it you want?"

"I want to invite you to come to Washington and meet our executives. I understand that you are the only survivors from your planet. Wait a minute. There are three of you. Where's the third one? Hiding in the building?"

"He died a few days ago, murdered actually." Jeliko replied.

"What a pity," Carlson said. "Who would do such a thing?"

"It's a long story so we won't bore you with the sordid details," Jeliko said.

"Nevertheless we would like to hear about your civilization and see your disks. I can help you, make you celebrities."

Darz said, "Mister Carlson, thank you kindly but we don't want to be celebrities; we want to be left alone. Now, if you don't mind, we have a schedule to keep. We're going to board that craft—he nodded toward the lander—and leave. Good day, sir." Then he and Jeliko turned and walked brusquely toward their lander.

At the same time, the engines of the Peyrian ship came to life and it seemed to be straining at some invisible bonds.

Carlson was furious: "I don't believe I made myself clear, Mr. Tureesh," he yelled after the Senoobians over the sound of the whirling blades. "That was more an order than an invitation. You may not realize it, but you two are in a lot of trouble. You killed three government men. The punishment will likely be life imprisonment or death. It would be a shame if anything like that happened to you two. Now, why don't you come along and let me help you with your little problem."

Darz stopped and turned toward him, "By the way, this is Peru, Mister Carlson. I don't believe you have any authority here."

"Obviously you don't know how things work here on Earth, Mr. Tureesh. Your extradition would be a mere formality. Now tell whoever's in that ship to shut it down. Now!" He gestured threateningly toward the ship that seemed to be straining to lift off. The two security men raised their M-16's.

"I won't do that. We're leaving and I wouldn't try to stop us," he shouted at Carlson as they turned and began walking quickly toward the lander again.

The sound of the Peyrian ship's engines reached a higher pitch and it lifted lightly off the ground and maneuvered into a position between Carlson's chopper and the building with its open hatch facing the building. At that moment Argrulee and Klyregit bolted from the building toward their ship.

Carlson saw them. *What the hell! There are four of them! These two don't look anything like Darz and Jeliko* he thought. *There are two kinds of aliens here!* He bellowed into the mouthpiece he was wearing. "Stop them! They're trying to escape. Disable both aircraft." One of his body guards started to call the chopper, but Carlson grabbed him by the arm. "Wait! No missiles. Don't destroy them."

Sonny was worried that Darz and Jeliko were going to be shot. Things were spiraling out of control. *These choppers are going to be blown to bits and me with them,* he realized as he unbuckled his seat belt and pushed open the chopper door.

"What're you doing?" the pilot yelled at him.

"I've got to talk to them," Sonny yelled back as he leaped from the chopper.

Sonny sprinted after the Senoobians. "Where the hell is he going?" Carlson yelled in dismay. "Stop him!"

The Senoobians were running now. "Stop them," he ordered, pointing toward them.

The two body guards in the second chopper opened fire, spraying bullets at Sonny and the aliens.

Darz and Jeliko broke into a desperate dash toward their lander as Sonny ran after them. In their haste they didn't see him behind them and, because of the whine of the Peyrian fighter and the sound of the three helicopters, they didn't hear him yelling to them. Before they could reach their ship, one bullet struck Darz's thigh and another hit his forearm.

Several yards behind them there was an ugly thud as a bullet struck Sonny in the back. He crumpled to the ground and lay still.

Carlson and his two bodyguards turned back toward their chopper as he called his orders to the pilot. As soon as they were on board, the pilot fired a Hellfire missile at the Peyrian ship just as Argrulee and Klyregit tumbled aboard and closed the hatch. A second later and they would have been killed instantly by the impact. The *Kornassin* was rocked by the deafening explosion of the missile's warhead against the ship's hull, throwing the two stunned Peyrians violently against the deck. But the hull was not breached.

"No missiles, damn it!" Carlson yelled at the pilot.

When he glanced back at the fighter, however, the missile had failed to disable it. *What the hell?*—he stared at it in surprise, realizing they were in trouble: the alien fighter was undamaged and would retaliate immediately. He threw himself from the *Black Hawk*, rolled over, scrambled to his feet, staying low and running hard for cover.

In the *Kornassin*, the Peyrians were dazed, not seeing Carlson escape. In seconds they had recovered and were furious. Argrulee lifted off, rotated the ship and fired a missile at the *Black Hawk* that was peppering it with cannon fire.

From some scrubby brush, Carlson watched the missile streak toward the *Black Hawk*—the attack on the alien ship had been a fatal miscalculation. Their choppers didn't have strong hulls like the alien craft; the *Black Hawk* disintegrated in a fiery shower of metal, killing Wentworth and the two body guards.

In the Apache that was firing at Darz and Jeliko, the pilot was distracted when he saw Carlson's chopper explode. His few seconds of inattention allowed them to reach the lander and scramble aboard. He looked back to see the two Senoobians leap aboard their lander as he lifted off, flying toward them and firing his machine guns.

The second *Apache* also became airborne as the pilot launched another Hellfire missile at the Peyrian ship. Again the ship absorbed the blast that rocked it violently but did not destroy it. Argrulee slid into the pilot's seat as Klyregit responded with a barrage of fire at that chopper.

Lifting off, the Peyrian ship quickly gained altitude above the two *Apaches* as the one fired two missiles at it. Klyregit's fingers moved deftly over the controls, however, releasing a cloud of metallic chaff to prevent the missiles from finding their target; then he acquired the target, pressed the weapon release and another missile streaked toward its target. The *Apache* disintegrated.

Seeing the other two choppers destroyed, the pilot of the remaining *Apache* decided he was hopelessly outgunned. Its engines roared as he slammed the throttle forward, tipped its nose down and banked sharply to the right. He flew as low and fast as he could toward the mountainous areas around Machu Pichu, hoping to disappear before the fighter could follow him. But it did.

The Peyrians noticed the *Apache* that was now desperately trying to escape. They immediately turned in pursuit of it, determined to take full retribution on the humans who had attacked them.

Inside the building, the three humans watched helplessly as the battle raged around them and Sonny lay face down on the open ground. Seeing the *Kornassin* in pursuit of the *Apache*, they bolted from the building and ran to his body. He was dead.

Jeliko and Darz reached the lander and she leapt aboard it, pulling Darz up with her. Just as she turned to close the hatch, she saw Sonny motionless on the ground. She jumped back out of the lander and ran to the humans who were gathered around him.

"We have to go NOW before they return," she warned. "Let's get Sonny's body into the house." She grabbed Luis by the shoulder. "Come with us to our new home. It's going to get ugly around here when the local police, the military and the CIA find out about this. There will be a lot of questions about the deaths of Sonny, Carlson, and his men and the destruction of three military helicopters. Let's hope the officials conclude they were all killed in a drug war."

Luis didn't know what else to do so he nodded, "Okay, let's go."

She turned to Phillipe, "You can come too."

"I can't," he said. "Right now, I need to take care of Sonny's body, and I've got to carry on my father's work."

The chopper was more maneuverable than the fighter as it twisted and turned, hugging the ground. But in the end, looking down on its prey from a higher vantage point, like an eagle swooping down on a frightened hare, the *Kornassin* was impossible to evade. When the chopper reached a short stretch of open ground, after a frantic 30-minute chase, there was no escape; the target was acquired. The chopper exploded in a spectacular fireball.

Pleased and triumphant, the Peyrians turned back toward Naksoris, ready to destroy the lander and kill both the Senoobians and all three humans, but the lander was gone.

On the lander Luis said to Jeliko, "Sonny was trying to reach the lander and they shot him. Shouldn't we call Luke and tell him what's happened?"

Darz shook his head no. "There will be an investigation by the Americans and the Peruvians. I don't think we should tell Luke about the Peyrians at this point. It's best to keep you and us out of it. We can tell him everything that happened later, after he's been through the investigation and we're safely away from here."

Luis thought a minute. "Yes, I guess you're right. If the authorities learn that I was here when this happened, I'll be in hot water for sure."

Marco dialed Luke's cell phone for Darz. When Luke answered, Darz said, "Luke, I'm sorry. Sonny's dead."

"Sonny's dead!" Tears came to his eyes. He and Sonny had been close friends for years. They had been through so much over the last few days; now he was dead!" The emotions drained out of him, leaving him numb.

"What happened?"

"He was trying to reach us when he was shot by one of Carlson's men." Darz told him about the confrontation with Carlson but said nothing about the Peyrians.

Darz's voice on the phone, sounded distant and surreal. "Luke, they're all dead!"

"All dead?" Luke repeated in a daze.

Darz said, "Yes. You're the only one left from Carlson's group. I suggest you give some thought to what you're going to say when you're asked about all this."

"What I'm going to say! I don't know what happened. Who killed *them*?" he asked.

"Luke, I can't say. You have to trust us. We can't get mixed up in this."

"What can I say about it then?" Luke shot back, in a panic.

Darz said slowly and firmly, "We didn't kill Carlson and his men and it would be best if you don't know who did at this point. Tell them you weren't here and you don't know. That's the truth. We're leaving for good as we planned. I once heard Captain Markovin say this planet is cursed and now I believe it."

Luke sat down and tried to collect his thoughts. "Carlson did say he had told everyone he was down here to look into drug trafficking. It seems there were reports that the drug lords had gotten their hands on some sophisticated weapons like Stinger missiles."

Darz said, "Then let's leave it at that."

29

APANOO VAHLEET

The race was on. When the Peyrians returned to Naksoris, the lander was gone, but eventually they got a radar fix and took up the chase. The Senoobians were northbound, flying at full throttle in their aging lander. The *Kornassin* was in pursuit and the Peyrians were determined to shoot it down and kill everyone on board. They were only two hours behind the lander but gaining on it rapidly when it blew by Mexico City.

By the time the lander reached Central Arizona, the *Kornassin* was only 30 minutes behind them. A Cessna Skyhawk was flying north toward Flagstaff when its pilot looked out the window, startled to see an unusual aircraft overtaking him. "What the heck is THAT?" he elbowed his passenger as it blew by them.

"Jim, I believe it's a U.F.O.!" his passenger stammered with eyes wide.

Twenty minutes later another aircraft, heavily armed and more menacing, shot past them and quickly disappeared from sight. The pilot's face was green and not human.

"Harold, THAT was a U.F.O.!" muttered the pilot, rubbing his eyes.

When the lander reached the narrow valley that sheltered the small settlement of Detza Keeska, its flaps came down, it made an abrupt landing and its passengers immediately deplaned. Jeliko pushed Cdr. Stovaris' Krayzur into the holder on her belt. "*Sog ko rojee,* welcome!" she shouted to the others as she jumped down to help Darz from the lander.

"Hurry!" she urged, "The Peyrians are right behind us." She pointed toward the brushy ravine behind the largest building. "Luis, help Darz find cover over there. Marco, you and I will take them on when they land. Are you up to it?"

"*Meegaht!* Bring them on," he whooped.

"They could sit back in their gunship and chew us to bits with their guns or destroy Detza Keeska with their missiles," Jeliko said. "Let's hope their arrogance obliges them to flaunt their superiority by fighting us hand to hand."

Luis and Darz made their way to the ravine while Jeliko and Marco waited anxiously by a large boulder that they hoped would offer some cover if they were fired upon.

Ten minutes later the *Kornassin* appeared low over the walls of the canyon and made straight for Detza Keeska as it slowed to land. The Senoobians had put the Peyrians to a lot of trouble. As soon as the fighter set down and the dust cleared, the canopy opened and they jumped to the ground, furious.

"Look at this: the pitiful old Senoobian and her human cur!" Argrulee howled in disbelief. "How foolish! Where are the others?"

"They're gone," Jeliko said calmly.

"Where have they gone?" Argrulee demanded impatiently.

Neither Jeliko nor Marco answered.

"Tell me where the *Mankuriun* went," he snapped.

Jeliko and Marco remained silent.

Argrulee turned to Marco, "What is your name, human?"

"Marco," he said, rattled. He had no idea what the Peyrians might do. *Can I beat them in hand to hand combat?* he wondered.

He closed his eyes, summoning all the years of training he had received from the Senoobians. He thought of Amara and all the times they had fought each other, neither one willing to concede defeat.

Argrulee's eyes burned into Marco. "What of the others and where did the *Mankuriun* go? Tell me or we will tear her to pieces before your eyes."

"Really," Jeliko chortled. "Good luck," she said sarcastically. She had hoped the Peyrians would leave their aircraft and fight them hand to hand instead of killing them on the spot.

Argrulee's scowl turned into a sadistic smile. "Your luck has run out, Old One. Your deaths will be slow and painful."

"We'll see," she said wryly. She glanced at Marco, "Show them what a human can do."

Argrulee nodded to Klyregit and Vahleet, "Teach *Maaarco* to cooperate." He spit out the word *Marco* in a sarcastic tone and nodded toward Jeliko. "I'll take care of her."

The threat to Jeliko made him mad. "If you harm her, I will kill you," Marco growled at Argrulee.

Klyregrit snarled at Marco. "No, we will kill you but first you will beg for mercy. We will beat you to a pulp until you ask us to kill you, and she begs to tell us what she knows."

Marco's blood was boiling.

"You look soft, human. Are you afraid, Maaaarco?" Vahleet taunted.

"Not of you," Marco sneered.

Their advance was arrogant and careless, as a cat sometimes torments a mouse before taking its meal.

Marco eyed them warily, but calmly, as they closed in on him. He began to weave back and forth like a cobra hypnotizing its prey. Suddenly he launched into a sidekick, his heel striking Klyregit on the side and knocking him off balance.

Pivoting toward Vahleet, he followed through with a front kick. The ball of his foot connected with Vahleet's stomach and sent him flying backward.

Klyregit's fist shot out, landing a powerful blow on Marco's jaw, sending him sprawling on his back, dazed, his head hitting the ground hard.

As his head cleared, Marco sprang to his feet and bounded into the air, delivering a spinning kick that caught the Peyrian squarely on the side of the head. Klyregit staggered backward and fell to his knees, stunned.

Marco whirled around to find Vahleet on his feet, ready to kick him in the stomach. Marco ducked to the side and then leaped into the air to deliver a forward kick but Vahleet was too fast. He grabbed Marco's foot and twisted hard, throwing Marco face down on the ground. Vahleet was on top of him, his arms around Marco's neck, trying to choke him.

They rolled on the ground, each one struggling to gain the advantage; they grappled, strangled and slammed each other against the ground until they were soaked with sweat. Klyregit scrambled to his feet and charged Marco in an attempt to grab him around the legs and pull him down but Marco kicked him back hard. At the same time, Argrulee lunged at Jeliko who nimbly sidestepped him and kicked him on the side of the knee bringing him down. He sat there for a minute seething, then straightening up, readied himself to renew his assault. He attacked her with a flurry of blows. He was so fast and strong that it was all she could do to fend off his attack. She raised her palms, parrying his blows, and grabbed his wrists, managing to hit him hard in the stomach, but her age was against her and she was out of breath.

Argrulee pulled free, spun around, kneed her in the groin and, in a one-two punch, battered her face with his fists, knocking her down. The Krayzur she had counted on as a last resort fell to the ground. She lunged for it; he kicked it away. As she lay there gasping for breath, Argrulee stood over her, reared back, and delivered a savage kick to her side and another one to her head. He watched with satisfaction as she coughed up blood. He planted one foot on the Krayzur that lay in the dirt near her head and kicked her again. She rolled into a fetal position, her arms pillowed around her head and tried to protect her face.

Out of the corner of his eye, Marco saw Argrulee give Jeliko a brutal kick to her ribs and heard her cry in pain. "Nooooo!" he screamed at Agrulee. With his chest heaving and his stomach churning, he put all of his strength into breaking free from the two Peyrians. Vahleet loosened his grip for a moment and Marco flung him aside, clambered to his hands and knees and then bolted to his feet, scrambling to get to Argrulee. At a full run, he plowed into the Peyrian, his arms flailing, knocking him away from Jeliko. Marco pelted him with several quick blows to the face; the surprised and enraged Peyrian went down.

Marco turned to Jeliko and cradled her in his arms to protect her, but Argrulee scooped up a handful of dirt and threw it in his face, blinding him. Argrulee eyed Jeliko's Krayzur on the ground and reached for it. "Leave him to me," Argrulee roared. *He would make Marco suffer.* "Kill her now!" he ordered Klyregit.

"With pleasure," Klyregit muttered. As Marco tried to blink the dirty sweat from his eyes, Klyregit pulled his sidearm from its holster, walked over to Jeliko and pointed it at her as she sat helplessly on the ground. He looked down at her, gloating, a cruel and twisted smile across his face, enjoying his power over her.

Jeliko looked up into the barrel of the weapon that Klyregit pointed at her, the blood draining from her face. She was badly hurt; she knew she couldn't move fast enough to escape the death sentence she faced. She closed her eyes; time seemed to stop.

Hating the decision forced upon him, Vahleet struggled to his feet and held his breath, his mind wavering between Jeliko and Klyregit. He jerked his sidearm from its holster and fired—.

There was a loud pop as a narrow beam of energy struck Klyregit in the chest. He straightened up briefly, stared at Jeliko blankly and crumpled to the ground, dead.

Argrulee saw what Vahleet had done and for an instant hesitated in confusion before raising the Krayzur to fire but he was too late. Another pulse of energy killed him at once.

Jeliko stumbled to her feet, bloodied and barely conscious, still expecting to be killed.

Vahleet, looking shaken and contrite, dropped his weapon on the ground and approached her slowly, extending his hand to help her up.

Her mouth fell open. She regarded him with a mixture of gratitude and confusion. "Why did you do that?" she stammered.

He lowered his head. "I didn't want to kill them but I couldn't let them kill you. I've dreaded this day but I did what I had to do."

They heard the crunch of gravel and turned to see Darz, helped by Luis, hobbling toward them. "Is it over?" Darz asked, watching Vahleet suspiciously and trying to sort out what had happened.

"It is for now," Vahleet replied. "But I expect the *Grunashar*—the same class of starship as the *Upaksanochin*—will be on its way here soon. The crew has probably begun preparations to depart the sixth planet from your sun by now. It will take about six months to wrap up operations but it can be here in about four years. There are two other starships that can be here in seven to ten years. They'll be looking for the *Mankuriun*, so I don't know what their plans for humans might be."

Darz turned to the humans. "He's referring to the giant planet Jupiter."

Finally able to see clearly and totally bewildered to see the two dead Peyrians, Marco stammered, "What's going on?"

Vahleet leaned over and extended his hand to help him up. "I made a promise a long time ago. There was a rebellion by the Obeldazi against the Frunjin on Peyr—"

Darz said, "Yes, your captain spoke of it and said that, as a result of it, your people became a more peaceful race."

"Argrulee mentioned that too," Jeliko reminded.

Vahleet grimaced, "Captain Idannup told that story to mislead you. I resented his dishonesty but that's the way of the Frunjin. There was a rebellion—it began after Athrumos attacked your ship—and there were many years of bloody fighting, but the Frunjin were eventually victorious and have ruled Peyr ever since. They did not become more peaceful.

"The rebellion by the Obeldazi rebels was put down but those that survived didn't give up. Instead they went underground, more determined than ever to prevent the Frunjin from dominating every other race in this part of the galaxy. The movement has continued until this day with agents within the Frunjin government and even the military. Their numbers are growing."

Darz cleared his throat. "You were a young Frunjin pilot and yet you joined the Obeldazi! Why? Couldn't that have gotten you killed?"

"Yes, tortured and executed publicly. Why did I do it? I grew up in the isolated Fahree region on Peyr; you see that my skin is not green like Argrulee's and Klyregit's. We are different: by nature independent and respectful of life, so we tend to think for ourselves. Before I was assigned to the *Upaksanochin*, I met someone I wasn't supposed to meet: a wise old Ovlodian, a survivor from the war that the Frunjin waged against his people on Krees when he was only a child.

"His people were peaceful but they were annihilated anyway. Their lands held thorithium and other mineral deposits that the Frunjin coveted to build their war machine. He and a few other Ovlodians were kept in a section of the Hall of History in a sort of diorama, a living exhibit that commemorated the triumph over them. There were others imprisoned there as well from other races that the Frunjin had defeated in their wars to master all of Peyr."

"It was forbidden to speak to those in the dioramas but one day I was assigned to research some military operations during the war. I had never met anyone with such courage and dignity as Hishtahr Mobis. I was gifted in languages and quickly mastered his language, Nejou. In spite of years of imprisonment, his nature was remarkably resilient.

"He made me see the evil of using war to subjugate other races. I was disheartened anyway because I had seen so much death and suffering caused by the power-hungry and cold-blooded Frunjin. I resolved then to join the cause he described to me.

"It was dangerous but he put me in touch with a member of the Obeldazi and I joined them. They needed someone who could pass on inside information about the missions of the Frunjin star fleet so I applied for duty on the *Upaksanochin*."

"So, you've been a secret agent of the Obeldazi for years!" Marco exclaimed.

He heaved a deep sigh, "Yes, it's been hard, keeping a dangerous secret while living with heartless fanatics. I wouldn't have survived on the *Upaksanochin* if it weren't for another one of our agents there. We had to be careful but we kept each other from going insane. Of course, she died when the ship was destroyed. If only she had survived . . ."

His voice grew softer and trailed away, "When the *Upaksanochin* was destroyed and I lost Tazangah, my whole world collapsed. I hated you Senoobians and almost gave up the cause but, in the end . . ."

Everyone fell silent, saddened by what had happened.

Vahleet continued. "There is a small group of Obeldazi, descendants of the first colonists to come to Chookuvot, and a few humans. They refused to allow humans to be exploited and they've foiled every mission by the Frunjin to found a colony here."

"It was the Obeldazi who destroyed the colony in Egypt!" Darz exclaimed.

"Yes. Tazahna was in communications. She passed on coordinates and other useful information to the group on the surface."

"What will you do now?" Marco asked.

"I will join them, of course."

"What about your fighter?" Marco asked.

"Ah, the *Kornassin*. I couldn't be without her. Anyway, she'll be put to good use by the Obeldazi here."

Jeliko said, "By the way, thank you for saving my life."

He smiled slightly, "It was the right thing to do."

He paused for a while, apparently unable to find the words he needed in Kuterin. "I'm sorry—I've said too much," he said. He walked over to the bodies of Argrulee and Klyregit and slid down beside them.

"What about them?" Bayn asked, nodding toward the two bodies.

"I'll find a suitable place and pay my respects tomorrow," Vahleet replied.

"I'll help you if you'll let me," Marco offered.

The next day, with Marco's and Luis' help, Vahleet buried the two Peyrians on a small rise near Detza Keeska. He remained by their graves for most of the day, mourning the loss of his comrades.

Late in the afternoon, Jeliko quietly approached Vahleet and sat down beside him. Neither one said anything for a while. She remembered some of the myths of the native peoples of South America. Finally she asked, "Vahleet, how many times have the Frunjin been on this planet?"

He looked at her and seemed pleased at the chance to talk. "Over several centuries the Frunjin sent three missions to this planet, establishing a presence in the areas that humans call Egypt and Mexico. From the earliest time in Egypt, the colonists interacted with the primitive peoples there who treated them as gods. Because of their influence, a strong class of priests arose and created one of the first organized religions on this planet. Isis, Osiris, Anubis, Thoth—all of them were named after our Peyrian ancestors who taught them how to build pyramids, temples and many other things. We even taught them about Sirius, the *Star of Isis*."

Vahleet went on, "Several of the ancient texts about flying machines were inspired by our ancestors. One primitive group of humans, the *Hebrews*, actually recorded a visitation by one of our aircraft."

"Really! What about this area?" Jeliko asked as Marco and Darz joined them.

"We came to the area north of here later but it was difficult for us. The humans here were more primitive than in Egypt; we taught them how to shape and move large stones and introduced the pyramid to this area as well but that didn't work out. The geography was too rugged, compared with the flatter terrain of Egypt. Besides that, the population was too sparse to undertake major projects like those in Egypt; there were only small, loosely-organized tribes who, having not yet mastered agriculture, still depended mostly on hunting and gathering for their survival."

Darz said, "We've heard confusing myths about two powerful individuals who were nothing like the local people and seemed to be at war with each other. There was a tall one known as Viracocha who traveled about this area in ancient times and tried to help the local peoples. The other was named Quetzalcoatl, I believe, and he seems to have been brutal and even associated with human sacrifice. Do those myths have a connection to your ancestor's presence here by any chance?"

Vahleet said, "That was a long time ago and the records from that time are incomplete. There was bad blood between the two leaders of the first mission to this part of the world. They came from different backgrounds on Peyr. The one named Viracocha connected with the humans here and made an effort to help them in matters such as health and building. But the other one looked down on the humans and sought to exploit them as a source of labor. Because of this and other personal differences, the mission split into two factions and hostilities ensued between them. Eventually Viracocha was forced to withdraw from this part of the world and he disappeared. We never knew what happened to him."

Early the following morning, Jeliko was awakened by the whine of the *Kornassin*'s engines ramping up. She walked stiffly to the porch to watch the craft.

From the cockpit Vahleet seemed to study her as the *Kornassin* began to taxi slowly down the short and uneven runway. Bright blue flames roared from its engines, pushing it skyward, and, before she could blink the sleep from her eyes, he was gone.

Back in Washington three days later, Ruger Carlson sat down with his boss and Senator Gordon to assess the damage: nine men killed and three D.O.D. helicopters lost. He went over the whole incident in detail, describing the aliens, their craft and what had happened.

Montgomery Scott swore under his breath.

Their losses were not the most remarkable aspect of the battle, however; there were not one, but two kinds of aliens, meeting for some unknown reason. The second kind in their lethal black fighter looked nothing like the Senoobians.

"Well, they're here! The green guys were obviously Peyrians," Carlson concluded.

Gordon gasped. "My God! Are we going to be invaded?"

"Walter, I don't have a clue, but I don't think Pearson and Campbell gave us the whole story. Something big's going on. I don't know what it is, but we'd better find out fast," Carlson replied.

"Why the hell would they keep the green guys a secret?" Scott mused.

"Monty, I don't know," he repeated, sounding annoyed.

Gordon was rattled. "Well, how are we going to explain all of this without letting the cat out of the bag?" he fumed.

"Our cover for the operation was gathering intelligence on a drug cartel, I think we'd better stick with that," Scott said.

He turned to Carlson. "What do you think we should do now?"

"We've got quite a body count, Monty. Broucelli is dead. So is Campbell. The old priest is dead too. The first thing I'm going to do is grill Pearson. I'll find out everything he knows, if I have to water board him. There were a couple of locals, a policeman and a priest; I'll check them out too. And there's that hick professor, Martin Connor— he'll talk. Then we're going to hunt some aliens."

The next day Carlson reviewed the reports that Broucelli had turned in before going to Peru. Then he cornered Luke at lunch and peppered him with questions. How many Senoobians were there? *Three after the one named Bayn was murdered. (Luke didn't mention Marco.)* Who murdered him? *I don't know.* Who killed Broucelli, Baker and Johnson? *Darz Tureesh.* Why didn't you stop him? *I couldn't. We were all knocked out by some kind of gas.* Where are they now? *I have no idea.* I saw another kind of alien with some kind of heavily armed aircraft at Naksoris with the Senoobians. What do you know about them? *I don't know anything about any other aliens.* There was some kind of explosion high in the atmosphere a few days ago. What do you know about it? *Nothing.* The questions went on and on.

Carlson was extremely frustrated. Finally, he said, "Luke, you sure don't know much to have been hanging around these aliens for a couple of weeks. If I find out you've been lying to me, you can kiss your ass goodbye. I hear you're on administrative leave until this is all sorted out. It would be unwise to leave town without checking in with me. If you hear from your alien buddies, call me day or night. Here's my cell number." He handed Luke his card.

Luke got up to leave. "Luke—," Carlson called after him in an ominous tone, "Don't leave town and don't do anything stupid."

Within days, Luke's apartment was bugged, his phones were tapped and he was placed under 24-hour surveillance.

Broucelli's report to Carlson had told how Luke had been been contacted by Dr. Connor who had gotten his name from Floyd Cates. The report mentioned that Dr. Connor was a retired college professor living in Jeferson City, a small town in East Tennessee. A few days later, Carlson showed up at the Connor home.

Martin was sitting on his porch, reading *The Standard Banner* and enjoying a morning cup of coffee when the black sedan pulled into his driveway. Ruger Carlson stepped out of the driver's side, strode briskly up Martin's driveway and introduced himself. "Dr. Connor, I'd like to ask you some questions," he began.

How many Senoobians were there? *Four.* Where are the Senoobians now? *I don't know.* Do you know how to contact them? *No, they didn't tell me. They were paranoid about some human agency apprehending them and exploiting them and their technologies.* What do you know about the other aliens who were with the Senoobians at Naksoris? *I don't know anything about any other aliens.* There was a huge explosion in the sky over southern Peru a few days ago. What do you know about it? *Nothing.* Carlson peppered Martin with questions but learned nothing new. Exasperated, he threw up his hands. "Dr. Connor, if I find out you've been lying to me, you will . . ."

Martin interrupted. "Mr. Carlson, we have been warned about the possibility of an invasion by the Peyrians, a hostile race more advanced than we are. The Senoobians wanted their technologies to benefit all of humanity so we might defend ourselves from this race. If you do succeed in finding them and you insist on misappropriating their technologies to your company's narrow benefit, you will regret it. Humans will be unable to defeat this alien race's invasion and it may mean the end of the human race. I suggest you think that over."

Two days later, while Martin and Ellen were out, their home was bugged, their phones were tapped and they were under surveillance.

30

DETZA KEESKA

The crater was on the way; I-40 went right by it. "Why not!" Ellen had agreed enthusiastically. Luke and Karen were half asleep in the back seat but curious to see it as well. It was still a three-hour drive to Kayenta on the way to Detza Keeska and they were all ready for a pit stop anyway. All four of them were eager to see their old friends from Nazca, but some unknown force seemed to draw them to the crater. It had been almost 25 years since the Connors had been there and the anticipation of seeing it again mounted as Martin turned off the interstate near Flagstaff onto Meteor Crater Road.

Thirty minutes later they were standing on the viewing platform, looking out over the huge crater formed 50,000 years ago when a meteorite, 160 feet across and traveling 28,000 mph, slammed into the Earth. It was a dramatic reminder of the kind of event that could happen again, causing a global catastrophe.

This time, seeing the crater made Martin feel uneasy; it reminded him of what had happened to his Senoobian friends. *One of the most singular events in human history has occurred during my lifetime! At last, the arrival of intelligent beings from a different world answers one of the most intriguing questions ever asked, the subject of speculation for centuries, and somehow, until now, I've failed to grasp the significance of that event. Remarkable and friendly beings from another planet with so much to tell us.* He grimaced. *How much longer will they live before their knowledge is lost to a humanity too morally impoverished to appreciate it or use it wisely?*

A carefree young couple approached him, smiling, and asked him to take their picture together. He was glad to oblige. Then he turned back to the great crater, becoming somber again. *They revealed grave perils we may face in the future: the risk of destructive meteors or*

Peyrians—what will happen if they show up someday, intending to colonize the Earth? In his imagination he conjured up visions of a galactic Ghengis Kahn, leading hordes far more powerful and menacing than those that had ravaged Eurasia in the 13th century.

He glanced at his wife, napping peacefully in the front seat, unconcerned. *Maybe I'm overreacting,* he thought. *Maybe the real threat is from humans who will stop at nothing to gain more power.*

Luke had used his position with the CIA to lobby different agencies to investigate the Peyrian threat. But Hayman-Angler, with the help of its government connections, had done everything it could to discredit him and squelch any investigation of aliens. Only a handful of astronomers and physicists took him seriously, but there were no resources to follow up on such vague information. He was mostly shunned as a crackpot.

At least Luke had tried, Martin thought. *He recognized the potential benefit for humanity. And he realized the danger if we don't take the alien threat seriously. So he stuck his neck out.*

In his conversations with Luke, Martin had heard the growing frustration in his voice. Only a few hours earlier, Luke had complained, "How do you find someone with the wisdom and the means to act on this kind of information? Is there anyone at the higher levels of government who is uncorrupted by their rise to power and able to see beyond their own parochial self-interests? If something happens to Darz and Jeliko, we may lose the opportunity to advance our civilization by solving problems that have plagued us for centuries."

Darz and Jeliko had finally agreed to turn over the disks to any morally responsible organization that could evaluate their information and apply it to the benefit of all mankind. But Luke had been unable to find such an organization. Those he approached either didn't take him seriously or they left him with an uneasy feeling about their moral culture. If the information fell into the hands of some predatory organization such as Hayman-Angler, it might be used to dominate and exploit the rest of humanity.

Thirteen months after the shootout at Naksoris, Luke was at a dead end, so he resigned from the CIA and moved to Knoxville to be near Karen while he sorted out his future. After settling down in Knoxville, he often talked to Martin when he visited Jefferson City, mostly to see Karen. There had still been no follow-up by anyone on the warning he had delivered to the government about the Peyrians.

On one of his visits to to see Karen, Luke had brought some electronic gadgets with him and he and Martin discovered that the Connor's house was bugged, their phones were tapped and GPS tracking devices installed in their cars. Just as Luke had done for himself, they left the surveillance items undisturbed.

The only communication from the Senoobians was by mail to Martin's post office box in Jefferson City. After he had written to Darz at a post office box in Kayenta that he was going to take his family on a vacation to the Grand Canyon, he had received a terse invitation for the Connors and Luke to visit Detza Keeska. Martin and Luke had readily agreed. At Luke's suggestion, they took additional precautions, switching out their own car for a rental car and taking short detours, to be sure they weren't followed.

As they left Meteor Crater on the final leg of their drive to Detza Keeska, Martin grew quiet, lost in his thoughts. Ellen had seen that troubled look on Martin's face before and tried to cheer him up. "Honey, look, maybe the Peyrians will never get here. If they do, maybe it will be a thousand years from now. Maybe they'll have a civil war that will ruin them. Maybe some nebula like the one that destroyed Senoobis will pulverize their planet. Or maybe some deadly virus will wipe them out!" She smiled blithely. "Come on, Honey, lighten up. We'll probably destroy ourselves before they can get here to enslave us anyway."

It was one of the qualities he loved about her personality: optimistic to a fault. "Well, there's a sobering thought," he beamed. "No need to worry—we'll just muddle through until we blow ourselves up." He turned to the back seat, winked at Luke and grinned at Karen. "Sounds like a plan to me. Gosh, Dear, I feel so much better. Thanks for cheering me up. It's a good thing I've got you to keep me grounded!"

They all had a good laugh as the straight highway rolled on relentlessly beneath them and in the distance magnificent reddish buttes rose up out of the desert flatness. Before they knew it, they were approaching Kayenta. Then there was 45 more miles of two-lane asphalt that gave way to a tired and desolate dirt road that snaked on westward across the desert, endlessly it seemed, for 20 more miles before reaching the small canyon near Lone Wolf Creek that sheltered Detza Keeska.

When the travelers finally reached the small cluster of adobe buildings that seemed to melt into the stony landscape, they found Darz, Marco, Phillipe and Luis hard at work, finishing the new building that Phillipe would occupy with the Navajo woman he planned to marry. Darz stood up and stretched his back, "*Meegaht!* We were beginning to worry about you!" The four workers dropped their tools and trotted over to meet the two weary couples.

"Welcome!" Jeliko called out to them as she rushed out of the main building to greet them.

The travelers were surprised to see Phillipe. Ellen hugged him. "I didn't expect to see you here; we thought you were still in Peru."

Martin added, "I thought you planned to continue working at the church."

Phillipe smiled broadly and took off his hat to wipe the sweat away. "That was my intention, but without my father, it wasn't the same. I couldn't get along with Bishop Hervias—all the man cared about was filling the coffers! Some men from that corporation came around a few times to question me and they kept following me. I got tired of it all.

"So, about six months ago, I decided to take Jeliko and Darz up on their offer; I slipped out of town and here I am. Things are simpler here. In a way, I feel guilty that I've given up the church but now I'm happier. I've actually gotten to know a few of the Navajo who live not far away and, through them, I met Mary Lou Nez—you'll meet her tomorrow, from a proud Navajo family. This is all new to me, but we're going to be married as soon as our home is finished."

Luke and Martin clapped him on the back and congratulated him.

After some lively conversation and a tour of the settlement, Jeliko said, "I can see you need a drink. Let's get in out of the sun; the mornings and evenings here are tolerable, but the afternoons can be brutal."

They all went inside the main adobe building and sat down while Jeliko poured them a drink. Martin looked at Darz and Jeliko. "You're happy here?"

Darz said, "Oh, yes. It's hotter than we're used to, but . . ." He stretched out his arms to include Phillipe and Luis. "We have our family here, a few Navajo friends and lots of privacy."

Ellen and Karen regarded Marco. He looked well-tanned and more muscular than when they had last seen him in Peru. He also appeared older and more confident. "How are you doing, Marco?" Ellen asked.

He smiled. "Fine. I'm staying busy. Lots to do around here—I'm glad Luis and Phillipe are here to help."

He leaned close, lowered his voice and nodded toward Darz and Jeliko. "They're feeling their age, so they've given all of us a great deal of responsibility."

He paused, drew a quick breath and took on a worried look. "They constantly remind us that we're still at risk and that we have to be ready to carry on without them. And then there's Amara. It's been two years but I still miss her and worry about her every day. Sometimes it hurts so bad I want to curl up under one of these damn cactuses and die. The only thing that keeps me going is hoping that—," he glanced up at the sky, "she's safe and happy out there."

Ellen and Karen hugged him.

Marco turned to hear Luke who was raising his voice. He was bringing the others up to date on what had happened to him since they had last seen each other. He told them about his work and its frustrations. Darz asked him about Hayman-Angler: "Was it crippled by the deaths of Broucelli and Carlson?"

"Far from it," Luke said. "In fact, it's become more determined and insidious than ever. Carlson himself survived, by the way, became even more obsessed with acquiring the alien technologies that he believes will make it a major power, and recruited new members. Even now, he continues his relentless search for you two." He eyed Marco. "He knows about you too, Marco, and wants to get his hands on you, as well.

"When Sonny and Carlson's men were killed, Hayman-Angler was so paranoid about stories of *aliens among us* getting out that they covered up the deaths. They were afraid some other group might get to you before they did and acquire the technologies that they crave so badly."

He paused as a slight smile came over his face. "Oh, and the U.S. government has stepped up its aid to Columbia and Peru to fight the drug traffickers; they're rumored to have acquired more-advanced weapons."

They all chuckled as Jeliko raised her glass in a mock toast. "Let's hope that bunch never finds us again!" she laughed.

Finally Luke said, "Speaking of Sonny and Carlson's men, now can you please tell me who really happened to them, since I'm no longer connected with the CIA? The Hayman-Angler Group pushed the story that they were killed by the *Evigado* cartel."

Jeliko glanced at Darz and then said, "Luke, there are Peyrians on Earth now."

"Did you say *Peyrians*? Peyrians are here—on Earth!" Martin stammered, not believing his ears.

"Yes, that's right. We decided it was best if you didn't know about them until you had been through the grueling investigation that we knew would come after Sonny and Carlson's men were killed. You and Carlson were the group's only survivors—no need to complicate things even more. That's why we wanted to wait until things cooled down to tell you what really happened. We figured the less you knew then, the better."

Darz turned to Martin, "We also decided against getting you and Ellen involved by telling you what had happened. We expected that you, as well as Luke, would be interrogated. Besides, we wanted to tell you all of this in person."

"So what actually happened?" Luke pressed.

"Luke, Sonny was killed by one of Carlson's own men. We were at Naksoris with Phillipe and Luis when a Peyrian gunship appeared."

Luke and Karen gasped. "At Naksoris. Holy smoke!" he said.

"Yes, that's right," she continued. "We didn't know where it came from, of course, until two Peyrians rushed from the gunship and stormed our building. They and a third crewman were the only survivors when their starship was destroyed by the *Mankuriun* . . ."

"The *Mankuriun*?" Luke interrupted. "Another starship showed up!"

"Yes, the *Mankuriun* was a Bretin ship. You may remember that the Bretin were hybrid Senoobians. They launched their ship after the *Volarion* to a planet called Nanzema. We never knew what happened to them and they never knew what happened to the *Syzilian*. When they came to Earth looking for us, a Peyrian starship showed up and they destroyed it. A Peyrian gunship that was on board escaped, however, and its crew decided to take revenge on us for the loss of their starship: we were the only 'Senoobians' they could get their hands on—they didn't know the *Mankuriun* was a Bretin ship."

Jeliko continued, "Before they could murder all of us at Naksoris however, Carlson and three choppers showed up. He didn't know about the Peyrians.

"He wanted to take us and our disks to Washington where we would be treated as monstrosities, no doubt. When we refused, he tried to stop us from leaving. Sonny jumped out of the chopper and tried to reach us, but one of Carlson's men freaked out and started shooting. Sonny was killed and Darz was wounded during the melee.

"I'll bet he wet his pants when he realized there was another alien right under his nose! The Peyrians lifted off and easily destroyed Carlson's choppers. In the meantime, while Phillipe took Sonny's body to the church, we took Luis on board and left for Detza Keeska with the Peyrians in hot pursuit. Where else could we go? They arrived just behind us and Marco and I fought them hand to hand."

Martin was incredulous. "What was it like fighting them?"

Marco said, "Tough! Jeliko and I were pretty badly beaten up: we're lucky to be alive. They could have killed us on the spot, but they wanted to make us suffer; they were tough and they didn't fight fair."

"But here's the strangest part," Darz said. "One of the Peyrians was about to shoot Jeliko point blank when another one saved her life by shooting the other two!"

"What!" Luke exclaimed. "That makes no sense!"

Jeliko said, "Yeah, well believe me, we were shocked. But get this: this one is a member of the Obeldazi, an underground group that rebelled against the Frunjin on Peyr. His name is Vahleet and, as far as I'm concerned, he's a hero. He told us the starship that was destroyed was in contact with another Peyrian starship within our solar system that will likely be diverted to Earth. He said the Peyrian government will be furious about the loss of the starship they mistakenly believe we Senoobians destroyed so I don't know what will come of it."

"So war may be coming! How long do we have?" Ellen asked, worried.

"It's hard to say, maybe two more years, if we're lucky," Marco replied.

Martin sat down stunned. Now he understood how the gravity of the situation.

Karen asked, "So, what happened to Vahleet?"

Darz said, "He joined the Obeldazi group here on Earth. He comes by on rare occasions, but spends most of his time helping monitor our sector."

"Where is their base and how many of them are there?" Martin asked.

"Don't know," Darz said. "It's a closely kept secret. Vahleet never talks about things like that. Peyrians don't look like humans so they can't move around freely. They have to be more secretive than us."

Martin asked, "Since the Obeldazi are monitoring our sector, will they warn us if they learn that Peyrian starships are coming here?"

Darz replied, "I hope so."

Before the travelers said their goodbyes, they talked about what to do with the disks. Luke was convinced that Hayman-Angler would persist in its search for the Peyrians, the Senoobians, and their disks and that eventually Detza Keeska would be found. Marco believed that the disks placed the colony and the planet at risk. After a heated debate, Darz and Jeliko decided to destroy the disks, but Martin had a better idea and together with Marco they came up with a plan.

The colonists continued to worry about the arrival of Peyrian starships, but none came while Darz and Jeliko were alive. The two Senoobians and five humans lived together peacefully at Detza Keeska, enjoying the exotic blending of their cultures.

Although the colonists mostly avoided outside human contact, a few Indians from the Navajo Nation came to know them well; Phillipe married Mary Lou Nez and brought her to live at Detza Keeska. They eventually had three children who made them proud but Phillipe missed Father Tony and told their children many stories about him.

Not a day went by that Jeliko didn't miss Amara and wonder what her life was like. *Was she safe and happy? Had she made the right choice? Would there someday be grandchildren on Nanzema that she would never know?* There were children born to the humans, but there would be no more Senoobians.

Marco was heartbroken without Amara. He never forgot her and he never married. For a long time, he was bitter about the path his life had taken, but his friends saw him through his sorrowful loss of Bayn, Darz, Jeliko and amara.

When Darz died a few months later, everyone took it hard, especially Jeliko. After his ashes were spread on the waters of Pigeon Creek, there was a week of mourning and funereal Proxima. All of the humans there adored her and fretted over her, but they could not console her. She gradually lost her will to live.

A few months later, Darz beckoned to her in a dream. The next morning she announced resolutely, "My time has come." She gave away her few possessions, thanked them all for their kindness and said goodbye with the grand emotion that was typical for a Senoobian.

She insisted on climbing alone to the top of Bothus Butte where she sat down in the meager shade of an ancient Joshua tree. The events of her life played out in her mind, allowing her to revisit all the joy and tragedy she had known since the *Syzilian* had brought her to Karyntis. She missed Amara and Bayn terribly; now Darz was gone. Closing her eyes, she recalled the *mishugah* she and Darz had shared and how it had changed her life. Then, in the whispers of the cool winds swirling around her, she could feel him coming to her and hear him calling her to him impatiently.

She thought of the humans, especially Marco, and smiled—yes, they were worth saving. She took in the view of Detza Keeska one last time, sat back against the rough trunk of the Joshua tree that, like her, had lived long enough and died, her spirit at peace. With great ceremony, her ashes were spread on the waters of Pigeon Creek and another week of mourning and funereal Proxima began.

Soon after Jeliko's death, Hayman-Angler found Detza Keeska. Ruger Carlson appeared one morning with a sizable force, determined to capture the Senoobians and take their disks. To his dismay, there were no Senoobians and no disks.

At the same time, having left Europa far behind, speeding past the giant planet Jupiter and beyond the orbit of Mars, the starship *Grunashar* relentlessly advanced toward Earth on its mission of revenge.

PRONUNCIATION GUIDE

This is a guide to pronouncing the Senoobian names in this book. Consonants are pronounced the same as in English. Vowels are written and pronounced as follows:

Written As	Or	Pronounced As	Written As	Or	Pronounced As
ū		*u* in sun	ē	*ee*	*ee* in seem
ā	*ay*	*ay* in day	o	*oh*	*o* in note
ă	*ă*	*a* in father	ö	*oo*	*oo* in moon
a		*a* in bath	u	*uh*	*u* in dull
e	*eh*	*e* in edge	i	*ih*	*i* in fish
ī	*ey* or *y*	*ey* in eye	ŏ	*ou*	*ou* in out

The stressed (accented) syllable for each example below is shown in **bold** type. When two vowels are together, they are pronounced separately and distinctly. Here are the rules for determining which syllable is stressed:

Two- and three-syllable words ending **in a vowel** are accented on the FIRST syllable.

Nayta	*nā-ta*	Rikay	*ri-kā*
Amara	*a-ma-ra*	Jeliko	*je-li-ko*
Nanzema	*nan-ze-ma*	Muthasi	*mu-tha-si*

Four-syllable words ending **in a vowel** are accented on the FIRST and THIRD syllables.

Ilaybahknoo	*i-lā-băk-nö*	Portineyhe	*por-ti-nī-he*
Parkopia	*par-ko-pi-a*		

Words of two or more syllables **ending in a consonant** are accented on the SECOND syllable (and the FOURTH syllable, if there is one).

Kener	*ke-ner*	Hanahban	*ha-nă-ban*
Tureesh	*tu-rēsh*	Karyntis	*ka-rīn-tis*
Senoobis	*se-nö-bis*	Mankuriun	*man-ku-ri-ūn*

A GLIMPSE OF KUTERIN

The Ancient Language of Senoobis

Here are some common expressions in Kuterin. Refer to the pronunciation guide for proper pronunciation.

ⲧⳑⳝⳡ	*gānu*	Hello
ⲯⳑⲧⳡ ⲯ⋀	*dogu dă*	How are you?
Ⳑₒ⳼·ⵝⲒ	*ē-mitā*	Greetings
Ⳑₒⵗⵀⵋ ⲯⳑ	*ē-jövā de*	Congratulations
ⳝⵀⲧⳡⵝⳡ	*nögutu*	Goodbye

ⲧⳑ	ⵕⳑ	*go shē*	Yes No
ⲧⳡⴲⳡ		*gulu*	Please
ⳑⳑⳝⳡ⁼ ⳝⳑ		*ponz ne*	Excuse (pardon) me
ⵣⵕⵔⳡⲯⳡ		*wīsudu*	Sorry
ⵝⲒ ⵔⵀⳝ ⲯⳑⳝ⊥⋀		*tā sön dēna*	What was that?

ⳝ ⵕⴲⳑⲕⵀⳡⲟ·ⵝⳝ ⲯⳑⳫ⋀	*nă shēpă sotin de*	I'm glad to meet you.
ⲯⵝⲯ ⵗⳑ ⵆⳑⵀⴲ	*dād ko rojē*	Make yourself at home.
ⴺⵔ⳼ ⲯⳑ Ⳑⳡ ⵦⵡⵦⳡ⋀	*lās de fu pāpu*	Thank you very much.
Ⳛ⊥ ⲧⳡⴲ ⳝⳑ⋀	*sa gul ne*	You're welcome.
ⴺⵔ⳼ ⲯⳑ ⵕⴲ⋀	*lās de shē*	No, thank you.

ⵛⳑⲧ ⵗⳑ ⵆⳑⵀⴲₙ ⲧⳑⵣ	*sog ko rojē, găr*	Welcome, come in.
⊥ⵕⴺ Ⳑⳡⳡ ⲯ⋀	*aba ētu dă*	Where are you from?
ⳝ ⵛⵀⴲ ⊥ⵕⴺ ⊥ⵦⳫⴺⳝⴲ⊥⋀	*nă söt aba atlanta*	I am from Atlanta.
⁼ⵕⳲⳝ ⵠⵕ⳼ⳡⳝⵜ ⵛⳡⳝ⋀	*zīdă hīmună sen*	Are you ready to go?
ⳝⵕⳝⳡₒⲯ⊥ⵋ ⲯ ⵋⲯⳡ⋀	*nīnu-dar dă vādā*	Would you like a drink?

⁼ⵕⲯⴲ ⵗⴺⲕ ⵛⳡ⳼ⳑⵗⵋⵝ⳼⋀	*zīdă kal kuterin*	Do you speak Kuterin?·
ⲧⳑₙ ⳝ ⵗⴺⲕ ⵛⴲ⋀	*Go nă kal sā*	Yes, I speak it.
ⵝⲒ ⲯ ⵚⵀⵗ⋀	*tā dā böj*	What do you want?

ᔓ ᎓ᑎᎿ Oᐣᔕ⌃	*nă böj sen*	I want to go.
ᑭᒪᘓ ᐖᏋ ᖪᏋᕂᒷ⌃	*tēl dī polā*	What's your name?
ᔕᏋ ᖪᏋᕂᒷ ᙭ᐢ᎒ᐣ᙭ᑭ⌃	*nī polā robert*	My name is Robert.
ᑭᑊ ᐖᏋ ᔕᏯ᎒ᐢ⌃	*tā dī nāke*	How old are you?
ᔕᏋ ᔕᏯ᎒ᐢ ᒪᙓ ᐱᒪ⌃	*nī nāke ēl ăkēm*	I am 30 years old.
ᔓ ᎐᙭O ᎒ᓒ᙭ᙣ⌃	*nă kās kură*	I have a cat.
ᖅ ᎒ᐩᔕ ᖪᏗ ᒪᵒᕊ⊥᙭ᙣⵏ	*thă kin po ē-tară*	She buys some apples.
Oᐧᑀ ᙭Ꮧᖪᙣⵏ	*sog vopă*	Be careful.
ᑭᑊ ᐖ ᎓ᑎᎿ ᙭ᑊᐖ⌃	*tā dă böj vād*	What do you want a drink?
ᐦᏋᐖᙣ ᐃᏋ᎐ᓒᔕ᎒ᙣ Oᐣᔕ⌃	*zīdă hīmună sen*	Are you ready to go?
O⊥ ᔔᖪᖪ⊥ Oᐣᔕ⌃	*sa wāpa sen*	It's time to go.
᎓⊥ᙣ ᔕᑎ Oᐣᔕ×	*băk nö sen*	Let's go!
ᑭᑊ ᖅᏗ ᖪ⊥ᔕ⌃	*tā tho pan*	What are they doing?
Ꭼ⊥ ᎓⌃	*la bă*	Who is he?
᎓ ᎒O ᎓ᙣᐦᐖᒪ⌃	*bă kās băzdē*	He has a brother.

Ꮛᕂᑕ ⊥᎓⊥ l ᑀᐣ lX ᑀᓒᎬᓒ⌃
shof aba āb ge ābūn gulu   Please count from 1 to 12.

l	ᙣ	⊥	ᐣ	Ꮻ	Ꮮ	ᐧ	ᑎ	ᓒ	ᐩ	∠	lX
āb	*ăk*	*ath*	*ej*	*īz*	*ēm*	*oks*	*öd*	*ul*	*ish*	*ŏt*	*ābūn*
1	2	3	4	5	6	7	8	9	10	11	12

Ꮿᑀ ᐣ ᒪᵒᕊ⊥᙭⊥ ᎒ᑎOᏯ⊥⌃	*īg ej ē-tară köska*	There are 4 apples left.
ᐣᑀ Ꮻ ᒪᵒ᎒ᐩᏮᙣ⌃	*eg īs ē-bimā*	Here are 5 shirts.
ᔓ ᎒O Ꮮ ᒪᵒ᙭ᙣᏮᐣ⌃	*nă kās ēm ē-rāmo*	I have 6 books.
ᖅᒪᖅ ᐩ ᒪᵒᐺᐩᔕ᙭ ᑀᐣᔕᐣ⌃	*thath ish ē-yinũ gene*	Give me 10 copies.
ᑭᒪᘓ ᔔᖪᖪ⊥⌃	*tēl wāpa*	What time is it?
O⊥ ᑎᐖ⌃	*sa öd*	It's 8:00 A.M.
O⊥ ᑎ ᎒l ᖴ⌃	*sa öd kā īz*	It's 8:05 A.M.
O⊥ ᑎ ᎒l ᐣᔕᑀᎬ⌃	*sa öd kā onglē*	It's 8:20 A.M.

324

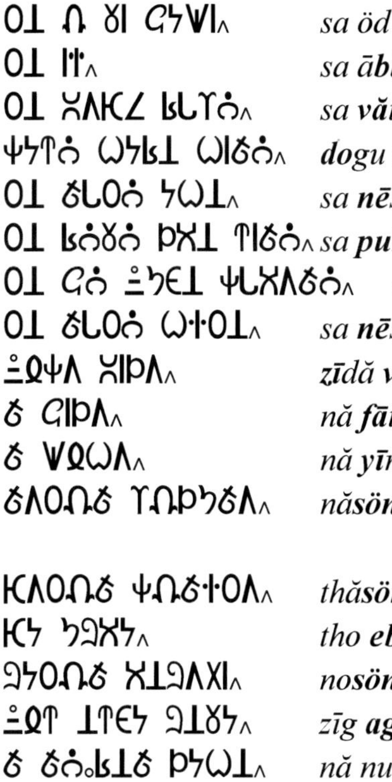

ᎤᏞ Ꮄ ᛪᛁ ᏣᏴᏉᏒᎸ	*sa öd kā foyā*	It's 8:30 A.M.
ᎤᏞ ᛁᛱᎸ	*sa ābish*	It's 10:00 P.M.
ᚼᎯᏦᏃ ᛒᏞᏔᎤᎸ	*sa văthŏ pēju*	It's almost noon.
�326ᎤᎤ ᏯᎲᛒᏞ ᏯᏍᎤᎤᎸ	*dogu mopa mānu*	How's the weather there?
ᎤᏞ ᎤᏞᎤᎤ ᏴᏯᏞᎸ	*sa nēsu oma*	It's quite warm.
ᎤᏞ ᛒᎤᎤᎤ ᎠᏧᏞ ᎧᎤᎤᎸ	*sa puku tra gānu*	It's too hot here.
ᎤᏞ ᏣᎤ ᷵ᏴᏋᏞ ᚼᏞᎲᎠᎤᎤᎸ	*sa fu zela dērănu*	It's very sunny today.
ᎤᏞ ᎤᏞᎤᎤ ᏯᎱᎤᏞᎸ	*sa nēsu misa*	It's quite nice.
᷵ᎹᚼᎠ ᛪᏆᏇᎸ	*zīdă vātă*	Are you cold?
Ꭴ ᏣᏆᏇᎸ	*nă fătă*	I'm busy.
Ꭴ ᏉᎹᏯᎠᎸ	*nă yīmă*	I'm afraid.
ᎤᎠᎹᏔᎤ ᎱᏔᏆᎴᎤᎸ	*năsön jötenă*	I was thirsty.
ᏦᎠᎹᏔᎤ ᚼᏔᎤᎱᎴᎹᎠᎸ	*thăsön dönisă*	She was tired.
ᏦᎲ ᎴᎲᛪᎲᎸ	*tho ebro*	They're late.
ᎮᎲᎹᏔᎤ ᛪᏞᎹᎠᎲᎥ	*nosön rabăsho*	We were hungry.
᷵ᎹᏔ ᏔᏔᎲᎲ ᎲᏚᎲᎸ	*zīg aglo bako*	Is there any tea?
Ꭴ ᎤᎤₒᛒᏞᎤ ᏆᎱᏯᏞᎸ	*nă nu-pan toma*	I am taking a walk.

Want to learn a really foreign language?

Try Kuterin, the ancient language of Senoobis

For a complete guide to **Kuterin**, see the following paperback with a complete grammar and vocabulary:

KUTERIN: The Official Guide to the Language of Senoobis
by Sam Bledsoe.

Go to **www.sector3309.com** for more information or to order your copy.

Available from Amazon.com.

The Alien Strategy Game from *The LAST SENOOBIANS*

You're Face to Face . . . The Pressure's On . . .
Let the Fun Begin!

A new board game for players who enjoy the challenge of face-to-face competition. It's a futuristic strategy game with a science fiction twist.

Its unique qualification system ranks players by class. Players can challenge each other and, by winning, advance to the next level. There will be tremendous pressure and lots of strategy as the smartest players compete for the title of *Surgee* (Top Gun).

For two players.   Playing time: about 30 minutes.

Go to **www.zanoba.net** for more information or to order your copy.